About this Boc

Since first contact w̲ı̲t̲h̲ ̲t̲h̲e̲ ̲a̲l̲i̲e̲n̲ ̲M̲o̲t̲i̲e̲s̲ ̲t̲h̲e̲ ̲e̲x̲p̲a̲n̲s̲i̲ ̲ ̲on of the Second Empire of Man has slowed. The Fleet's attention has become consumed with blocking Motie access to human space—and holding that thin line now depends upon a shaky alliance with the horrifically prolific, technologically brilliant, three-armed Moties themselves. And under the terms of Horace Bury's will, human and Motie shareholders have assumed joint control of industrial giant Imperial Autonetics.

Against this backdrop, the Empire decides the fate of worlds. Those already in possession of space-worthy craft may join as Classified systems, and enjoy the benefits of access to new technology, trading rights, and Fleet protection. Those less advanced may be parceled out as colonial concessions. Outworlds that refuse to join risk conquest by zealous commanders intent on preserving the hard-won peace at any cost. Those boasting great riches are targeted for quick accession. Those presenting any danger are targeted for quick destruction.

Yet, though their very planets depend on guessing the right questions, and delivering the right answers, few of these details are known in the remote backwaters of Imperial space. Set in the first chaotic year following Horace Bury's death, this fresh sequel to *King David's Spaceship*, *The Mote in God's Eye*, and *The Gripping Hand* introduces Asach Quinn, a wily, genderless diplomat as enigmatic as the Mote-space aliens. With Quinn as guide, it shifts point of view from the vast race across the stars, to that of one small outworld, already deemed irrelevant, and gives its "outie" citizens a voice.

Other books in the Mote Universe

Pocket Books by J.E. Pournelle
King David's Spaceship

Pocket Books by Larry Niven
and J.E. Pournelle
The Mote in God's Eye
The Gripping Hand

Outies

J. R. Pournelle

New Brookland Press
www.newbrooklandpress.com

ISBN-13: 978-0-615-43271-7 (e-book).
ISBN-13: 978-0615-43414-8 (paper).

ISBN-10: 0-615-43271-9 (e-book).
ISBN-10: 0-615-43414-2 (paper).

For my father. It's his world, we just try our best to live in it...

Contents

CONTENTS

List of Characters

Imperial Autonetics Majority Shareholders

SIR KEVIN RENNER, owner and pilot, *Sinbad*; five percent plus one share.

ROBERT PEELE BURY, oldest grandson of Horace Bury, twenty percent less one share.

ALI BABA, Mediator, fifteen percent.

EUDOXUS, Mediator, representative, Medina Traders, fifteen percent.

OMAR, Mediator, representative, East India Company, ten percent.

VICTORIA, Mediator, representative, Crimean Tartars, 2.5 percent.

Other Humans

Imperials

AMARI SELKIRK ALIDADE CLARKE HATHAWAY (ASACH) QUINN, Analyst and Advisor.

SANDRA (SALLY) LIDDEL LEONOVNA FOWLER, LADY BLAINE, Co-Director, the Blaine Institute, New Caledonia.

RODERICK HAROLD, LORD BLAINE, Earl of Acrux, Co-Director, the Blaine Institute, New Caledonia.

COMMISSIONER (DR.) ANTHONY HORVATH, Minister of Science, Sparta.

HG, Horvath's delegate and representative on New Utah.

COLCHIS BARTHES, Curator of American Collections, Imperial Library, Sparta. Information delegate to New Utah.

SIR LAWRENCE JACKSON, Governor, Maxroy's Purchase.

Saint George, New Utah, and Environs

ZIA (UMM HUGO) AZHAD, Procurement Agent, Orcutt Land and Mining.

CHARACTERS

OLLIE (ABU HUGO) AZHAD, Chief of Security, True Church Militant Contract Security (TCM Security), Zia's husband.

HUGO AZHAD, son of Zia and Ollie.

DEELA AZHAD, daughter of Zia and Ollie.

MARUL, Zia's niece.

LADY LILLITH VAN ZANDT, Margravine Batavia, Entrepreneur.

HARLAN CLEGG, Security Contractor.

ALOYSIUS GEERY, Chair, College of Technical Science, Engineering, and Urban Planning, Zion University.

Saint George True Church Militant (TCM) Security Zone

CAPTAIN JERI LEGRANGE, Zone Operations Security Officer.

SERGEANT SHEILA THOMPSON, medic, Zone Operations support company.

PRIVATE SWANSON, LeGrange 's driver, Zone Operations support company.

PRIVATE THEO PARKER, Zone Operations support company.

MAJOR JOHANNES TRIPPE, Executive Officer, TCM Saints ("Mormon") Battalion.

LINDA LIBIZIEWSKY, Zone Operations Administrator.

Bonneville and The Barrens, New Utah

COLLIER (COLLIE) ORCUTT, rancher.

LAUREL COURTER, rancher, Orcutt's niece.

MICHAEL VAN ZANDT, opal meerschaum broker, Lillith Van Zandt's son.

NEJME SILELYAN, major domo to Michael Van Zandt.

LENA SILELYAN, Nejme's daughter.

MENA SILELYAN, Nejme's wife.

JOHN DAVID SWENSON, New Utah Founder's Era surveyor, provisioner and naturalist.

Other Moties

JOHN, Farmer. Agricultural concession-holder.

LONGSHANKS, Runners. Post-Watchers in the employ of Farmer John.

LEICA, Runners. Offspring of Longshanks.

SARGON, Master. Procurator, Northern Protectorate, Mesolimeris.

LAGASH, Keeper, Northern Protectorate, Mesolimeris.

ENHEDUANNA, Master, Side Captain, House of Sargon.

ALHACEN, Miner.

LORD CORNWALLIS, Master, East India Group. Associate Master of Inner Base Six; presumptive parent of Ali Baba.

Other Species

AGAMEMNON, a horse.

Chronology (Standard Years)

Events preceding the opening of this story...

2450   Jasper Murcheson explores region beyond the Coal Sack.

2452   In New Caledonia system, domed colonies established on New Scotland and New Ireland, following terraforming.

2456   Maxroy's Purchase (MP) settled by dissident Mormons.

2546   Domes removed, New Scotland and New Ireland colonies.

2552   Mountain Mover asteroid mining registered, Purchase system.

2553   100,000+ transportees settled on Maxroy's Purchase.

2567   Temple of the True Church moved to Glacier Valley, Maxroy's Purchase. True Church colony sent to New Utah. Founder's Report to the Elders of Maxroy's Purchase filed.

2600   Imperial Navy Initial Assessment Report, New Utah, filed.

2603   Secession Wars begin. New Scotland loyalist; New Ireland secessionist. Maxroy's Purchase and New Utah are distant and largely neutral.

2640   First Empire collapses.

2800   Interstellar trade collapses in Trans-Coal Sack sector.

2820   In absence of Imperial contact, Loyalist New Scotland continues prosecution of war against "Rebel" New Ireland.

2862   "Motie" Civilization on Mote Prime launches a solar sail-guided probe into human space, using a laser cannon.

        Coherent Light from the Mote reaches New Caledonia.

2867   City churches, Maxroy's Purchase destroyed. Temple

of the True Church proclaimed Governing Church of Maxroy's Purchase. Swenson's Ape paper authored.

2868 Alderson tramlines collapse between Purchase system and New Utah.

2870 Secession Wars end. New Ireland defeated.

2882 Howard Grote Littlemead founds Church of Him on New Scotland.

2902 Coherent light from Mote ends abruptly. Howard Grote Littlemead "hastened to meet his God." Under intense persecution, many Himmists flee to New Ireland.

2903 Leaonidas IV of Sparta proclaims the Second Empire of Man.

2908 His Mission dispatched from New Ireland to Maxroy's Purchase. Expands rapidly among "false" Church remnants.

2963 Hannifin Mines registered, Pitchfork City, Maxroy's Purchase. True Church begins secret, periodic shipments of selenium supplements and fertilizer to New Utah, in exchange for opal meerschaum.

2964 His Mission to Heaven dispatched from Maxroy's Purchase to New Utah.

2967 Imperial contact with New Caledonia re-established. INSS *Terrible* bombards Derry, ending New Ireland secession. New Scotland designated sector capital.

2984 General Metals registered, Pitchfork City, Maxroy's Purchase.

2986 New Ireland designated sector naval shore leave destination.

3005 Union Planetoids registered, Maxroy's Purchase.

3007 Maxroy's Purchase joins Second Empire of Man.

3013 Prince Samual's World discovered by units of Imperial Navy. **Events of *King David's Spaceship* begin.**

3016 New Chicago Revolt. **Events of *The Mote in God's***

Eye begin.

3017   First contact: Motie light sail reaches human space. *MacArthur* dispatched to investigate Mote System. Mote Blockade Treaty concluded with representatives from Mote Prime, preventing Motie exit from Mote Space.

3026   Tanner Metals registered, Pitchfork City, Maxroy's Purchase.

3035   Sir Lawrence Jackson, Governor, Maxroy's Purchase, dispatches Bury-owned ship to New Utah to invite Empire membership. The New Utah True Church refuses.

3047   **Events of *The Gripping Hand* begin.** The "Motie scare" on Maxroy's Purchase. Renner investigation reveals True Church use of a periodic tramline from Maxroy's Purchase to New Utah. Collapse of The Curdle opens a second Alderson point from the Mote system into Imperial space.

3048   Motie Medina Trader Alliance concludes and polices the Second Mote Blockade Treaty in exchange for exclusive trading rights with the Empire. Motie access to Empire Space prohibited without infection with contraceptive C-L parasite.

        Horace Bury bequeaths bulk of Imperial Autonetics voting stock to a combination of his own and Alliance families.

3049   Second Jackson Expedition to New Utah planned. **Events of *Outies* begin.**

Model of Trans-Coal Sack Space

Annotated to indicate probable location of major planetary systems.

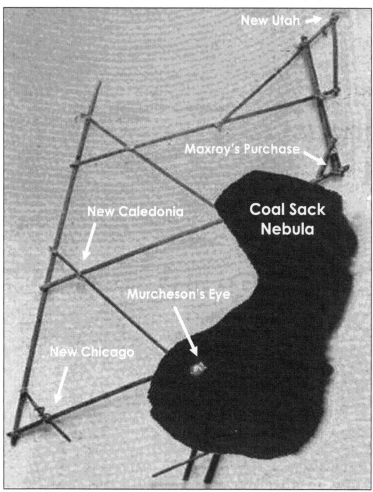

Provenance: Himmist Mission to New Utah, c.2964. Artisan Unknown.
Materials: stems, twine, black wool, uncut ruby ("His Eye").
Image courtesy Mena Silelyan

Prologue

Nauvoo Vision, en route to Saint George, New Utah, 3035

Ship's time, it was well past midnight. Reuben Fox padded silently through the empty corridor. The Delegation all slept like exhausted children, thanks to a generous dollop of melatonin in their evening nightcaps. "It's a Mormon Tea," he'd said, passing around the steaming cups, "No caffeine. Help you sleep like babies before we descend tomorrow."

And indeed they did. He stopped before a door just outside the cargo bay, marked only by a small plate that read "Maintenance Access." He tapped softly. Barely a tap, even. More like stroking the door with his fingertips. It opened, silently. "Twenty minutes to Fling," he murmured. Asach Quinn nodded, stepped into the corridor, satchel in one hand, a sealed hard case in the other. Fox pulled the door shut noiselessly, and led the way.

Inside the cargo bay, they skirted two enormous, white, blunt-nosed cylinders cradled in Fling racks. Each bore a square red cross, half-encircled by a bright red crescent. They stopped at a double-walled safety lock beside the bay door. Quinn knelt on the floor, and unlocked the case. Three objects were lodged in form-fitting impact foam inside. The first was cylindrical, the size of a man's fist, with several fittings around a collar at one end. The second was a spider of tubing, laced through a solid tubular framework with quick-connectors at either end and couplings at the ends of each hose. Third, there was a sphere, small enough to be enclosed by a woman's hands cupped fingertip-to-fingertip, made of a tough, flexible composite compound.

Asach locked one end of the frame to the cylinder, then dogged a set of couplings to the collar fittings. Next, from the satchel came a tough, turgid, multi-celled, doughnut-shaped bladder, with more fittings ringing one base. Asach slipped it over the hose assembly, fitting side away from the cylinder, dogged down the other end of the hose couplings, and snapped the sphere to the top end of the frame. The whole thing—sphere, upon toroid surrounding the frame assembly, upon cylinder—was little longer than the distance from Asach's elbow to wrist, and light enough to lift easily with one hand.

Fox tapped a code sequence, then pressed his thumb into the pad beside the safety lock. The door slid open. Coils of retractable lifeline were stowed neatly at four anchor points on the inner walls; it was otherwise empty. Asach slid the assembled contraption inside. It fit, just. Fox closed the door with another key sequence. It was still air-filled; still pressurized. It would not be for much longer.

A disembodied voice echoed in the quiet. "Commander Fox?"

"Present."

"Cargo Bay cycle commencing, sixty seconds. Clear, or abort?"

"Clearing."

"Aye-aye, sir. Clear to commence in fifty-nine. Fifty-eight. Fifty-seven…"

It took only a few moments to traverse the bay, exit the hold, and seal the door. Fox remained at the view panel. The faint hum as air was sucked from the bay and recompressed somewhere in the bowels of the ship was audible for a few moments, then faded as the hold neared vacuum. The fling racks began sliding along their rails. The bay doors opened to space. A few stars glittered. Most were obscured by the Coal Sack.

Fox put the readout on audio. "…Three. Two. One. Cargo Bay cycle complete. Commencing Fling sequence. Fling in F minus…"

The rail extender arms rolled the medical supply canisters out the doors, injected them into the Flinger, then folded back inside. The bay doors closed. The faint thrum of the charging Flinger pulsed through the hull.

"…Five. Four. Three. Two. One."

The ship shuddered slightly as the linear accelerator shoved twenty tons of medical supplies toward the Sorting Station in the Oquirr foothills outside Saint George on New Utah. As *Nauvoo Vision* slowed and prepared to drop into geosynchronous orbit, the canisters would blaze down through the atmosphere, ablating heat from their noses, drogue chutes jerking them to drop to the ground, spilling their contents like Santa's reindeer making a clumsy chimney-top landing.

And, unnoticed alongside the Flinging, the safety lock cycled. Or rather, failed to cycle. Instead, its outer door merely opened, and the donut with its ball-nose and soda-can tail puffed out into space like so much jetsam. Floating alongside *Nauvoo Vision*, the assemblage coasted in toward New Utah for awhile. Then, as the medical cargo raced off to its mountain rendezvous, and as the ship dropped into its parking space, the little ball sailed on by itself, a speck, alone with its own thoughts in the vastness.

Its own thoughts were simple. They went something like this:

"…Four. Three. Two. One."

And then the tiny rocket fired.

1
Visitation Rights

Sargon came, to fill the sanctuary like a cargo-ship; to fuel its great furnaces; to see that its canals spew waters of joy, to see that the hoes till the arable tracts and that barley covers the fields; to turn the house of Kish, which was like a haunted town, into a living settlement again.

—The Legend of Sargon, Segment A

Farmer Moties tend crops, which grow on whatever land is not covered by buildings or roads. They ignore anything except plants and anything that seems to threaten the plants, being essentially agricultural relatives of Engineers. Their hands and feet are adapted for digging and tamping down soil. They can operate machinery such as tractors.

Runners are employed carrying messages and are much taller than other Moties, but the Runner is mostly leg. One variety of Runner has multicolored layers of erectile hairs that allow it to camouflage itself while delivering messages.

—Wikipedia

The Barrens, New Utah, 3049

Laurel stopped. Rather, Agamemnon stopped, eyes bulging, a thousand purring cats roaring in his nose, shoulders quivering, hunched down on his hunkers ready to whirl, or bolt, or spring Pegasus-like straight up into the sky.

But Agamemnon did none of those things. He waited, trembling and snorting, anchored like lichen to a rock, because Laurel told him to. Not in words, but in body: a faint flinch of her shoulders, and he would have whirled fast as a wind devil; a faint rock of her seat, and he would have crossed the plain as a flaming chestnut rocket. Given an almost imperceptible scrunch-and-release of all her muscles at once, he would have imploded upward, coiled as a springbok, lashing backwards with steel-shod heels and screaming a battle roar.

But Laurel froze stock-still, not breathing, not blinking, paralyzed with shock. Because before her, spanning from rim to rim of what should have been the prickly scrubland of the Borrego Valley, stretched a shimmering haze of aquamarine. It rippled like a gentle sea. And, lurching upright, staring straight into Agamemnon's white-rimmed eyes, was the most enormous mole she'd ever seen. A disfigured mole. A deformed mole. Not a cutesy, myopic mole in a children's storybook, but a brute of a thing, with hands big as garden spades, tipped with claws strong as the tangs on a bucket loader, muscles thick as bridge cables locking its head to its arms.

For its part, the mole leaned forward, glared, and let loose a low-pitched chittering whirr, like the scolding of an angry wren. This proved too much for Agamemnon who, teetering among left, right, forward, and up, lurched backward in a valiant attempt to do what was demanded of him, while nevertheless exercising prudent equine judgment. At this, the giant mole paused, turned, trundled back to the field's edge, and disappeared into the aquamarine sea of wire-grass. Laurel blinked, then rubbed sweat from her eyes. A gap remained where the stalks had parted, and an iridescent shimmer streaked toward the horizon, trilling like a hummingbird, answered by a buzzing wren-whirr from deep inside the reeds.

Laurel winced left, and Agamemnon whirled and blazed toward home.

Farmer John felt the danger well before he heard it, and heard it well before he saw it. Both "felt" and "heard" being misnomers for what he sensed, but the best translation possible for what was transmitted to his brain by two specialized sets of bones.

The first, dense as tusk and capped with a claw hard as dentine, articulated to the knobkerrie that passed for a wrist, and thence up his arm directly to his skull. With hands buried in earth, Farmer John Felt the regular plonk-plonk-plonk-plonk of Agamemnon's hoof beats, far in the distance, reverberating through his skull like timbales on tympani.

The second, a cluster of tiny, moveable pitot tubes surrounded by a pliable sail of skin, concentrated whispers of air-propagating frequencies well above the range of human hearing. When standing erect, Farmer John could bend the sail at whim, absorbing sounds as faint as the squeak of grating sand or air cavitating past nose-hairs. So having felt the ground tremble in his hands, Farmer John stood up, and heard wind whistling far away in Agamemnon's nose and Laurel's ears, beyond his line of vision.

He then crouched low again, two fingers thrust into the ground, his ear bending the shape of the wind. His leathery face, incapable of expression, did not register his horror as a flame-red, six-limbed obscenity topped the small rise not ten paces before him, then lurched to a stop, quivering and whistling, but saying nothing that he could understand.

Farmer John had no Warriors. He had no Master within earshot. He had no idea what the *far moon* he was looking at. So he did what best he could. He stood bolt upright, leaned forward, and screamed "get the far moon off my land, you mooning pest of a herbivore!"

Of course, Farmer John did not really say "herbivore." He said something probably better translated as: "you brainless, gluttonous progeny of vermin." Further, he had no way of knowing for sure whether the thing *was* an herbivore, but if it wasn't, he didn't want it plonking through his fields, and if it was, he didn't want it chomping through them, either.

In any event, it backed away. He kept his ear on it, but turned and trudged down to his concession, maintaining full height to connote his full authority. The two Runners at Post 10 shifted uneasily, their colors rippling in tune with the shimmering field behind them. "Hey Longshanks," he barked. "Go tell Lord Sargon that we've got company."

Actually, it took him a lot longer to say this, because he barked orders until the runners were out of earshot, and conveyed rather a lot more information than that, including the height, color(s), number of (apparent) limbs, eyes, nostrils, and other various protuberances demarcating his unwanted visitor; plus his best assessment of sentience (none) and numbers (one). Also, as the Runners sped toward the far horizon, he made them repeat back every line of the report, to ensure that they'd gotten the full message, and that correctly.

Then, immediate danger past, and duty done, he got back to soil testing. He had to figure out how best to cope with all those toxins.

Longshanks watched Farmer John and his sweet field of blue-green manna. It was not their job or duty to watch anything else. It was their right and duty (the two words better being combined into an indivisible whole that meant both things at once) to stand like gateposts, their iridescent hair rippling with the breeze, rendering them all but invisible. They watched Farmer John closely, for Farmer John bore immense responsibility, including the (to them) paramount responsibility of feeding Longshanks.

More accurately, their name was something like: "Longshanks, Post 10, Concession John, Eanna House, Sargon Protectorate, Mesolimeris, Mannaworld." As a pair, they'd Watched Farmer John faithfully their entire lives, inheriting their post from their parents, never falling into land debt, and never aspiring to any other Post. For his part, Farmer John might address all Longshanks as if interchangeable, but Longshanks 10 John had been Mentioned in Dispatches for their speed and accuracy, and Sargon himself had appointed them to that Watch.

There was no better posting. Runners in Farmer John's employ always ate. They were never sent on spurious missions. They were never beaten or tortured. They were given clear orders and drilled to succeed. So when Farmer John bellowed "Hey, moonbrains, get moving!' what happened at Post 10 ceased to be their responsibility, and from that moment, poised on tiptoe, they cared only for four orders: Speed. Direction. Recipient. Message. When they heard the code most dreaded by any Runner: All Due Haste, they did not pause to flinch. They lit out like silent typhoons, catching and repeating the remaining orders on the fly, burning every last reserve to maintain near-invisibility as they streaked toward the horizon.

Other Runners might have held something back, terrified of being left like gasping fish at the end of that most dreaded journey's end, too depleted even to stand, used up in a final dash for an employer's whim. But their great race anchored on one end by Farmer John's meadows, and on the other by Sargon's fealty, Longshanks sped toward the certain knowledge that, at day's end, they would eat. Along the way, they repeated and drilled one another on the message, as insurance, should either fail the mission.

Agamemnon stood spread-eagled, head hanging, chest heaving, sweat steaming from every pore, air blasting through his nostrils with the force of bellows. A stock tank stood within five paces, and his belly ached with longing. But, throwing herself from his back before he'd even staggered to a lurching halt, Laurel had shouted "Stand!" So he stood, heaving and gasping, a good boy, doing as he was told.

There were significant benefits to being a good boy. Chief among them was Laurel. When Laurel was there, he knew everything. He knew his purpose. He knew his rank. He knew that nothing would harm him. He knew that there would be hay. He knew that sometimes, if he was a *very* good boy, there might be treats. Agamemnon did not always understand why there could not be hay now (or, for that matter, water), but if Laurel said no, she meant no, and hay or water would have to wait. In any case, at the moment Agamemnon was chiefly preoccupied with air, so even though he was fairly sure that he *had* been a very good boy, he was willing to gasp and fix his rolled eyes on the ranch house door, through which Laurel disappeared with a bang that made him jump a little.

Agamemnon did not like banging. in his memory, banging went along with screaming, which was of itself unpleasant, but where there was banging and screaming there was generally also an aching insufficiency of hay, water and air, and the dread possibility of biting and kicking. However, at the moment, nothing unpleasant seemed to be happening, except for his thirst and the absence of Laurel, so he relaxed a bit. As he caught his breath he nickered once, in a low, snuffley, hopeful way, but the door remained steadfastly closed. So Agamemnon sighed, cocked one hip to rest the opposite leg, pricked his ears to listen for her return, and settled in to wait.

Collie Orcutt sat, elbows before him, head in hands, hunched over accounts, the remaining litter of paper shoved to one side of his desk, near tears.

Beyond the window, through which he could not bear to look, sprigs of dead grass extended in neat rows from doorstep to horizon, crunchy with the heat. He had slaughtered or sold most of his stock. His wells were nearly dry. His stores were depleted. What had once been a mountain view was ground down to dust and slag, the line of haulpaks gone, the boom over, with nothing to show for it all but debt. He was in too deep to leave, he was in to deep to stick it out, and he was long past imagining real solutions.

So there he sat, silently damning the land man, staring numbly at the unrelenting columns of terrible news, listing to the terrible, drying wind, mourning for his dream, with no idea how to tell his friends, let alone his creditors.

He started from his chair at the sudden banging of the back door, followed by boot steps thundering across the porch and through the kitchen. He had no time to react before his office door flew open, cracking against the wall behind, and a dust-caked Laurel, stinking of horse-sweat, burst in, shouting.

"They've come! They've tapped the aquifer at Borrego Springs! There's salt meadow growing from Butterfield Station to Ocotillo Wells!"

Orcutt stood stupidly, frozen in place. The Borrego seep was a pathetic trickle of alkaline water, supporting nothing but poisonous crustaceans. The aquifer beneath its ancient soil was a hell-worthy soup of sulfurous brine. Nobody went there. Nothing grew there. Nothing could grow there. It was a wasteland: a waste of space, and a waste of time.

"Uncle Collie!"

He looked at her, still uncomprehending.

"They're making *hay!*"

Which was followed by a sharp whinny, accompanied by emphatic banging at the back door that made Orcutt jump.

Then he burst into tears of joy.

Then he plunked back into his chair, sobbing, "Praise Him for Salvation!"

A ripple wavered up the vast, mud-brick staircase as Longshanks, now a pall of matted grey fur, blurred past and upward, their chittering All Due Haste code preceding and following in a Doppler blur. Behind the ripple, Warriors snapped back into present-and-lock-arms position, rumbling in a dull roar, "Make Way, the Protector's Courier!"

Their message delivered even as they ran; their encrypted code for Lord Sargon's Ears Only; the great Lord was roused from his accounting chambers and met them where they collapsed, spent, on the glassy floor of the entry hall.

Doctors converged, hovering without acting. Sargon clenched the gripping hand.

"Let them Eat!"

A sharp prick, and the Runners felt the sheer bliss of Manna, flooding calories, electrolytes, antioxidants, analgesics, and blessed, pure water into what passed for their bloodstreams.

Sargon bent over them, emoting so softly that only they could hear, and enwrapped each small head with two gentler, softer hands. Longshanks wriggled slightly.

"Let them Rejoice!"

The Runner's eyes rolled, the only expression of which they were capable. Their bodies arced in unison as a new substance, sweet as pure euphoria, flooded every pore of their being. Their hair pulsed with all the colors of shattered light as they rolled upright, springing to their tiptoes as daintily as if they had spent the day merely watching, and faced one another in ecstatic disbelief.

Holding light hands steady upon them, raising the gripping hand still clenched, Sargon roared or screamed sounds lower and higher than all hearing. In frequencies felt (or heard) by every caste, The Sacred Words poured from Sargon's very head and feet:

"Let them Marry!"

Longshanks 10 John leapt, and locked in union. They had been Very Good Boys, indeed. Their Messenger days were over. They were retired to stud, so to speak.

Fifty miles away, his hands buried in soil, Farmer John muttered at his plants. He hoped to far moons Lord Sargon quit mooning around, and gave him decent replacements for Post 10 until Longshanks's first litter came of age. He had a thousand sar of manna to re-seed.

New Scotland, 3049

Alone, unwatched by anyone, Kevin Renner stopped playing the role of Kevin Renner, and instead sat, eyes closed, forehead resting on one hand, leaning on one elbow, propped against the wing of his formidable chair.

Absorbed in thought, by feel alone, with his free hand he opened the edenwood case beside him, and ran his fingers across the contents. Silky silver tongs, buttery resin chunks, the crusher, the clicker, the tin of fermented leaf, the rosewood cradle, the amber bit, and finally, the bowl itself. He rubbed one fingertip along the cool, soapy, luscious feel of spiral galaxies whirling away around the lip of his pipe, laser-carved at his direction from a pristine chunk of New Utah opal meerschaum by a Motie Engineer. Its draw was impeccable, as was its feel. He cupped it to his palm and felt it warm to his hand.

Sighing, he opened his eyes, turned, and assembled the pipe. With the tongs, he dropped a chunk of resin into the bowl, then used the crusher, first to powder it, then to evenly smear the powder around the inside. Laying that tool aside, he flicked open the battered tin, rolled a plug of leaf between thumb and forefinger, used it to blot up any stray resin powder, and tamped it into the pipe. Finally, he raised the pipe to his lips, and with one long draw lit the mass with the clicker. The resin flashed red from bottom up, then glowed with an even white light. Renner smiled, and cupped the pipe with both hands. That last warmth of body heat tipped the scale, revealing the magic of the stone. The soapy meerschaum became translucent, rippling with opalene fire. With each draw, the galaxies sparkled in a milky blue field, as colors played across variations in temperature and the depth of the bas relief.

Anywhere he had ever been or ever seen, his pipe was the finest of its kind. Renner breathed deeply, pulling cool, opal fire through every pore, exhaled a chain of smoke rings, and smiled again. He smoked, and thought, and cleared his mind until the last pale flicker faded to white. High above him, blue, wispy swirls vented through the roof, into the starless night, as he slammed the door behind him and strode downstairs to meet Governor Jackson.

Jackson—now *Sir Lawrence* Jackson, and Governor of Maxroy's Purchase, was momentarily flustered. "But Sally Fowler said—"

Renner, now playing Renner, knocked back the thimble of poisonous brew, smacked the table, leaned forward, and looked Jackson straight in the eyes.

"Governor, let me make one thing perfectly clear." He held the pause for one heartbeat, then continued, earnest as a boy scout.

"Sally Fowler, Lady Blaine, is a dear, old friend; the wife of one of the damned few members of the inherited aristocracy who has outright earned his titles, a do-gooder extraordinaire, and the mother of my Godchildren."

Renner leaned back a bit, and cocked his head.

"That makes her a wealthy, useful, well-intentioned dilettante. But her *actual* credentials? One year of so-called graduate education, most of it stuck in a prison camp, followed by a cloistered life surrounded by the Fleet, Fleet officers, and aristos while she decorated her husband's arm and patronized her pet projects. That does *not* make her an expert on *anything* except how to wrest money from people who have more of it than sense. It sure as hell does not make her a geomorphologist, anthropologist, or ecumenist, nor does it make her conversant with any reasonably current list of people who *are*. You had better dodge her request, and put somebody on that accession expedition who *is*—both expert, and stupid enough to speak truth to power."

Renner straightened completely, grinned, tossed back another shot, and grinned again.

"Preferably, somebody expendable. Because I would bet my pipe that you ain't gonna like what you hear."

Jackson toyed with his drink, calculating, resenting that charming grin. He wasn't stupid. Renner had him in a triple bind. On the one hand, he needed Lord Blaine's support if he was to succeed in reclaiming New Utah for the Empire. Absentmindedly, he slid the glass toward himself across the polished surface. On the other hand, the Mormon True Church Militant despised Renner, personally, and deeply. If the TCM dug in, there would be war, not trade, and he himself, Jackson, Governor of Maxroy's Purchase, would be blamed for another failed mission to New Utah. Jackson slapped the glass from left to right, and caught it mid-glide toward the end of the table. On the gripping hand, Renner was Bury's man; Renner was his inside to Imperial Autonetics; Renner was, so to speak, the man behind the Moties behind the—behind the what? He didn't know. Nobody knew, yet. But in Jackson's experience power followed wealth, and not the other way around.

"I suppose," he said, lifting the glass to toasting level, "you have someone specific in mind?"

Renner smiled. He had the man's tell. "Oh, yeah," he replied. "I thought Quinn."

"Quinn!"

"Uh huh."

"Asach Quinn?"

"Uh huh."

Jackson nodded, once, downed the drink, and looked preoccupied. Then, to no one in particular: "Asach. Quinn. Oh yes. Indeed. Asach Quinn will do just fine."

He stood sharply, and donned his man-of-the-people face. "C'mon, Kev," he said breezily, "we'd best get moving, before the Commissioners accuse us of plotting things we shouldn't."

Horvath's face was literally purple. Spittle flew from his mouth as he ranted.

"*Quinn?!* Asach *Quinn?!* Asach Quinn is—" but his words were drowned out by the babble that ensued:

"the most dedicated servant of truth this Empire has ever…"

"living in a mucking hut on Makassar…"

"arguably the most brilliant ethnographer since…'

"a political hack unfit to…"

"utterly incorruptible…"

"*not* a team player…"

"a polymath genius…"

"used-up and overrated. Did you hear…"

"a deft negotiator, with an uncanny ability to *fit in*…"

"irascible, incorrigible, inscrutable, impossible to…"

"singularly persuasive. Writes like an angel…"

Among them, only Lord Blaine did not raise his voice. Nevertheless, all speech stopped when he spoke.

"The only social scientist Horace Bury personally designated as useful to the Empire of Man."

All heads turned in shock.

Horvath regained control, barely, biting each word in half. "Asach. Quinn. Is. Not. Morally. Suited—"

"I am well aware of your *personal* differences with Quinn's—*demeanor,*" continued Blaine, unruffled. "But you must agree that what is here at issue is of rather more import than—*attire,* wouldn't you agree, Dr. Horvath?"

"With all due respect *My Lord Blaine,* you know that I am not referring to *attire.* I am referring to—"

"My *dear Dr.* Horvath," smiled Blaine. "You are not about to tell me that, after all we have been through, you are frightened of—*hair? Are you?"*

Despite themselves, most of the table chuckled, infuriating Horvath even further, were that possible. His hands were actually trembling. Little patches of foam had congealed at the corners of his mouth. *"You know full well that I am not—"*

"Excellent!" cheered Blaine, flashing his best old-school smile. "Glad that's settled, then. We'll have that vote, shall we? By acclamation, I think, don't you? Shall I move that? Kevin, you'll second? All in favor?"

Of course, the vote carried unanimously. At least, out loud.

2
Accrual
Methods

Now it is unmistakable that even in the German word Beruf, and perhaps still more in the English calling, a religious conception, that of a task set by God, is at least suggested.

—Max Weber, The Protestant Ethic and the Spirit of Capitalism

Makassar, 3049

On Saturday afternoon, the eighteenth of August, Amari Selkirk Alidade Clarke Hathaway (Asach) Quinn sat down with a silk-smooth pen and a stack of creamy blank parchment, and commenced to write a novel. A book, in any case. A novel perhaps. It was a decision on the order of marriage or advanced degree-taking. It was not that the completion would mark an entirely new life. It was rather that the decision itself was life-ordering. On Saturday morning, Asach Quinn would not have made such a decision at all, but on Saturday afternoon did, and in so doing ended an era of waffling, and pondering, and unending waiting for some kind of unnecessary permission, and just got on with it.

It was unapparent why Asach had taken so long to arrive at this literary gate. Asach sported the requisite advanced degrees, the marriage, no end of supporters, and even talent. And the experience: that elusive life experience, intense, and intended to inform.

Asach had *lived in* the Americas. Not in the sense of an Old Earth America, the United States of, as opposed to some other land. The Americas, as in *all* of them. All of those planets that had taken their names, and tried to resurrect some version of their customs, from the cities and states of that ancient republic.

That meant Asach had lived in many flavors of revivalisms and pretenses of resurrection on a dozen member worlds, and another score at least passed through. Had drunk deeply of millennium-old, Pre Empire, Pre-Secession, Pre-transport nostalgia.

Had lived in towns where wheat and monotony were punctuated only by rampant gossip. In villages that had only ever existed as adjuncts to slave markets or recruitment centers or training posts for grunts and jarheads and navvies. In world-class cities big enough to be Targets; cities old enough to have flown five flags before the Crown was welded to The Seal. In cities that remade themselves each decade with such enthusiasm that their natives became economic refugees, fleeing the booms that transformed fishermen's shacks into priceless boutique-side properties.

Had lived in desert vastnesses so unending that news of rain was carried on late-night breezes spiced with the scent of sage and desert varnish. In rolling hills so dense with trees that travel anywhere was like being catapulted through green tubes of foliage, with nothing to see for a hundred miles but litter and fat beasts browsing in the verges. In America the beautiful, America the urban, America the wild, America the suburban, America of the (pseudo-)potato salad and (mock-)apple pie.

And Asach had not just traveled geographically. Asach had known poverty, and at least seen rich; had known position, and had stood next to power. Most people had, at best, some dim opinion of parochial rivalries, but walked, at best, in the footsteps of their high school valedictorian. Asach had seen levels of society so low, and so high, and so bizarre, as to be unimaginable to broadly-defined middle-class harmony. Or working-class dissent. Or upper class segregation.

Yet, for fifty years, Asach had written nearly nothing of import. Reams of drivel—term papers, and white papers, and reports daily, weekly, monthly, and annual. Proposals, and abstracts, and summaries, and overviews, and briefing notes, and speaking points, and outlines as uninspired as obligatory postcards home. All, in the end, barely necessary, and even less memorable.

It began with a cup of coffee. Asach wrote: <u>About Coffee</u>, and underlined both words with one stroke. And then sat and pondered for a good long while about every angle, drip, and smell related to coffee. A diner, with chicken-fried steak. And pie. Asach wrote: <u>Pie</u>, and underlined that, then thought some more about coffee. Coffee could carry you anywhere. Just the geography of coffee could fill walls of maps. Just the price of coffee—Oh Brother! Can you spare a dime?—could fill hours with economics and trade news, fair and unfair. Midnights of exhausted wakefulness: that was the taste and sludgy smell of bad coffee, instant coffee, reheated coffee, coffee ersatz and chicory.

Asach sighed, and put down the pen. The problem with writing was where, and what to begin. The mind begged to write into being every moment of intensity, or imagination, or serendipity. The pen demanded rather more organization than Pie and Coffee. It demanded a sense of place, and a sense of being. Coffee's place was everywhere Asach had ever been or cared to go, and its being was most of humanity. It was exquisitely broadening, but insufficiently narrowing. A book needed characters. Asach sighed again, picked up the pen, and wrote: <u>People</u>. And then pondered some more.

Saint George, New Utah, 3049

Zia stopped, half whirling, and tugged in exasperation at her billowing black dress, snagged on the iron stump of a sawed-down street sign.

It was just too typical. Nothing worked. The streets had not been swept in a month, and trash was drifting around a desiccated dog that no-one wanted to touch because it was, well, dead, and a dog. For three days, there had not been enough electricity to fill the water tanks on the roof, so now the laundry was piling up to the rafters and the kids were whinging with the awful pouty, edgy crankiness that is the inevitable aftermath of sticky drinks and too little sleep.

Ollie had been gone for hours in a probably vain attempt to fill the transporter's fuel cells, so that they could tap the fuel, in order to power the generator, in order to run the equally cranky air conditioner and get at least a few hours respite from the heat. *Ollie*— the head of TCM Contract Security; the man of a thousand eyes. Ollie Azhad, who recruited the local lads; the silent lads; the lads impossible to notice, and had thousands of plain-clothes troops assigned all over Saint George. Ollie-the-rock, now reduced to waiting, himself, personally, in refueling lines.

Dirt was everywhere, billowing down the street in dust devils and forced by the hot, dry wind through every crack. Not that the city government could do anything about the wind, but it just seemed to illustrate the point, in that it was the wind that had snatched her dress and wrapped it around this damnable post—because the one thing the city *had* managed to do was enforce the signage easements. There might not be fuel, or electricity, or even dead dog removal, but what there was,

was a row of sawn-down signs denoting some bureaucrat's bizarre notions of progress.

It was just too much. Furious, framed with a quavering halo of brown, wind-whipped dust, sick to death of the outfall of economic embargo and frustrated nearly to tears, Zia jerked again at the snagged hem, muttering curses alternately against her ridiculously conservative mother-in-law and the ridiculously officious city bureaucracy. The struggle was its own sort of respite: the world shrank; life shrank; into this one, dress-wrapped, but imminently winnable battle. She dropped her shopping bag and seized the offending fabric with both hands, yanking and swearing and just daring them to win. All of them—the heat, the wind, the dirt, the kids, the mother-in-law, the bureaucrats—just daring them to even try to make even one more day even one bit more miserable then it already was. She just dared them, and yanked with a fury.

Tanith, 3049

Rain lashed the driveway, running in sheets under the truck's wheels; giving life and body to the heavy weight of humidity. Harlan Clegg folded over his keyboard, tap-tap-tapping in the disjointed hammering of a four-finger typist who nonetheless stabs out sixty words per minute regardless of weather or circumstance. Folded over, around, peering through the little porthole of a view screen, hunched into a little universe of safe, virtual space defined by secrecy, unconnected to the gentle peeping of tree frogs emerging to dance their little rituals of increase.

Tap-tap-tapping; peering, the screen glare casting his shirtfront with a bluish glow. He paused a moment. His brow furrowed slightly. He inhaled sharply. He stabbed the transmit key, sending his resume hurtling through the torrents with electronic certainty.

Then, staring blankly at his now-blank screen, he sat a while, still folded around his blue virtual space, while the rain sheeted in a solid grey mist through the trees.

There was a kind, hard edge to certainty. You could decide, right or wrong, but just decide, and then you stopped being virtual, and started being hard and certain as the rain-pelted trees. As certain as the peepers in their quest to spawn in the midst of a hurricane. The wind could blow and blow; the trees could lash; you could just laugh at the rain hitting the truck like a shower of lead pellets, and all of that became real and green and smellable, and not hunched and wavering and peering. One keystroke, and you could walk right through the screen and into another life.

New Scotland

They were back upstairs in the anteroom. Back at the table. This time, Rod Blaine was with them. Renner was not playing Renner. Neither was he smoking. Blaine said nothing, for a very long time. Jackson feigned relaxed, patient interest, but clearly he was bored, and tired, and wanted to go home.

Blaine's fingers lay flat on the table, his thumbs wrapped beneath the edge. Still flat, they drummed a random, rhythmless sequence as he stared fixedly at the two men. Finally he seemed to reach some decision.

"I'd rather hoped that *either one* of you might have carried that debate."

Jackson stopped feigning patience. Renner merely shrugged.

"Let alone *both* of you?"

Renner shrugged again. "You saw what it was. We made the pitch, and—"

"And lost control of the Commission. "

Jackson was visibly irritated. "I'd hardly say lost control. You got your—representative—in, didn't you?"

"*My* representative? How amusing. I should have thought Quinn was *your* representative?"

"Whatever. In any case—"

"*Whom*ever. *In any case,* at the cost of showing my hand."

"I have no idea what you are talking about."

"Oh, I think you do."

Jackson widened his eyes and shook his head in mock abject ignorance. "Please! Do enlighten me!"

At this, Blaine's thumbs slipped from beneath the table, and pressed into two thumb-shaped indentations on its edge. His fingers tapped that a-rhythmic sequence again.

"Perhaps this will jar your memory. It is a report on the First Jackson Mission to New Utah. The so-called *failed* mission of 3035? When, according to your report, New Utah *refused* accession to the Empire? Was formally declared an Outie world? Anathema? Placed under permanent Trade Ban? Anyway, this is *another* report, written by someone Bury termed 'useful to the Empire of Man.' "

Milky light glowed in a square just below the polished surface. Blaine dragged his fingers downward over the glow, twice, then dragged his index finger rightwards across a row, then tapped twice on a point about a hand's breadth above his navel. Text appeared, floating in the milky haze. He placed one finger in each of the topmost corners, crossed his hands, and shoved his fingers across the table toward Renner. The text page rotated one-hundred eighty degrees, appearing right-side up to Kevin. Renner glanced at it briefly, then with two hands tapped once in the uppermost corners, then again to the left of the page. A copy appeared. With his left palm on the table, he shoved it toward Jackson, who reached out, dragged it palm-wise the rest of the distance, then re-oriented it.

Jackson was visibly annoyed that he'd been second-in-line for the handout. Until he began reading.

PERSONAL AND CONFIDENTIAL

His Excellency Horace Hussein Bury

Sinbad

Eid-al-Fitr, 3035

My dear Abu Nadir,

A pleasure, as always, to find myself in your service. I trust this letter finds your family well.

Attached is my full report on the Jackson Mission to New Utah. I believe that you will find it interesting reading. Here follows a summary of the most salient issues.

Bottom line: The delegation is deeply divided, and have papered over their differences with the creative fiction that New Utah has "refused" accession to the Empire.

The reality: The New Utah True Church has become dominated by its paramilitary arm, the True Church Militant (TCM), over which the Elders of Maxroy's Purchase (MP) have ever-diminishing, but desire total, control. Insofar as there is a New Utah planetary government, it is *de facto* the TCM. However, TCM authority does not penetrate deeply beyond Saint George, where it has nationalized city-state lands and therefore dominates most of the food supply. Whatever the Jackson delegation may report, the vast majority of New Utah's citizens are at best barely aware of the Empire's existence. The term "Outie" is a fiction conjugated by the TC on Maxroy's Purchase, to divert attention from transgressions against the Empire perpetrated by external actors and their own paramilitaries.

Key issues: To boost short-term agricultural yields, the TCM has sanctioned return to "traditional" industrial agricultural practices, with predictable results. Soils surrounding Saint

George are essentially dead, and the TCM is now dependent on commercial agrochemical inputs to maintain food production. As these must come from Maxroy's Purchase, the True Church is desperate to maintain its monopoly on agricultural input deliveries—in order to maintain its hold over the TCM.

Most of the non-Mormon Saint George civil population, weary of the constant infighting among the TC/TCM factions, have drifted ever-further into the New Utah outback. I managed to travel as far as Bonneville, at the edge of TC authority on New Utah, where the TCM does collect annual "tithes," but does not provide basic services. A vibrant Levantine quarter has grown up in the old Founder district there, with intermixed Muslim, LDS Sixer, Armenian, Chaldean, Fijian, and other Christian communities.

As you know, on Maxroy's Purchase, following the self-proclaimed True Church purges of urban LDS Sixer wards around 175 years ago, missionaries from the New Ireland Church of Him made great inroads among the displaced victims of that pogrom. What is less well known (few on MP would admit to it), is that in 2965 these Purchase Himmists dispatched what they called "His Mission to Heaven" to New Utah. Most passed through Saint George, directly onward into the outback.

I am told that everything beyond Bonneville is "pilgrim country," wherein not even the TCM holds sway. I did not manage to visit there, but did manage to speak with so-called "pilgrims" traveling incognito, en route to visit what they called their "gathering" in the outback. More they would not tell me, unless I joined them, which given time constraints I could not do.

Why, you are no doubt asking, am I conveying this colorful religious history? Because it is key to the factionalization within the Jackson delegation. "Pilgrim country" is clearly the source of opal meerschaum, on which the TCM depends for revenue to purchase agrichemicals. Yet, because of TC strictures, effectively only non-Mormons may travel and trade there. The Purchase TC position is that all Himmists are worse than non-believers: they are "excommunicants." Therefore, no TC Mormon may missionize there, on pain of the same fate. They have got themselves into a real internal dilemma regarding church, state, and mammon—and any number of off-world opportunists (among them ITA entrepreneurs) have moved into that vacuum.

I have great fear as to how this dilemma may be resolved. Rumor has it that Lillith Van Zandt is bankrolling the so-called Outie piracy, and has secreted a battalion of Friedlander armor in the Oquirr mountains outside Saint George. How or if the Van Zandts intend to weigh in is unclear to me, but if true, the presence of Friedlanders could only mean that there will likely be civil war to break this impasse over control of the pathetic trade in outmoded agrochemicals and shiny rocks.

In summary: Horace, you and I already know that there is nothing of sufficient *financial* interest to tempt Imperial Autonetics into this backwater fray. It is too remote, the trip too costly, and the products too few to justify the expense.

But New Utah is a big world. The First Empire Naval surveys were only perfunctory, and concentrated (a) geographically, around Saint George Province, and (b) in scope, primarily in search of commercially viable weapons-grade metal ores. While TC/MP claims to control the planet are absurd, New Utah is certainly neither of threat or of interest to the Empire. What *may* interest *you* is the vibrant, peaceful, and in its own way cosmopolitan Levantine community in

Bonneville—and the attendant possibilities for further exploration of parts unknown.

Please commend Capt. Fox for his alacrity and discretion. I assure you that no one aside from Fox and the Governor himself were aware of my presence, let alone my mission.

Warmest regards to Cynthia,

Asach

While Jackson read the letter, Blaine's eyes never wavered from his face. Renner finished first. He let out a low whistle, then sat back. With his finger, he circled the "bottom line" paragraph, then stroked and stabbed it with his finger. A crimson oval surrounded the text, with an exclamation point in the margin. He then ticked next to "Outie is a fiction," and finally "the Governor himself." Red checkmarks appeared beside the text. He then put his hand flat on the desk, centered on the message, and pushed it back across the table to Blaine.

Blaine nodded curtly, and turned it right side up, without actually looking down. Jackson looked up, confused; uncertain.

"Did you meet Asach Quinn during that first mission to New Utah?"

"Well, yes. Quinn was—"

"And do you agree with the substance of this report?"

"Well, it wasn't made to me, and I—"

"That's not what I asked you. Do you agree or not?"

"I stand by the *official* report of the Commission."

"I'd advise you *not* to hide behind your Commissioners. After all, *you* appointed them."

"I don't know why you would trust a private letter written by a low-level advisor over the official summary of the Governor's Commission."

"There! You see? *Your* Commission. Able Spacer Lawrence Jackson's Commission! As against the word of an *independent* advisor appointed by—"

"My *Lord* Blaine! I may once have been a mere able spacer under your *junior* command, but I now hold a Knighthood that stands me credit against anyone, even if I had to *earn* my title. As for Quinn, Quinn's a well-known class traitor who denies any responsibility for—"

"Ah, indeed! Just the point, *Sir* Lawrence. *Governor* Sir Lawrence. Governor Sir Lawrence Jackson, what is the unofficial motto of this Empire?"

Jackson was clearly confused as he delivered the schoolboy response. "The Empire of Man decides the fate of worlds."

"And who embodies the Empire?"

"The Emperor, of course"

"Yes."

Blaine let that soak in a moment. "The Emperor. Not Commissioners. Not the ITA. Not the aristocracy. Not his *appointed Governors*. And *especially* not *ex-Able Spacers.*"

"Now see here—"

"*No, you* see here, *Sir Lawrence.* That's the deal, you see. It's a deal as old as the Magna Carta. It's a deal that anyone with *inherited* title gets drubbed in from their first suckle, whatever way their family decides to gamble thereafter. And *it's the deal you sign up for when you accept the Knighthood.* The Barons get to run their realms however they see fit, *but the King gets to pick the Barons.* They *do not, ever,* under *any* circumstance, *get to appoint themselves.* And it is the *sworn duty of the King's Chivalry to defend* that principle. Or did you miss that little part of the oath when the sword tapped your *manifestly unworthy* shoulders?"

Renner twisted in his seat. "Look, Rod, don't you think you are being a little—"

"*Sir* Kevin. Do not presume upon our friendship. You have always suffered the cheerful delusion that the aristocracy works for you. *It does not.* It works for itself. *It works to earn and preserve its Baronage.* In furtherance of that aim, we may delegate *privilege*, but we *never, ever* delegate *power. As you well know.*"

Renner was frozen. Blaine turned back to Jackson. "I carried a grudge against Horace Bury, *the richest man in the Empire*, for *three decades* because he had played a *minor* role, hedging his financial bets during a *local* insurrection on a *useless* planet that was already an *active threat* to the Empire."

He shot an aside to Renner. "You quite charmingly believed that grudge was personal? Because Sally got caught up in the mess and fell into my gallant, youthful arms? *Don't be ridiculous.*"

He went on. "*For merely falling under suspicion,* Sir Lawrence, Bury paid with a lifetime of service, with annual capital contributions to the Crown that exceeded the entire tax revenue of your pathetic backwoods planet to date, and, in the end, his life. So now, *Governor,* faced with this little piece of Bury's payback, just how do you propose to earn back your neck, let alone your liberty, *when you have clearly suborned the Commission's report, attempted to hold New Utah as a vassal of Maxroy's Purchase, and thereby committed outright treason against the Emperor himself?*"

Jackson blanched, while his intestines attempted to escape through his navel.

"But you can't prove that I knew *any* of this!"

Blaine's voice was ice. "Ah, there you go, missing the point *again*. If you *didn't*, as Governor you *should have*. If you *did*, well, *then*. And *in any case*, there is always that problem of *suspicion.*"

He watched Jackson's lips turn slightly blue. He did not rise. "I will give you twenty-four hours leave to ponder my question. I trust you can see yourself out?"

To his credit, the Governor's hands were almost steady as he latched the heavy door behind him. Renner and Blaine faced one another and broke into wicked grins.

"I trust you have people outside?'

"Oh, better than that," nodded Renner.

"Ah. Of course. Now, let's see which way the rabbit runs."

Renner reached for his pipe box, still smiling. Blaine rose and poured himself a stiff drink. And for his part, shivering outside in the warm night air, Governor Sir Lawrence Jackson silently vowed to personally strangle Asach Quinn.

Blaine Institute, New Caledonia, 3049

"But it's not *fair,*" whinged Ali Baba. Glenda Ruth Fowler, a human child raised by a Motie Mediator nanny, marveled at this, a Motie Mediator child raised by—well, by nobody, really, at the moment. By her, if anyone. If Ali Baba had *been* a human, she'd call his—her—its—behavior acting out. Clearly, Bury's death had deeply upset the—she was about to think *child* again, but aside from the fact that Ali Baba was not human, Ali Baba also was no longer really a child. Moties grew, and matured, very quickly.

On that horrible day on *Sinbad,* when Bury had died, during the final jump out of the Mote system and into the red star that meant *home,* in the midst of the panic—*Sinbad* hot on *Atropos'* stern; Moties hot behind; *Sinbad* forced to stand alone against the Motie Khanate fleets; the Flinger going on and on and on, tossing nukes into the hearts of dozens, maybe hundreds of Motie ships still too jump-shocked to respond—on that horrible, horrible day, Glenda Ruth's heart breaking, had Cynthia known? She'd charged the paddles, shouted "Clear!," then "Glenda Ruth! Take Ali Baba!"

Ali Baba was howling then; ranting; furious that Bury was gone. But Glenda Ruth's heart was breaking too, for a different reason, as the killing went on, and on, and on. She knew it then; couldn't understand it then: the baby mediator willed and willed and willed *Sinbad* to win, while part of her willed that they would not. She did not wish *Sinbad* to lose, but she could not bear that all those Moties would die. So, it wasn't at all that Ali Baba clung to her, it was that she clung to Ali Baba. Had Cynthia known? That on board that ship, the closest thing to her, a Motie-raised human, was Ali Baba, a human-raised Motie? Or was it just the off chance that she'd stood nearby?

He was not howling now. With the fluid shift of a Mediator-in-the-making, Ali Baba changed tactics, ceased to whine, and momentarily caught her off guard. She knew what was happening, but that did not change the flutter in her hindbrain as she responded to the summation of posture, pitch and tone that no longer signaled *you have power*, but instead signaled *you have none,* despite the paucity of words.

"Excuse me," said Ali Baba, who, with a slight bow, left the room. To any other observer, the exit would have seemed a polite apology and graceful exit. To Glenda Ruth, it was a clear, and final, dismissal: of her; of her own desperate wish to be, if not a mother, then at least a friend, to this fragile, alien child.

Glenda Ruth's lips narrowed to a white slash, and she closed her eyes. Her blunder was absolute. She had been forewarned, and ignored the warning. She had made the arrogant human presumption that she wasn't *meant* to see Ali Baba's personal log; that Ali Baba had been too young; too naive to adequately hide a babyish what-I-did-on-my-first-trip-to-space schoolbook exercise.

Well, she had seen it, which actually left little doubt that she *was* meant to see it, even if it was designed to *look* as though she wasn't. If Ali Baba, or any Motie, didn't want a log read by Glenda Ruth, Glenda Ruth was hardly likely to even become aware of its existence, let alone break into the file. So how much more arrogant to presume that what she'd read indicated childish misunderstanding; that it was something she could *fix* with patience and time. Babyish it might look, but it wasn't a confessional cry for help. It had been written with *intent*. That she'd been allowed to read it meant—what?

She replayed the text in memory. She *willed* a clearer mind. She opened her eyes. Stupid, stupid, stupid.

It was not a lonely cry for social contact. It was a declaration of allegiance. Only she, Motie-raised she, could know how profound a line she had transgressed; how insulting she had been to Ali Baba's very person in demanding allegiance to her own emotional desires.

Aboard Sinbad, Mote System, 3047

Auntie Omar took me to see Grampa Horace. He was weird. He only had two arms. He had no gripping hand. He had no ear. He was all thin and pale, like a Runner, or a Doctor. But he was warm. He scratched my ear. I liked that.

Auntie Omar said the Tatars were afraid. Auntie Omar said they "do not know what they have." Grampa Horace said "They're holding a wolf by the ears." That sounded scary and strange. I was not sure about *ears*. I knew what *my* ear was. But *ears* was something *Wolves* had more-than-one of. I thought maybe it meant Warrior scythes. I thought maybe a *Wolf* was a kind of Warrior. Auntie Omar said I was *never* to go to a Warrior unless MaPa, personally, said so. Not even MaMa. Not even Auntie Omar. Only MaPa. Auntie Omar said Warriors made quick work of the likes of us. Auntie Omar said *only* a Master could give orders to a Warrior. Auntie Omar said only my MaPa could give orders to a Warrior that I could trust.

Then Grampa Horace said my name was Ali Baba. That's how I knew he was a Grampa. Because Auntie Omar said only Auntie Omar, or my MaPa, or a Grampa could name me. That made me sad. Grampas are old. They always die soon.

That's what Auntie Omar said. You have to learn everything they know, as fast as you can, because Grampas will die soon.

Later, Auntie Omar took me to see Grampa Horace again. He said gravity did not make him tired. He said he was *attracted* to me. He said I gave him *pleasure*. I was very proud. Auntie Omar said it is always best when your Grampa likes you. She said it does not always happen.

Then a Runner came. It said that *Tartars* were coming. That's what Auntie Omar called them: *Tartars*. It said the Tartars had valuable *Guests*. It said the guests were *Humans*. It said the *Humans* were all *safe*. That's what Auntie Omar told Grampa Horace: *guests, humans, safe*. Then Grampa Horace asked Sir Eudoxus to send a message to *Lord* Blaine that *his offspring are safe.*" Auntie Omar called MaPa *Lord* Cornwallis. And Grampa Horace said this message was important. And Sir Eudoxus worried that *Lord* Blaine would send warships. So I knew these *Humans* must be young Masters! Maybe that's why the Tartars were afraid. Maybe *Wolves* were enemy Warriors who would kill young Masters!

So I was very afraid, too. I wanted to go to MaMa. But I did my Duty. I watched Grampa Horace. I watched and watched him. It was very hard. His arms did not move. His hands did not move. He was in his g-force bed. It was full of water, so he would squash down into it when the ship accelerated. You had to watch and watch his *face*. That was hard too, because it got all squashed flat. But that's when I noticed that Grampa Horace had two *ears*. They were very small. They were hard to see. They were flat against his head. At first, I thought he was afraid.

But then Auntie Omar *speaked* to MaPa! And Sir Eudoxus *speaked* to *their* Master! And I could hear: *their* Master was afraid! Their Master was very afraid that *Lord Blaine* would send many warships. But even when Auntie Omar *speaked* to MaPa, Grampa Horace was not afraid. I was very proud. My

Grampa must have been a very powerful Master, and Auntie Omar and MaPa had given him to me!

And then I thought: If *Wolves* have two *ears*, then maybe they are like Grampa Horace. Maybe *Wolves* are a special kind of *Humans*. Maybe *Wolves* are very powerful young Masters. Maybe *Wolves* are *Lord Blaine's children*. Not just his *get*, like me. If Lord Blaine had many warships, I was very afraid for the Tartars. I should have been afraid for us.

After that, whenever I was not with Auntie Omar, or MaMa, I went to Grampa Horace. He was mostly in bed. We were on a warship. It was going very fast. Everyone got very heavy. Grampa Horace had to stay in the waterbed, so he would not squash completely. Uncle Kevin said that we would *jump* soon. I call him Uncle Kevin, because he was very close to Grampa Horace. But he was not one of Grampa's *offspring*. He was Grampa Horace's pilot. A pilot is like an Engineer, but an Engineer who can talk. Grampa Horace and Uncle Kevin talked a lot. So Uncle Kevin was like a Master too. So that was like Auntie Omar, or me. Somebody who has a MaMa who is an Engineer, and a MaPa who is a Master, and can talk to anyone. So I called him Uncle. He called Auntie Omar a *Mediator*.

I did not know what *jump* was. It was something they had to make the ship do, to send this message about the wolves. Uncle Kevin was afraid Grampa Horace would die. Doctor Cynthia was afraid too. I told Auntie Omar that it was my Duty to stay with Grampa Horace if he was going to die. Auntie Omar was very proud.

Grampa was very warm. The bed was very soft. I fell asleep. And then! Oh, the horror! I wished that I would die! Everything went—silent! I could not hear MaMa! I could not hear MaPa! I could not hear Uncle Kevin, or Auntie Omar, or Doctor Cynthia, or anyone! I tried to hold Grampa Horace, but my arms could not hear my brain! I could not hear Grampa Horace! I was sure Grampa Horace had died!

And then, just a little, I could hear Uncle Kevin. He was making noises. They were not words, just noises. I crawled. I crawled and crawled. I thought I would die. I wished I would die. I crawled onto his chest. I grabbed his clothes and rocked and rocked. "Uncle Kevin!" I screamed and screamed. But he did not hear. And then I remembered that Uncle Kevin could not hear *screams*. I had to think in Anglic. I tried and tried. I had not spoken Anglic before. I had listened and listened, but I had not spoken. I tried again. And then the words came out. "Ali Baba is sick," I said. "His Excellency is sick. So is, am I. Sick in the head, scrambled brains, wobbly eyes. Kevin?" It was very hard. But I made sure to say "His Excellency." Uncle Kevin was just a pilot. Grampa Horace was a Great Master.

Uncle Kevin said it would be all right, but it was not. Everyone was sick. Everyone had died a little, inside. The ship was sick. Doctor Cynthia was sick. But she crawled to Grampa Horace's side. She did things. She was his Doctor. He just lay there, on his back. But then I could *hear* him again. I thought: he is a very *old* Grampa. He should have died. It is too soon. I don't know anything. What will I do, if my Grampa dies? What will I do without Doctor Cynthia beside his bed?

I went back to him. He did not speak. I just listened. I did my best, but I cried and cried. Uncle Kevin could not hear. Doctor Cynthia could not hear. But I thought MaMa could hear. And MaPa, and Auntie Omar, and Sir Eudoxus. I wanted them all to know: I am doing my Duty. I will do my Duty. Even this horrible sickness will not make me stop my Duty. I will not leave his side.

And then Uncle Kevin said he would do it again. Make the ship accelerate. Squash Grampa Horace down into his bed, so he could not even breathe. They were talking about the Eye. They were talking about a *jump* through the Eye. It would kill him! So I jumped first! I jumped as hard as I could, and hit Uncle Kevin in the chest, and said, "NO! Not Again!" But

Grampa said "Here, Ali Baba," so I went. And then the Engineers moved Doctor Cynthia's travel couch right next to Grampa Horace's bed. I hid my head under Grampa's arm, and just *listened*. And then we *jumped* again.

This time, she was there. Doctor Cynthia. She was a Doctor, but she could talk to everyone too. And when the others were gone, she often talked to Grampa Horace. Uncle Kevin passed out, but she never did. I never did. She breathed for him. Breathed for Grampa. I heard her breath go into him, and come back out again. Again, and again. Again, and again. I thought *there is a machine for this*. But I also knew: she is doing her Duty. She is doing her Duty for him.

I could hear his heart. It never stopped. It boomed. Lub-dub. Lub-dub. Lub-dub. On and on it pounded. I timed my breathing to it. I timed my breathing to her breathing for him. And then I heard his breath go into her. Again and again. Again and again. I was sick and afraid with joy. I thought: it is over now. It is done. He will be safe.

Even when Uncle Kevin said "Cynthia, how much can he stand?" Grampa answered. He said: "Anything. Kevin. Do what you must It is now in the hands of Allah." I did not know who Allah was, but his heart was so strong. Grampa's heart was strong. They all still listened to him. Whatever he said, they listened, and so did I.

3
Sanctum, Sanctus, Sancta

On the other hand, we shall expect to find that the influence of Calvinism was exerted more in the liberation of energy for private acquisition. For in spite of all the formal legalism of the elect, Goethe's remark in fact applied often enough to the Calvinist: "The man of action is always ruthless; no one has a conscience but an observer."

—*Max Weber, The Protestant Ethic and the Spirit of Capitalism*

Makassar

Asach stared out into the dusk, awaiting the first twinkling stars. People were clearly the problem, always and everywhere. People were unfixed, and needed fixing. Unfixed in place, in time, in purpose; unfixed in principle or intent. Unfixed in their aims or views or desires or even likes and dislikes.

Or, alternatively, entirely fixed, in all these things. People were, generally speaking, slippery and contrary things: saying one thing, doing another, and oblivious to the contradiction. Generally speaking, the only things truly fixed about them were rut and routine. Ruts so deep that they never peered out to any horizon.

And down there in their little ruts they stayed, bored and boring, changing aims and principles alike in a daily quest for the preferential familiar. Familiarity substituting for—Asach was going to write "character," but stopped to ponder this presumption. A preference for the known *defined* character, rather than negating it. Familiarity was not a substitute for character at all. Merely for purposefulness. Familiarity was a substitute for purpose—or at least for purpose of the rut-busting sort.

Hence the need for fixing. Down there in the deep well of rut-ness, a few found true solace and contentment, but in Asach's experience *most* found a deep well of resentment, and spent a good part of every waking day trying to affix this resentment on some blameworthy party.

Which was tough news for Asach, now fixed to a purpose, which the unfixed smelled like hot blood at a fresh kill. Asach the finally-motivated, the living contradiction of rut-ness, the past practitioner of constant movement, the perfect focus for veritable wellsprings of hostility. Asach, bearer of the unforgivable flaw: Asach, the *different*. Asach underlined different.

And yet, somehow, to Asach they trooped (and always had done) for fixing—hence the decades-long stream of reportage. At this juncture, some days Asach simply wanted to stand up and scream: *go see for yourself!* Open your eyes, open your ears, open your petrified, suburbanized, rut-encrusted brains and for once in your predictable life, *think!* But knowing better: knowing the sheltered [fill in class name here] class's insatiable thirst for talking to itself about other people, out there, unseen beyond the rut, Asach, hermeneutic chronicler extraordinaire, donning keyboard and point-of-view, would set out once again to *explain.*

Yes, the food is different here. No, those people over there are not criminals. They are just poor. In this [village, town, city, country, planet] those are not the same thing. *Ad nauseum.* A lot of the explaining was more prosaic, having to do with enabling a warehouse operations chief to talk to an ITA implementation team, but it all boiled down to the same thing: amazing but true, other people do not live in your rut! They live in a different rut!

The explanation went that this made them *actually* different. But in Asach's mind, the opposite was the case: they were all exactly—*exactly*—the same. Hide-bound, parochial, inexperienced, defensive, and, generally speaking, hostile, although they papered that over with varying degrees of hubris. In need of fixing.

It was late evening. The soft air and crickets recalled so many other evenings, filled with crickets, or peepers, or cicadas, or all three. A lot had changed in Makassar over thirty-five years. A lot more might have changed—and not for the better—if the ITA hadn't originally dumped the Prince Samual's World exiles into the most god-awful, pestilential armpit of the continent. Thankfully, MacKinnie's successors were still fully occupied with re-creating Church, State, and the Silk Road among the winter-frozen peasantry scattered from Jikar to Batav. Which had the added benefit of occupying the jihadists allied against them, and leaving the warm, gracious, civilized realms of the Bungar delta to the (thankfully largely absentee) colonials and Tambar traders. The local wealth generated by all the movement of exotic woods, spices, and coffee made life here quite comfortable indeed. And yet.

Asach underlined: fixing, and reassessed. So far, Pie, Coffee, People, Different, Fixing. Asach decided, personally, to head into the kitchen, fix some pie and coffee, and give up on this book thing. It just seemed safer that way. Asach was, generally speaking, profoundly tired of being different. It was probably a fair trade for the heaven-sent experience of knowing fifty-seven different ways to explain coffee, but right about now a little rut would be nice. Just a different rut. Somebody else's rut. A rut that didn't require so much fixing.

The light faded. Wind played through the makassar trees. Asach sat on the roof, wolfing down pie and sucking down aromatic draughts of coffee. Watched curiously as a hefty shape made its way down the lane, raised a fist, and pounded on the door below.

It took Asach half an hour to throw essentials into a hand grip, lock up, pass the keys to a neighbor, and hitch a rickshaw into the authorized ITA landing zone in Ujung Pandang. After that, an interminable wait for a pinisi up to the space hub, where Horvath's Goon was, inexplicably, waiting, accompanied by the Librarian.

The Librarian was understandable. Contrary to know-it-all opinion, librarians actually thought long and deep over, were meticulously trained in, and knew a lot about information archives. That included not just what to stuff into them, but how to establish and maintain integrated resources, data maintenance and recovery, remote access, redundant storage, cataloguing, search and retrieval, unpowered access, and all the other arcana that went along with ensuring that locals got, and kept, and kept up with, what they needed. Or what the Empire thought they needed. Or both.

Horvath's Goon was another matter. HG, as he had already been mentally christened by Asach, was a graying, impatient, imperious version of Horvath, and like Horvath utterly without any social grace known in any civilized society. Alternately whining and blustering, HG's express purpose seemed to be—well, Asach was not sure what HG's purpose might be. Presumably to Represent the Academic Might and

Gravitas of the Empire, for whatever that might count to the failing stock farmers of New Utah. Why that required travel halfway across the galaxy and back, just to escort Asach to a meeting, was even less clear.

Of course, HG had a real name, a title, a doctorate, and a reputation, but Asach didn't much care. It was the sort of name and title that came with birth; the sort of doctorate that came from privilege (via a grandfather clause at a prestigious university), and the sort of reputation that came from snapping up and claiming as his own the works and limelight of a parade of graduate students and lesser-known scholars who had actually done most of the slog, made most of the insights, and slaved over most of the write-up and lecture prep. HG just showed up to make the pitch and collect the accolades, not to mention the honoraria.

Apparently, for this stint The Goon had claimed "lifelong" experience in the "remote regions" of "the New Caledonia and Purchase systems," and "intimate acquaintance" with those societies, their religious practices, and the doctrines of the Mormon True Church. In fact, Asach knew, two decades earlier as a graduate student HG had spent a smattering of summer weeks over the course of several years out in the boonies, unsuccessfully prospecting with a rock zapper and chemical test kit. While playing with his chemistry set he'd probably met about a dozen people total, including his paid field crew and the drivers who hauled him out to the middle of nowhere. He did not speak one relevant language aside from Anglic, was appallingly inept at negotiating through interpreters, and wouldn't recognize a religious zealot if it smacked him over the head with *The Book*. But, like most suburbanites, he fancied his little camping trips as *real adventures*, a fiction that he probably actually believed. His audiences certainly did.

In any case, there he sat, and Asach would have to endure him throughout the long slog, via Sparta, to the

Commission's prep meetings on New Scotland, and thence until arrival at Saint George on New Utah. Thankfully, thereafter, true to form, The Goon would reside in the safety of the TCM Security Zone, while Asach flew on to Bonneville, and from there to—to where?

To wherever necessary to answer the Imperial Questions. There were eight. They were the questions that determined the fates of nations:

1. Does New Utah possess a planetary government?

2. If yes, is that government controlled by the True Church theocracy?

3. Is the True Church on New Utah politically subordinate to the True Church on Maxroy's Purchase?

4. Is New Utah disposed to willing accession to the Empire of Man?

5. If yes, under what terms?

6. If yes, can sufficiently profitable opportunities be identified to justify the costs of Imperial accession?

7. If yes, in what accession class?

8. If no, does New Utah pose immanent, credible threat to the Empire or any of its members?

It was The Goon's job to answer these from within the cloisters of the TC safe zone on the outskirts of Saint George. It was the Librarian's job to establish a "knowledge mission" to "rebuild capacity" for "education in the rule of law" at the largely gutted university. And it was Asach's job to go anywhere and everywhere else, and then report back directly, and discretely, to the Commission. But only Asach knew of those latter instructions. They were unknown to The Goon and The Librarian. As far as they were concerned, Asach was "coordinating with locals" to "set up offices" for a trade mission in Bonneville.

SANCTUM, SANTUS, SANCTA

Sparta

Of all things, Peet's coffee at JCF Interstellar! A whiff of Makassar in a sea of Anglos. Horvath's designated minion insisted on handling every cent, clearly thought Asach's quest for fair trade dark roast an eccentric extravagance, and yet also insisted on paying for it. Conversely, the extravagance of forced meal consumption was nothing short of amazing. Dinner outbound at the JCF sector hub, dinner on the jumper, then lunch on arrival at Sparta Imperial Spaceport, then dinner on the planetside shuttle (again). Total actual elapsed time between meals: about 3 hours.

Asach could not keep up, and enduring dour glares skipped the SIS lunch in favor of leftovers saved from a boxed breakfast from the inbound shuttle. Clearly, there was a minefield of food control issues there. They hadn't really had any business on Sparta itself, and no-one felt the need to play tourist, but they had a few hours to kill and decided to freshen up and catch some good sleep under gravity before making the Trans-Coal Sack trek. So, down they went, and checked in for a couple of hours at the SIS Crown and Thistle. It was clean, pleasant, and close to the gates.

HG paid for that, too, then forced Asach to endure a nightcap accompanied by an interminable lecture on Alderson Drive technology. Being amply convinced by decades of experience that they did so, Asach did not really care to hear yet again the details of how tramlines opened between some stars, nor how the drives exploited these to play interstellar hop-scotch, nor the theoretical basis for why onboard systems flailed through multiple checks and restarts on re-entry into normal space. Nor—especially nor—how many times HG had or had not puked his guts up while recovering from jump shock. At a momentary lull during the third recounting of his outbound trip to Makassar, Asach mad brisk apologies, abandoned the unfinished, unwanted drink, and bolted for a shower and bed.

Maxroy's Purchase

The trip had already taken forever. Asach detested pretty much everything about space travel. The jumps were excruciating. The boredom transiting between jump points was interminable, but it at least allowed time for writing. Then came the agonizing waits at orbital hubs for planetary shuttles, where the cramped little seats and disorienting floating about in search of the right exit corridors made any more writing impossible. Finally, the even more cramped shuttle descents.

It was Asach's personal purgatory. Trapped forever in meetings and shuttle diplomacy with HG and The Librarian. To soften up New Utah for the Imperial Pitch, Maxroy's Purchase was formally ordained with provisional authority to supervise a three-month lifting of "Outie" status and the attendant mandatory trade embargo. This made New Utah exempt from all import and export duties—at least on anything that was close to worthless. Anybody willing to run the risk was free to run any cargo they chose. Given the risks and costs, there were, unsurprisingly, few takers.

First, just getting there was tedious and expensive, requiring two jumps past red dwarfs and a long crawl past a lump of rock in an E-class star system. Then, once you got there, there was nothing to buy, and the poor sods there had nothing to barter with. It certainly wasn't worth the expense of running containers, let alone cargo ships. A steady stream of relatives, adventure seekers, and speculators now passed to and fro, packed into any available transportation, but it was hard to see how this was going to add up to sufficient economic activity to be of much impact or interest.

Finally, the place was a mess. It certainly was not the Heaven that true believers of the Pitchfork River True Church on Maxroy's Purchase claimed it to be. It might be united now—the True Church claimed it was—but if so, that unity had come at a price. Nothing worked, and wrecked military junk was everywhere.

HG's approach to this chaos was to institute shuttle diplomacy. For reasons unclear to Asach, HG, who felt himself in charge of the mission, insisted initially on "establishing a beachhead" on Maxroy's Purchase, and "staying in close coordination with" the Commission, in order to "provide orderly reports of progress." In other words, to suck up to whoever would listen and report whether, in HG's august opinion, New Utah had been sufficiently impressed by their new economic boom to welcome the Fleet with open arms. From Asach's view, what this meant in practice was that most of their time was used up tramp steaming across the stars, attending meetings, and planning the next trip, with precious little time focused on The Questions.

Trapped next to The Goon's coughing, snorting, gouging, yakking, and fidgeting, Asach gave up on work and feigned sleep, admitting full consciousness only once standing in interstellar baggage claim. HG, who earned more money per year than the average laborer would see in a lifetime, refused to shell out five crowns for a porter to wrangle the trio's luggage. Disinclined to endure late-night scenes, Asach yanked bags stuffed with indefinable lumps of unnecessary gear from the carousel. The Librarian wrestled them onto a trolley. Asach steeled for the remaining trudge to the air taxi depot, to catch the hop to Hand Glacier. HG checked into a "nice" hotel in downtown Pitchfork River.

Saint George, New Utah, 3049

The fringe of concrete slab construction, hung with sorry laundry gone limp with grey drizzle, was called

"Moorstown." Nobody remembered why. All army barracks have their half-light fringes, their frontier lands suffering from the garish combination of all the worst elements of occupier and occupied. The loutish testosterone haze that inevitably accompanies conscientious and coltish males infuses everything it touches with a massive, cacophonous, masculine aesthetic. Wherever troops imagine themselves as some brand of muscle-professional (hired heroes, or hired killers), only the aggressively-strapped-to-industrial-workbench survives the filter of breakage and brigandage to compete in their payday marketplace. The inevitable scatter of dusty children and under-, over-, or otherwise malnourished mothers must make what way they can among the swagger, personal weaponry, techno-gadgetry, and nasty-smelling drink.

In Moorstown, their lot was this sad line of postwar pre-fab apartment blocks. There were no gardens, no neat landscaping. The only colors relieving the unremitting grey were bright splashes of bedding, skirts, and bonnets hung from windowsills to air in the pre-dawn breeze.

Marul's footsteps echoed down the stairwell, and she shivered against the gooseflesh raised by the dirty air. It seeped through her yellow bonnet; fingered her cheap knit cardigan, and blew past in a swirl of dried, muddied leaves. Across the still, she heard jody calls, echoing like water slapping boat hulls in a foggy harbor. Not that she had ever seen, or would ever see, a harbor.

Troops running in formation had already cleared the main gate and would soon wind their way up the post perimeter, headed toward the last shaggy patch of grazing commons—what was left of a landing safety zone for the old TCM airfield, long since built over into a maze of warehouses attached to a shipping depot. All of what had once stood secreted in a foothill forest belt beyond the city proper was now surrounded by SunRail container yards, FLIVRbahns, and the backwash of immigrant and military housing.

All, that is, except the little patch of commons abutting the post on one side, and across it, at the end of the winding, wide walking path the troops would follow on their morning run, the thin greenbelt along the river's edge ironically named the Philosopher's Way. It was doubtful that any philosopher had walked there since Foundation times, when it had connected a vast parkland here to a footbridge crossing the river into the old city.

Marul started as a patch of damp air suddenly magnified a cadence call, as if someone standing not a foot away had shouted inexplicably:

"My old lady was ninety-THREE,"

But the breeze tugged again; the sound dimmed. Her heart pounding, Marul turned toward the commons, eyes steadfastly on her feet, and began trudging in the direction of the distant trees. Every morning she walked this way, part of a long trek toward her Uncle Ollie's stall in the farm market on the edge of the old city. While he met his clients and discussed men's business over tea, she measured out olives and nuts; fruits and seed pastes; fermented milks and clotted creams. He was a busy man. He provided security guards to everyone, everywhere, and that meant a lot of meetings in these troubled times.

So every morning, Marul rose before the soldiers, prepared her brother's meals and clothes, laid them out ready for them to speed their way to school, readied herself, dressing in the dark, then began her trudge across the field at half-light in order that she might open the stall, receive and set out the wares, and prepare her uncle's coffee.

And every morning, every step of that way, she was watched, or directly accompanied, lest she meet some chance encounter that would irretrievably stain family honor. Her little brother, Wayan, took his breakfast perched at the window, half-heartedly tracing the path of her yellow bonnet in the melting frost as she made her way across the field in the weak morning sun. Her cousin Hugo met her on the bridge, riding her on the handlebars of his bicycle if he was in a good mood; scowling and pinching and telling her to hurry and keep up if he was not.

But on days like today, when she was tired and cold and had lingered for just a minute's extra sleep, she emerged like now, heart in her throat, fear pounding in her ears, tears choking her eyes at the approaching uniform tramp of running feet. For although, for years, she had stopped and smiled and waved at the soldiers who, grinning, waved back as she continued to the bridge while she turned right along the stream bank, last week she had turned thirteen. And with that her father, for no reason that she could see or understand, on hearing from cousin and brother that she had looked full face on the soldiers; had smiled and waved as usual—on hearing that, he had flown into a fury and had slapped her so badly that her face was still mottled purple and green. Screamed at her for a harlot. Pulled her out of school. Made her don the bonnet. Made her work all day, under Uncle's eye, instead of just helping in the early morning.

She hurried on, determined to make the bridge before they passed her, the stiff grass and battered ground hard and unyielding to the passing of her swishing skirts and rushing feet. The formation pulled closer, feet crunching in unison as they left the pavement for the trackway. She could hear their steamy breathing, a great, puffing dragon of a beast bearing down. She was jogging herself now, trying to stay ahead. Her own feet followed the rhythm as they half-sang, half-shouted:

> "A yellow bird
> > A yellow bird
> With a yellow bill

With a yellow bill
Was perched upon
Was perched upon
My window sill
My window sill!"

She joined in, under her breath. She had learned most
of the Anglic she knew this way, listening to the jodies, every
day, day after day, morning and evening, for thousands of days.
Until, somehow, a word at a time, they'd seeped in along with
Pisin and Dutch and were just part of her vocabulary. Part of
the multilingual patois of the Moorstown community.

At "window sill," she glanced up involuntarily, looking
over her left shoulder to the third storey window, now far
behind her. But if little Wayan was tracing little pictures in the
glass to mark her way, she could not see him.

It was just a glance. A quick peek. But in that moment,
as she still jogged in time with the singing and crossed from the
field into the dark of the trees, her right foot splashed, then slid
on a patch of wet, slick on the pavement of clay beneath.
Marul flew headlong forward, the cadence calls echoing
through the tunnel of trees:

"I lured him in
I lured him in
With bits of bread
With bits of bread
And then I SMASHed his LIT-tle head!"

The turn of her own head meant that she slammed
down onto her right shoulder and tumbled before she had a
chance to think. She landed hard on the right elbow pinned
beneath her, rolled to her back, and in one desperate move
scrambled to her feet, facing away from the bridge, looking
face-on to the oncoming troops plowing among the trees four
abreast like a train derailing, as the first ranks splattered into
the same patch that had sent her sprawling.

They skidded to a halt, song stopped mid-word, to keep from running her down, and stood gaping and gasping, the NCO in charge already trotting forward to reach for her arm, saying "Are you OK, honey?" They gaped at her, skirt matted with chocolate mud and debris, bonnet askew; at the red smeared down her right cheek and soaking the shoulder and arm at the back of her white sweater. They gaped at much too much red.

The battalion medic was already jogging forward, already saying "It's OK honey, it'll be OK. It's probably just a little cut on the scalp. They bleed a lot. They always look worse than they are. It'll be OK. Let's have a little look-see, OK?"

But Marul was not looking at the steaming soldiers, in their baggy yellow jogging suits, milling around her in a smelly yellow gaggle, those rearward still lurching to a stop as the accordion affect made its way to the most distant and slow-moving among them. Nor was she looking at the thin line of those too short, or tired, or hung over, or sick, or lame, or unfit, or slow, or just plain lazy to keep up with the gazelle's pace set by the lead battery's best runners. Nor was she listening.

Instead, Marul was staring straight up into the trees. Not at her feet. Not at their faces. Rather, far above their heads. She clutched her hurt right elbow hard against her stomach with her opposite hand. Her breath came in short, deep pants. Her bonnet slipped back from her head. She did not notice. She began trembling. And just as the medic reached out to her, saying, "Just let me see your arm, honey," Marul let go of it, so that the medic alone looked down at her and saw her bruised cheeks.

The others, following the line of her shaking, outstretched left hand to the end of her pointing finger, stared with her, on beyond it, up into the century-old tamarisk. They now saw what she had seen during that frantic instant on her back, twenty feet above the ground. Upside down, his throat a crimson gash; something pink and sloppy covering his chest; a crimson spike pinning him to the trunk by his ankles, hung Marul's cousin Hugo.

The medic heard the XO's bark: "Secure the scene. I'll secure the gate. You. You. You. You. Detail, follow me." Heard, but did not see, the tramp of retreating feet, as Marul's breathing became ragged, her knees shook, and she slumped to the ground, her arm still pointing. Sergeant Thompson gently lowered the arm, wrapped the girl in her jacket, knelt beside her, and only then turned to survey the scene. She watched the XO's retreating back. Heard a slow drip-drip-dripping from the tree. Watched the XO stuff a 'tooth into his ear. Pulled the girl closer and said "It'll be OK Honey."

Far above, high in the Oquirr mountains, seated before a glass wall that overlooked the smoky, fogged-in plains below, Lillith Van Zandt felt a warm buzzing pass through her desktop. Still soaking up the sublime scene of a dewy, early morning, she pressed her thumb to the table's edge and said: "speak."

A characterless electronic voice responded. "Confirmed and secured."

Lillith smiled, pressed her thumb again, and returned to her steaming coffee. The sun broke over the clouds below, burning through in spots to patches of brilliant green. It was a beautiful morning, indeed.

Aboard Sinbad, Mote System, 3047

We went on and on, for a very long time. Once Uncle Kevin asked how Grampa was feeling. I was always afraid now, when Uncle Kevin asked that. It meant he was going to do something to the ship that would be bad for Grampa. Grampa said he'd been better, which meant he did not feel well. He said "I've been altering my will." I could not imagine how Grampa could alter his will. His will was iron. His will was obeyed even though he was old and dying. Even strange Masters bent to his will. Auntie Omar said that's why it was the greatest possible honor to be given to him.

Then he and Uncle Kevin made a cube. Glenda Ruth helped. I do not like Glenda Ruth. She lies. And I will not call her Auntie. She moves like a Mediator, but she is no Mediator, and no mistake. I will bet Uncle Kevin's pipe that she has two MaPas and no MaMa.

It went on for five days. And then came Grampa Horace's greatest hour. It was like this. Glenda Ruth was sitting on Grampa's bed. I did not like that. It made the bed move, and that disturbed Grampa Horace. He did not say so, but I could hear it in his heart. It went lub-dubby-dub, just for a moment, whenever she moved. She did not even notice! Calls herself a Mediator! Can't even see the obvious! She was scratching my ear. I can lie too. I pretended to like it. I held very still, because the scratching made it hard to hear. Imagine! A Mediator! Interfering with my Duty!

And that's when I began to know for sure what she was. She began talking to Uncle Kevin about Warriors. She began instructing him on how Warriors would behave. And then she said; "Remember the mission and look again." So there it was. She knew what Warriors might do, and then she ordered Uncle Kevin to provide a new analysis. Only a Master could do that.

But Uncle Kevin wasn't up to it. He is not a Master. He is an Uncle. But Grandpa Horace was. Up to it. He said it was about the fuel. At first, Uncle Kevin did not care. He said that enemy ships would be too late. He said we would move too fast through the *jump point*. But Grampa Horace knew. He said the enemy would send a mass of junk through the jump point just when we needed to cross.

Grampa Horace was a Great Master. I could hear his heart. I could hear everyone's heart. Whenever he spoke, Uncle Kevin's heart slowed. So did Glenda Ruth's. So did his own. Great Masters can do that. They speak, and hearts are calmed. He was brave and strong. For the next twenty minutes, he laughed and kept their hearts all steady. He knew what enemy Warriors would do. He knew what our Warriors would do. He knew what the ship would do. For twenty minutes, his heart never wavered, and lub-dub, lub-dub, lub-dub was the last thing I heard before we *jumped.*

Doctor Cynthia was everywhere. She was doing everything. But there was nothing a Doctor could do. When a Great Master dies, there is nothing a Doctor can do. I did my Duty. I *screamed.* I *roared.* I *howled* in every pitch and language I knew, so that everyone, everywhere, would hear and know: A Great Master has died. Beware, his Warriors are loosed! And then Doctor Cynthia gave me to Glenda Ruth! It was not her place! She was only his Doctor! Not to Auntie Omar! To *Glenda Ruth!* Glenda Ruth made *stupid* noises. She said I was to *stop!* And Auntie Omar made no move to take me back. So then I knew it was true. Glena Ruth pretended to be a Mediator. But Glenda Ruth was a Master. Glenda Ruth was who the Tatars had captured. Glenda Ruth was a *wolf.*

I stopped listening. I refused to *listen* to another Master. I refused to *listen* to the howling of *wolves.* I clung to my Duty. I closed my eyes and listened to Auntie Omar, who spoke with Grampa Horace's voice. I practiced every conversation I had heard before the fatal *jump.* I listened to his great heart, beating again and again, lub-dub, lub-dub, lub-dub, beating away in my head.

We were through Murcheson's Eye. We were on the way to New Caledonia. It was Uncle Nabil who called them all together. I called him Uncle, but he was really a Warrior. He was Grampa Horace's personal Warrior. Proof, again, of what a Great Master my Grampa had been. They obeyed him as if he were a Master himself; as if my Grampa still lived. Even Uncle Kevin asked "Should we be looking at this?" And Uncle Nabil said yes, His Excellency had instructed it. So I knew Uncle Nabil was like me. He had been loosed, but not from his Duty. He still served his Great Master. That's why I call him Uncle.

They were all there: Uncle Nabil and Uncle Kevin, the wolves Glenda Ruth and Frederick, Auntie Omar, Sir Eudoxus, Sir Victoria, Sir Harlequin, many others. They played a cube. Then I understood what Grampa had meant by *alter his will*. He was not in his bed. He was on his couch. He looked very bad. This is what he said:

> I am Horace Hussein al-Shamlan Bury, trader, Magnate Citizen of the Empire of Man, pasha and citizen of the planetary principality of Ikhwan al-Musliman, known commonly as Levant.
>
> This is a codicil to my will and testament left in the safekeeping of Nabil Ahmed Khadurri. I hereby confirm all bequests made in that previous testament, except as may be directly and explicitly contradicted in this codicil. I dictate this document in the full knowledge that neither it nor this ship is likely to survive our present mission; but Allah may will differently.
>
> I hereby name Kevin Renner, commodore of the Imperial Space Navy, as executor to my will and confer on him full executive power to execute my wishes and dispose of my property in accordance with my original will as amended by this codicil. This supersedes the appointment of Ibn-Farouk named as executor in the original testament. Kevin, I suggest but do not require that you delegate the detailed implementation of my will, and particularly supervising the

bequests of entailed property on Levant, to the law firm of Farouk, Halstead, and Harabi, and I commend to you its senior partner, Ibn-Farouk, as a longtime friend and counselor. I believe you will recall meeting him from time to time.

I confirm the bequest of my house, my lands, and all entailed properties on Ikhwan al-Musliman shall be divided among my blood relatives by the laws of my home planet; except that to my great-nephew Elie Adjami I leave the sum of one crown and what he has stolen from me. It is less than the law would have given him, but the choice was his.

It is my strong recommendation to the Empire that Kevin Renner be appointed the first governor of the Mote system, and it is my belief that the Empire will make that appointment.

Governor or not, I know that Kevin Renner will be ridden by demons if he cannot observe future events in the Mote system. I confess I wish I could be there myself. To aid Kevin Renner in satisfying his compulsive curiosity, I bequeath to him my personal ship known as *Sinbad*; and since I know he has not stolen any of my money, and certainly has not enough to operate my ship, I leave to him the sum of ten million crowns in cash to be paid after liquidation of assets other than Imperial Autonetics as described in the main body of my will, such to be deducted from the residual properties; and also I leave to Kevin Renner ten thousand and one shares of voting stock in Imperial Autonetics. Kevin, that's five percent plus one share of the company, and there's a reason I want you to have it.

The balance of my holdings of Imperial Autonetics, amounting to an additional sixty-five percent of the total voting stock, shall be divided as follows:

To my oldest living grandson, thirty-nine thousand nine hundred and ninety-nine shares.

To Omar as representative of the Motie family known as the East India Company, twenty thousand shares. To Victoria as representative of the Motie Family known as the Crimean Tartars, five thousand shares. To the Motie Mediator known as Ali Baba, thirty thousand shares.

The remaining shares are held by partners, banks, business concerns, and other humans scattered through the Empire. If you care to contemplate the possible voting blocks, you will find the combinations interesting. Kevin, Allah has willed that you shall live in interesting times, and I do no more than abet His will.

One final bequest: to Roderick, Lord Blaine, onetime captain of the Imperial cruiser *MacArthur*, I bequeath the personal sealed files designated with his name. They contain information about agents who have been useful to the Empire of Man, but who may now be dangerous. I know that Lord Blaine will satisfactorily carry the moral obligations of this knowledge.

As for the rest, you will find the details in the cube I have entrusted to Nabil. I have provided generously for those who have served me faithfully. I believe that I have faithfully discharged my duties to Allah, to my compatriots, and to the Empire; and whatever Allah wills for my future, I am content that we have done all that we could do.

Witness my voice and signature, Horace Hussein al-Shamlan Bury, aboard the sip *Sinbad*, somewhere in the Mote system.

And then Glenda Ruth witnessed.

And then I understood. Doctor Cynthia had not given me to Glenda Ruth. Grampa Horace had *altered his will*. Grampa Horace had given me to—me.

4
FairServ

The earliest form of nationalism — one that I have called Creole nationalism — arose out of the vast expansion of some of these empires overseas, often, but not always, very far away. Such Creole nationalisms are still very much alive, and one could say are even spreading....A second form of nationalism...official nationalism...arose historically as a reactionary response to popular nationalisms from below, directed against rulers, aristocrats and imperial centres. The most famous example is provided by Imperial Russia, where the Tsars ruled over hundreds of ethnic groups and many religious communities, and in their own circles spoke French—a sign of their civilized difference from their subjects... But as popular nationalisms spread through the empire in the nineteenth century..., the Tsars finally decided they were national Russians after all, and embarked on a fatal policy of russification of their subjects. In the same way, London tried to anglicize Ireland (with substantial success), Imperial Germany tried to germanify its share of Poland..., Imperial France imposed French on Italian-speaking Corsica (partial success) and the Ottoman Empire Turkish on the Arab world (with no success). In every case...there was a major effort to stretch the short, tight skin of the nation over the vast body of the old empire.

—*Benedict Anderson*

Hand Glacier Civil Spaceport, Maxroy's Purchase

What makes a thing worth doing? An unpleasant thing; a thing of minimal import, a thing hardly guaranteed of success? Asach began the trip to New Utah with profoundly mixed feelings as always. Trepidation. Excitement. Ennui. At Hand Glacier Civil spaceport, FairServ's operations had already become nearly routine. The jump point still had not opened, but the True Church's no-longer-secret spaceport actually had long experience in shuttling dubious personnel to rendezvous with New-Utah-bound small craft in near orbit. On the other hand, FairServ had long experience with working alongside the Empire in getting various non-governmental humanitarian missions into and out of Outie worlds. The single TC ship was on station, under Imperial supervision, loaded with medical supplies, awaiting the imminent opening of the transient Alderson tramline that would provide near-instantaneous connection between systems. So it was natural that, meanwhile, FairServ would set up what was jokingly referred to as the trudge line.

Approaching the routine. There was still a funny little pre-check stand outside, with a young clerk and clipboard verifying names. She locked in long and serious negotiation with a missionary manager in sweat-stained suit, his Dutch sibilants excoriating poor communications between the back office and this operations shed. He has paid. No, he has not. Yes he has, and he can prove it. Sir, that is no receipt. It is a receipt, or what should pass for one. No. Yes.

On and on this droned, a bizarre riff on a muzak background hum. Coffee being off the menu, Asach sipped decaf tea and contemplated the meager selection of snack foods: they were a crossroads mix of stale imports from around the Empire. Asach passed on salted fish and plums; contemplated—were they cheese?—puffs; settled for salty, sun-baked veggie crisps.

They passed the red dwarfs and rock ball with the predictable tedium, but without incident. Asach spent most of the trip semi-comatose, there being absolutely nothing to see but black space and the red suns. Then the yellow one. Then the rock ball. When they fell out of orbit HG threw up. The Librarian blanched. Asach sucked a salt crisp, pinched one wrist, and stared straight down the wing, in a straight line through the center of a corkscrew.

It was a tactical landing, done to hold the craft within the safe airspace of Saint George's only functioning airfield and minimize susceptibility to ground-based small arms fire—a fact lost on HG, but noted wryly by Asach. The Lynx 3000 wheeled left, in a deft spiral anchored along its left wing tip. Like a gull, a large cheeky seagull, eyeing a tourist's sandwich and oblivious to its own acrobatic feats, it flashed over ruined tabernacles; water gardens turned turquoise by a bloom of blue-green algae; oblong fields stretching fanwise from the river; heliports; tent cities; graveled lots shimmering white in the summer heat; green slashes of reed cane choking disused canals; bomb craters; tank traps; rows of defunct militarized aircraft, ranks of rusting armored vehicles; passing cross-wise to the runway in a blur of screaming rocket motors that suddenly stopped with a soft pop, leaving the gull to bank, glide and drop deftly onto the taxiway.

Asach stopped, the first out the door and onto the ground transport pick-up point. Friedlander security stood out a mile, khaki ballistic body armor stuffed slick with Protector Plates riding high on their chests, 'tooth seeds stuffed into their ears, bleeping invisible signals into a mystery of electronics buried within the sandwich-board protection zone of half-inch-thick hardened Plate.

Designed to flatten any projectile up to and including a high-velocity round fired at point-blank range, Plate was to executive body armor what double-boxed bubble wrap was to a padded mailer. If shot while wearing Plate, a man might well be slammed fore or aft with the full kinetic energy of that explosive slug, heated red by the friction of its passage through the air at Mach whatever, with a force equivalent to being struck full-on by a battering ram. Like as not, the hit might stop his breathing; his ribs might crack; certainly his pleural sac and every internal organ would be bruised by slamming with equal force into the interior of his rib cage first when he was hit, then again when he hit the ground. But the Plate would instantaneously spread the force over its entire surface, and redirect much of the shock laterally, out its edges. With luck and an iron constitution, he'd stand and breathe again.

Rather less protection was provided by their wrap-around shades, raked-backwards caps, and scowls of grim determination. Their desert-weight pants bulged in enough places to suggest entire concealed arsenals, in addition to the bristling array of personal side arms brashly unconcealed in external holsters. They were the very poster children of "personal security," and as such appeared to confer upon their various besuited charges a confident air of relaxed machismo; of dangerous operations well-in-hand.

They stood out a mile, and that scared the crap out of Asach. They had "target" painted all over them. Asach presumed that anything sufficiently armed and hostile as to require Plate as a defense was likely to view these characters as bounty prey at the peak of hunting season. Asach sidled as far away from them as was possible on the narrow platform. A cleaner slid past, muttering apology. Asach gave him a small tip.

Saint George, New Utah

Harlan's eyes rested briefly on the odd character at the end of the platform. He could not quite make it out. It belonged—nowhere really. Anywhere. Dutch, maybe. A

Dutch trader, maybe. Or a Missionary. But not. All the wrong mannerisms. More—fluid than most Eurasians. There, but not there. Not jutting forward, pulling rank by just being there, the way most Imperials did. But not shrinking back, either. Not embarrassed for living. Nor nervous, for all of the shifting away down the platform. No idle, chatty, over-bright conversation. No shoulder sporting a hefty chip.

Preparation was mostly letting go. Draining. Draining away ambition; draining away desire; draining away intent. Letting go of any thought of who you were or who you had wanted to be. No false imagining of joining first families or making fortunes. No heartfelt sense of failure at what you'd taken for granted as achievement, and harsh reality of achievement unmet. No expectations. Only planning.

Planning was a different thing. Planning meant living in the now. Now you were a set of eyes, and a set of ears. Now you watched, and watched, and listened, and listened. You watched and listened to everything, and planned how to get from the now here, to the now there, without ever once, even for a moment, letting your mind or eyes or ears leave the now that was now—right here, right now.

It was the Zen of city driving; the Zen of city waiting; the Zen of being eyes and ears so that the eyes and ears that you were for could entertain the luxury of that other kind of planning: that kind of planning wrapped up in hope and ambition and aim and desire and maybe a future state and place where auxiliary eyes and ears were no longer necessary.

A cleaner scuttled past with mop and bucket, muttering apology in a language familiar to half the populations of half the transport worlds. Preoccupied with something else, the Dutch character answered in kind, and with an automatic gesture slipped the cleaner a token.

Clegg smirked inwardly at the thought of all the New Scotland aristos dutifully mastering unintelligible Anglic dialects. The actual diasporas had been less romantic than imagined communities transplanted from the Scottish Highlands. They were blithely unaware that their broad-nosed, flat-faced, brown-skinned, curly-headed predecessors were probably transportees sporting startling tattoos, displaced from drowned islands in Earth's Pacific Ocean, who had never once laid eyes on a haggis—as was obvious to anyone who actually bothered to travel outside the capital and listen to real natives speak.

No, the real story began as so many did. On twenty-first century Earth, while politicians squabbled, sea levels inexorably rose. Rich cities, like Venice, or Dubai, designed barrier gates, or created land where none had ever been. Poor islands slowly drowned. The evacuations began with the entire population of Tuvalu. At first, Australia rejected them. New Zealand finally agreed to resettlement, but only under draconian terms. Then came Vanuatu. Then Carteret. Other drowning residents fled to New Britain—the earth island for which the terraformed planet was named— then fled New Britain for New Ireland (ditto), and then fled New Ireland for New Guinea. Or fled Fiji for New Caledonia (ditto again), then New Caledonia for the selfsame fate.

But New Guinea was neither far nor big enough. Polar caps kept melting. Sea levels kept rising. Prime coastal zones were drowned. Farmland disappeared beneath the sea. Marine catches plummeted. In the end, most wound up in Queensland after all, packed into tents and shantytowns, where they joined the greater Southeast Asian labor pool. One month, construction contracts in the Gulf, building indoor ski slopes. The next, vertical towers in Singapore. Never resident, never citizen, rarely managing even to stay on the same work crew for two jobs running.

What were left of Melanesia's islands survived as breaker-washed ridgelines with no navigable harbors, their people departed, their languages subsumed into the what had started, in the seventeenth century, as a regional trader's pidgin, and ended up, in the twenty-fifth, as the first language of most "blackbird" kids. Trainloads, shiploads, planeloads of workers, all highly skilled, all classified as "unskilled" by simple virtue of ubiquity and liquidity, washed from shore to shore, the shores of their own islands long gone. So, when the Alderson Drive flared into life, promising release from the tiny prison of the solar system, for these, and for their labor contractors, it was just One More Jump.

Transportees? Only in the sense that they were transported. They worked their way across the stars. They erected gantries. They cleaned the toilets. They installed wind collectors. They folded and shrink-wrapped blankets. They blasted mining shafts through asteroids. They mopped up puke by the bucket load after every jump. Every day, they paid their way, until they finally managed to pay their way out of the very real tiny prisons of the labor pools. For some, that took half a millennium.

Thus, the *lingua franca* of labor contractors sending cheap, skilled work crews from Australian ports became the *lingua franca* of interstellar mobile service industries catering to hot, sticky, miserable corners of the Empire where people of better means would not even travel without heavily armed escort. Want to *really* know what's up in a Tanith (or Makassar, or New Caledonia) hotel? Don't talk to the manager. Talk to the maids. Talk to the construction workers. Talk to the liveried security guards. Talk to the service contract engineers. Talk to the concierge. Talk to the ticket agent. Talk in the language spoken by anyone descended from those heaved out of drowning refugee camps, and anyone dumped there with them. Talk in Tok Pisin.

The cleaner gave a curt nod. "*Tenkyu. Yumipela Kasin. Yumipela pundaun tudak wantaim. Yumipela wanwakaaout arere bilong kantr. Mipela yupela hous pekpek clinim. "* Thank-you. We're cousins. We once jumped together. We could travel to the frontier together. I could clean your house toilets.

"Narakain, pren. Mipela stap bikples dispela. Lukim yu behain." Another time, friend. I'm staying in the city this time. See you later.

So, just a regular. Not a threat.

Then two others strode up, obviously Imperial Suits. Obviously nervous. The conversation switched to Anglic.

Harlan's eyes moved on.

"I don't see *why*," whinged HG, who Asach was beginning to think of as His Goonship," we *can't* have *real* security accompany—"

Asach cut him off. "*Because*, mi*lord*, here on an outworld, *real* security depends on a lucky combination of flying beneath notice and posing no possible threat whatsoever to anyone. Driving around surrounded by a Friedlander security detail accomplishes *neither* of those objectives." *And in your case, faint hope of the former in any event,* thought Asach. HG might fancy himself the great expert, able to blend in by doffing a workman's cap or some such nonsense, but despite only average stature, his ego swelled to fill all visible space. Not to mention audible. His every breath was so obviously *not* Purchase, or New Cal, or anywhere else Trans-Coal Sack it was painfully offensive.

What Asach did not bother to point out, because HG would assuredly turn it into cocktail chatter at the earliest opportunity, was that their little entourage was in fact *extremely* well-protected. The grinning, leathery, skinny farm boy in the driver's seat looked exactly like any other local farm boy, precisely because he *was* one. However, unlike most farm boys, he had a burp gun concealed beneath his feet, and his driver's side door panels were stuffed with Plate. Riding shotgun, in shades and a buzz cut, armed with, well, a shotgun, was a big dumb lummox clearly more at home taking potshots at dinner. Except that behind his shades, his eyes never stopped moving. The battered old wreck of a transporter bore ancient reg plates, dating well before Maxroy's Imperial accession. Anywhere they went, frick and frack up front smiled and waved and chatted up the local traffic cops.

In brief: for anybody looking, who did not know what they were looking at, a couple of yokels were making a quick crown ferrying third-class nobodies. And for anybody who knew what they were looking at, this little troop traveled under a local Mormon Stick's protection. Maxroy's Purchase was a long, long way away. Here, as the saying went, scratch a Stick, feel the club.

The Librarian said nothing: merely stared out the window. They wove their way through dust-choked streets. They'd never been elegant, but decades of blockade had trashed even the major thoroughfares. In the traffic islands, dead palms wept brown fronds over shanty huts tacked together from reed mats. Alternately, garbage blew everywhere; trash was sifted into towering recycle piles, whence it blew away again. Kids sifted through debris, picking out bits that glinted in the sun.

Eventually, they arrived at what passed for the University. Supposedly, work was already underway, in preparation to receive an Imperial Cultural and Trade Exchange Library, the better to "bring these primitives up to speed," as HG had so graciously put it. HG made a beeline for what passed as the most richly appointed office, and settled in to suck down what Asach guessed to be a month's supply of tea on this cash-strapped planet.

Meanwhile, Asach completed an inspection walk-through with the civil engineers. They had done a stunning job, but the local librarian was clearly overwhelmed. She had not made any orderly plan for transitioning materials from old to new systems. Nanos were piled in haphazard mountains in the adjacent room, with hundreds of 'tooth fones scattered about the floor. No effort had been made to clean the library area before re-sorting. Everything—shelving, nanos, desk surfaces—was covered with a thick layer of construction dust mixed with stirred-up muck and soot—of which she complained, showing her begrimed hands.

Asach decided to let them get on with it a bit, but also to set up another working meeting specifically to deal with library issues. That would keep both librarians occupied—for clearly she had prepared none of the promised reports, would not be ready to receive shipped d-sets, and would not be ready for the next academic term—and this without even addressing the issue of system training for her.

Asach explained carefully to the Librarian, an intelligent man, but one who clearly had little experience outside the sheltered halls of Sparta: "You need to appoint someone here that can provide close supervision of this. You need to give her the support she needs to do her job well. She is trying, but for her our gift imposes a tremendous burden of work and responsibility."

HG blustered, but the Librarian nodded, and took careful, meticulous notes.

On the surface, Saint George life, fueled mostly by an injection of hope, seemed improved since Asach's visit fourteen years before. More shops were open. More people were working. The suitcase imports brought by visiting family members were percolating through the consumer economy. Everyone was excited by the opening of a Retread Emporium with dirt-cheap clothes.

Road traffic was heavier—even congested—and better policed. People had returned to following normal rules of the road. Lines were shorter at fuel cell charge points. Construction was booming, everywhere. There had been a lot of cleanup of outright rubble, but trash collection seemed to have fallen by the wayside. There were drifts of garbage and a dead dog even outside Orcutt Land and Mining's new offices. Asach got the impression of a strain on managerial capacity. There may have been spare laborers about, but the city was clearly short on people to effectively train and supervise them.

Ensconced within the TC Security Zone, HG was buffered from electricity outages, but everyone else suffered in the summer heat through rolling blackouts. As spare parts trickled in, more capacity was brought online, but the grid was absorbing mountains of repaired and replaced refrigerators and air conditioners.

Crime seemed less overtly violent. Weapons were no longer openly carried on every street corner. Boxes of large appliances remained outside on the sidewalk overnight, with only a few sleeping watchman to guard them. There were no sounds of nearby or distant gunfire. Despite all this, people themselves were grim and tense. The murder rate was extremely high. There were rumors of revenge and reprisal killings—of whom? By whom? For what? Chained to HG's leg, which was chained to the oligarchy inside The Zone, Asach could learn little.

Zone operations were retrenching, with offices moved into dug-in concrete shelters surrounded by blast barriers. The True Church Elder insisted that this was merely "precautionary," pending accession talks. Asach was unconvinced. Ominously, their old hotel—with many apologies—would no longer accept Imperials. While HG blustered his credentials as a True Friend of The People at the front desk, Asach pulled a waiter aside and switched to Tok Pisin.

"Mipela pret." Was all he would say. *"Mipela pret TCM. Mipela Kristen. Emtupela longlong. Emtupela setan setan."* We're afraid. Afraid of TCM. We're Christian. Those guys are crazy. Those guys are devils.

Clearly all was *not* love and roses on New Utah. Everyone *claimed* that the killings and kidnappings were being done by outsiders pouring in from Maxroy's Purchase, New Ireland, New Scotland, who knows where—but nobody knew what to do about that. The high prevalence of Tok Pisin speakers amongst the security forces, laborers, and service staff perhaps leant credence to that notion, or perhaps was just a by-product of the appalling penchant for contractors smelling Treasury money to bring in their own workers, rather than employ locals. The second night, just after two a.m., a man was gunned down across the street from Asach's hotel room window. Police sirens blared and flashed; he was taken away in the back of a flatbed. Asach could not tell if he was dead or alive, or whether he was a criminal shot by the police themselves.

Everyone seemed nervous about standing in the shadow of foreigners, yet clearly they were grateful for the change and wanted to help as much as they could. The Saint Georgians, inured to the dangers, asserted the right to act as if things were normal, while the Zonies dug into their bunkers. Blending in was increasingly important. Asach found a little safe-ish triangle bounded by old offices, the hotel, and new offices, which were half a block away. The hotel was several notches down from past accommodation, but the price was right and the food was excellent and cheap. The weather was blisteringly hot, which felt right at home.

HG barely ruffled the sheets and choked down a meal before deciding to "head on back" and "report in," as if (a) they actually had much of any substance to report, and (b) a report could not be sent by outbound courier. Asach had finally had enough, ignored HG's insistence that they "keep the team together," and just failed to show up at the spaceport. It was time to get out of the moon raking capital and find out what was going on.

Saint George, New Utah

According to the duty log, Captain LeGrange took the first garbled report over the landline from the gatehouse at 7:03. Specialist Theo Parker, the unit's fastest runner, had been dispatched from the scene to summon the duty officer. Nobody had a 'tooth, because the commander had forbidden their use during runs. It had not occurred to Parker to check for one at any of the nearby military housing; he had accomplished his mission by sprinting the two-thousand-plus meters back to the main gate, a feat he accomplished in slightly under seven minutes.

This left Parker doubled over, head between his knees, gulping for air while the guard on duty contacted the operations desk. On top of his airlessness, Parker was a supply clerk. He could balance an ammunition accounting ledger down to the last bullet without error, but he could not construct a coherent sentence to save his life. Between his agonizing thought processes, and his agonized breathing, LeGrange had trouble ascertaining what, precisely, he was reporting.

She gathered that it involved a girl, the woods, and a great deal of blood. For a moment she thought that a military vehicle had run over a child and struck a tree. Finally, after much quizzing, LeGrange came to understand that there had (clearly) been a murder, not an accident; that the victim was in the tree (and did not appear to be military); that there was a girl on the scene who seemed to know who the victim was; and that a detail, with a vehicle, was wanted to secure the scene pending the arrival of civil authorities.

It was the luck of the draw that LeGrange had pulled duty the night before, and equally happenstance that the duty NCO, not herself, was out making the hourly checks just as the call came in. But as chance would have it, LeGrange was the post security officer, and would have been called in any event. Indeed, had she not been on duty, she'd have been out with the troops on the run. She was also a linguist. These two facts—security, linguist—had landed her the additional joy, among her many additional duties, of serving as the installation liaison officer to the local police authorities. Murder of a local civilian in the philosopher's woods well outside the installation perimeter clearly fell in their jurisdiction, not hers.

Under normal circumstances, the duty officer would have simply made a call to the local police like any private citizen, and sent a patrol to keep military personnel clear of the area until the green-and-whites took charge of the scene. However, the proximity to Moorstown, bordered as it was by a patchwork of leased military housing, installation warehouses, and the warren of apartment blocks full of cheap flats rented by private soldiers made LeGrange uneasy. She didn't like sending those Maxroy's Purchase boys on public duty at all, but that's what she had suited up and ready at that hour of the morning. She told Parker to go and find the duty sergeant, contacted the police, then got through to her civilian counterpart.

His desk sergeant informed her that he would not be in until seven-thirty. She asked for a callback when he arrived, then called the Maxroy's Purchase detachment for a two-person detail, stressing "Hancock, give me somebody with civil patrol experience, not any of your deadly-force-authorized watchtower rats." Ringing off, LeGrange kicked the dozing duty driver on his boot soles to wake him up.

"Sorry, Swanson. One more run. Get down to Charlie company. There'll be a detail waiting. Pick 'em up, then come back for me. We're going over to the road apples."

The TCM contracted the commons out for grazing, and the public trails were shared by riders with mounts stabled within and beyond the industrial fringe. The more intrepid among them used the greenbelt section of the Philosopher's Way, where it cut along the river past the warehouses, as a pass-through to open hill-and-orchard country beyond. This remnant of old agriculture was the subject of much scatological merriment among the urban troops, who jogged past (and over) the results every morning. Their children had a kindred, unofficial appellation: "the wee-wees," derived from the Founder name on the sketch map included in welcome packets: "the Wiese," meaning, simply, *the meadows*.

LeGrange updated the duty log, signed off the end-of-shift inventories, and was just pulling on her field jacket when Porter reappeared with the duty sergeant and Charge-of-Quarters. She opened the cage door.

"It's all in the log, Top. I don't know any more than what Parker's told me, and if he hasn't told you by now, make him. As soon as the Civvie checks in, fill him in and ask him to please meet me at the scene. Remember: Civil. Liaison. Officer. Don't forget the please. The police will be there already, and I'll need that C-LO to make sure that we find out anything that we care about. And call the main gate. Tell 'em that we're coming through."

The First Sergeant grunted, and then grunted toward the pot of bilge sludge stewing in the corner.

"Parker. Coffee. Report."

LeGrange bolted out of the headquarters, dragging her cap onto her head with one hand, zipping her field jacket with the other, and jumped into the shotgun seat of the FLIVR. At the main gate, not a hundred meters away, already backed up past the external buffer strip and around the corner along the main traffic way, the installation rush hour had begun, with civilian employees racing the clock to be at their desks by seven-thirty. This vehicular tidal surge was already spilling into the first waves of regular commuter traffic, pouring past the post and on into the city. In an attempt to minimize the congestion, from seven to eight the installation police designated both lanes at the main gate as inbound-only. LeGrange would catch hell for having the gate block traffic to let her out, but so be it. Meandering across post to exit by the back gate would add another quarter-hour delay.

The duty driver didn't even slow down as he gunned it past the guard. At the checkpoint, LeGrange returned his salute on the fly, shouting "Thanks Conway!" as the FLIVR careened past the second guard. No doubt Parker's garbled story was already known to half the Maxroy's Purchase company by now. Those MP boys were a tight little bunch.

The FLIVR bounced overland, ignoring marked pathways, in a beeline for the crime scene. They covered the distance to the meadow in just under two minutes—urgency or no, LeGrange did not want her driver flattening some schoolchild—and halted where the pavement turned into gravel.

Her face went rigid. She glowered across the expanse, teeth gritted in fury. A little blob of banana suits was clustered at the edge of the trees. Fanning back from that, like lines of ant trails, cutting across the fields toward the back gate; toward Moorstown; toward post housing, were the tracks of nearly one hundred-fifty soldiers, obviously released to return to their homes and barracks to prep for the duty day. It was seven-twenty-four. The police had not yet arrived. So much for controlling the crime scene.

LeGrange looked back at the two MP troops. They were traffic cops, maybe. Housing Patrol officers, at best. And they had not yet been briefed. She sighed.

"OK you two, time to go earn some of those hero's wings."

They looked at each other, then responded in unison. "Ma'am?"

"We're gunna secure a murder scene."

"Yes SIR, Ma'am." They bolted from the FLIVR, but the driver was already dozing. He'd been more-or-less awake, at that point, for twenty-six hours. LeGrange bellowed, not out of anger: just to get his adrenaline flowing.

"SWANSON!" He jerked.

"Unass that machine!"

He jumped.

"I want YOU, AT parade rest, RIGHT here, right NOW!"

She stabbed with a forefinger at the spot where the concrete ended and the gravel path began. He scrambled to.

"Swanson, listen up! Nobody. I mean NOBODY, brings any vehicle down here unless the police tell them to, you hear me?

"Yes Ma'am!"

"And nobody, but NOBODY, walks across this field, or down this path, EXCEPT the police, you got that?"

"Yes Ma'am."

"Say it back."

"I ain't spozed ta let nobody cross here 'cept the p'lice, and I ain't spozed ta let nobody walk down there 'cept the p'lice." 'Police' had no 'o', and rhymed with 'grease.'

"You got it. And who am I?"

"The D-O, Ma'am."

"And what does that make me?"

"GOD, Ma'am."

"And who does God report to?"

"Colonel Slam-Dunk, Ma'am!"

So who's the only one who can change that order?"

"Only you or the Hoop, Ma'am!"

Colonel Roger A. Hooper, aka Slam-Dunk Hooper, aka The Hoop, was the installation commander. Until he arrived on post, the Duty Officer acted with his authority.

"C'mon, you two," she grumbled, turning to go, but then stopped abruptly and faced back.

"Swanson!"

"Ma'am!"

"You are NOT authorized to hurt anybody, you hear me?"

"Ma'am?"

"Do not so much as *breathe* on a civilian. *Politely.* Tell people *politely.*"

"Ma'am." He looked crestfallen. Swanson was still new enough to suffer from the delusion that he was owed a hero's welcome as part of a post-war occupation army helping to save the New Utahans from themselves and, inexplicably, Outies. When the New Utahans quite naturally, and *not* always politely, proffered differing views, Swanson still tended to take things personally. His toolkit of social skills being fairly limited in scope, this had the potential to lead to ugly scenes.

"Just say 'tasol polis' if they don't speak Anglic."

He nodded.

"Say it."

"Taser p'lice." It still rhymed with "grease."

"PO-lis," she stressed. "It's PO-lis."

"Taser p'lice," he repeated.

She sighed. "Good, Swanson. That's really good," and turned down the path, the MPs in tow, as the neeer-nor, neer-nor of the police sirens finally wailed in the distance.

5
Knowledge Management

May my hymns be in everyone's mouth; let the songs about me not pass from memory. So that the fame of my praise ... shall never be forgotten, I have had it written down line by line in the House of the Wisdom in holy heavenly writing, as great works of scholarship. No one shall ever let any of it pass from memory .... It shall not be forgotten, since indestructible heavenly writing has a lasting renown.

—The Electronic Text Corpus of Sumerian Literature 2.4.2.05, lines 240–248

Saint George, New Utah

Asach and the Lads set off just after dawn, on a jaunt down the Bonneville highway, into the panhandle. They trundled through the old city, into and through the house furnishings market: rolls of flooring stacked against sleeping windows; parking lots lined with velvet-upholstered furniture. Out past Gazelle Springs, where Founder horse burials inhabited limestone caves above the source.

Through the industrial district of Zarkel, choked with smog; lined with vehicle graveyards that escalated from diminutive taxis to rusting tractor rigs, the latter incongruously piled on rooftops. The highway was lined with transporters, teamsters, cart traffic: a free zone with tarp-covered trailer loads of every make and model; then water tankers in line after line.

Their main destination for the day would be the Ezekiel wetlands: prior to Foundation the once-vast marshes were fed by aquifers seeping from beneath the Oquirr mountains. Pumping had so lowered the water table that exposed peat sloughed off and blew away. Vast tracts of desiccated land outside the marsh were demarcated into lines and squares by piles of basalt stone. Within these censurations sprawled herder encampments, brown wool burlap tents fluttering in the wind, the livestock grazing thin pasturage somewhere out of view.

A small percentage of the water back into a small fraction of the marsh was kept as a desolate tourist park. Reed brakes choked the seeps. Water grazers kept pond-sized patches open. The springs were divided by a Founder wall designed to keep salt from fresh. One end had stone arches carved in animal reliefs. An abandoned rehabilitation project had aimed to add a second pool system: all that remained was cracked mud and dust.

Staff poured the visitors honey-sweetened tea in little glasses, and then left them to wander through the brakes to an adobe observation hut overlooking a bucolic wallow.

Refreshed, Asach and the boys next headed north through Ezekiel itself for a two-dinar wheel repair. Shops catering to the highway trade were bedecked with plush and plasticene and plaster Tweety Kitties (did people here even know of Tweety Kitty?). Asach wondered: in this teamster world, is it plush for girls, plasticene for boys, and plaster for the garden? Cascades of nuts and seeds and spices and tins; cheeses in oil; unidentifiable fruits in syrup lined shop shelves. The road into town crossed onto basalt fields as sharply as crossing a watered pitch, past a series of once grand, now abandoned guest houses, and then the black blocks of Ezekiel's castle loomed: the Founder's wartime headquarters, with its two-ton solid basalt door.

They rolled onward toward Bonneville along the southern road, through horizon-wide pebble plains, trackless and capped with desert varnish, grazed clean of any puff of chaff. Along a long-dry wadi lay Amra Tabernacle—a little Founder-era bubble with a roadway tourist sign. Concrete cones, a meter high, ran parallel awhile: markers along the old First Empire Mandate track. They careened behind, through, alongside truck convoys ferrying limestone nodules the size of squashed dumpsters to facing-tile plants on the outskirts of Saint George. Foursquare, turreted Castle Peery rose above a second wadi, overlooking a Founder's-Era landfill. Dust devils boiled past flocks of desolate sheep, fed with trucked grain; watered by tankers; allowed to graze to scorched earth any seed that dared germinate under the moisture-sapping wind. They passed a transporter overtopped with green reed headed toward the sheep camps.

Bonneville, New Utah

They were ten days on the road, and arrived in Bonneville at the last violet of dusk, rolling to a stop outside a battered hotel just as stars punctured the vault of heaven. By the time they clambered over one another and milled toward the grimy door, the black of night had sapped all color, flattened objects to silhouettes, and sharpened every footstep into a staccato echo. Asach, wrapped in a shapeless, hooded cloak, faded to the rear, allowing the farm boys to shove their way ahead into the shabby lobby. They did all the talking.

"*Rum long tripela man bai kostim hamas?*" How much is a room for three?

The desk clerk feigned indifference. "*Yu no save long tok anglis, a? Man bilong wokim gaden, a? Pilgrim, a?* " *You don't speak Anglic, huh? Farmer, huh? Pilgrim, huh?*

"Well, yeah, grinned the lummox with the shotgun, still sporting his shades. As a matter of fact, I do. Speak Anglic."

The clerk snorted.

"Umm, yeah," grinned the driver. "About 12,000 hectares." Still grinning. "Farmer, I mean." Still grinning. "You know, Saint George? Little TCM—*garden plot*—just outside Saint George?"

The clerk blanched. These weren't Himmist hicks.

Shotgun leaned elbows in the desk, which rather emphasized the sling crossing his several acres of chest. Still grinning. "Imagine!" he chirped brightly, "You're right three for three! That one," (he jerked his head rearwards) is the— pilgrim? Is that what you said? Did you actually say *pilgrim?*"

Now thoroughly confused, the clerk gaped until rescued by the driver who, still grinning, gave a little shrug. "Thing is, best not to *Stick* your nose in, if you follow my meaning?"

The clerk nodded.

"So then, *brother,* "he smiled, "*how much is a room for three?*"

They trudged upstairs, past sallow walls, into a poured concrete wing that at best had only ever been elegant in a developer's imagination. The flimsy door banged open, revealing a tawdry suite with smoke-stained walls. A wheezing air conditioner struggled unsuccessfully with the heat. Asach pulled back heavy curtains, sodden with the odors of ages, to reveal grimy French windows that opened onto a miniscule balcony. The balcony could accommodate two chairs, or two people standing, but not both at once. To sit, you had to pull the chairs into the room, then plunk-and-scoot your way back out to the rusty railing.

Not that the view was worth the trouble. The balcony faced an inner courtyard; far-below, stained concrete circled an algae-rimed pool. Bad music blared from a makeshift bandstand in one corner. Bored guests attending a bad suit convention stared into their drinks.

"And to think," said Asach into the murky air, "this is the *luxury* wing."

"At full rack rates," nodded the brothers.

"Come on," sighed Asach, not bothering to close the doors, "I know a better place."

Saint George, New Utah

In the end, Asach's "defection," as HG called the no-show status, proved to be The Librarian's own ticket off the transport returning to Maxroy's Purchase.

"Got to have somebody to keep tabs on things," said HG, though how, concretely, any report of this was to be accomplished, given the absence of any direct communications means, was unclear to The Librarian.

The Librarian did have a name: Colchis Barthes. A long-limbed man with silver hair, Barthes would appear quizzically unruffled and immaculately pressed in the midst of a hailstorm. Or, more appropriately, as the case might be here on New Utah, in the midst of a dust storm.

Barthes had distinguished himself as head of American Collections at the Imperial Library on Sparta. It was an odd sort of division within the library: The "Americas" were a grab-bag of worlds that shared only one common denominator: their names were derived from millennium-old names of states and territories on Earth.

Actually, this implied a second (and really, a defining) denominator: these worlds tended toward self-styled traditionalisms, linguistic revivals, and archaic information preservation societies. Hence The Librarian's slow, patient rise through the ranks. He could read Old and Middle Anglic fluently, and was an adept at locating and recovering the flotsam of a previous information age. It was amazing what people had, figuratively speaking, tucked into their shoes across thirty generations; what church records they had defended with their lives; or what just plain turned up in long-forgotten archives. One entire city library had been miraculously preserved on a thousand-year-old flash drive, disguised (or designed?) as a piece of jewelry. Of course, no machine now existed that could decode the thing, but that's where Colchis came into it.

As the home world of the Imperial line, New Washington had naturally been of special collector interest, and that is where Barthes had earned his reputation. After the Imperial Restoration, interest also surged in archival recovery on New Chicago—his first assignment in the Trans-Coal Sack sector. Naturally, that work done, he'd been handy, so it seemed useful that he be assigned to the second New Utah accession mission.

But New Utah was a far cry from his previous career postings. He had, of course, been assigned to a cultural attaché here or there several times during his younger years, but always during less interesting times. He had enjoyed rambling through street markets and media stalls, rifling through junk and stumbling upon entire collections turned out of some grandmother's locker.

To his credit, he was appalled at the state in which he'd found New Utah's (well, Saint George's) Zion University library. He stood, hand pressed to his face in horror, before the melted wreckage of one Scriptorium—Scriptorium!—Actual, hand-lettered manuscripts, pre-dating First Empire!—now reduced to a gutted, ash-filled shell, inhabited by mangy dogs.

Three small boys appeared with rocks. They pelted the dogs. His guide pointed to what had been: *There* was the melted slag of a stained glass wall that had once soared above the foyer, casting flower fields of light on the reading benches on every floor. *There* was where the genealogical archives had stood: the papers, diaries, notes and bibles that hung flesh on the bare bones of the begats. *There* had been an alcove, where the notes and diaries and unfinished research plans of retired and deceased professors had been stored. Colchis stood aghast, contemplating a massive charred beam, a double-hand span wide to a side, adze-marks preserved in charcoal. It was all that remained of the timbered ceiling. He reached out and shoved it with his foot. Unsteady on its bed of rubble, it rolled lazily over.

Colchis scuffed absent-mindedly through the incongruously unburned stripe of shattered brick and mortar that had been insulated by the timber. Clearly, the fireball had exploded though from the floor above, collapsing the ceiling before consuming all below it. He traced the grey stripe, amazed at the intensity of heat that had reduced everything else around it to white ash. Then he stopped. A charred edge poked through the wrack. Expecting a flake; a fragment, he was surprised when a light tug failed to dislodge it. He brushed away the fist-deep overburden. The charred edge belonged to a clipped sheaf of hand-written paper, miraculously preserved.

It was a conference paper, a little over eighty years old. Something to do with the biology of something called a Swenson's Ape. Sad, that of all the things that might have been saved, all that remained of the vast collection was a random draft of a minor bit of academic arcana. There was no name on it, just the date.

"Any idea who wrote this?" He showed the title to his guide.

The student shrugged. "Some dead professor or other. Hard to know now. The catalogue went up with the library. You might check with the Temple archivist. Some of our collections were backed up there. Not all of them."

Barthes handed her the paper. She shrugged again, then swiveled, hands out, to take in the ruin. "If you're going to the Temple, you might as well hang onto it. I have nowhere to put it. Maybe they can find a related file."

A week passed before Barthes thought of the paper again. The reconstruction effort itself had been all-consuming. It wasn't just that New Utah had a different language and business culture for all things informatic (which it did). It was not just that it had its own mature bureaucratic system, accounting methods, and paperwork (there were bit streams of that, too). The biggest impediment was that it was clearly a post-war reconstruction zone.

He couldn't just pop in a 'tooth and call anyone, because the dish system still didn't work, and anyway most people didn't have them. He couldn't just set an appointment, because that would tell the assassins (yes, he discovered, there were assassins) exactly the time and place to murder whomever he was meeting. So he had to just show up, and hope that the office he was visiting was open, and that whomever he needed was there.

When he did that, traffic was utterly unpredictable. Whenever the TCM, private security teams, or a True Church VIP was moving (unannounced of course), they closed half the roads through the city, turning freeways into parking lots. About half the time—and an unpredictable half of the time—offices were just closed. Whenever there was a big security alert, which happened in unpredictable clusters, everything just shut down. At Zion University, there were no summer classes, so to save salary and electricity the campus was closed. If contractors showed up, they were turned away three times out of four, for lack of guides.

And the big True Church construction contractors and projects—Titan-Van Zandt, Tumbridge, Orcutt Land and Mining—were sucking the city dry of qualified managers. There was just a lot more money to be made working for them than for one stray Librarian. So there might have been plenty of workmen, but there were few to direct them, and even fewer to manage routine back office matters like invoicing.

Then there was the 130-degree heat. That was not an exaggeration. The city electricity cycled in two-hour on, (hopefully only) four-hour off increments, on an unpredictable schedule. Usually it cycled off-phase, which meant that it wouldn't actually run many appliances, like air conditioners, and it fried computational electronics. So, everyone sweated through the night and arrived to work exhausted. There were backup generators, but in Saint George most of those were True-Church contracted, meaning that they ran on fuel cells, not solar, and the hydrogen extractors down on the coast were only operating at about twenty percent capacity. You couldn't legally fill fuel cylinders (to prevent black marketing), so to refuel the cells you had to wait in line, fill a FLIVR, drive it home, and in a bloody dangerous operation siphon the fuel out of the FLIVR's tank and into the generator's.

Colchis was buffered from this somewhat at his hotel—they managed to keep the air conditioning going some of the time, so his room temperature at night stayed down to barely-livable with a fan—but the people working for him did not have that luxury. Compared to those unpredictabilities, sorting through a budget variance felt pretty minor, and tracking down the long-dead author of a paper presented at a Xenobiology plenary session was nowhere on his charts.

Lying on his bed one night, spread-eagled to enjoy the full cooling effects of his fan, Barthes glanced again at the title page. It was dated 2867, for a conference somewhere in New Caledonia. He amended his assessment. For a paper never even presented at a conference. That was the year of the True Church uprising on Maxroy's Purchase. That's when its newly-hatched military wing had burned and looted cities across that planet, destroyed their churches, withdrawn its Temple to Glacier

Valley, proclaimed itself primate, transported thousands into exile, and established its Security Zone on New Utah.

And then, were that not enough, came the collapse of New Utah's Alderson tramline, effectively ending interstellar travel for all but the extremely wealthy. Barthes wasn't sure that the New Caledonia conference had ever been held, but it was dead cert that the poor biologist, beavering away in the backwaters of Zion University, had not attended. Making the paper's lone survivorship all the more poignant. He held it up in the guttering light from the indifferently-powered bulb, and fell asleep before he'd finished the first paragraph.

New Scotland

HG arrived back in New Caledonia in a flurry and a huff, so puffed with self-importance and wounded pride that Horvath himself felt obliged to talk him down from his high horse.

"Now look here," said Horvath, "are you saying that Quinn violated the technology ban? That's a serious charge. Don't levy it unless you've got proof that will stand up in a formal inquiry."

"Well, no. It's just that Quinn's so impossible to—to—*control*."

Renner snorted. "I'm impressed. I don't know anyone with any sense who'd even *try.*"

Horvath noted, but ignored, the implied insult. "Young man,"—only in comparison to Horvath could HG reasonably called *young*—"it's not my position—and therefore not yours—to *control* Quinn."

"But I was Chief of Party!"

"No. *I* am Chief of Party. You are the science delegate on the advance team. Your sole function is to ensure that there are no inadvertent science and technology breeches during preparations to receive the Accession Delegation."

"And to do that—"

"To do that, you look over Colchis Barthes' shoulder during Library installation—though I daresay the man knows his job—and, as far as I care, give Quinn enough rope to hang."

Renner rolled his eyes and waved the Quinn comment away, grunting. "Umph. Stay on point. Quinn's mission is—to do what?"

"To set up extension offices in Bonneville."

"Pending your full Science and Technology assessment?"

"Yes."

"And so far as you know, that's where Quinn's gone?"

HG blustered. "Well, yes, but—"

"So, there's no problem, then, right? You'll just compare the pre- and post-assessments for evidence of technology leaks."

HG flushed, but did not answer. Horvath's eyes flashed. Renner pounced. "You did *do* a pre-assessment in Bonneville?"

"Well, no, actually." HG's lips disappeared. He addressed his answer to Horvath, but glared sideways at Renner. "It's not precisely easy to get there."

"But your own report shows air, rail, and road lines-of-communication. Aside from the Lynx."

"Road takes ten days. 'Air' is the solar glider, and that takes four, weather allowing. The SunRail runs overnight, but—but…" He trailed off.

"But what?"

HG squirmed. "There are no sleeper cars. No berths. Just—*seats.* And I was told there could be *bandits.*"

Renner laughed. "Well, Horvath, you've got to hand it to Quinn, the fool who rushes in where Science and Technology fears to tread."

Horvath was furious, grim. "Are you at least in communication with Barthes?"

HG shook his head. "No. I couldn't even get through to *you* until I was well out of atmosphere. I had to use Naval relay communications. We're close to the tramline opening, I think. I'm no astrophysicist, but I'm guessing that neutron star is getting close enough to suck matter off its mate. New Utah's sun. And spitting it back out as RF energy. Or pulling sunspots from the sun. Or both. " He glowered at Renner. "It's touch-and-go even getting through to Bonneville from Saint George on anything but landline. Even then."

Renner nodded. "That's the old report. A good yellow star; a neutron companion in an eccentric orbit around their mutual center of mass. And the TC's little secret was that every twenty-one years, they both swing in close enough to each other to open up the Alderson tram—"

Horvath cut in. "They have *landline?*"

"Oh, yes. Backup fiberoptic, you know. Especially out into more remote areas. Old mining camps and such. Simple emergency communications. Ancient, but they keep it patched together. But sometimes it's so bad even *that* doesn't work right. As far as contacting *you,* there's just the one TCM satellite, and it has to bounce the signal down the whole relay chain and through to you via the jump point messenger shuttles, so of course that's bloody expensive and even less reliable. Anyway, they control it, so I was hardly going to use it for classified communications. Even encrypted."

Renner said nothing. Horvath became thoughtful. "OK, so you came back here to report. Damned waste of time, all this traveling. Still." He sighed. "I suppose it couldn't be helped. One way trip, and all that?"

"Yes, precisely. I think the mate's exact words were: 'On, or off, mister-bloody-scientist. This is a scheduled ferry, not a personal-bloody-chat line.' So, I got on. And told Colchis to stay and keep an eye out for Quinn."

Renner smiled. "Sounds like a business opportunity, that." He knew he shouldn't be goading HG, but it was just so easy to raise his hackles, he couldn't quite resist. And he was gearing up to do Renner again for the crowd. "OK, let's get the others in here. Sounds like opportunity's knocking. That tramline opens, we need to be first through the door. Time to finalize the Accession Delegation."

HG didn't rise, though. Dry as dust, level as a playing field, finally, he looked directly at Renner. "And you, Sir Kevin, are involved in this process—because? I should have thought it was the Governor's prerogative?"

Renner grinned. "Ah! Doctor Science Minister, didn't you let him in on what good friends we're all going to be?" He leaned forward, and dropped the grin. "Because I own—and pilot—the ship that's bringing the delegation in. Because if it weren't for her previous owner's commitment to *proper* investigation, there'd *be* no New Utah, let alone a second Jackson delegation."

Horvath sighed. "You really should know, I suppose. Sir Kevin and I go way back. I don't *like* him—never did." He didn't even bother to look at Renner. For his part, far from flinching, Renner resumed grinning. "Before he died, Horace Hussein Bury detected certain financial—irregularities—in the system. Given the relative proximity to the blockade—"

His social failings aside, HG was not stupid. "—he suspected Motie involvement?"

Kevin nodded. "Feared, more like. Sent me in to check things out—"

"His *own* initiative? His *own* expense?"

"Yes on both counts. Not that it constituted much of an expense for him—*just let me finish!*"

HG bit off his next word before it began; nodded; sat.

"I went down to Maxroy's Purchase, and the whole damned planet was "gripping hand" this, and "gripping hand" that. Made *me* more than a little suspicious, and then I got mugged by some True Church goons when I tried to report in. Bury was ready to nuke New Utah and hand Maxroy's Purchase off to the Empire for the Navy to deal with in an equally draconian fashion."

Horvath was twiddling with his fingers, bored to death by Renner's grandstanding. He'd heard this story at least a dozen times. But it was new to HG, who looked horrified.

"But *wh*—"

"*Let me finish.* So I went on a little hunting expedition. Got a nice double catch: one snow ghost; one secret spaceport under Hand Glacier. That's when we copped to the periodic tramline. True Church was getting all primed to jump a big shipment in. Scared the crap out of 'em. Told 'em that if they didn't prove to me, on the spot, that there was no Motie technology involved in any of it, and no Moties anywhere, Bury would turn New Utah into glass just to be on the safe side, and ask permission later. Which he would have done."

HG was even more confused. He looked from Renner, to Horvath, to Renner, to Horvath, waiting for a volley of salvation.

Horvath sighed. "Now you see the earnestness of this mission."

"No, I don't. I'm sorry, but I just don't—"

Horvath continued. "A little over thirty years ago—my God Kevin, has it been that long?—thirty years ago I was—about your age—and science minister for the Trans-Coal Sack sector. I was assigned to the First Contact mission."

HG nodded vigorously. It had made Horvath famous. My God, the first scientist to have exclusive access to a newly discovered sentient civilization, with unimaginable technology and—

"Kevin here was sailing master on the *MacArthur*. We disagreed on just about everything to do with the Moties. Did. Disagree. Don't now. Once we understood their phenomenal reproduction rates; their endless internecine warfare; their sheer capacity to *overwhelm* our own economies with their constant technological innovations—"

"Yes, yes, I know this. Everyone does. Every *taxpayer* does. The blockade is hideously expensive."

"Yes, and hideously necessary. Even I have come to understand this. But even *then*, Bury was positively adamant."

"Yes, yes, but since second contact and the C-L worm—"

"Now let *me* finish. Think about that. Horace Bury, Magnate of *Imperial Autonetics*, fully supported absolute blockade and a Motie technology import ban. He could have made—well, he already *had* made billions. Trillions maybe. But he saw the Moties as a direct, personal threat to the existence of humankind. After that, Bury made Kevin an offer he couldn't refuse. Kevin signed on as *Sinbad's* pilot."

"Bury's personal ship."

"Yes. Kevin and Bury did a lot of things together, but one of them was to fully, rigorously investigate anomalies that could indicate that Moties had somehow broken the blockade."

"But there are no Moties on Maxroy's Purchase!"

Renner cut in again "Nope. Turned out all that "gripping hand" crap was Jackson himself. Making much of his tour as an Able Spacer on the first expedition."

"Yes," said Horvath, "but more to the point, it meant *Sinbad* was on hand when the Crazy Eddy jump point from Mote Prime shifted last year; the Sister opened; all of that."

HG's eyes widened. "You mean Sir Kevin—"

"Yes. Fewer than two dozen people have ever had direct contact with Moties. Precious few of us have ever been to the Mote system. Sir Kevin Renner's done it twice, and lived to tell the tale. The second time, with *Sinbad*. Bury did it twice as well, but didn't make it back the second time. Died on the final jump. Like Moses, who saw, but could not enter, the promised land."

He let HG chew on that. Renner continued. "So, here I am again. Like a bad penny. Johnny on the spot. The Navy's strapped beyond limits maintaining this blockade, plus policing the Motie Consortium blockade at the Sister. It's not going to dedicate a ship just to play ferryboat. The Imperial Traders Association—"

"—and the True Church, and Governor Jackson—"

"yes, all of them, offered, but they aren't exactly *neutral ground*, are they?

"Neither are you."

"Well, no, neither am I, but Imperial Autonetics already passed on the opal meerschaum trade when Bury was alive. And profitable as a few containers of selenium supplements and medical supplies might be for a *small* trader, not really my style, is it? Get bogged down shipping vitamins, fertilizer, and rocks? I'm as neutral as you're gonna get right now."

Renner gave that grin again. HG detested that grin. Renner was getting too old to play fighter-jock cocky. "I still don't see where Moties come into it."

"They don't. Let's just say I'm curious. Back to where it started last year. The True Church thinks New Utah is Heaven, all evidence to the contrary. Thought I'd take a break and see what all the fuss is about." *And*, he thought, *Bury always felt there was too much money in this system, opal meerschaum aside. We never found out why.*

Horvath looked at him sharply, but let it slide. "So, from a science and technology standpoint, the earnestness of this mission is twofold. First, all the normal accession concerns— accurate assessment of existing levels and accomplishments; whether introduction of Imperial technology would be destabilizing, and so forth. And related to that, prevention of S&T leaks *during* the assessment and classification phase. No leading questions; no idle chatter, all that."

"Yes, yes." HG was flapping his hand. He really was good at that part of his job, which is why he'd been chosen as ground man.

"But in this case, given the proximity to the New Caledonia System, and the Crazy Eddy jump point from the Mote, there's the added concern of inadvertent transfer of *Motie* technology."

"*What* Motie technology? I mean, Imperial Autonetics pretty much has a lock on what's available for public sale." He trailed off. "Oh. I see."

This time, Kevin did not grin. He smiled. "Yes. And Imperial Autonetics would very much like to maintain that prerogative. We have a keen interest in preventing—and detecting—piracy."

"So your interest *isn't* just personal."

"Let's call it *professional* curiosity."

In the end, like most well-run meetings, there were no surprises. Kevin and the *Sinbad* crew would host; Kevin would pilot; Kevin would have broad discretion to determine whether any violations of Imperial Autonetics licensing, production, trademarks, or copyrights had occurred.

Governor Jackson would head the delegation, not in his official capacity as governor of Maxroy's Purchase, but as Emissary of the Viceroy. The True Church would send Bishop Ohran, who had led the secret supply missions from Maxroy's Purchase for decades.

Horvath himself would not go. He was not a young man. He had other duties elsewhere in the Empire and, since the

Trans-Coal Sack Science Minister was tied up with Motie issues, HG would have to soldier on.

To his mortified disappointment, the Maxroy's Purchase ITA representative was upstaged by another from out-of-sector. Officially, *there had been no* trade with New Utah during the embargo, so initial ITA representation was reserved for a "neutral," meaning not-Maxroy's-Purchase, party.

Since he was already on the ground, Colchis Barthes would get a temporary appointment as cultural attaché. There would be a small uniformed Marine bodyguard. No mention was made of Asach.

So, all-in-all, Jackson was satisfied: he and Ohran covered Church and State; HG was from New Cal, so local and presumably sympathetic; Barthes didn't matter; the ITA rep could angle all he wanted, but MP held proximity, which was the biggest fact on the ground; and Renner was, well, Renner. Nominally acting on behalf of himself; Imperial Autonetics; of service to the Empire. Renner was the loose cannon, but it couldn't be helped.

They'd be ready to leave within the week, as soon as the ITA rep arrived. *Sinbad* would travel to Maxroy's Purchase, and then hold station at the jump point. Jackson would keep a shuttle on standby, so that the delegation could work planetside as needed, and then rejoin *Sinbad* once the jump point opened.

6
Hostile Takeover

I came to hate nations. We are deformed by nation-states. I wanted to erase my name and the place I had come from…not to belong to anyone, to any nation.

—Michael Ondaatje, *The English Patient*

Mesolimeris, New Utah

The Masters' dais, warmed by geothermal swells, glowed faintly in the crisp air of The Keep. Sargon lounged, the smooth curves of the seat cupping the lines of his hips to provide effortless repose. Stragglers were still arriving. some with finesse; some grandstanding, using the gripping hand to lever themselves, with one brute-force jerk, over the final ascension step into the cave. Only old Lagash had been too weak to complete the climb.

A pity, thought Sargon. Old Lagash had been a good ally. Lagash had tended to his *ar,* kept three counties, and in a pinch could lend a Master's Hand for planting. A pity. Now redistribution of his *ar* and cattle would be decided, for Lagash had no offspring. It would make for a long, dull meeting.

Sargon was tempted by this, but only briefly. A mess, indeed. No doubt, most of the *ar* would be wasted settling fictitious land debts. A better tactic: watch for the Landholder most eager to grasp the least of the *ar*. That Landholder would be the one to court. That's how he'd come by Farmer John, and look how well that had turned out. Started with a Field, turned it to a Grasp, and that very nearly to a Hand. Not that John admitted to it all, but all you had to do was count his cattle, all the result of increase. Anyone could *buy* cattle—foolish ones by selling *ar*. Sell the bowls; sell the cattle; but never, ever part with *ar*, and the cattle will see to themselves. And of all your cattle, treat your Farmers best. Buy the best; raise the best—and they will deliver you a post for a span.

The dais was filling—nearly full. Head to head, feet to feet, only Lagash's place empty. The sun had climbed enough to send liquid rays slanting up into the ceiling. They reflected off that glassy dome and suffused the chamber with warm light. As senior Keeper, Gilgamesh began the round, and each joined in response:

> By the light cast from
>> beneath the waters
> By the light cast from
>> the rim of the world
> By the light cast from
>> within the mountain
> By the light cast from
>> the vault above
> By the light cast on the fields of
>> Uruk
> By the light cast on the fields of
>> Ur
> By the light cast on the fields of
>> Eridu
> By the light cast on the fields of
>> Umma
> By the light cast on the fields of

Shurruppak
By the light cast on the fields of
Mesolimeris
By the light cast on the fields of
—

But of course, Lagash did not answer.
"Does no light shine on the fields of Lagash?"
"The light of Lagash has not risen."
By the water cast on the fields of
Uruk
By the water cast on the fields of
Ur
By the water cast on the fields of
Eridu
By the water cast on the fields of
Umma
By the water cast on the fields of
Shurruppak
By the water cast on the fields of
Mesolimeris
By the water cast on the fields of
—

"Does no water flow on the fields of Lagash?"
"The fields of Lagash lie barren."
This went on for rather a lot of formulaic time, in
Sargon's estimation. Long enough, presumably, for the dead to
rise, hand-over-hand up the mountain. But Lagash's days of
rock-climbing were over. Old Lagash had left it too long to
induce a successor; had nearly died giving birth to a stillborn
rat, and the mourning howls had been heard all the way to
Mesolimeris. Rumor had it that all but the bedside Warriors
had already been put down, and it was only a matter of time.
Finally, the ritual invocation was done:
"Let us rise and deal justly with the *ar* of Lagash."

At which point the accountants really got into it. Sargon ignored most of this juridical clamor: depositions from wailing dependants of every stripe; reputed creditors; their antagonists. Of more interest was the Farmer's Council. Farmers didn't talk much; when they did, it was generally worth listening to. Interesting was a green, weedy stalk of a lad, more like a planter than a Farmer, who was quietly but furiously clacking the fingers of all three hands. Finally, at a lull in accountancy, the stripling chirped. All heads turned.

"Lagash Post 3. Eighty *ar*. Two planters."

Most of the Farmer's Council rumbled amusement. Umma and Shurruppak flipped back their hands: *no sale.* Interesting, thought Sargon. Lagash Post three was a useless bit of scrubland abutting the northeastern periphery of Mesolimeris. The stripling was offering to hold it, to the value of eighty *ar,* and to throw a payment of two planters into the bargain.

Sargon looked over at Farmer John. Farmer John was very, very carefully staring at the floor, and sitting on his hands.

"Assessment?" barked Sargon.

The estate Accountant looked shocked. It was a worthless scrap of land, but heavily indebted. Sargon would be mad to settle the ledger. "Two post, five span, five hand small cattle. Freehold"

Had his face been capable of such an expression, Sargon would have smiled. Instead, he flipped his gripping hand.

"Well, my young Farmer. Let's see if you can earn some get."

A low murmur circled the room. All attention was on Sargon. Which had rather been the point.

"On the subject of Lagash Post 3," he flipped the gripping hand again, "that is, *Mesolimeris Post 27*" —accountants scribbled furiously— "may we move on to *new* business?"

There was no dissent.

Sargon stood. He used The Voice. The Voice rumbled and screeched in registers above and below the human range of hearing.

"*Anathema* has come. Their *vermin* have arrived at my western Posts! John, inform them!"

A moment of chaos, and then a hush, as John trilled an amazing, sophisticated, detailed data stream, most of which was lost on the Masters present. But they gathered the critical points. For two side less two hand years, Post Watchers had observed these creatures. At first they would arrive by ones and twos, then, every two hand years, their numbers would swell. Hands, Sides, Grips—half of a Master's Hand—would trek from the wastes by various paths, through the badlands, into the realms of the mountain light. They passed respectfully, carried their bowls, left their beasts to graze the wilds, and returned whence they came again. They never crossed into Council lands: by the wastes they came, by the wilds they went. The Council had discussed options; made contingency plans, but in the end agreed that they had done no harm, and posed no threat, and therefore were not worth wasting an *ar* of regard.

But Sargon, with Lagash as ally, had never been *quite* content with that. Sargon'd had them followed. Had them followed, at incredible expense, by relays of Runners, and Porters carrying a Farmer, the last of whom had reported on their deathbeds, collapsed from starvation. And *what* they had reported! These creatures—these *anathema*—had laid *waste* to their own lands! Clearly, they bred *Engineers*. Monstrous machines had crushed entire mountains. They planted without regard to *ar*. They kept cattle in such abundance that soil was laid *bare*. They flooded their fields, and then despaired when the inevitable salty crusts caked in drifts across the furrows. Then they wept, and watered the ground with their salty tears.

The Council was horrified; the Farmers nearly berserk. So they had agreed: the day *anathema* threatened the western *ar*, they would act as one. Every Master would breed Cavalry. Every Keeper would open a storehouse. Every Farmer would tithe provisions. And the Council would appoint from among them a Commander.

Sargon flipped his hand again. Sargon, Procurator of the Northern Protectorate, Master of all wilds and wastes between the mountains; Master of all lands not accounted to any city's *ar*, now had a Master's Grip. He had begun with wasteland, and created plenty. The Keepers still held the storehouses. The Masters still commanded the city walls. But by the end of the Meeting, Sargon commanded the Army that protected all.

They disbanded the Meeting. They climbed down the cliff-face. They marshaled their trains and continued to the levees, where many piled into pole-boats. Some set out for their island cities in the delta: Shurruppak, Umma, Uruk, Ur, and Eridu. Sargon's delegation zigged and zagged through a mesh of reed-choked byways, until they abandoned the waterways completely for the dust-cloaked hinterlands of Mesolimeris. Everywhere, as far as they went, exhausted pannes bloomed anew, the checkerboard aquamarine shimmer a living testament to the miracle of Sargon's *ar*. In Sargon's train, the saying went, there was no waste. *Ar* blossomed where Sargon stepped.

Or shat, more like, snorted Farmer John. It's the Farmers do all the steppin'. Good call, though, on that young one. Young'un'll be an *ar*-buster, and no mistake.

The Barrens, New Utah

Collie shook his head emphatically. "Young missy, I really think you'd better let me—"

"Uncle Collie, *it is the duty of every island to give aid and support to the Seers, that they may be of aid to all pilgrims.* My mother gave her life to make me a Seer. I think they will—"

"Missy, your mother didn't 'give' anything. She was just a venomous old cow who refused to listen to reason. She insisted on Gathering even though—"

"You can't talk about my mother—"

"No, missy, but I *can* talk about my own sister. I loved her like my own eye. But she had no business trying to conceive a Seer at her age. There's plenty of younger women more fit to trek. She'd already seen one Gathering, and she was a late-comer to that. She'd no business trying to schedule your birth at her age, let alone schedule it to happen on top of a mountain!"

"How can you say that? How can you talk like that about The Gathering!"

"Because I am trying to make you see reason."

"But it is your duty too! Your duty to support the Seers—"

"Missy, let me remind you, that in His Gaze, we are all pilgrims, we are all Seers, and all islands are One. It is also the *duty of every pilgrim to honor the wisdom of the pilgrims of Gatherings past, who have gazed into his earthly Eye and believed.* I have done so. You have not, yet. That's just how people are. You need all the support you can get right now—not just the support of the third and fourth Gatherings."

"But I've Seen—"

"—the path to the gathering place. Which none but Seers are allowed. You've Seen the Waking of His Eye. Which none but Seers are allowed. And now, you've seen the Revelation of Angels! Praise Him! In His Gaze, I do believe! *But you have not yet seen His earthly Eye awake!* How will gathered pilgrims believe? How can an *ungathered* Seer prophesy?"

"Well, why do you? Believe, I mean?"

"Because He was revealed in *my* hour of *grievous* need. I lifted *my* hands from my face, and saw *His* face in your Gaze."

But at this moment, Laurel's face was set, hard and grim. "Well, *it is the duty of every Seer to maintain the Watch for the Waking of His Eye*. It is my *duty* to announce the Waking. "

"Missy, I can't change your mind for you. You are our island's Seer, and you are my own blood. I trust you with my life. I trust you *to guide all pilgrims in safety and secrecy to the Gathering*. But please, trust me in this one thing. Tell them. Tell them that He Wakes. Tell them to assemble. Tell them to begin the march. Lead them. But do not announce Revelation now. It will only awaken jealousy. Either leave it to later, or leave it to me."

"But when will we tell them?"

He smiled at the "we."

"Laurel, let it be Revealed on the mountain. You won't be alone. You will have led them in safety. They will be drunk in His Gaze. You will be thronged with His angels. And then, when you return, Gathered and Seen in Glory, you can leave the old codgers to me."

Collie winked. Finally, Laurel smiled. "Well, Agamemnon knows, too," she said. "Agamemnon believes."

"Sweet Pie, Agamemnon would believe if you told him fire was water."

Captain LeGrange 's mood became even grimmer as she approached the small knot of people at the edge of the trees. The girl was seated on a log to the left of the bridge entrance, hunched over, head between her knees, shoulders shaking. Yellow sweat jackets were piled on her back like so many remnants at a jumble sale, leaving the concerned-looking troops clumped around her like half-peeled bananas, puckered and shivering in their singlets. Sheila Thompson, the medic, was crouched down beside her, rather pointlessly waving a crushed ampoule beside the girl's running nose with one hand, and patting her shoulder with the other. Under the jackets, LeGrange saw a hint of shadow-khaki, and realized that the girl's right arm was supported and tied to her body by a field sling. It never ceased to amaze her what Thompson could pull from her pockets, even on a morning training run.

One of the bananas looked up, then jogged up the path to meet her, dropping to a walk as he saluted, already blurting, "He's still up in the tree, Ma'am." He did not direct his gaze above LeGrange 's own height. "We was worried that people would start walking and shite, you know, over the bridge and shite, and it's pretty awful, but we thought we shouldn't touch him, I mean…" He trailed off, with a furtive glance at the grim reality above him.

LeGrange looked stolidly up at the horrible, waxy, crimson-washed face; at the bulging, staring eyes, and then down at the girl.

"You did right, Sergeant."

He nodded once, and then turned to rejoin the milling gaggle.

LeGrange looked back down at the slip of a girl, and felt a sudden burst of anger. "Sergeant, why the hell haven't you gotten her out of here?"

She regretted snapping even as she did it, but Thompson just took it in stride. "I know, Ma'am. I know, but she won't leave. I tried to have a detail walk her home, but she just starts yelling and crying and finally I said flock it, 'scuze me Ma'am, goldam it, leave her be until the police get here."

She said it the same way Swanson did: p'leece.

LeGrange 's nostrils narrowed as she surveyed the scene. Bloody footprints were spread everywhere, the result of the first ranks splashing through the blood puddle, then being allowed to mill around aimlessly, and then being allowed to leave without wiping their feet. Worse, she could see a wet trail scuffled through the leaves leading into the woods off to the right along the Philosopher's way. Somehow, she did not think it had been made by the killer.

"Sergeant, who passed through here?'

"That would have been the detail, Ma'am."

"The detail?"

"The XO, Ma'am. He said we should make sure nobody came through from the back gate. He led the fallouts down there to block the way."

And in the process, thought LeGrange, obliterated the tracks of anyone else that might have gone the same way.

"Sergeant, who the hell is going to come *from* post *to* Moorstown *on foot* at this hour of the morning?"

She shrugged. "Ma'am, I didn't say it was my idea. I didn't say it was a good idea. I just said that's what the XO did."

LeGrange said nothing, but everyone there knew what she was thinking. They were probably thinking the same thing. Major Trippe was that hopeless combination of dull and keen; uninspired and ambitious, most dreaded by every soldier. He never seemed to grasp the important in anything, but could be relied upon to pursue the unimportant with vigor, annoying everyone involved with pointless supervision, overtime, and cheer-leading even as major problems crashed and burned around them.

"Let me guess," she said tersely, "he also released everyone to quarters."

"Oh, yes Ma'am. He said he 'wasn't going to hold up the duty day over some A-rab getting his throat cut in a blood feud.'"

With that, the girl jumped to her feet, shaking her head, scattering yellow sweat suit jackets as she ranted.

"No! That's not true! Hugo's a good boy! He's never,

never, fighting!" Her eyes burned bright, deep within the shadow of her bonnet.

The group started, stupefied. It had not occurred to them that she spoke any Anglic, despite the fact that they had been speaking it to her, unremittingly, for half an hour. The MPs shifted from one foot to another, looking at her, then at each other, then at her again, wondering if they should do something. Or secure something. Or something. Caught off balance by Marul's sudden movement, Sergeant Thompson stopped waving the ammonia capsule and thrashed to her own feet. The shivering banana cluster took a step back in unison, then remembering the grim artifact in the tree above them, lurched forward again. Even Swanson, at the far end of the path, turned to see what was going on.

The girl switched to Tok Pisin and continued ranting.

"See, Ma'am? She just goes off!"

LeGrange looked down at the child, dwarfed by this forest of strangers, and made several snap decisions.

"Sergeant," she barked, pointing to the banana bunch, "why are these people here?"

"They—uh—live in unofficial barracks? I mean, you know, in Moorstown? They was gunna take her home, only she won't go."

"Were any of you first on the scene?"

"Ma'am?"

"In that gaggle of 150 heroes chasing each others' afterburners through the road apples, were any of you up at the front of the formation?"

"No, Ma'am."

"OK, Sergeant, get these people out of here, and get the first rank back here, ASAP."

"But Ma'am, it was a Brigade Fun Run."

The implication of this was not lost on LeGrange . Fun Runs were not in the least fun. Fun Runs were an opportunity for officers twice their age to demonstrate the tortoise principle to eighteen-year-old hares. Said tortoises comprised the primary headquarters staff. The Personnel, Security, Operations, and Supply Officers would have formed the first rank, led by The Hoop himself or, in his absence, his Executive Officer—the selfsame Major Trippe. And, since LeGrange had herself been absent, by virtue of the previous night's Duty, the Communications Officer would have run in her stead. Sending a buck sergeant medic to entreat the entire headquarters senior staff to abandon their desks and return to Moorstown was not only impolitic; it was extremely unlikely to succeed.

LeGrange looked at her watch. It was 7:30. "OK. Take Swanson and the FLIVR. Tell 'em the DO says Command Call, Staff Conference Room, oh-eight hundred. I'll bring the civil liaison officer to them to take their statements."

The cluster shifted a bit uneasily. One spoke up, looking rather horrified at his sweat suit jacket, now half-trampled under Marul's bloody feet. "Uh, Ma'am, I mean, it don't really matter, but what about our gear?"

LeGrange just nodded, and unzipped her field jacket. "Leave straight up the *middle* of the path. Do *not* under *any* circumstances cut across that field!"

They grappled with their clothing while LeGrange directed one of the MPs.

"You. Go straight to the far side of the bridge and stop *anyone* from crossing. Watch your feet every step of the way. If you see footprints, *do not* step in 'em. If you see blood, do *not* step on it. You are the Last of the Mohicans in those woods. You disturb nothing. You hop like silent fleas."

"Yes Ma'am," he said, eyes already darting over the ground, obviously comprehending nothing of what he saw.

She sighed. "Footprints."

"Ma'am?"

"They'll be sort of like scuff marks. Places where the leaves have been squashed or kicked off the gravel."

"Yes Ma'am."

She called after him as he moved off. "And *politely*. Tell people 'Tasol Polis' *politely!*"

The second MP was now panting for a mission of his own.

"You. Same thing, only go about a hundred meters down the Philosopher's Way *away* from post. To the left. Follow your buddy's tracks *exactly* until you turn off, then same instructions."

He looked disappointed. He kept looking up at the body and fingering his utility belt. He clearly did not see much of anything heroic about standing around on the Philosopher's Way in case some fresh air nut came blundering onto the scene. He wanted to log evidence, or arrest somebody, or just plain knock heads.

LeGrange eyed him as he turned, somewhat sullenly, and threw him a bone. "And watch yourself, Poole. That killer's still out there somewhere."

She smiled slightly as his shoulders squared and he stalked off, shadowing his partner's footsteps to the millimeter.

The banana bunch had finally finished sorting out their jackets—a pointless exercise, it seemed to LeGrange , for they all looked to be the same shapeless size and well-ripened color. They filed past. LeGrange softly, tenderly, lowered her field jacket onto Marul's shoulders. She then unwound the field scarf from around her own neck and handed it to Sergeant Thompson, who had begun to shiver, teeth chattering.

LeGrange looked at her watch again, impatiently. It was now 7:35, and there was still no sign of either the civil police or the Civil Liaison Officer. Sirens or no, they were obviously stuck in the crush of morning traffic. She was tired, she was cold, she was hungry, she hoped to God her troops would handle any confrontation with civilians appropriately, and she did not look forward to the tongue-lashing she would no doubt receive for the absolute bollocks the troops had made of the murder scene.

LeGrange squatted, facing the girl, and spoke softly, bilingually.

"Are you sad?" She thought the girl nodded, but Marul was rocking, still shivering and sobbing, and it was hard to tell.

"Are you afraid?" This time, Marul definitely nodded, slowly.

"I can imagine. It's horrible." The girl continued rocking.

LeGrange glanced upward. "Is that what you're afraid of?" Nothing.

"What are you afraid of?" Still nothing.

"Of him?" Marul shook her head, slowly.

"Of me?" Again, a slow shake of the head.

"Of somebody else?" The rocking stopped, and the girl gave one short nod.

"Of whom?"

Marul did not answer, but she made one quick, involuntary glance in the direction of the bridge, and then another up the path across the meadows. There, her glance froze, then relaxed. She actually smiled slightly, tears still welling.

With gritty eyes, LeGrange followed Marul's look, then muttered "Damn!" under her breath. She'd sent the trooper off with Swanson and the FLIVR, but had posted no-one in Swanson's place to block access. A lone, wiry, slight figure was approaching.

Every third Friday at six a.m., Linda Libiziewsky parked her oxide green skater, named Kermit the Magnificent, at the far end of the leased housing block and began a systematic trek from stairwell to stairwell, toting a touchscreen, cross-checking and verifying repair reports, fire extinguisher inspection tags, work orders, grounds maintenance, and anything else that caught her meticulous eye.

Her powers were broad. Nominally, she was the post housing coordinator, responsible for ensuring that each and every soldier, civilian employee, school teacher, and attached family member obtained and moved into safe, approved, adequate quarters, preferably within seven days of arrival in the TCM security zone.

But that mandate gave her secondary, sweeping authority to inspect housing conditions in general, in order to assess availability and adequacy. She chose to interpret "conditions" fairly liberally, and was on the lookout constantly and especially for signs of strain; stress; community breakdown. By the time soldiers earn several stripes and several children, their habits are well-entrenched. They come to prefer ordered lives. Too many shaggy lawns; too many toys and appliances left rusting alongside walkways; too many stairwells littered with unclaimed junk; too many bloody noses and black eyes were signs, not so much of bad upbringing, but of families stretched by grueling duty hours; short tempers; fatigue. Absent these factors, the few bad apples were quickly polished by the orchard police.

This morning, as she wound her way down the inevitable Brigham Young Way intersection with John Smith Lane, Linda stopped to ponder the inordinate number of cracked window panes, missing insect screens, unsealed fire extinguishers, and untrimmed hedges. Dirt, leaves, and graffiti marked an imperceptible but inexorable transition into Moorstown. Where once had stood a demarcation line, like foursquare farmland abutting a wilderness, was now more like the brackish pooling of an anastomosing river into a saline estuary—impossible to tell, through mangrove roots or cypress knees, where river left off and sea began. If anything, although drearier, simple lack of possessions made for neater exteriors outside the Moorstown buildings.

Linda's teeth set. This change was not the result of some long decline. She could date it, and document it. It was very recent indeed. In another era, she would have been housekeeper to a great estate on New Washington or Sparta, aware at any moment of the location and condition of each and every piece of crockery. This state of affairs offended her sense of order.

It had taken about an hour-and-a-half to complete her peregrination, and she set out briskly to reach her office, a temporary partition in a temporary building erected in haste forty years before, by eight o'clock sharp. She could, of course, have simply gone back to retrieve Kermit the Magnificent, but a brisk constitutional along the banks of the river was part of her routine, for she made several more checks and paperwork stops at the various warehouses that intervened.

As she turned toward the meadows, she could barely make out several figures at the forest's edge. Clearly, something was amiss. At this point, she should be hearing the Doppler mumble of Jodie calls carrying over the bright morning air, and preparing to dodge a couple of hundred running feet bearing down in banana-yellow glory. She squinted, and as she drew close enough to make out faces she broke into a run.

"Marul! Jeri! Sheila! What's wrong?"

LeGrange stood abruptly; frantically waved her back; alternately stabbing toward the ground with one finger, then pointing up into the tree. "Lindy, stay back!"

But with LeGrange's attention occupied, Marul, too, jumped to her feet, and in one motion bolted into Linda's arms, as Linda's touch screen bounced across the path into the grass. Linda's feet froze in place as the girl's arms enveloped her; gripped her, and her own body shook with the force of Marul's sobs.

"He kill me! He kill me! He say it is stain on his honor! Lindy! Lindy! You have to help! Please, you have to help! Please, help me get to Uncle Ollie!"

"Jeri?"

LeGrange hesitated only a fraction. Two hundred troops had already seen what happened. "The run came down through here, and plowed into this poor kid just as she slipped and fell in the—" she looked down at Marul, "in *his*—" and looked again, "as she slipped and fell. There." LeGrange pointed to the skid marks in Hugo's blood. "She says his name is Hugo? I got the call, and came around. The XO had already released the troops."

Linda nodded. "Can I—can we—it's hard shouting like this."

LeGrange nodded and pointed to a safe path around, through the trampled mess made by the troops, where any clue was well-buried now. Linda gently peeled Marul's arms apart and tried to take her hand, but the girl clung to her side like a toddler as they made their way to LeGrange .

"So she was alone here, with about a million soldiers. *Male* soldiers?"

"Well, yes. I mean, not all male. You know, it's about sixty-forty on a Brigade run."

"And the front rank was?"

"Command staff, of course."

"Then why weren't you—"

"DO. I was duty officer. So Sergeant…." She trailed off, as Linda groaned.

"Did anyone touch her?"

LeGrange turned. "Sergeant Thompson?"

Sheila was staring at the ground. "Yes Ma'am. Me." But she did not look up.

"Anyone else?"

"Not really."

"What do you mean, not really? Did they, or didn't they?"

"Ma'am. It happened pretty fast. I mean, the guys just wanted to help, you know? They didn't do nuthin.' Just put their jackets on her, helped her sit down."

But Linda was already shaking her head. "Oh, Sheila."

"I know ma'am. I know. I'm so sorry. It happened so fast. I was at the back and it took me a minute to get up there. And we was kind of—well, even me. You know."

Linda followed her eyes up into the tree, nodded, sighed.

"She's right. He'll kill her."

"Who?"

"Her father."

"Oh, surely that's ridiculous."

Gently, Linda cupped Marul's chin and turned her face toward LeGrange . The sun was higher now, reaching beneath the bonnet's cowl. One eye was black; the cheek below mottled purple and green. "He did this to her because she *waved* when they *ran past*. She wasn't even on the path. She wasn't within thirty paces of them. Imagine what he'll do if he finds out that she was *manhandled* by a bunch of unrelated, healthy, young men, without a chaperone."

"But it's ridiculous! I mean, it's utterly irrational. Nothing happened. Nothing *could* have happened. There's a hundred *witnesses*."

Linda sighed. "Jeri, you are missing the point. This isn't *rational*. It's not about whether or not 'anything' happened. In his twisted view, something *did* happen. An honor violation, plain and simple. So somebody has to pay. And since he's an

MP TCM fundy himself, it'll be the girl who pays, not his troopy buddies."

"But how does it 'defend his honor' to kill his own child?"

"If it makes you feel any better, he'll probably cry when he does it. But he'll do it. They talk a lot about defending church and family, but in the end, it's really all about themselves."

"But that's—*illegal*. He'll get himself court-martialed."

"Nevertheless." She smiled thinly. "And maybe he won't do it himself. Or maybe he'll do it, but somebody who owes his family a favor will confess to it and serve the time. In any case, it'll get done."

The police sirens, wailing in the distance, suddenly lurched closer. The morning traffic was breaking up.

"So what do we do? We need to do it fast. The civvies will be here any minute."

"I'll take her to her Uncle."

"Her Uncle? But won't he just hand her over to her father?"

Linda was already shaking her head, but LeGrange suddenly blanched and interrupted whatever she might have said. "Oh God. The MPs. I brought two with me."

"Did they see her with anyone?"

"Yes. No. Wait." LeGrange struggled with fatigue, trying to remember who had seen exactly what, exactly when. "Sheila?"

"No, ma'am. When you got here, I was sittin' with her on that log. And the jackets was already on. And her face was all hid anyway. She was lookin' down at the groun'."

"What about the rest of the troops?"

"Ma'am, I bin sittin' here thinkin' on it. It happened so fast, but see, when she fell, she got up lookin' *away* from anyone. An she's wearin' that big ole' bonnet. An' then I was with her on that log, an she was mostly lookin' *down*. An' those boys with the jackets, they was our boys. They weren't none of that MP shite. Sorry ma'am. I jus' don't like them boys. They make me a lot of trouble over nuthin.'"

LeGrange merely nodded. Thompson went on. "So, I don't think anybody could say for certain it was her. I mean, some of 'em might know there's a girl walks this way every mornin,' but mos' of the regulars, like me, was way at the back and didn't see nuthin.'"

"Are you sure? She told you her name, didn't she? Didn't they hear that?"

"No ma'am. I don't think so. Even Major Trippe was all, like, do this, do that, come here, go there. He ran off with that detail, and sent Theo to get you, but nobody really talked to her 'cept me. An,' an'—honey, did you even tell *me* your name?"

Sharply, emphatically, Marul shook her head *no*.

LeGrange thought a moment. "Did you tell anyone your cousin's name? Before I got here, I mean?"

No, again.

LeGrange turned to Thompson. "So the banana boys with the jackets know that she recognized the body, but that's all?"

"Ma'am I think that's pretty much it. I mean, I think a bunch of people might know that she *recognized* him, but only those boys with the jackets, and me, and you even heard his name. And nobody knows her name but us."

But Marul started shivering again, uncontrollably, and new tears welled. "Wayan! Wayan knows!"

Linda was already in motion, grabbing Marul's hand, towing the girl behind her. "That's it. That sniveling little shite will tell. He's a typical, pampered, spoiled brat of an eldest son, and he'll *delight* in telling. Her Uncle's her only chance."

LeGrange jogged after her, shouting, "But how can he help?"

Linda stopped abruptly, incredulous. "Jeri, haven't you put this together? That's Hugo *Azhad* in that tree. *Ollie* Azhad's son. Marul's *cousin*." And when the penny still did not drop, "Jeri, Ollie *Azhad*. Chief of TCM Contract Security. His youngest sister married the piece of crap that did this to her. You see how that boy was murdered. It's nothing to do with Marul. This isn't personal. It's professional."

"But they'll want a witness statement!"

"I'm getting this girl out of here. They don't need her. She witnessed nothing. You could get anybody in Saint George to identify that boy. Anybody *local*." And with that, they sprinted for the bridge.

LeGrange jogged to a stop, turned, walked back to Sheila Thompson. Thompson's face was stone. "Ma'am, that girl was jus' walkin' by. Didn't see nuthin,' didn't know nuthin.' I will swear that to a Magistrate."

LeGrange smiled wanly. "What girl was that, Sergeant Thompson?"

7
Forty Thieves

You follow the laws because they are your laws—not always, because you perhaps cheat on your tax forms, but normally you do. Nationalism encourages good behavior.

—*Benedict Anderson*

Bonneville, New Utah

They wound their way through the city center, working vaguely uphill, finally squeezing into streets so narrow that they must have dated to Foundation times. Individual buildings gave way to long, massive walls punctuated by small, massive doors. The streets became rougher, then narrower, then rougher again, until the street proper ended at a cul-de-sac broken by footpaths fanning off into the blackness. The lads were no longer grinning. As he dismounted, the driver rummaged under his feet—until Asach stopped him with one curt shake of the head.

"But—"

"We'll be fine."

"But this is—"

Asach smiled, and finished the sentence. "—my world, now. It is possible, you know, to leave the Ward, and leave the Stick, and live to tell the tale. Think of it as a Mission."

The Lads nodded sheepishly, and fell in step behind Asach.

They wound down a short alley, turned a sharp left, and halted before a door barely visible in the black. Asach balled a fist and pounded three dull blows. They were swallowed up into what sounded like a vast cavern within.

They waited. The Lads fidgeted, standing back-to-back facing opposite ends of the alleyway. Asach smiled privately, without moving. Eventually, footsteps echoed within, a light snapped on above them, and a disembodied voice said, "Yes?"

"Is Michael in?"

"Who asks?"

At which point Asach pushed back the cloak hood and stared up into the button camera. "Quinn. Asach Quinn. And two friends. If he's not there, we'll just go on back to—"

But the door burst open before the thought was finished, and a tiny man was already pulling Asach into the compound with one hand, waving the others to cross the threshold with the other, and shouting to two even tinier women across the courtyard.

"My dear friend! My dear friend! What brings you here! What brings you here! We did not think we would ever—Lena! Bring—Asach? What do you need? We will—Lena!—How came you to be here? How can we help you, my friend?—Lena, get the—"

"Sleep."

"The cots! Lena, three cots!—I am sorry my friend, the rooms are all—"

"The roof is fine. Better, even."

"Lena! Three cots! On the roof! And towels. And—are you refreshed? Do you desire—"

"We've eaten," Asach lied.

"Just tea, then! Lena, hot towels, and tea!"

Much banging and clanking ensued just out of vision, as the little man finally turned full attention to the little entourage, one hand patting the center of Asach's back to punctuate each sentence. For a moment, he looked downcast.

"You know there is trouble in the House?"

Asach scanned the immaculate courtyard, floors, square columns, walls washed white with gypsum. Lamplight flickered over the intricate lacework, carved from soapy rock that covered each ground floor window. Stone steps, made from solid blocks stacked one above the other, led to the second story, where the pattern was repeated in carved wooden shutters, now thrown open to the nighttime air. In the opposite corner, a river of basalt, clad in green tracery, plunged from the roofline, through the balustrade, to the entry yard, as backdrop to a gentle spray and fall of water. The stone was cratered with fist-sized holes. Warm air gushed through, was cooled by passage through the mist, and made a gentle breeze as it sank into the courtyard. The Lads gaped, dumbfounded.

"Trouble? What trouble could there be, here in Heaven?"

The little man grunted. "As I love you, do not blaspheme."

Asach smiled.

"Michael's mother—"

"She has returned?"

"No." He frowned. "No. She has withdrawn her share, and so Michael cannot—"

"But surely the major work is done?" Asach scanned the fresh plaster, restored shutters, rebuilt staircase, waterfall fountain. Even the cross, carved into the lintel beneath which they had passed as they entered, was carefully cleaned and repainted, with polished stones set into each of the trefoil tips that terminated the corners of each arm. Above it was inset a glazed tile depicting an eye: blue-green iris, black pupil, enclosed within a triangle overlaid on radial rays of aquamarine and white.

The script enwrapping all was archaic, flowing, not at all Anglic. Asach made out: May His Eye be upon us.

"Ah, Excellency. It requires so much to run this household, and Michael—"

"Do not call me that. I work for a living."

Asach's voice had not risen one decibel. Nevertheless, all three men winced, but relaxed again under Asach's jolly smile.

At which point, Lena arrived with tea, accompanied by a mountain of little cakes. They huddled together around a pretty stone table, dragged to the cool corner beside the waterfall. The Lads said nothing, and drank no tea, but finally removed their shades and wolfed their way through the mountain, pausing occasionally to cup a handful of water from the fountain.

The little man was Nejme Silelyan; Lena was his daughter. The tea-and-cake elf was his wife, Mena, who bubbled forth briefly, smothered the top of Asach's head with kisses, then disappeared again, Lena in tow. The household was in a frenzy, preparing for a wealthy group expected the following evening. A small army, under Mena's direction, was pressing linens; making beds; airing rooms; dressing suites. A group of what, the Lads could not quite make out: Asach and Nejme shifted among languages, none of them Anglic or Tok Pisin. The Lads did not ask. If they needed to know, they'd be told. If they did not need to know, it was best that they not find out.

"Michael of course resents having to—to—to—"

"To run a *hotel*?"

Nejme's eyes sparkled. "For me, it is not so…it is only…it is a *way*, you know? But for Michael, it is—demeaning. Well, not demeaning, exactly, but—"

"Oh, I can imagine Michael's views. Is that why he's away?"

"Oh, no. Michael—"

But not wishing to tax Nejme's hospitality, before the last cake was devoured, Asach rose, declined three offers to remain at table, and motioned The Lads to follow. They trudged up the stairs, then around a turning into an unrestored, ramshackle staircase that took them up to the flat, beaten-clay roof.

The view of the city was stunning. Up there, above the urban canyons, it was windy, and the night was turning cool. It was amazingly soothing to hear late evening traffic in the distance. Fireworks sparkled over some celebration or other further off in the hills. A wedding was going on down below, with attendant laughter, chatter, music, song, arrivals, departures, and fireworks of its own. Finally, a muezzin made the midnight call to prayer, the aching poetry of that timeless call to God washing over the sleeping Lads, who neither heard nor stirred. It was everything Asach remembered a wonderful time in New Utah to be: that easy-going mix of Mormon and Muslim; High Church and Himmist. Heaven, in fact.

What had happened?

Bonneville, New Utah

Next morning, after washing down nutty-flavored mush with hair-raising coffee (for Asach) and bright red tea (for the rest of the household), Asach sent The Lads on a payback mission. The house Stirling was acting up. It sucked up heat from a solar collector on the roof, and used it to pump water, power the house electrics, and run an air compressor for mechanical jobs. Or, it sucked up motion from the rooftop wind turbine, and used that to pump heat out of the house in the summer, and into the house in the winter. However, at the moment, it was doing none of these things with any great efficiency, providing The Lads with potential hours of fascination as they poured over house energetics diagrams.

If that failed, according to Nejme, there was a coop daisy field not far away? Set up on the bulldozed remains of an old industrial warehouse, with the collection tower retrofitted into the old crane deck? The daisies were small, self-orienting parabolic dishes. Anyone could add one (for a fee). Anyone could buy power from the coop (for an even bigger fee). But the coop had not yet wired this neighborhood, and Michael had not wanted to bear the expense, personally, of a rooftop line? So the house was dependant upon the (thankfully low-maintenance) Stirling? So if it needed a part, maybe The Lads could run down to the souk and get it fabricated? And if not, maybe lug some backup cells down to the daisy field, and wave their TCM badges around?

No problem, said Asach, and sent the ecstatic Lads off for a day of mechanical engineering. Meanwhile, Asach returned to the roof. The early morning sun had broken over the horizon, and its shadow was slowly climbing an opposite wall. Asach moved out of what was soon to be the shadow of the parabolic collectors that fed the house Stirling and kitchen cooker, spread the cloak out flat on the deck, and then unzipped the hood.

From within the collar, Asach pulled a thin wire, ending in a connector. Asach then inverted the hood, and jerked a toggle near what had been the throat tie. The hood, now with a shiny side out, snapped into a rigid, octagonal shape, with stays connecting each point to the center. From the cloak facing, Asach extracted what looked like a disjointed snake. Another tug on its end, and this became a rigid staff, about a meter long, which socketed neatly into the center back of the hood-parabola. From a pocket, Asach extracted a pencil-sized tripod, which worked to stand and stabilize the staff.

Then, from the cloak hem, Asach extracted four objects, each the size of two thick thumbs. These fit together to form a four-pointed star, with another short staff that socketed into the dish center. Asach sat cross-legged, plugged the wire into the base of the dish antenna, wiggled the tripod around so that the whole thing faced roughly the opposite horizon, and then pulled back a flap on the cloak, revealing a flat keypad below a flexible view screen. Fishing around in a pocket, Asach found two nano-clips. One snapped into place on the back of the hood-dish; the second just above the keypad.

Asach waited for the sun to clear the roof and power the solar cloak. It climbed slowly. Asach daydreamed, and wondered about all those things, on all those worlds, that were known and unknown.

For example: Asach knew what a duck-billed platypus was. Asach knew about its leathery beak, aquatic habits, mammalian kinship, and bizarre reproductive habits, including now-forgotten details of courtship and its near-uniqueness among mammals of laying leathery eggs. The egg-laying somehow loomed larger than their absolute uniqueness among mammals of possessing venomous—spines? The method of poison delivery had dimmed, but Asach was nonetheless sure of the fact, despite never actually having seen one of the creatures, now a millennium away on another, unvisited world.

Sure. With an absolute, stalwart, evangelical faith, of the existence and hard, objective reality of the duck-billed platypus. It was reassuring to know that, on a distant planet, in a touchable closeness of memory, there lived sleek, furry little mammals that might be cute, save for their toxic, egg-laying, leathery qualities.

That Asach knew this was at the same time immensely disturbing, because Asach did not know *why*. The *how* was easy: it was depicted in school texts; there were explanatory panels at zoos (not that Asach ever saw an actual platypus there, either); there had been video excursions to a sort of duck-billed platypus theme park, which Asach found most bizarre. But *why*? Of all the things of this galaxy that are known or knowable, *why*, in the end, was it so sure, and so certain, and so *ensured* that Asach knew of the duck-billed platypus? Was there some hidden institutional wisdom in teaching the truth and palpability of a bizarre little creature, based upon the evidence of things unseen?

Asach was not at all sure that the Empire was—that Asach was—at all doing the right thing, on the right path, in the right way, here. Asach was not at all sure that the Empire was not merely planting seeds of disappointment. Asach was not at all sure that they had not made a cascading series of enormous mistakes, ending up in a backwater of obscurity, with nothing much to show for the dislocation and travail but the evangelical depths of a montoreme faith. See the platypus, and believe: anything can happen. Anything often does. Insh' Allah.

The sun broke. It crept lazily across the roof. Equally lazily, Asach waited for it to reach the cloak, rather than moving the cloak to greet it. At last, its warming rays crept out of the morning chill, each nano-cell embedded on the fabric sparkling for a nanosecond, then soaking the light into its black depths as the line of rosy light marched on.

Only when the entire cloak was basked in rapidly rising heat; only when the photovoltaics were pumping at full power, did Asach stir and rub on the keypad. A chart appeared. Asach tapped an icon, then took a bearing and tapped on a point at the hemline that was directly aligned to the sun. Another tap on the chart. Another tap on the cloak, this time in line with the setting chip of a moon. The moon was only a pathetic lump of asteroid, but it glittered on the dawn horizon. Another tap. A pause. Then the fabric of the dish began writhing, as if it wished to twist off the tripod, reinvert, and rejoin the cloak. At last, it settled on an orientation, and a shape.

Asach unsnapped a 'tooth from beside the keypad, and stuffed it into one ear. One more tap. An inaudible sound burped into the ether. It hurtled across the roof, away from the hill, away from Bonneville. It raced across scorched fields; past wastelands. It raced the sun across the plains, trying to beat the light to the horizon. It met the horizon; left the horizon; raced to the edge of atmosphere. Where Air met No Air, it bounced, just a little, then plunged out of the sun's reach altogether, into New Utah's black shadow, sheeting through the ice of space. It was a tiny message. It was only one word. It was:

"[Ping!]"

The little composite sphere, left to drift alone for thirteen years, snapped awake from its reverie. Thirteen years, and an eon of technology later, it still knew what was wanted. It still knew what to do. It answered.

An agonizing second later, Asach laughed out loud at its cheery reply. It was: "[Ping!]"

Saint George, New Utah

Michael Van Zandt was *not* having a good day. Because he was having a bad day, he was having a bad tantrum for the benefit of the clerk at Orcutt Land & Mining. The office was hot and stuffy. City electricity was out again. It was incomprehensible to him *why*. People in Bonneville managed to keep their buildings cool. People in *Pahrump* managed to keep their buildings cool. He managed to keep his *own house* cool. So why was air conditioning out of the reach of Orcutt Land & Mining?

Zia sighed, and tried again. "*Myneer* Van Zandt, I *cannot* give you a receipt for deliveries that you *have not* made! If you—"

"*Why* is this so hard to grasp? Deliveries *have* been made. We stockpiled *twenty-two kilos* at *your* depot in Bonneville! The chit is—"

"Is *not* OLaM scrip! It is—"

"Not *scrip*, because it is *not* scrip! It's a full-fledged promissory voucher, and—"

"It can be a full-fledged whatever you like, but it is not going to fly! I cannot validate a voucher issued by a contract buyer I've never heard of! If you needed—"

"If I needed what?! He was standing in the middle of your mucking warehouse. How am I supposed to—"

Zia slapped her hand on the counter, then stabbed for emphasis on one of a dozen ID facsimiles pressed beneath the laminate. "Any 10-year old on this planet knows: No badge, no deal! I don't care if your *promissory voucher* came from the Prophet himself. If you can't give me a *valid badge number*, I can't give you a *tithe receipt.*"

Michael had sunk beyond anger, beyond frustration. Now he was plumbing despair. His face was ashen. His voice caught on every word.

"TCM tithe collectors are booked into my House for the night. Tonight. My *House*. If I can't show them a tithe receipt—" and then his shoulders collapsed. He stood vacantly for a moment, and then paced to a seedy chair next to the grimy window overlooking the sidewalk. He sank into the hard, cracked seat. He stared out at a row of rusting signpost stumps, and muttered, to no one; to anyone: "I'm ruined."

Zia had crossed a line herself. Detached, disembodied, sick to death of the scam she knew full well had happened. An illicit cargo. A midnight rendezvous. A dark warehouse. An efficient, knowledgeable buyer. The conversation: "Of course, we can't issue *commodity scrip* Mr. Van Zandt. Not for *this* cargo. What we can do is give you a *for services* promissory voucher. Just exchange it for tithe receipts at the Saint George office.

Safer for you, anyway. Full value, right? Even if the price fluctuates? Better all 'round, eh?" And then twenty-two kilos of prime opal meerschaum just—ceased to exist. And Michael Van Zandt left holding the Stick. No scrip to exchange for company stores; no tithe credit to settle the TCM books.

Yes, any ten-year-old from New Utah would have known that score. But Michael Van Zandt wasn't a ten-year-old, and he wasn't from New Utah. She looked at him, slumped in the rickety chair, languid and patrician in his Bonneville whites, trying so hard to look the part, but New Utahan he definitely wasn't. She looked beyond him, to the window, grimy and yellowed because water could not be spared to wash it. Through the window to the filthy, littered sidewalk, until her eyes, too, came to rest on the rusting stumps of signposts. And came to a decision of her own.

"*Myneer* Van Zandt."

He looked back at her, sharply.

"Perhaps we might come up with some more—*creative*—clerical arrangement."

His eyes narrowed.

"Perhaps I could issue a receipt for this year's tithe, against your promise of *future* deliveries to that value."

Michael shot to his feet. "Now look here! I've already delivered twenty-two kilos at *current* prices. You know full well —"

"That prices are about to drop? Yes. That's the gamble, isn't it? The price rises, and then it drops. And we both know *why*. The difference is, *I* know someone who knows exactly *when*."

"Why should I care? I already—"

"*You* already fell for a sucker's deal, *Myneer*. Consider it a sunk cost. Think about it. *I* know someone who can tell you exactly—*exactly*—when the next shipment will flood the market. And exactly—*exactly*—when it will dry up again. Surely *you* know someone who knows what to make of that? How to recoup your losses?"

"And how do I know that you will keep *that* promise?"

"A time-honored tradition, *Myneer* Van Zandt. Hostages."

Michael looked confused. Zia smiled.

"If you agree to what I'm about to do, you will move me, and my family, into your House in Bonneville."

"I do not need any more household *help* in Bonneville."

"Oh, you'll find us useful, *Myneer* Van Zandt. But it goes with the deal. Because if I do this, I'll have no choice."

Michael shook his head. "It doesn't matter, anyway. The TCM collectors are already there by now. At my House. They're probably already at my House."

"Well, there's where you're in luck. As it happens, I'm making a depot run. Today. To the Bonneville warehouse. FairServ hop leaves in an hour. Two seats left."

"FairServ? But that would cost—"

"Next to nothing." Zia grinned. "Remember? Not-for-profit. TCM-registered, TC-sanctioned charity. With any luck, we'll be home for dinner. Tithe certificates in hand."

And they were.

Blaine Institute, New Caledonia

At first, it seemed inevitable that Ali Baba would return to the so-called East India Group. But Ali Baba was past nursing; there was no *nutritional* need, and Lord Cornwallis herself, Ali Baba's sire-turned-dam, seemed strangely indifferent. The Motie Engineer nursemaid who had born the pup had no voice in the matter. The pup's closest remaining relationship was that to Omar: Omar the "Bury Educator;"

Omar, the Motie shadow to Bury himself. It was eerie, even now, to round a corner and hear the dead man's voice, complete in every pitch, timbre, and sub-tone. It still made even Glenda Ruth start.

From the human perspective, it seemed a strange relationship: on First Contact in 3017, Motie Mediators were assigned as *fyunch≠* to humans, and to humans, that pairing still seemed the "natural" one. But of course, as they'd learned during that horrific dash through the Mote system last year, many Mediators were assigned to learn from other Mediators, and many more were assigned to no-one at all. Motie Masters had learned that lesson early on: choose *fyunch≠* targets wisely. From the Motie perspective, the gulf between Motie pragmatism and human innovation—well, *some* human innovation—was just too wide. Mediators could be made "insane" by the effort to learn, internalize, and emulate every thought and action of their subjects. They played their parts too well. They started acting in terms of what *should be*, instead of acting in terms of *what is*. But not "Bury Moties"—those educational descendants of that first Bury *fyunch≠*. They were pragmatic in the extreme. They were also extremely valuable.

When Bury named him in his will, Ali Baba's real troubles began. S/he was coveted, reviled, or both by nearly everyone.

First came the status issue. Was a Motie a *person* under the law? *Whose* law? Could a Motie be *adopted*? That point was moot. Bury's family wouldn't have him. Cynthia couldn't take her. Even the pronouns were a problem.

At stake was not semantics, but inheritance: Under Imperial, or Levantine, law, *could* a minor Motie hold property? As a *person*, or as *some other* legal entity? As nearly everyone pointed out, Ali Baba now held the swing vote in any possible Imperial Autonetics shareholder alliance (human, Motie, or otherwise). In the end, an injunction held: all or none. The

Empire *could not maintain* a second blockade of the Mote System without the cooperation of the Motie Trader groups endowed by Bury's will. For their part, they *would not* cooperate unless the terms of that will were deemed valid. A legal battle, framed against the Empire itself could bankrupt even Imperial Autonetics. The will held. Bury's *fyunch‡* descendants had learned their lessons well.

So, with this decision, the Little Prince(ss) was crowned, and the struggle for its allegiance began. To whom would Ali Baba be assigned? Who would be neutral, but qualified? Where would Ali Baba even be *safe*? In the end, as Bury's executor, Renner was appointed Ali Baba's guardian. Omar was retained as Ali Baba's "Bury Educator." When Renner traveled, Ali Baba stayed with Glenda Ruth in the Blaine Institute compound in New Caledonia.

But Ali Baba was re-assigned as *fyunch‡* to no-one, because Ali Baba was adamant on this point. Everyone by now knew the watch phrase that presaged a tantrum: "I belong to myself!" Where did this temper come from? From Bury? Bury was gone. From Omar? Mediators were not given to angry outbursts, and Omar least of all. From Glenda Ruth herself? Her mother had said it, laughing: "that sounds just like you, as a little girl. You would put up with anything, but you never could stand injustice."

But it seemed unlikely. Ali Baba's relationship to her was simply—cold. Not that other humans could tell. Motie faces twisted up into uniform, inscrutable smiles. They did not move. Insofar as Ali Baba used body language, it was all Bury's gestures, the three arms notwithstanding. Cool, calculating, graceful, even. Giving nothing away. But Glenda Ruth could—feel—it. In the timbre of Ali Baba's voice. It sounded like Bury's. It could be impassioned when angry. But when addressing her, it was missing all subtones of emotion.

"It's not right," said Ali Baba. "If I am to exercise prudent judgment regarding my voting shares, I must be allowed to travel. How else will I get to know—"

"It's just not *safe*," she pleaded. "You know that. We can protect you here at the Institute. But out there, beyond the Trans-Coal Sack—"

"I will be as *safe* on *Sinbad* as anywhere." She hated it when he did that. Switched to Bury's Voice. It sounded—chilling—coming from one so small. Chilling, and frighteningly intelligent, which s/he was.

"I will put it to Renner."

"But I—"

"Lady Blaine, I appreciate your concern. I will put it to Renner. It is *Renner's* responsibility, as my Guardian."

And with that, the conversation was simply—over. She used every guile she knew, human and Motie, but when Ali Baba was in this mode, nothing penetrated. Nothing at all. In desperation, she'd even asked Omar. "What's to be done? What do you do, when an apprentice Motie loses a *fyunch≠?*"

"Loses a *fyunch≠?*" answered Omar, with that inscrutable smile and body language indicating: *your question is nonsensical*. "Assigned a new one. Retained as a trainer. Apprenticed to other duties. Spaced. As the Master desires."

"But Ali Baba refuses to be re-assigned!"

"*Re*assigned? As *fyunch≠?*" Omar's arms indicated bemusement. "Ali Baba was never *assigned*."

"To Bury. You gave Ali Baba to Bury."

"*I* gave? No. Lord *Cornwallis* gave."

"Yes, of course. But I mean, Ali Baba was assigned to Bury as *fyunch≠*."

Omar suppressed mirth at this, but Glenda Ruth caught it.

"Lady, I will say this: there's a difference between *assigned* and *gave*, even in *your* language."

At which point. Glenda Ruth had had enough, and barked, "Explain!" with full Master's bearing and posture.

Omar merely smiled with arms posed in respectful deference, not obeisance. "Ah, Lady Blaine. We all know our Master's Voice, and you do not speak with mine."

Subtly, Omar's hands conveyed: *think, don't demand. You are no longer a child.*

She was stumped. She was raised by a Mediator, but not this one. This one was as alien as any outworlder. "Please, you *were fyunch≠* to Bury, right?"

"Yes, milady, I had that honor."

"And you are saying that Ali Baba was not?"

"Yes, Milady."

"Then please, as Bury, tell me: what does Ali Baba need? What is his problem?"

"Ah," with mirth, "for a *Bury fyunch≠*, this is no problem. Ali Baba seeks his Master's Voice."

And Omar left her with that double—no triple—maybe quadruple—entendre.

8
The Gathering

A man has no religion who has not slowly and painfully gathered one together, adding to it, shaping it; and one's religion is never complete and final, it seems, but must always be undergoing modification. So I contend that...honest, fervent politics are religion; that whatsoever a man will labour for earnestly and in some measure unselfishly is religion.

—David Herbert Lawrence, *Letters, vol. 1*

Bonneville, New Utah

When Zia and Michael arrived, the house was the pandemonium of hand-waving, room-changing, orders-bellowing, and petty officiousness that accompanies any gaggle of minor officials unaccustomed to holding either real respect or real authority. Asach and The Lads had retreated to the roof: Asach to avoid being observed; The Lads to avoid being dragooned. They might have been a TCM detail, but they were locals, and it didn't take long to grow fond of Mena's cooking. They had no particular love for these foul-smelling, book-touting zealots from Maxroy's Purchase, and they didn't much like what they were hearing down below. This lot was outright *bragging* that they'd "tithe the last tenth" and put this "band of mammon-grubbing *pilgrims* out on the street."

So, much mirth was suppressed when Michael burst into the compound, and confronted the assessors with the black-frock-clad Zia, who was the *last word* in officiousness. Accounts ledgers, sealed TCM security certificates, and perfect Anglic diction were laid on with a spatula. Then, in the good-cop counter to Zia's bad-cop berating, Mena and Lena appeared with *mountains* of food, topped off with *genuine* Mormon bush tea. It was lights out in short order; then in what seemed barely five minutes rousted to *another* mountain of breakfast, and slightly confused by their sense of well-being, the True Church tithe team was on its way. The Lads' joy at one pulled-over at the expense of the MPs quite overwhelmed any sense of obligation they might have felt toward their brethren-in-faith, and they cheerfully volunteered to head off as escorts to whatever hinterland Asach might next direct.

Their second shock came when they headed downstairs later that morning, after the tithe-collectors had finally departed. Michael stood, not triumphant, but stooped, crushed and crumpled, face sallow, patrician demeanor evaporated. Zia's hand wrapped that of a small, hooded girl with purple bruises marbling her face. Both their faces were wet with tears. But the worst was Ollie, slumped at the little stone table, face in hands, shoulders wracked, sobbing like an infant, while Zia explained to Michael.

"They came on the SunRail. The overnight. They left right after we did. Right after the MPs let them go."

"Who's the girl?"

"My niece. Ollie's niece. He couldn't leave her. Her father's a TCM pig—" she spat, then looked sharply at the Lads. "Sorry. I don't mean you or the rest of Ollie's contract security boys. I mean MPs, you know? A private, joined up on the Purchase. One of those MP fundies who—you know? Just look at her."

Their eyes widened in horror, and they nodded. The wiry one suddenly blurted: "Where's Deela?"

Zia looked at him. Tried to remember him. There were so many. All of them sweet on little Deela, with her little smile and her emerald-green eyes. The light of Ollie's eye.

"With the boys. Ollie came ahead on the SunRail when he heard, because—"

And now Michael blurted: "*Where are Deela and the boys?*"

Ollie shot from the bench, sobbing and pulling something from his shirt, shoving it forward, half lurching, half falling into Michael's face. The Lads crowded around. They couldn't make out the image. A dark glade. Something butchered. Something hanging, butchered, but with much too much red.

And Ollie shouted: "That's Hugo. Look what they've done to my Hugo!"

And Zia's voice joined in, sounding very far away. "We don't know. That's why they came ahead. We don't know. Except, of course, poor Hugo."

Michael sagged; suddenly looked old. "That's it, then. They know." Then he looked up, wild-eyed.

"You can't stay here! They'll know! They'll come here, and they'll know, and we'll all—"

But somehow, all at once, Zia and Ollie and Marul were ringed: by Nejme, and Mena, and Lena; by the house staff; by the Lads, who stepped into the circle. Suddenly, Michael stood on the outside, and everyone else was on the inside, ringed around their own.

Asach reached out, gently, and took the image from Ollie's quavering hand. Examined it carefully. Rubbed a finger over one portion several times, enlarging the detail. Looked at it thoughtfully, dispassionately.

"Ollie," Asach said, "do you hire Saurons for your security details?"

He stopped blubbing with one breath, suddenly sober, suddenly back on the job.

"No!"

"How about Tanith? Hire any Tanith jungle boys?"

He was already shaking his head. "No! No offworlders! Only locals! Only lads from wards I know!"

Asach looked up from the image, slowly. "Only, feathery thing, a tamarisk. No limbs that'd hold that weight. That's why they—that's why his weight is borne by the trunk. It took somebody strong as an ox to get that boy up that tree. But there're no tracks."

And then Asach was looking at Michael. "And then there's the method."

Asach looked at Zia and Ollie. Then down at Marul. "I'm sorry. But you've already seen it. I think you should know. And I suppose they'll tell you anyway, once they've figured it out for themselves. Or not. Which would say a lot in itself."

Back to Michael. "It's a nasty death. It's a nasty death, because it's meant to send a signal. Question is, who was the signal for?"

Michael was pale, on the verge of fainting.

And then to Ollie. But clearly, the boy's father already knew. Asach handed him back the image, and pulled Michael aside, out of Mena's hearing. "It's called reverse kosher, for some pinch-minded, sadistic reason I don't care to pursue right now. You can tell by the bleeding. First he was pinned to the tree. Then he was gutted. Then his throat was cut. It isn't pretty, and depending on what bastard does it, it can be very slow."

And very, very slowly, Asach looked Michael full in the face. "So, tell me, Michael. Who on New Utah pays hired goons? From offworld? From the nether regions of Hell?"

He cowered.

"See, I don't think sending these folks away will make much difference now. Do you?"

He shuddered, as if a spell had lifted. He shook his head. "No."

"Michael, I think it's time to start spilling your guts to your dear, old friend. Because these people," Asach waved a hand to take in the assembled behind them, "*desperately* need our help."

He nodded.

"OK, so, do you believe me now?"

He nodded.

"Evidence of things seen, or unseen?"

He shuddered again. "Seen. Unseen. Both."

"So, who was this message intended for?"

"I don't know."

"Michael?!"

"*I DON'T know.*"

"Then let's try it a different way. Michael, *where* is your mother?*"

Nothing.

"Michael, *where* is *Lillith Van Zandt?*"

Nothing.

"Michael, *is Lillith Van Zandt here on New Utah?*"

He nodded, slowly.

"Well, then, old friend, I think it is time to spill."

They trundled poor Marul off to bed, in the company of Mena, Lena, half the household, and The Lads, who swore on their mother's heads that they would trade watch to ensure that no harm came to her during the night.

Asach, Zia, Ollie, Michael, Nejme, and later Mena, lullabies complete, huddled around a table in the kitchen, with Lena on the periphery tending refills. And oh, did Michael spill. It had all been the opal meerschaum trade, he said. Lillith wanted in on the action; the TCM had a lock; and good son

Michael had been dispatched to ooze his way around the margins and insinuate himself.

He'd insinuated as far at Bonneville. He'd sniffed and sniffed, and found that the TCM seemed to hold a bunch of warehouses there. Officially, they were tithe-houses, secured for the annual collection. Michael wasn't so sure. Seemed to be a lot of to-and-fro, especially this past year, and well before the collection and debtor's assizes.

So he'd gone to Bonneville. Bought the house. With Lillith's money, not his. Found a staff. *Settled in.* Put it about a bit, quietly, that he'd broker. It was Nejme, really. Nejme and Mena. People came, spoke with them. It trickled in. Never much. Never much from one seller. No really big chunks. Bits and pieces, packed in sand, direct from wherever it came from. But nice quality. Even a few pieces of black—old family pieces, you know? It trickled in.

"What did they want for it?"

"Excuse me?"

"The meerschaum. What did they want? Selenium?"

Michael looked confused. So did everyone. "Selenium? Vitamins? Fertilizer?"

"Oh, no. Nothing like that. No barter. Strictly cash."

"*Crowns?*"

"Whatever. Crowns, local, credits, scrip. TCM tithe credits are favorite here. Sort of cuts out the middleman."

Everyone nodded.

"And the other end?"

"There was no other end. I only worked here."

"So you still have it all?"

"No." He looked over at the grim-faced woman in the conservative black dress. "That's where Zia comes in." He re-told the story: the meeting; the Bonneville warehouse; the twenty-two kilos, sold, supposedly, fair-and-square, to a TCM contract buyer from something called Orcutt Land and Mining.

The promissory voucher for full, one-to-one tithe credit. The notice of the impending auditor descent, and the subpoena to the debtor's assizes. His hideously expensive, panic-driven flight to Saint George. Zia's deal for salvation.

Asach thought for awhile in the exhausted quiet. Looked over at the plump, tough little woman with the pinched, grim face cowled by her severe, black frock and bonnet.

"And, you had in mind—?"

Zia felt nothing. Business was business. Hugo was dead.

"The warehouses," she said. "I had in mind the warehouses. The warehouses for Orcutt Land and Mining."

Ollie started. "Zia, No!"

She shrugged. 'What does it matter now? Hugo is dead."

"But Deela! And—"

"What does it matter? If they have them, if they want them, they are gone now too, no matter what we do."

She turned back to Asach. "I know when the warehouses will make delivery to the TCM in Saint George."

Michael jumped in. "But how can you? That's what you never explained. How can you know *when?* I'm telling you, there isn't enough product out there! There isn't—"

"There will be. Very soon now, it's coming."

"But how do you *know*"

Zia glowered at him, her face pinched, and hard. She detested him. Detested his patrician manners; detested his phony Bonneville whites, detested his caviling clinging to his Mama's purse. She barely, just barely, refrained from name-calling.

"I know, because we *all* know. Anyone from *here.* Anyone from *Bonneville.* Don't we?"

She scanned the table. Nejme, Mena, Lena: they met her gaze briefly, then averted their eyes. But everyone nodded, slightly.

Asach knew too, of course, albeit in a different way, and from the other end. Had been briefed that much. Knew that a neutron star, in an eccentric orbit, opened a tramline — an Alderson point—from New Utah to Maxroy's Purchase on a roughly 21-year cycle. Knew that the True Church had, every twenty years or so, briefly registered some mining company or other on Maxroy's Purchase, and used its books to mask illicit shipments of fertilizer, vitamins, medical supplies—and in return pull in prime opal meerschaum. In between those decades, the price would climb and climb. The end game speculation was the stuff of dreams for small players.

And now, the Jackson Delegation was more-or-less hanging around, awaiting Asach's report; awaiting the opening of the tramline, ready to offer free trade in fertilizer, in exchange for the munificent benefits of Empire membership. Munificent for some. Not so very munificent at all, if you had neither planetary government nor space travel. In which case, you enjoyed all the benefits of being colonized, as on Makassar.

But this seemed a different conversation. This was not a question of TCM stockpiles waiting to ship *out*. This seemed a question of TCM warehouses expecting goods *in*. And everybody *here* seemed in on it.

Asach took a stab in the dark. "So, what you mean is, you know when the opal meerschaum will start coming *in?*"

Zia nodded.

"As in, *in* to Orcutt Land and Mining?"

Zia nodded again.

"And that is—*how?*"

Zia did not answer. Shifted her glower to Nejme, who still did not meet her eyes.

Finally, Mena spoke. "It's just a bit—*embarrassing.*"

"Ma, there's nothing *wrong* with it, you know! That's just a superstition. There's nothing *wrong*—"

"No, nothing *wrong* at all," affirmed Nejme. "Which is why we all agreed, together, to work with Michael."

All three of them raised their eyes to the Eye above the doorway.

"We call them *tangiwai*—His tears." Nejme nodded. Mena continued. "They come from the Gatherings. We pick them up—pilgrims pick them—on the way too and from the Gatherings. They are just—souvenirs—you know? To show that you have been?"

Lena nodded enthusiastically. "And they're stony cool, you know? Elthazar found a big, flat chunk once, and carved it into a fire screen. *Carried* it all the way back, and carved it into a fire screen. It's really beautiful at night. You light the fire, and—"

Nejme glared. "Now *that's* going too far! You should treat *tangiwai* with respect. Just because—"

"Oh, like selling them to *offworlders* and carving *pipes* is more respectful?"

"That's different."

"Different how? Different because—"

Mena spoke, softly. "Different, because people need the money." She turned to Asach.

"It is hard to come by cash, you know? For the tithe? And so of course in the end most of them keep the littlest pieces, but sell the best to a broker."

"Like Michael."

She smiled, softly. "Yes, like Michael. None of us would do it, you know. Take the stone in exchange for money. Not from another islander. It would just—in the end—it makes trouble, you know? People get jealous? And we don't deal with the TCM if we can help it." Her face suddenly clouded, saddened. "It's too dangerous for us. They hate us. Anyway," she brightened, "somebody from outside. Somebody—"

"Like Michael."

"Yes, High Church, like Michael, or Muslim— somebody like that, is better. Even Mormon LDS—Sixers, I mean, not True Church. Just not TCM. We weren't brokers, before, but Michael—"

"—needed someone he could trust to run a House, " finished Nejme.

Asach nodded, doodling idly with one finger on the table. Didn't look up. "Michael?"

He jumped.

"Michael, why were you messing about with middlemen in the dark of the night?"

He squirmed, uncomfortable, but did not reply.

"Michael, if Lillith Van Zandt wanted to horn in on the opal meerschaum trade, why another wholesaler? Why not deal direct?"

He squirmed again. "Well, we couldn't, really. And anyway, like I said, I didn't know—"

"Didn't know what? Didn't know something that, by the sound of it, at least half the children on this planet knows? Oh, please, Michael. That's not like you at all."

He bridled. "Now look here, Asach, I've been completely frank with you. I don't know—"

"*Frank*, yes, but completely? I think not. There's more. Isn't there Michael? More? Something *more* that Lillith Van Zandt wants to know."

"Well, the source, of course. She wants the source."

"Why? Why would she bother? Sounds like it gets trotted right up to her front door. Well, *your* front door, anyway."

"I don't *know*." He was really whinging now. Asach hated it when he whinged. There wasn't much to Michael but charm, and when that evaporated, what remained got under the skin. "She just said I *had* to. Had to deal with Orcutt. Had to follow Orcutt to the source."

"The *source* of *what?*"

"Well, I just thought the meerschaum. Why not? I mean, there's a market for it. I just thought she wanted to corner the market."

"Oh good grief, Michael. Whatever for? Can you honestly see your mother bothering to corner the market in etched pipes and fireplace screens?"

But, again, just: "I don't *know.*"

Exasperated, Zia interrupted. "Well, maybe Collie Orcutt knows."

Michael looked blank. Asach looked interested. Nejme looked up. Mena froze. Lena began to speak, but Mena waved her down.

"Who?"

"Collie Orcutt? The previous owner? Went bust, oh, eight, ten years ago? TCM took his paper?"

"His paper?"

"His paper. His claim."

Nejme filled in: "The mining rights to his land."

"Oh, more than that, in his case. He was way, way in. Had a vision? Had a vision, of a united Church, here in Bonneville? But thought he was beyond the tithe. Way out there, in The Barrens, where they never go. Thought wrong. Borrowed from the wrong people, at the wrong time, at the wrong rates. True Church Militant got it all. Well, most of it. Mining, minerals, water: left him with a chunk of barrens and a solar well. Took in haulpaks and chewed up a couple of mountains. Made a fortune. That's about when I was hired, clerking in the Bonneville warehouses. Then they dumped it all. Some consortium bought the claim. It's still filed in Saint

George and Pitchfork River. TCM still uses the warehouses, though. I've never met the current owners."

"Yes," said Lena, glaring at the ceiling, "Collie Orcutt got *the wrong end of the Stick,* as we say around here."

"Not too loud, I hope," said Ollie, dismally.

The night cold fell upon the courtyard. The House was quiet. All but Mena and Asach slept. A low fire burned in a ceramic stove, pulled close to the table, radiating warmth. Mena spoke softly.

"No, they won't harm you. But you have to be prepared. That's all Himmist country, out there, in The Barrens. They keep to themselves."

"But you worship Him, yes?" Asach looked thoughtfully on the Eye above the doorway.

"Yes, of course. He sees us everywhere."

Asach waited, patiently. Mena shook her head. "But you must understand. *We* look on you as an ally, a guest. We truly believe, as it is said: '*In His Gaze, we are all pilgrims, we are all Seers, and all islands are One.*' But the backlanders?" She shook her head again. "They won't harm you, but they won't help you."

"Why not?"

Mena sat a moment, finding the right words. "It's hard for them, you know? They may help. But more likely, they will see you as a threat. They see everyone as a threat, and who is to blame them?" She shook her head sadly. "It is the history of our church: congregations smashed, driven into exile—first from New Scotland to New Ireland, then from New Ireland to Maxroy's Purchase, then from the Purchase to Saint George, then out of Saint George to Bonneville—until there was nowhere left to go. Except The Barrens."

"But *you* are still here in Bonneville."

Mena nodded. "Yes. It's the MP converts who fare the worst. Most of them were Mormons, you see. Sixer LDS, not True Church. People like us—direct descendents of the New Scotland Church of Him—" she waved her hand to indicate the household— "who were never Mormon to begin with, we're all right. As long as we pay the tithe. But the former Sixers?" She shrugged her shoulders. "They are considered the descendants of heretics. Shunned. Cast out into The Barrens."

"How is anyone to know?"

"You mean the *Church*?" she countered, aghast, then lowered her voice. "The *True* Church? Not know who an immigrant is descended from? Of course they know. That was one of the tenets of the schism. The primacy of reconstructing the genealogy of *everyone,* all the way back to Adam and Eve. The Sixers didn't care so much about that any more. Didn't think it was possible, anyway."

Asach smiled. "I take your point. So, The Barrens Himmists won't help anyone—because?"

Mena sighed. "Well, they cite scripture, of course. But really? I think it's sort of tit for tat. Payback for exile."

"Scripture?"

" '*May we turn our Gaze from those who refuse to See, praying fervently that they may not remain blind.*' They *are* pacifists, and open to evangelizing, but they feel no obligation to help nonbelievers. The most extreme fundamentalists won't even *look at* a non-believer. If you head out there, you're on your own."

Asach nodded. "What else do I really need to know?"

Mena walked through the catechism. Fundamentalist Himmists believed, really believed, that the Coal Sack, with its bright red sun called Murchison's Eye, was *actually* the face of God. That once, during the Secession Wars, the eye had opened, awaking Howard Grote Littlemead, founder of the religion. That His Face represented the *fourth* arm of the Cross, which had nothing to do with crucifixion, but represented a quadrine, or quadripartite, God: Father, Son, Holy Spirit, and His Face, or Eye, with which he saw all. That, appalled by the sins of those who waged war in His presence, refusing to believe, he closed his Eye on them once and for all. That Himmists on New Utah could not really see that face directly in the heavens, being far from New Scotland where the phenomenon was most visible. Himmists in The Barrens felt closer to "His Earthly Eye" and Gathered once every score years to visit it. About *that*, Mena would say no more. She handed Asach a tract, entitled "The Catechism of the Great Weep," and said only, "Read it. It's what every child should know."

Asach thanked her, pocketed the tract, looked tenderly at this sensible, helpful woman. "Mena?"

"Yes?"

"Do you believe? I mean truly believe? Do *you* believe in the Face of God, with Howard Grote Littlemead as His prophet?"

Mena smiled, and took Asach's hand in her own, patting it gently. "Littlemead? I don't know. I think Littlemead was one small man, in the vastness of space, who despaired of his lot on earth and looked for God in the heavenly lights. Who among us has not? Who among us has not, in the secret vaults of the heart, prayed for salvation in the dark of night?"

"Indeed," said Asach. "Indeed. Don't we all. Mena?"

"Yes?"

"What's a Seer?"

She shook her head. "Read the Catechism, first."

"OK, I promise. I'll do it before I sleep tonight. But, please tell me, so that I'll understand it after I do."

Mena thought a moment. Sighed. "Ok," she said, "I guess it does no harm." Crow's feet crinkled around her eyes. "A Seer is born at a Gathering, so a Seer spans two Gatherings, so a Seer learns to See the way and lead others to the next Gathering. The Seer spans the Gathering past, to the Gathering next. Understand?"

Asach smiled, reaching for the pamphlet. "Clear as mud."

They departed early next morning. Just Asach, and the boys. They made a detour through the market quarter, catching pre-dawn deliveries before the stalls were even open. The boys packed the rig full with water; dried fruits; dried meats; dried nuts; blankets; self-erecting shelters. They bolted extra fuel tanks to the outer hull, and extra solar chargers to the roof. They stripped out the heavy Plate in the driver's door and the floor. A lot of tithe credits changed hands. They gulped tea at a teamster's stall, then headed east.

Back at the house, Mena and Nejme traded off, sending the same message, over and over, by satphone, by telegraph, by 'tooth, with no assurance that it would even get through to the remoteness of Orcutt Station: *Asach Quinn comes, a friend of truth. Meet at Butterfield Wells. We beg you: do not avert your Gaze.*

The swing from cold of night to heat of day was sudden, and incredible. Before dawn, they had to chip a haze of frost from the view screen. After sunrise, they peeled away every layer of clothing decency allowed. The boys hummed and bounced to internal tunes. Bonneville fell away. Heat shimmered on salt panne and desert varnish.

It would have been more comfortable to drive at night, and sleep by day, with reflector shelters to keep them cool. But they needed the solar boost. Once up to speed, while the sun was bright and the road was level, it saved a lot of juice. With it, Butterfield Wells was the turn back point; as far as the boys could go with any guarantee of getting back before running out of fuel. Without it, they'd be marooned. There was no traffic. They were utterly alone.

The desert varnish gave way to surface glaze: silty flats, the thin crust polished smooth. Mirage shimmered in the distance, showing what had been, perhaps millennia before: vast lakes of water; lagoons and islands; estuarine pools. If anything was alive out there, it did not move. Sometimes the breeze would carry the faintest scent of water; of aromatic herbs, blown like whispers across the desert from the far, far mountains.

They passed an adobe bubble, with a minaret barely taller than a man. Once a shrine, or a roadside mosque, now fallen to ruin. "Making good time," said the driver. They drove on.

Eventually a tiny blob rose above the road at the horizon. It hovered, upside down, a reflection in the shimmering heat that floated above the pavement. For a good while, it stayed there. Then, it set, like a tiny moon, and a real blob, a right-side-up blob, grew in its stead. At first it was nothing. Then it was solid. Then they rumbled to a stop, at a tiny public square.

The lads were disconsolate. At first, they refused to leave Asach there. But Asach was adamant. "You have to go back. You have to get Ollie back to Saint George. You have to help him find Deela and the boys. You have to help him find out what happened to Hugo."

They could not argue with that. They tried to leave water. Asach waved them off, indicating the miniscule fountain: a rusty pipe, sticking out from a concrete block, trickling cold, clear water into a grate, where it disappeared. They tried to leave blankets, but Asach wanted no more than the cloak. They tried to leave food, and Asach acquiesced.

"Go on," Asach waved them off. "You're burning daylight."

Butterfield Wells, The Barrens, New Utah

The square was little more than a dusty crossroad with a water tap. Not so much as a tree, nor anything natively tree-like. There was a good deal of wind, and a windmill to power the water pump. They sat in its thin stripe of shade. Asach entertained three pleasantly grubby children by using one handful of pebbles to knock another handful of pebbles from a circle scratched into the gravel.

Each would giggle, then throw down a pebble with that universal awkward, jerky toss of children everywhere old enough to walk and talk, but not yet old enough to be truly helpful at very much. Then, as Asach aimed and tossed in reply, in delighted unison they would shout encouragement: "WANpela! TUpela! TREEpela!" In variably, Asach would "miss" at least once, and the ecstatic associated child would run in a little circle herself, hands stretched overhead, shouting "GOOOAAAL! Mi Winim! Mi Winim!"

The game went on and on. The children were tireless. Eventually, a boy appeared, slightly older. From where, it was difficult to say. There seemed nowhere to come from, and nowhere to go to. The Barrens appeared to be utterly flat, horizon to horizon, but it was their vastness that tricked the eye. There were actually folds in the ground big enough to conceal a rail car; slashes deeper than a building that raged with water when rain fell in mountains that were mere purple stains on the rim of the horizon.

The boy scowled at Asach. *"Yu save long tok Anglis, a?"*

The girls stopped, unsure, then clustered nearer to Asach, who answered simply, "Yes. Do you?"

At this, the little ones erupted: "Me too! Me too! I speak Anglic too!" then ran around the windmill and giggled, playing hide-and-seek from behind the pole.

The boy scowled again. He was at best a year or two older than the others, but very serious. "Are you a pilgrim?"

With puckered eyebrows, Asach matched his earnestness. "I'm waiting for Collie Orcutt."

This seemed to satisfy him for the moment, but he clearly felt the need to assert some kind of authority over the situation. He picked up a pebble, and with one vicious swipe from where he stood, hurtled it against the polished white stone still lying within the scratched ring. With a *crack* the white stone went flying across the gravel. He stalked over, picked it up, pocketed it, and said, "Mine now!"

The littlest girl, still clinging to the windmill pole, shouted, "That's not fair!" She began to sob. "It's my best one! It's my favorite! It's *mine!*" She stamped a foot.

The boy shrugged. Asach assessed the situation. Pulled a handful of stones from somewhere within the cloak. Opened one hand to reveal a child's treasure of purple, pink, green, and speckled red. "Double or nothing," Asach said. Eyes wide, the boy nodded.

Asach played skillfully—or rather, lost skillfully. By the end, the boy held all the colored stones; Asach held only the white one. "You win!" Asach said, folding the white pebble into the little girl's hand. Unsuspecting and smiling, the boy counted and re-counted his new stash as the little girl bounced over to Asach's lap. "I'm Jolly!" she announced.

"Yes, I can see that."

"No, silly. My *name* is Jolly"

"Her name is Jo-*lynn*," the second one said. But everyone *calls* her Jolly."

"And what's *your* name?"

The girl's eyes widened in horror.

Damn, thought Asach. *I forgot. Never ask a child's name. She'll think you are trying to steal her spirit.*

"Never mind honey. Don't be scared. I forgot. We—we do things different, where I come from. Names don't mean the same thing there."

The boy nodded, sagely, promoted to ally by his recent acquisition. "The *Anglis*, they don't know *anything.*"

The horrified girl regarded Asach sternly. "What's your number?" she blurted at last.

Mystified, Asach gambled. "Three hundred and fifty-seven."

The horrified one giggled. Jolly peered up from Asach's lap, little brow furrowed. "Are you a boy, or a girl?" she said.

Asach looked down, smiling. "What do you think?"

"I think you're a big silly!' she answered, exploding in a frenzy of knees and elbows to run rings around the pole. "You're a bi-ig sil-ly! You're a bi-ig sil-ly!" The third girl, obviously her sister, joined in. "Sil-ly, sil-ly, SIL-ly!"

No-longer-horrified girl bounced forward. "I'm a four. We're all fours. Well, four is really nine, but we say fours. Only papa says we're too little to Gather. But mama says this is the big one, so we should, and wouldn't you be sorry if it was and they not even there? But you're a pilgrim. So you must be a four too. Only you look old. Are you a three? Mama's a three. Did you Gather before? Sometimes people are really old before they Gather." Her eyes went wide again. "But you're waiting for Uncle Collie. Maybe— are you a *Seer*? You're never a Seer, are you? Like cousin Laurel?"

At which the other two gasped and stopped running. The little boy's face went white. Un-horrified girl looked re-horrified, and just stood gaping.

Asach thought fast. Whatever was meant by the question, there could be only one answer. Asach took a calculated guess about the rest.

"No, honey, I'm not a Seer. I'm going to visit your Uncle Collie, that's all. And I hope to get to meet Laurel while I'm there. We have some things to talk about."

Color returned to the boy's face. He nodded sagely again, then leaned over to stage-whisper into horrified-girl's ear: "They're gunna talk about *the Gathering.*" Then he announced: "Well, *I'm* a four, and *I'm* not too little to Gather!"

With that, horrified girl broke into a gale of giggles, and led the trio in a new romp around the windmill. "Sil-ly's gunna Gath-er. Sil-ly's gunna Gath-er."

Asach leaned back and smiled as dust boiled toward them from the distance. Threes and Fours and Seers, oh my. They'd have a lot more to talk about than mining claims.

9

Angels in Heaven

Naturally we would prefer seven epiphanies a day and an earth not so apparently devoid of angels. We become very tired with pretending we like to earn a living, with the ordinary objects and events of our lives.

—Jim Harrison, Letters to Yesenin

Saint George, New Utah

The Librarian also had an early start, punctuated by a scary moment entering the TCM Security Zone. Entry was controlled by double barriers. As his FLIVR was held up between them for inspection, the guards suddenly dived behind the concrete bunkers, leaving him stuck like a little rat in a have-a-heart trap. He thought for a chilling moment that they'd found an explosive in the undercarriage. It was a deadly-force-authorized zone, so he also thought it inadvisable to simply leap from the vehicle. He slowly opened the windows, then the doors, to ask what was up. Finally, a shivering clerk motioned that he was to come inside. Apparently, mortars were falling somewhere so distant that he could not even hear them. After five minutes they received the all clear, without actual incident. It was his first brush with the dark underside of Saint George that they had all felt, but never seen, on previous arrivals.

He questioned the clerks, but they were not very forthcoming. "Troubles!" they answered, shaking their heads. "More troubles! It starting again!"

"What's starting again?"

They just looked disgusted. "You people, you *Imperials* come, it starts. Before you come is OK, but then you go away again it starts. Like last time."

Barthes frowned. They were suddenly frightened; quick to clarify. "Not you! You OK, we know. But bad people—" he spit—"bad people, they start. From outside. We tell them: Go Away! If you want to kill Imperials, go away and kill them somewhere else. Stop killing us."

But the Temple was closed that day, for some ecclesiastical procedure that he'd never heard of, as was the university. With nothing to be accomplished, he decided to return to his local office. And then "it started" in earnest. He drove back amid reports of bad fighting in the East of the city, and sporadic outbreaks elsewhere. So they closed up early, his assistant grabbing her skirts and running full bore down the street, now empty of anything but the usual stench and swirling dust.

It was a rough night. He was repeatedly awakened by explosions rattling the building, from where he could not tell. One was close enough to send spent gravel pattering gently against the glass. He gave up trying to sleep and, with some sense of irony, watched an old war video. He was somewhat reassured by the lack of actual gun ships, police sirens, or ambulances. His street was a major thoroughfare, so had anything really bad happened nearby, it would have lit up. He heard distant shouting; a rattle of gunfire. Then the generator died.

Still sleepless, he switched on a battery lamp; pulled out the charred old conference paper, and settled in to read. He got about half-way through before his eyelids began to droop. It was a somewhat more interesting, and clearly more valuable, document than he'd thought. As he fell asleep, two phrases whispered in his mind. *New Utah would not now be dependent upon selenium supplementation....this data is directly relevant to questions of how life begins on and propagates across many worlds.*

But in the morning, all was as if he'd dreamt it. The shops along the way opened as usual, albeit a little late. He set off groggily. Then, once at the office, he had trouble concentrating on the work at hand. He decided to try the Temple again. The more complicated University installation was nearly complete. It was time to coordinate the Temple archives hook-up.

This time, Barthes entered the Zone without incident. He parked at the back of the Temple, near the delivery bays, and knocked on a side door marked "Service Entrance." As a non-member, the main sanctuary was closed to him; in any case, he'd come for a working meeting, not a Temple tour.

He was in luck. The clerk who answered nodded, gestured *follow me*, and led him directly to the Archivist's office. Not only was she in; she was delighted. "Delighted!" she said, pumping his long, graceful hand with both of her tiny ones, "What an honor! Never did I think to meet so august a colleague in our remote little corner!"

"You've heard of the Imperial Library, then?"

"Heard of! How could I claim to be a professional, and not dream of going there one day!"

She was grateful he'd come.

She was grateful for this tacit recognition of her archive as a library of merit.

She was grateful for his offer of the Imperial Pre-accession Package.

She was grateful for any assistance in re-establishing the trunk connection to the Zion University Library.

She expressed no interest whatsoever in eventual live LM linkage to the Imperial Newscast Networks. "Oh no," she said, "I don't think the Bishop would approve *that*. We're not *backward*, you know. It's not that."

He remained impassive.

"It's just that we take seriously our responsibility to avoid *confusion* among our flock."

Colchis briefly nodded.

"So we prefer to preview recorded cubes *before* distribution."

Colchis patiently explained Imperial policies regarding non-interference with local science and technology. Explained that the feed would be filtered in any event, depending upon how New Utah was classified.

She marveled at this.

Suspecting that her personal technological expertise might not be up to this discussion, he asked if he might speak with her technical operations manager. They spent a pleasant few minutes chatting about Temple collections while they waited.

"My guide at Zion said that you back up many of their collections?"

"Oh yes," she nodded. "To our great pride, this makes relevant work accessible to our flock directly from the main reading room."

"Relevant work?"

"Research results and technical innovations that further the True Church's Mission on New Utah."

"So you do not duplicate everything."

"Oh no." She looked appalled. "We wouldn't back up work that was *confusing.*"

Barthes paused a moment, sipping his tea. She seemed clear on her views, but open enough to discussion. It was worth a try.

"I toured the Zion Library," he said evenly, "what was left of it."

Her brow furrowed. Her lips pursed. "Terrible thing, that. Terrible." She set down her cup with a little clink; looked at him earnestly; clasped her hands to her chest, leaned forward. "I mean, of course, there was much there that was *confusing.* Which is why we create a *safe* collection here. But to burn a Library!"

"Is that what happened? I didn't know." *Nor did I ask,* he thought, *not at the time.*

"Oh yes!" Here eyes went wide. "Some of our youth— they are very sincere. But misguided. Some boys *firebombed* the Zion Library." She made a weak imitation of throwing. "It was unfortunate. And completely wrong. Of course, they will be punished. If they find them." Her hands collapsed to her lap. She picked up the teacup.

"It that what the fighting was? Last night? Something like that?"

Her face widened, an open book, as she sipped her tea. "Fighting? What fighting?"

"Perhaps I was mistaken."

There was a longer pause. The technician still had not arrived. Barthes grasped for a subject.

"Would you be so kind?" he asked, fishing the burned paper from a burnished portfolio. "It is just a matter of curiosity. I found this in the rubble. It's of no importance, really, but it seems to be all that survived. It makes reference to earlier research, done during "Foundation" times. Is this something you'd have copies of?"

He passed it over. She merely glanced at the title, then smiled broadly and jumped to her feet, handing it back. "Come!" she gestured, "Please, come! Where were my manners! I can't take you inside the Sanctuary, of course, but please, let me show you the reading rooms! Those are public!"

She scooted through the maze of corridors so quickly, black skirts swishing about her, that Colchis nearly had to jog to keep stride. They made a final turning to a nondescript door with a cipher lock. She punched in a code, and waved him inside.

Colchis gasped. The vaulted hall rose before him, suffused with perfect, even, milky light. The dome seemed to have been carved apiece, filtering the sun's natural rays through silky, translucent stone. Reader's desks with nano jacks ringed the room, the tabletops and benches forming staggered, concentric rings with a librarian's desk at the center.

"We call this our Temple of Light!" she beamed. "You can see why!"

"It's beautiful." His answer was simple, honest. He was awed.

"But come!" she said, towing him by one hand through the maze. "Lily, can we borrow the glass?"

The librarian nodded, fished below the counter, and handed over a small monocular even as they arrived at her station.

The archivist handed it to Colchis, pointing across the room and upward. "Look at the frieze." He raised the implement to one eye; fumbled. "Twist it to focus," she bubbled, "and look at the rim along the bottom of the dome. It's a carved frieze. Carved in Founder times."

He did as directed, while she chattered on. "You see, that's what I mean. About not being backward. About avoiding *confusion*. The early settlers, they were really very superstitious. They called it being devout, but it was really just ignorance.

They thought those were angels. Imagine! They really believed that those were angels. And that's why they were carved."

Fumbling, twisting, finally changing eyes, Colchis struggled with the monocular, finally walking it slowly up the wall until he found the frieze itself. He gave a final twist and nearly dropped the thing as an alien, smiling face suddenly filled his eye. He literally choked. Then ran the glass to and fro along the frieze in panicked disbelief.

Misunderstanding his reaction, the archivist laughed, and chattered on. "Ugly, aren't they?"

His patrician composure shattered, Barthes stammered his reply. "What—what—are—they?!"

"Why, Swenson's Apes, of course. The earliest settlers found them here when they arrived. And being superstitious, thought they were Angels. That's why they called it Heaven— *Heaven and all His Angels*. But they aren't of course. They're just animals."

But Barthes barely heard this. His mind was racing. Because, from his perspective, it was an unchanging, enigmatic, lopsided Motie smile that greeted his terrified eye. Heart pounding, he slowly lowered the glass. Spoke carefully. "Madam Archivist, you have seen Imperial news cubes from the past three decades, have you not? I realize *officially* no, but I presume—"

She laughed. "Of course!"

"So, have you not remarked the amazing resemblance of these—Swenson's Apes—to Moties?

She laughed again. "Of course! That's how we knew it was all a lie!"

Barthes was confused. "A lie? What lie is that, Madam?'

She was clearly delighted. "All of it—the blockade expenses, the so-called First Contact, all of it!" She leaned forward with a conspiratorial grin. "They think *we're* backward.

But *they* all swallow that tripe. It's just made up. It's just made up to justify whatever the Empire is doing with all that money. It's just the modern version of thinking they're Angels. We've known they're just animals all along. It's one of our teaching points now, on the *good* use of science. To avoid *confusion.*"

Barthes breathed deeply. "Ah. Well then. How very—interesting. Might I see the Swenson collection, then? While we wait?"

But she was already handing the glass back to the librarian, shaking her head. "Oh, no. I *am* sorry. That collection is classified now. You see—" she switched to stage whisper—"we think that's how they made all those fake newsreels. We think someone pirated an unauthorized copy of the Swenson archives and—*manipulated*—it. Not from here of course." She returned to full voice. "From the Zion U. archives. Their security is terrible over there."

Throughout the technical meeting, Colchis Barthes was numb. He remained numb as he left the security zone. He was numb as he looked in at his office, and left instructions on how to carry on. He was numb as he arrived at his hotel; numb as he climbed the stairs; numb as he entered his room. He slumped onto the edge of the bed without even bothering to close the door. He pulled the report from the portfolio again. The portfolio dropped to the floor. He rifled through the many pages, until he arrived at the second, unread section. *The Planet of the Apes*, it began.

He became more agitated as he read, eyes darting across the page:

> Lesser Ape species... bilaterally symmetrical... Greater Apes... only three arms... Colors included white, brown, black, and occasionally striped... colors were separate species... multi-species colonies... division of labor by species...

> watchdog species with sharp, chitonous, cutting spines... largest species usually white.

That was Moties. That was Moties, plain and simple. Masters —that was the white ones. Farmers. Mediators, even—that would be the striped ones. And the "watchdogs"—those were clearly Warriors. All described. Something else too— one that excavated the colony dens, or mounds, or whatever it was they lived in. Was that a primitive Engineer? He read on. It became biologically technical, but from what he could make of it, that matched too:

> Colonies were few and far between... hermaphrodites... chimeras...mechanism for apparent sex-change during reproductive cycle.

But none of this made sense. This paper referred to a time *centuries* before First Contact. These—apes, only Swenson was clear that they absolutely were *not* apes—were *already here* when New Utah was first colonized. But they lived like—animals. Where was the advanced technology? Was this a *fallen* civilization? If so, where were the ruined cities? He read on:

> Swenson's Apes cultivated marsh "grasses" that concentrated selenium and prevented it leaching from soils...Interfered with agricultural expansion... Most Swenson's apes exterminated; locally extinct... some Swenson's Apes fled...Founder era plowing destroyed root mats so that commercial irrigation resulted in rapid selenium depletion...

> We should investigate methods for re-establishing selenium-concentrating algal fields for livestock forage and local nutritional supplementation. *Doing so would eliminate New Utah's dependency on imported fertilizers and vitamins.*

Barthes felt ill. Tales of extinction were common enough. That was merely sad, but nothing that could be undone in the present. Actually, he momentarily forgot even the Motie issue, under the weight of that final sentence. He was ill, because Librarian or no, he did not actually live in an ivory tower. Well, he did, but that was beside the point. The point was, nobody was every going to catch the boys who had firebombed the University Library. They were long since safely back on Maxroy's Purchase.

And suddenly, it all made sense. The Jackson delegation came and went nearly twenty years ago—and New Utah had nearly plunged into civil war immediately thereafter. Or hadn't. They'd arrived—himself, HG, Asach, as the advance team for the Accession Delegation—and the city had hotted up, putting everyone on edge. Teetering on the brink. Never *quite* going over, but teetering on the brink.

And who benefited from that? Colchis sighed. Entrepreneurs, of a certain ilk. Colonizers. Maxroy's Purchase. Anybody who themselves gained from New Utah's *not* gaining Classified status. He hated this. He was a scholar, not a warrior, but that did not mean he was naive. It would get uglier before it got better. Color slowly drained from his hands as he added to this a potential Motie connection. Had they broken the blockade?

He reminded himself that they hadn't. They were here all along. Or had been. Surely, they were gone by now. If no, with their phenomenal reproductive rates, they'd have long since swamped the planet. So, sad it was, the extinction was for the best. Absent that, the likes of a Kutuzov would have vitrified New Utah. Kutuzov himself, even.

He rose, packed the paper away again, moved like a wooden nutcracker. Out of his room. Down the corridor. Up the back stairs. Climbed and climbed. Up to the roof. *Only in dire emergency.* Asach had said. *I can't tell you how, but in dire emergency, I can get a message off-planet. It will pass into—Imperial hands. I cannot tell you more than that. Barthes, I am trusting your discretion.*

So Colchis Barthes, data recovery expert, who had spent his entire life in Imperial service and understood exactly *what* Asach had meant by that, if not exactly *who*, nicked some cable housing, clipped a connector, attached his locator, typed in a direction. The small dish wobbled a bit, like a flower seeking the sun, then settled. He detached the locator, attached a nano, spoke to it.

Many kilometers across the ground, and several miles above his head, unheard by Colchis, a tiny, silent voice began a long sequence of electronic chatter.

Several hours later, and much, much farther away from that, spake an electronic voice on *Sinbad.*

"Kevin?"

Renner floundered awake. Joyce groaned, rolled over, pulled the covers over her head.

"What, goddamn it!"

"To your office, Kevin, All Due Haste."

Muttering, he marched down the corridor, barefoot and shirtless, pulling on a bathrobe as he went.

"Kevin, are you ready?"

"Goddamn it, yes. On desk."

And then he truly awoke as he read:

Priority: Flash

From: Colchis Barthes, on Behalf of Asach Quinn.

He raced through Colchis' summary, muttering again. The usual pre-accession jitters didn't bother him much. The usual crap. They'd get it together, or not. It was part of the test. But the *Motie* connection gave him gooseflesh. Unlike Barthes, he read the entire Swenson's Ape report immediately, and *extremely* carefully. So, unlike Barthes, he did not miss the crucial paragraph:

...in the case of Swenson's Apes, ... selenium deficiency resulting from collapse of access to the algae fields was especially dramatic in its effects on reproductive hormonal regulation. Absent selenium, reproductive drive increased, as did copulation rates. ... the immediate effect was a local population explosion. However, the second consequence ... became manifest in isolated individuals: spontaneous, habitual abortion and miscarriage. Outwardly, apparently "female" Swenson's Apes gradually sickened and died, as internal egg and sperm stocks were repeatedly fertilized, aborted, and reabsorbed...

"Damnation!" he blurted, slapping the desk. "I am *sick* of this crap!" Then, because his fingers were faster than his voice, he punched: Redirect. Flash. Directors' Eyes Only, Blaine Institute, New Caledonia."

And then he went back to bed. They'd wake him soon enough.

The Librarian did not nurse *Shadenfreude*. He was not pleased when his sour predictions came to pass. It began with the Christian High Churches. The Armenian and Syrian Catholic churches a few blocks from his office, the Russian Orthodox church across the river, and the Chaldean church on the south side of the city were bombed during high mass the following afternoon. Several of his colleagues' family members suffered minor cuts from flying debris, and bruising from being trampled in the ensuing confusion. After the bombings, the red lights and sirens went on for hours.

The first two explosions rattled the office building. He could also hear the second two in the far distance. Several people arrived at the office a few minutes later, shaken, bloodied, battered, but otherwise all right. Colchis showed a kindly, tender side. He cleaned them up, dressed their wounds, and offered what support he could. They reported that at least three were killed at the Armenian Church, and perhaps a dozen injured. Later that day, the death toll rose to twenty.

The community took the immediate precaution of closing the Christian clubs and offices, so communications were effectively shut down. Colchis himself was fine, and other colleagues even joined him at his hotel for coffee late in the evening. In the night, he was awakened once by gunshots in the street outside, but nothing seemed to come of it.

There seemed to be several local news outlets. One, which provided especially graphic coverage, was subsequently shut down by the True Church Bishop himself. Barthes presumed that it had become confusing. A competing piece, commenting on the muzzling of its competitor's reporters, ran a hyperbolic headline: "No Bad News Allowed!" It railed against suppression of the free press.

Colchis questioned this. No bad news? From Saint George? His impression was that there had been very little except bad news reported—despite concerted, obvious, and often successful efforts by a great many citizens to calm things down and move life onto a—if not normal, than at least hopeful—footing. The utter failure to report any of the good news was clearly demoralizing for a lot of people who had not had a day's respite in quite some time. They just wanted a little credit for what they had accomplished.

The next evening, after the office closed, Colchis went grocery shopping. The experience was utterly mundane. No-one harassed him. No-one closed the door. No-one nervously thanked him for his custom, then requested quietly that he not come back. He made selections from well-stocked shelves, paid predictably high-ish prices for imported items, and predictably dirt-cheap prices for local commodities, then went on his way.

Next stop was a roadside fruit stand. Much haggling ensued over a melon the size of New Scotland. He insisted that it not be cut for a sample. The melon was cut nonetheless, with a knife worthy of carnage. Once it was cut, Colchis didn't want it. Now that it was cut, he had to take it. A price was named worthy of a Spartan grocer. For an unwanted, uncut melon? Never! Colchis bought elsewhere. Despite much brandishing of melon knives, only fruit was threatened, and in the end he bought two monstrous fruits for half a crown.

Of course, he was hoping for archival news, mundane or otherwise. Much of the next several days was mundane indeed, spent reviewing invoices for equipment orders, making final decisions about placement of things, and figuring out what, if anything, they were to do about the leaky roof. It required the combined decision-making skills of four professors, the university president, a civil engineer, a security chief, a systems integrator, a budget analyst, and a secretary to accomplish this, but accomplished it was. Installation at Zion University, God willing, was to be finished the following week. Work would start in earnest on the Temple in the next several days, with Bonneville to follow.

One might well have asked what fighting in remote corners of the city had to do with installing archives. Nothing. Everything. Nothing, at any given moment, in that it was physically happening far from where Colchis was. Sometimes he heard gun ships flying overhead. Sometimes, if mortar fire and counter-fire was really intense, he heard a distant rumble, mostly drowned out by traffic noise. Everything, over the toll of days, because of rumored calls for, and threats of, violence. One day, a rumor would ripple down the street from the fruit stand: it's bad today! But Colchis would hear nothing. Two days later came footage of the extent of the fighting; the hundreds or thousands (hard to tell) demonstrating in the streets in some far-off neighborhood.

Barthes saw news interviews with locals, righteously indignant at the prospect of Maxroy's Purchase TCM troops entering this or that pocket. Any talk regarding Maxroy's Purchase and Accession resurrected fearful memories of the aftermath of the first "Jackson Delegation" visit. There was strong conviction that MP and Imperial factions were sponsoring a good deal of the violence. Local TCM members, formerly sympathetic to the Maxroy's Purchase troops, now saw the latter as spoilers who wished only to take over control of holy sites on New Utah. MP fighters, in the local view, were a bunch of hired thugs, and quietly most would allow that their True Church Elder was the worst kind of political opportunist. Colchis heard this from people of all religious stripes: Sixer, High Christian, Muslim, even True Church adherents themselves.

A rumor was circulating, supposedly corroborated by several witnesses: on the day of the church bombings, before the bombs went off, reporters were on hand, cameras trained on the doorways on the sheltered side of the church, just in time to catch the screaming victims burst out. How could they have known to be there? Who knew. Maybe it was coincidence. Maybe they were not there at all. But in that climate, calls to random violence certainly did not need any more media outlets.

Flyers appeared, circulated to non-Mormon shops. Convert to the True Church, they said, and you will no longer be in danger. The Bishop himself declared a curfew on all ministries, warning employees to stay home "for their own safety." "Hooligans" attacked ambulances and water-delivery trucks serving poorer, fringe neighborhoods. So although nothing overt happened within central Saint George itself, and certainly nothing within the Security Zone, events elsewhere cast a pall over street-level commerce. Some businesses closed up for the day; some just closed early; others opened late. Yet again the university was closed, and no work done. So, they would not finish the following week after all.

One Thursday night was exceptionally bizarre. All was normalcy: the shops, the traffic, the bustle of loading docks. All was awry: the brightness, the meetings, the walk home; the gun ships, the horns, the sirens. Then silence. Then cheerful sounds of an evening get-together next door: laughter, clinking glasses, a blaring tri-v. A game of some kind. The rising and falling cheers of a sporting match. A happy evening. He was lulled to sleep.

He awoke to discover that, instincts intact, he'd just hit the floor behind cover, as a roar of gunfire engulfed the city. It volleyed; it rolled; it thundered; it erupted from beneath his very balcony. Shouting erupted with it, from every direction: hundreds, it seemed thousands, of—of cheers? And fans screaming GOAL!!!!? He realized that he'd been jolted from sleep by—a winning side in a trophy match? Yes! Saint George defeats Bonneville! Securing the cup! The gunfire was deafening. It grew in intensity. It swept eastward, then westward, then eastward again. Then, in a staccato riff on dueling strings or howling dogs, distant burps were answered by local reports. As it began to fade, he could once again hear his neighbors clearly—unconcerned, laughing and clinking and happy. He became extraordinarily bright himself. He climbed sheepishly from the floor.

But what goes up, must come down. The velocity of a bullet, having reached the apex of its trajectory, and falling once again to the ground, is the same as it was when it left the muzzle of the rifle, discharged into the sky. Following the jubilation, came a different kind of rifle fire. More pointed. Single shots. With a different kind of shouting. Angry shouting. Angry fire. Some of it from directly beneath Barthes' window. Then silence.

Then horns. Then sirens. Then, finally, a less easy quiet, with night watchmen milling like disturbed ants on the street. Finally, relief, and, in the wee hours, sleep.

So it came as no surprise to hear on the morning news—having caught up at last with the wind—that fighting in the east of the city had been fierce on Thursday, with scattered fighting throughout the night. Colchis spent his Friday alternately doing normal things: a bit of washing up, a bit of writing—while plotting exit strategies and contemplating some security meetings of his own for Saturday morning. Then, in the afternoon, four explosions rattled his windows from about half a mile away. Then sirens. Then helicopters. And then an evening movie on the tri-v. And then he waited for the news delay that would tell him what had been.

The satellite on which Barthes' regular communication access depended remained inaccessible for days, leaving him feeling deaf, dumb, and blind. Tense, tense, tense: everything and everyone was tense. He spent one day twiddling with a presentation showing some of his progress. He queued it up to send once re-connected. Then, once the connection came up, solar flares, or something, had communications down anyway. Fierce fighting was rumored near the Medical College. Reports flowed in to the main Zion University campus: windows rattling on and off for three days; mortars falling in residential neighborhoods everywhere; security guards posted everywhere; TCM and civil police nowhere to be seen. Daytime curfews had shut down all transportation between city districts. Stranded at his office, he had good news from the Zion campus itself: no disturbances there, and work managed to limp along. Barthes was amazed by the courage exhibited every day, day after day, by those around him.

And then, abruptly as it had begun, came several days and nights of calm. The air was stunningly clear, lending Barthes to pensive consideration of the landscape, and agriculture, and history of New Utah. At Zion University, the large, new instructional lab and reading rooms were complete, and at both facilities the datasets were brought online. Evening Citizen Workshops were scheduled to teach all comers how to access public lecture, archival, and research media.

Colchis spent his nights troubleshooting, upgrading, and updating all the behind the scenes cataloguing, circulation, and reference support more-or-less taken for granted at home institutions. He emerged each morning to glorious weather. Cool, breezy, and clear. Finally, they were done. It was on to Bonneville for Colchis Barthes now.

10
Verbal Contracts

Faith has to do with things that are not seen, and hope with things that are not at hand.

—Saint Thomas Aquinas

The Barrens, New Utah

For all of Mena's warnings, Collie Orcutt didn't seem the least concerned about or interested in the status of Asach Quinn's beliefs. In fact, he wasn't particularly bothered about Asach's identity. "Get in," was all he'd said. Asach got in.

The girl in the front seat was another matter. About nineteen, twenty years old, Asach guessed. It was refreshing to see someone her age *not* in a cowled bonnet and long, black dress. Asach attempted conversation, but the girl just stared resolutely ahead. "Don't mind her," said Orcutt, "her position goes to her head."

He looked old as the hills. Older. Ages were always hard, on other planets. Differences in sun, wind, and work aged human skin more, or less, than one expected. Spacers were more predictable, but even then. It just depended on how much exposure, and to what kind of radiation, they'd had.

But in Orcutt's case, Asach had the sense that he really *was* old. Wiry, fit, agile, strong, but old. There was little else think about, as they went boiling overland. Asach had lost all sense of direction.

"Took a big chance, just waitin' out there like that."

Asach shrugged. "I had water, and patience."

"What would you have done, if nobody'd shown up to getcha?"

"Somebody would have. Somebody always does." Asach stared out the window. Collie laughed.

"Well, you've got faith. I like that."

Suddenly, the girl swiveled. Her eyes were still downcast, but she was at least facing Asach's direction. "And what about Hope? Charity?"

Asach tried to sound kind, but circumspect. "That's what I'm here to talk about, I guess."

Orcutt snorted. "We've heard that before."

They sank back into silence. For all the days already spent on the road, this leg seemed to last forever.

As they finally bounced into a packed-earth courtyard, sun low on the horizon, the evening chill dropped like a dusting of invisible snow. Asach groaned inwardly, and stretched. Too many nights sleeping rough. Too many days like this. Asach hoped for a comfortable bed, although looking at the state of the place, did not expect one.

"I'm going up to the barn," the girl said, without looking back.

"Sure, sugar. Say g'night to Agamemnon." And then, to Asach, "Her horse. That girl will marry that beast one day."

Asach turned for the door. "Just a minute," said Orcutt. He gripped Asach's upper arm; steered a new direction, pointed. "You see that?"

The evening glow suffused each little clump of dead bunch grass, glittering in ranks marching off to the distance. A pinky stain marked the stub of a mined-out mountain at their end. "Last one o' y'all to come here claimed that crap would be our salvation. Lies though and through."

"I know," Asach said.

Collie dropped the arm, looked critically at Asach's face. "Mena said you was comin.' Didn't say why."

Asach thought again about the answer to this inevitable question. Had thought all day. But there and then, locked in Collie Orcutt's gaze, decided not to lie. Not to tell the truth, precisely, but not to lie. "I've come to find the source."

Orcutt did not respond. Asach tried again, mentally reaching for the catechism. Found a universal line. *"In His Gaze, we are all pilgrims, we are all Seers, and all islands are One."*

Collie took in the cloak; the open, guileless face. Decided.

"We'll, you've come dressed for it." Then, in a bellow that carried all the way up to the barn, "Laurel, better get back down here. Got a pilgrim wants to Gather."

In the end, Asach was grateful indeed for Mena's insistent preparation. Laurel was neither patient, nor kind, but all business. "What are His Numbers"

Asach rattled that off without problem.

"What are His Tenets?"

Thankfully, that was short as well.

"Can you say His Creed?"

Asach struggled a moment with this. A mental picture formed of a chant-and-response, but the details were fuzzy. "Not alone. I—"

But Asach was saved by Laurel's impetuousness. "That's right," she said, nodding, "you can only say the creed together with your island. Or at another gathering, if you are a traveler."

Asach was getting a sense that there were Gatherings and gatherings, but the distinctions remained unclear.

"Can you sing the Hymn?"

Asach winged this one. "I don't know the tune. I've never heard it sung."

Laurel jumped on this. "Well, of course not, if you've never Gathered. But can you *say* it?"

Asach was out to sea now. "It's hard, without—"

"Oh, never mind. You'll learn it on the way, with everyone else. It's just that any *child* can say—" She stopped. "Wait a minute. Are you a *convert?*"

Asach looked back blankly, not wishing to outright lie. Thankfully, Laurel persisted. "You weren't *born* to Him?"

Grateful for the out, Asach pounced. "That's right. I was not born to Him."

But now, Laurel became suspicious, her eyes downcast again. "I warn you. If we find out that you are a TCM spy, you'll be abandoned on the high plains where *no-one* will come to get you."

Asach had no need to circumnavigate this. "I swear by the stars above that I am not a member of the TCM, or the True Church, nor am I a spy for either of them. Think on it. My name is *Quinn.*"

Laurel looked up sharply. The name meant nothing to her, but Asach's patent sincerity did. "OK. Name his Gatherings."

Asach felt like a graduate student wilting under oral examination. "I—I don't know them all. Only the New Utah ones. That's why I'm here."

"Well, do those, then. You need to know them all, but do those."

"OK. Um…" These were a little easier, since they rounded off in twenty-year increments. "Um, 2960, that's when you—I mean He, first came to New Utah. I mean Heaven."

Laurel was nodding, obviously bored.

"Then, 2980, that's the First Gathering—" and suddenly, this began to make sense—"that is, the first Gathering here on New Utah—Heaven—which is the sixth overall."

Laurel was still nodding. "And?"

"And…and…and His Earthly Eye was revealed!" Asach still had no idea what that meant, but it satisfied Laurel.

"Then, 3000—that's the second here, seventh overall; 3020—that's the third here, eighth overall; and 3040—that's the fourth, or ninth overall."

"And?"

"Oh, yes, and—and—and what *was* the Revelation? I mean, I realize that I should know, but—"

Laurel was clearly exasperated. "Well how could you know? It hasn't happened yet!"

"But it's already 3048, so—" But Asach stopped, as Laurel glared. *Stupid!* It was a liturgical calendar. It didn't *use* Standard Years.

But clearly this wasn't the first time Laurel had heard that particular error. She forged on. "So, what's your number?"

Asach was growing weary of this interrogation, and peevishly nearly answered "Scorpio," when the childish chatter at the windmill came to mind. Asach frantically counted back, trying to allow the correct slippage for the lag between calendars, and took a calculated guess. "Two."

Clearly, to Laurel this seemed about right. "Little old, aren't you, to make your first Gathering?" She eyed Asach critically. "Well, you seem fit enough."

Asach exhaled slowly. "I can go then?"

"Go? Of course you can go. Who am I to stop you?" She got up to leave. "More to the point, we'll bring you with our island, so long as you're clear in your mind." Then she paused. "You *can* ride, can't you?"

Relieved at an *easy* question, Asach smiled and nodded. Laurel turned to go, calling out over her shoulder, "Only, if you're a two, I'm not your Seer. You need to talk to Collie."

Asach's fears were disappointed. The bed was deep, soft, and warm. The night was dark and quiet. In the morning, Laurel was already up and gone, but Collie lingered over breakfast.

"I won't apologize, but I'll explain. That girl's got a lot on her mind."

Asach listened, patiently.

"See, she's of an age where she takes *everything* seriously. Like, being a Seer. Now, she really, really, way down deep *believes* that she was Seen in her mother's womb by His Eye." He shook his head. "Now, I believe that too, of course I do, but *mostly* it's just a way of stayin' organized." He looked at Asach intently. "You ain't from Purchase, are you?"

Asach indicated the negative.

"See, I figured that you was from New Cal. Maybe even farther."

Asach nodded.

"Well, OK, so. See, that's more burden on Laurel. *First* she has to see off everyone from her own island. All them little ones. *Then* she has to see off every Three or Four from The Barrens who don't have a Seer of their own. You follow?"

Asach made a slight inclination of the head. "Go on?"

"But at least all them folks knows their way to the staging areas; knows their way around. I mean, even if they can't see where theys' goin', they sure as hell know what to do once they get there. And the parents usually take the little ones. But then on top o' that, comes all the town-dogs from

Bonneville. At least there, we know our own, and a lot of them hook up with their kin in The Barrens islands. But the fun really starts when the city rats from Saint George start marchin' in. 'Cuz then, she's gotta figure out which ones're TCM spies, and keep 'em isolated until she can lose 'em or chase 'em home." He shook his head. "And all that's gotta get sorted before the tramline opens and sisters from MP and New Cal arrive. And most of them, well they usually come, because somebody in their island came, so they have some idea of what's goin' on. But the wild fishes like you, who swim in from the starry ocean?" He shook his head again "That's a lot for a kid her age to take on, on top of everything else."

"I'm sorry," said Asach simply, and genuinely.

Collie smiled. "Don't be. She *says* it's all about doin' it right,' but really it's just to get one more thing off her mind. Like I said, it's mostly just a way to stay organized. It's not *really* all on her. It's not like she's the only one. She picks up the Threes and Fours from her island, plus whichever else other ones gets sent to her island. There's other Seers, and other islands. They don't all go to her. So she wants to hand you off to a Seer for Twos. Twos and Threes. In other words, to the Seer whose done it all once, and taught her."

"I see," said Asach. "And who is that?"

Orcutt frowned. "Well, really, that was my sister. Her mother who died."

"I'm sorry," said Asach again. "I can see why she'd take this very seriously. With a lot of piety."

"Thank-you." Collie pursed his lips. "But I think it's worse than you realize. " He pursed again. His lips moved in, then out, several times. He cocked his head and decided. "You know how a Seer is made?"

"No. Are they?"

"Good answer. They're not. They're born. At a Gathering. They are born at a Gathering, in the Sight of His

Earthly Eye." He sighed. "And you'll find out just what that means soon enough. But just think on this. Laurel's too much like her mother. Too serious. Takes it too serious, when it's really just about being organized. Somebody born at the Second Gathering, they train to take Twos and Threes next time. Somebody born at the Third, they take Threes and Fours next time, And so on. You follow?"

Asach nodded.

"So, it's not even *meant* to follow in any family line. It's just a way to be sure the routes get passed on. But Laurel's Mom was stubborn as they come. Came the Third Gathering, she was no spring bud any more, and she was carrying Laurel. But she just wouldn't hear of reassigning her people to another island. And so she went up there, and He opened His Eye, and she bore Laurel, and on the way back she died." He stared down at the table. "I know her mind. She thinks He took her Mom, to make her Seer. But it's just a way to stay organized." Tears welled in his eyes.

Asach left him a moment with this remembered grief. "Perhaps it would be better if I sought another island?"

Orcutt coughed. "Oh, hell, no." He rubbed his eyes. Then he actually grinned. "See, this one's gunna be special, and you're already here, and she ain't the only Seer in our island." Now he had a twinkle in his eye. "How old you think I am?"

"Well, it's hard to say. You say your sister, so—" Asach paused. "Were you the oldest?"

"Yep."

"And your sister—Laurel's Mom—the youngest?"

"Yep."

"Big family?"

"Yep."

"Surely, not—"

"Yep. Ones and twos, that's me. So. I thought, when I saw you sittin' in the dirt playin' plink with the little ones: I thought, *that one's been around the block a few times.* So, I'll make you a deal. I'll get you prepped, get you up to speed, see you to the staging area, then hand you off to Laurel when she's got herself organized. For a price."

He grinned again. "Because, I figure, if you came all this way, you can afford it. And if you can't, well, it would do Laurel good to have somebody along more than a hand or two old. Somebody on her side."

Asach met his gaze evenly, did not waver, reached into the cloak. Did not even look down, just handed over the TCM tithe credit.

Orcutt looked, though. He saw the color. His eyes went wide.

Now, Asach grinned. "You're right. I can. And I will."

From Asach's perspective, it was preparations for a pack trip like any other. Asach picked a riding horse. Asach picked a pack mule. Asach packed light, but prepared for any weather. Asach picked a farrier, and had the animals shod with full plates and studs to cope with rocky ground. Asach overpaid for it all, and made clear that return favors for the custom were due Laurel.

Orcutt was impressed. There was nothing flashy about the animals or the gear. They were of a piece: sensible, serviceable, sound. "Don't much need me at all," he said. "We should keep you around."

"Mis-spent youth," Asach replied, but volunteered no more.

Even the staging area was predictable: stones marked numbered campsites; picket lines were set up between stakes driven into the packed ground. Most animals were hobbled. Feed and water wagons made a circuit, so that rations could be saved for the trek to come. Asach drilled the catechism until

The Hymn intruded into dreams, set to varying strains, including all the tunes the lads had hummed driving out from Bonneville. Asach hoped they'd returned unharmed.

Actually, Asach was surprised. There were not that many people there. A lot of them were children. "Mostly Barrens islands, yet," explained Orcutt. "We need to clear this lot out before we drown. Once that tramline opens, no tellin' how many rounds she'll have to make."

"You mean this is not the only Gathering?"

Orcutt clearly thought the question mad. "There's only one Gathering. And this'll be the biggest yet."

Asach thought about this a moment, and tried again. "So, how long will it go on?"

"No tellin.' Year, two three. At least, if it's the same as always. Only, this one won't be."

"The Revelation."

He winked. "The Revelation."

"But if I only have supplies for—"

"Oh, you don't worry about that. You can trust Laurel. His Eye will open by the time you get up there. You will stand in awe before his Gaze." His voice quavered reverentially, and then, quite matter-of-factly, he continued. "Then Laurel will see you back down, and see the next batch up. Unless, of course, you See and don't believe. In that case, you're on your own."

The next morning, Asach discovered why this could be a problem.

They mounted up. Asach saw at once why the appellation *pilgrim* had so often been presumed: everyone mounted, except Laurel and other Seers, wore long, split-backed, hooded cloaks not unlike Asach's own. Laurel proceeded down the line from back to front, handing each rider a lead line for the horse behind. Asach began to protest: "that's really not nec—" but trailed off at Laurel's glower.

"Just mind your mule," she said, moving up the line.

And then she was mounted herself. She made a flapping motion past her ear, as if waving off a bug. "Hoods up!" She shouted. "Hoods Up!...Hoods Up!...Hoods Up!" echoed down the line.

Confused, Asach fumbled to pull the cloak hood from the collar with one hand without dropping the pack mule's lead line. Another Seer trudged up from behind, checking something. It was difficult to see exactly what was going on. Asach jumped at a slap on the thigh.

"Hoods UP!"

Confused, Asach looked down. The Seer signaled furiously, as at a child. "Over the eyes! Pull your hood down over your eyes!"

Asach groaned. Seers. Clairvoyants? Shamans? Oracles? Prognosticators? No. Himmists had to be the most bloody-mindedly literal people ever imagined, apart from accountants. Seers were, quite literally, guides to the blind. Or, in this case, blinded. Mindful of the consequences of being abandoned in the middle of nowhere, Asach complied. It was going to be a bloody boring ride.

Asach wasn't *completely* blind. A patch of the horse's mane was visible. A patch of Asach's own chest was visible. A patch of the mule's pack was visible, wobbling off to the side. Occasionally, the mule's nose hove into view, as it slobbered on its new buddy's withers. The horse did not seem to mind. Asach became intensely aware of the need for clippers and a nail buffer. Asach began daydreaming of coffee and pie. The train trundled on.

Other senses became more acute. The smell of the dust changed. Less—clayey. Then, simply, less. Before the end of the first day, they had moved onto rocky ground. Asach had lost all sense of direction; tried to picture in what direction rocky ground might lie. Then noted the warmth beaming from the—back. Definitely back. And surely, it was late in the day now? Surely the warmth had—passed overhead? So, they were heading east?

Asach listened. There was nothing to hear, except the scrabbling sound of hooves on gravel. Sometimes a clop, more often a crunch, or a slither, or a scrape. And the squeaking of tack. And the clinking of harness. And the crickety bit rollers in nervous horses' mouths. And their breathing, and snorting, and snotty-nose-blowing sounds. The occasional squeal as one or another objected to the attentions of a pack-mule. Asach's feet, then knees, then butt grew numb. Asach's stomach made rumbling sounds. The horses trudged on.

It was the mules who announced camp time. As if on cue, braying began at one end of the train, then whipped along with ear-splitting fervor. As if on a cue of their own, the horses all pulled up. Asach reflected. None of these could have made *this* trip before. The last Gathering would have been twenty years earlier. But clearly, at least *some* knew what was going on.

"Dismount!" echoed down the line as the sun winked out. They made camp in the dark, on the rock-hard ground. The Seers encircled the camp with watch fires. They could pull their hoods off now. It was impossible to see where they were.

After three days, the air changed. It smelled of high, cold mountains. The ground was uneven now, rising and falling, the trail twisting across the fall lines. If it could be called a trail. It was as if Laurel was *seeking* the worst possible ground. Rocky, unlevel, horses lurching and scrambling to find purchase in spots. At one bend, Asach nearly pitched over from vertigo, as the fist-sized view from under the hood revealed a sloping granite face, plunging down, down, down, but no clear trail at all beneath the mule's feet. The animals seemed unperturbed. At camp that night, Asach sidled up to another fire, populated by what looked like a ten-year old. "How do they do this?" Asach asked.

"Who?"

"The horses. The mules. How do they know these trails?"

The boy wrinkled his nose and forehead. "They train them, of course!"

Asach said a silent prayer for Orcutt, who clearly had done more of the choosing than Asach had realized, and another for Laurel, out of new respect for a Seer's multifaceted responsibilities.

Another day of this, and they had passed the foothills, into the mountains themselves. Asach could not identify the smells, beyond something like leaf mold; something like earth. They had to unrope the horses now, so that the mules could drop back to single file. Then, even that became impossible, and they had to dismount, tying the mule to the horse and leading the horse on foot. Asach felt physically ill as they clambered across a scree slope one by one, the very trail, if it could be called that, cascading from beneath their feet, but miraculously, all made it safely, and not a single animal was lost.

Finally, toward day's end, they topped a rise, and slithered into a saddle of level ground. Asach leaned against the horse, exhausted, soaking in the snuffly warmth of its breath. It turned and nibbled hopefully at the mule's pack, then jumped as a raucous cheer swept the line. Unbalanced, Asach nearly hit the ground, and in sheer reflex swept back the hood—only to see everyone else do the same.

"Hoods off! Hoods off from here on!"

This time, they made camp in daylight. The animals were fed and rubbed down. As dusk fell Asach dozed, leaning on the mule's pack, trying to stir the energy to cook a meal, mind drifting to an eerie, half-heard sound. It echoed softly between the rock walls of the saddle; oozed down from higher on the mountain. Like a roundelay, of childhood. Like a desert wind. Like a—Asach stirred. Like a medieval chant. Asach sat up. Like a hymn. Asach stood. Which is what is was. For the first time, Asach was hearing The Gathering Hymn sung aloud. It was unbelievably alien. It was unbelievably beautiful. Picked up and carried beyond fatigue; carried away by the moment, Asach joined in. Surely, they were not far now.

Fog lay so heavily in the valley that morning was marked only by a lessening of darkness. People; shelters; animals, loomed suddenly from the grey, then sank back into the mist whence they arose. There was a shallow, rocky lake somewhere beyond their picket line. Asach led the stock to water.

"Not too much," cautioned Laurel's disembodied voice. Asach started. "This water's OK for them, but not too much at once. Don't let them wade in and muddy up the bottom. It'll make them sick."

The mule was fussy. It sipped, then raised its head to swivel its great, long, fuzzy ears, spooking at every noise. Eventually it was done, and Asach returned them both to the picket line.

"They rest today," said Laurel, materializing again. "Come on with me. We'll lead the others up. I don't want to lose you. "

"Thanks, but I'll be fine."

Laurel rolled her eyes. "No, you won't. Come on."

Asach worried briefly that the hoods were about to go back on; that they'd spend the day teetering on precipices, blind. But not so: it was trail craft that concerned Laurel, not visibility. "Stay off the dirt. Stay off the sand. See there? Stay on the rock." She pointed to an option off the obvious path; it required hopping across polished boulders, as if fording a stream. A light came on in Asach's head.

"Is that what we've been doing all along? Avoiding seeing the trail? Avoiding *making* a trail?"

Again, Laurel rolled her eyes. "What else?"

I don't know, thought Asach. *Initiation rites. Secret orders. Dark mystery. And so on.*

Laurel trudged upward. "We share His gaze. We don't hide it. But we're not stupid. If they found this place, what do *you* think the TCM would do?"

"I'm surprised they haven't already."

Laurel stopped and turned around. Her eyes were piercing aquamarine. They seemed to focus the dreary light. "A few have tried."

She turned, and continued on.

Eventually, the path became—a path, worn into dark granite. Asach did some mental calculations. The Himmists had been on New Utah less than a century. Either there were a lot more of them than anyone thought, which was unlikely, or the path predated them by a very long time.

"Who made this?"

Laurel's answer was matter-of-fact, as if Asach had asked the time. "The Angels." She did not look back.

The path wore deeper into the rock, and widened. The route became more boulder-strewn. They were old, and weathered, and lichen-encrusted. Lichen-*like* encrusted. Who knew what grew here of its own. Then suddenly they stepped through the veil of fog into the open sun. Asach was momentarily dazzled. Before them lay a barren, until the path rounded up over a lip and disappeared. Behind them lay a carpet of cloud, sparkling in the sunshine.

Finally they reached the rim. Asach gasped as their heads cleared the rise. They looked out over the edge of a tabletop; the truncated remains of an ancient cone. It dipped gently away from the eye, like a concave lens seen edge-on. Windswept, bare, it seemed paved with diamonds. As they climbed up over the edge and stood to full height, the reason became clear. The ground was littered with foamy shards, brilliant white in the morning sun. Asach picked one up in a hand heated by the climb, and saw the ghost of blue iridescence. It was opal meerschaum.

"His tears," smiled Laurel. "It makes me happy to be so near."

As they walked on, the scattered chunks consolidated; some streaked edgewise in exposed veins, crystallized in an ancient volcanic layer-cake. Their boots crunched in the gravel. Then, behind them, floated the eerie thread of the Hymn as the others joined them on the plateau. It came from all directions, as other parties also cleared the edge, converging toward the unseen center, obscured by the slope of the land. Asach looked up at the aquamarine sky, clear as Laurel's eyes. The day was crisp, clean; the sun warm. They walked on awhile. As the voices of one group joined the next, the singing became less a roundelay, but kept that exquisite polyphonic harmony. Then, as they approached a dip, Laurel held up a hand and turned, shouting back, "We stop here."

Asach looked about, confused as others crowded past and pushed forward, singing in full voice. Joining hands, turning to look one another full in the eyes, then turning to do the same to each neighbor, they waved Asach to join in; belting out the final stanzas:

> Arise! And leave no stone unturned!
> Arise! And plow each field!
> Arise! Believe! That all who yearn
> Will see His Face revealed!
>
> We fled in fear His awful Gaze

But with His Earthly Eye
He sees, He knows, He sends His Grace
Across all starry skies.

So shoulder all your burdens!
For when your time is done
Revealed at last! His angels
Will make all Churches one!

And as they ringed the rim and the final words echoed below, all looked down, and gasped again as one: even those who had been there before. Centered within a mile-wide bowl stretched a polished dome of white: a stratum of perfect opal meerschaum, nearly half a mile across, its overlying layers worn away by wind and time. It bulged upward slightly, perhaps due to pressures within the mountain core. At its center intruded— an old lava tube?—that radiated with crystalline depths in the sun, like a ruby set in gold. *Or more likely*, thought Asach, *like a garnet set in mica, but why spoil the magic of it all?*

Whatever the structure was that twinkled in the heart of the dead volcano, the effect was unmistakable: it did indeed, for all the world, look like an enormous red eye, complete with mica-speckled iris and a dark pupil staring up from deep within the mountain.

Unthinking, Asach stepped forward.

"No! No further! You could be consumed by His Gaze!" Laurel pointed to something at her feet.

Exasperated—it was, after all, only *rocks*—Asach followed the line of Laurel's finger. There was something carved there, in the stone. Peering, it was difficult to make out. Fist-sized, old, scuffed, weathered, it looked like—eyes, maybe, over a lopsided mouth, but highly stylized.

"Watch for the Angels," Laurel instructed. "Do not pass His Angels. Wait here. I must bring others."

So, it seemed there was to be more to the show. Asach sank down cross-legged next to the carving, and settled in for the duration. Another round-trip would take a fair stretch of time. Doodling aimlessly with one finger on the rock, picking away stray bits of mossy, lichenish gunk, Asach studied the amazing panorama. The crystalline structure was hauntingly flawless. It drew the eye into its depths, like staring into infinity. Like staring into space—the eyes played tricks, and it even seemed to twinkle from time to time. On careful study, the mica seemed to be *under*, or *behind*, or—well, Asach really couldn't decide, but anyway somehow layered with the gemstone, as if looking through the garnet to the reflecting mica.

The wind blew steadily across the rim, and eventually Asach worked out why the meerschaum seemed so polished: in a sense, it *was*. The prevailing wind passed over the lip at a nock, sending it into a swirl through the bowl. The heavier particles had long since piled up in the lee corner; only the lightest dust was blown across, sweeping and polishing the stone smooth before it. The rim was far from solid: Asach could see nooks and caves riddling the face. Some whistled spookily as the dust devils blew past, or in.

As the sun passed overhead, then sank, high cirrus played tricks with the light. A rosy glow suffused the dome, feathering like wisps of smoke. Abandoning the particle-picking effort, Asach stood and peered again, eyes squinted. Translucent light was dancing across the stone in milky swirls. Asach looked around in vain for a source; peered again. But the light was clearly coming from *within* the dome itself: swirling, pooling, blue and green for an instant, then winking out. Agitated, Asach looked to the others. They were smiling; clapping, waving: "He wakes!" they called. "Here come the Seers, now!"

As Laurel topped the crest, another singing band in tow, dusk fell with that sudden plummet of the sun felt only in the mountains. The pilgrims now stood hand-to-hand in an enormous semicircle around the rim, their Seers spaced behind them. The colors showed up stronger in the gloam, and the dome itself glowed brighter: now milky; now cloudy; now clear.

"Now!" screamed Laurel, "Now! Avert Your Gaze! He Wakes!"

In that instant, Asach became intently aware of standing on the top of a volcano. Of the implications of a magma surge close enough, and hot enough, to excite that much meerschaum beyond playing at iridescent halos, and into emitting clear, incandescent, light. Of themselves, Asach's eyelids clamped shut; of itself, Asach's head snapped down. But like looking at the sun, mere eyelids were not enough to block the dazzle of brilliant green that bathed the dome, or the long green line that shot from the crater's core straight up into the sky.

Carefully, face pointed resolutely downward, Asach opened and blinked one dazzled eye. The ghastly glow painted the little carved figure at Asach's feet in ghoulish light. Blinking furiously to erase the retinal image, Asach opened the other eye and tried to focus. Made out the odd little noseless face, with its floppy hood and twisted grin, two arms folded across its chest and—and—and—. And, Asach realized, as the enormous laser winked out, plunging the figure into darkness, a third arm stretching downward, three fingers extended, in the Motie signal for: *"Halt!"*

Involuntarily, still staring at the ground, Asach blurted: "Oh. My. God."

"Yes!" shouted Laurel. "Yes! Who among us could revel in His Gaze and not believe!"

But all Asach could think was: *Vacation's over. Time to get organized.*

The vermin crawled over almost every route leading into Beacon Hill, but never used this morning side face, because their cattle could not climb. From a distance, the cliff appeared to be sheer, but even one echo-chirp showed it to be a porous mix of tufa and tuff: easy to grip, and easy to climb.

Side Captain Enheduanna led the assault, with two hand of Warriors in column behind, the slight wind erasing their file of tracks even as they moved on. On crossing the final line of dunes before the base they spread in a horizontal array, so that no fall by one could take down another. The Warriors *kicked*, then *stepped*, then *kicked*, then *stepped* their sharp-toed, horny feet into the face and passed the time with a marching ditty, chanted down the rank one line per trooper.

> Her song sung
> With joy of heart
> In the plain
> With joy of heart
> She sings and she
> Soaks her mace
> In blood and gore
> And smashes heads
> And butchers prey
> With eater-ax
> And bloodied spear
> *All day*

They barked the final words in unison, then began again, on and on. Of course, the chant did not merely pass the time. It enabled each to know, at any moment, exactly where the others were.

It was not usual for a Master to accompany so small a Warrior detail into the field, but Lord Sargon had been quite explicit: "We would know the Enemy. Bring one to us. Unharmed."

Enheduanna shook off a wave of disgust. The notion of vermin owning cattle was *anathema*. Vermin they were: they slept in the field with their cattle; they drank the fluids of their cattle; they clad themselves in the hair of their cattle; they burned the dung of their cattle, they trekked without regard to the *ar* of their neighbors, even as they laid waste to their own fields. Like vermin; like scavengers, that swarmed on the outskirts of Houses, fashioning bowers of baubles stolen from trash-piles, consuming the garbage carefully layered for compost by the Farmers, and stripping the ground around them to bare dirt. In such a case, absent their Master's Voice, Warriors could hardly be expected to show restraint. They were what they were.

They cleared the softer rock, and now took greater care as they made their way up weathered laterite. A pair of Warriors flanked their Captain, each alternately driving home a *chrshnar*, the eater-ax, the razor-sharp and tungsten-tough Warrior's fighting claw, to serve as living pitons for the clawless Master.

They paused on a step, where the baked surface peeled away from a crumbling granite core. This would be the tricky part: from there, they would move laterally, to a large cave mouth called Esker's Tongue, named for the line of sand and gravel that poured from it to the plain below. There were almost no holds for the last post's span: the Warriors would have to leapfrog where needed as a living chain for the Master. So, to prepare, they rested for a very short while.

The night was dark, but the cave was black. It would be better to have a Miner. Enheduanna did not bother to think *too late now*. It was what it was. The Warrior's vision would get them most of the way. The rest, Enheduanna knew by heart.

Just shy of the exits, as a greenish glow made visible the porous walls around them, the hand leaders barked once. Enheduanna's nictitating membranes snapped shut, as did all the others,' shielding their eyes from the dazzling glare as they sprinted out.

It was not Enheduanna's job to get them to their prey. The hand leaders knew their mission. They hurtled up the rim, jerking to a halt just as the green beacon light winked out. They crouched among the rocks, two Warriors covering Enheduanna's white fur with their black. The opal meerschaum glow etched the bowl with stark shadows. They listened. The vermin had begun their hideous noises again. They waited, counting silently: *digit...thumb...palm...hand...* Then, just before they'd counted to five side, with their third eyelids again clamped tight shut, they burst upwards over the lip, their black shapes haloed, like demons shot from within the beacon.

The leaders snarled, and Enheduanna heard a *clack* as both posts spread their *chrshnar* in unison. "Hold!" barked Enheduanna, and strode forward between them, white fur glowing in the backlight as the beacon winked out again.

They opened their eyes for clearer vision, fully prepared to lunge, but a bizarre sight greeted them. They had expected— something. Stunners. Piercers. Shock-bolts. Poisons. Gas. Something from the centuries of recorded armed resistance. But these vermin merely—faced them. Some standing, some on their knees, but facing them, arms wide, palms forward, reaching overhead, bodies swaying side to side—some even swooning in their tracks, without a hand laid on them. Then one separated from the group, stepping forward slowly.

"Hold" snarled Enheduanna again, as the figure sank to its knees, clasping its hands in some incomprehensible gesture.

It Spoke; its voice reverberating for all to hear. "Behold! The Revelation of His Angels! It is the Prophesy! They *are* here!"

Enheduanna looked down at the jabbering thing. It had the strangest eyes. They were brilliant aquamarine, like manna in the early morning sun. *How odd*, thought Enheduanna, *that this—* thing—*should bear the color of* ar. Enheduanna gestured to the Warriors. "Take this one."

The vermin parted, making no move, as the remaining Warriors guarded their retreat. All save one. It made no threat, but it dogged their steps. Its face was white as a Master's in the opal glare; odd folds of skin draped and furled around it. One Warrior made to cut it down, but Enheduanna waved it off. "It's only the vermin's cattle. Let it come."

They trudged down the slope, finding the path in time to shield their eyes as the beacon flared again. They listened to the vermin on the rim screech and wail their animal gibberish.

"It is the prophesy! It is the Revelation! Seer Laurel is born away by Angels!"

Oh crap, thought Asach, hood pulled down against the blinding green, so that only the faintest view of the treacherous way was visible, *here we go*.

11
Communications
Update

What can be said at all can be said clearly, and what we cannot talk about we must pass over in silence....Everyday language is a part of our organism and no less complicated than it....Language disguises thought. So much so, that from the outward form of the clothing it is impossible to infer the form of the thought beneath it.

—*Ludwig Wittgenstein, Tractatus Logico-Philosophicus*

Somewhere East of The Barrens, New Utah

They approached a city, and Asach paused in awe. It was not large. Perhaps two hundred hectares in all. It shimmered above the fields of reed, glowing green and gold in the morning sun. It appeared to be one enormous, integral structure, pockmarked with entryways: a sponge of ochre brick and glass, carpeted with green fuzz. No roads appeared to lead into it, save the one they were on: a narrow pavement of laterite, barely two hands wide, disappearing fore and aft into a tunnel of arching reeds. Asach realized that there could well be dozens of such tracks; hundreds even, hidden within the surrounding marsh and invisible to the ground-level eye. The others did not stop. Asach hurried to catch up.

But a city, indeed, it was, and had Asach's sixth sense of that needed confirmation, it was soon to come. As they drew near, the paved track widened, and became lined with—industrial stalls, as best Asach could tell. The construction was the same: a low rise in ground, covered with young crop; one or more entryways; the doorways and, so far as Asach could see inside, the domed interior walls fashioned of what looked like glass; the floors and surrounds of laterite paving. Some forecourts included knee-high laterite benches with green-stained tops. Others had large, smooth, slightly concave, bluish-white circular surfaces, a double-arm span wide and a hand's-breadth deep. Still others had stacks and stacks of pottery bowls, the size of two cupped hands, inverted beside laterite stair steps leading nowhere.

As they walked, some of these stalls were empty; others alive with activity, and Asach became aware of an industrial process. Enormous, silent versions of the white-haired creature that seemed to be in charge of Laurel's progress delivered stacks and stacks of the fresh-cut reed to the work-bench stalls. There, wielding stone cudgels, others like them shoved and pounded the stalks until limp. The workbenches actually included narrow gutters at the top and base, which drained into larger versions of the bowls, that had one edge pinched into a pouring spout. Next, the now-limp reed was passed to the stone circles, where it passed under what looked like corrugated rolling pins that circled the dish, reducing the reed to pulp. Again, narrow channels drained juices into large spouted bowls. Then, bearers brought racks of bowls. Each bowl was filled, the pulp pressed flat to the rim. The racks of full bowls were then taken to the stair steps, where they were set out to dry in the dazzling sun. When partially dry, the reed-patties were turned out onto drying mats until they were hard. Lastly, the collected juices were poured into enormous ewers.

Reed-like, thought Asach, trudging along. *Not reed, exactly. More like Spartina—salt grass. Or something else entirely. That intense aquamarine color—like blue-green algae. A giant algae? A fruiting algae? Like seaweed, perhaps, only on land?* Absent-mindedly, lost in thought, Asach reached out and broke off a stalk with an audible snap. The hindmost Warrior swiveled at the waist in a shocking one-eighty-degree turn like an owl's head, then leapt. Within three bounds its clawed fist dug into the small of Asach's back while—something—scratched a thin line of blood at Asach's throat. In sheer desperation, arched so far backward that the only thing visible was the vault of the sky, Asach shouted, as loud as possible with a hyper-extended neck, a bad imitation of the hairball-hacking sound the white one had used twice before to order restraint.

Unfortunately, what Asach actually shouted was an obscenity, but it so startled the Warrior that he took a half step back, even as Enheduanna called back "Hold!" This time, Asach caught the variation in inflection, repeated it perfectly— and then repeated it again with the error. The Warrior froze a moment. Then, suddenly, it leaned forward, eyes locked on Asach, and began hissing like a steam kettle. The other Warriors turned as one in that back-wrenching pose.

Now Asach froze. Slowly, palms forward, Asach knelt, placed the broken stalk on the ground, then just as slowly stood. At this, all the Warriors began hissing. The white one was watching Asach intently. Asach was watching Laurel. The girl's upper arm was bruised to pulp by the gripping hands of her rotating guard. She looked pale and terrified.

Asach decided to gamble all or nothing. It needed only one move to bend down, snatch up the broken stalk, and take the first two steps forward. Looking squarely at the first Warrior, Asach shouted again, in its own tongue, "Hold!" and started walking. The Warrior made to grab, but the white one waved it off. Asach kept walking, looking directly at the white one, then directly at Laurel, then directly at the white one again, the green stalk thrust forward.

"Hey Top," called the one closest to Asach, "D'ya think it knows what it's saying?"

"Nah," answered the hand leader, "it's just copyin' the sounds. Like A Meat."

"Yeah?" answered the first one, "I ain't never met dinner before what said 'hold off, buttface!'"

All the Warriors began laughing again, their hisses pulsing in unison. The thing was no threat—any one of them could cut it down in an instant—and Enheduanna was cautiously curious. Mimicking like a Meat? Or mimicking like a *child*? It seemed purposeful. Before bringing it before the Protector, its status must be known. It approached; it stopped, its bizarre skin hanging about in folds. It looked directly at Enheduanna. Like a Farmer at a Post, it took a bite of the stalk; chewed, swallowed. Then it touched the manna-eyed one. It made noises. Exasperated, Enheduanna turned to move on, but the thing spoke again, this time softly: "hold?"

Enheduanna's disgust overflowed. The Warriors reeked of anger. *How dare it?* Thought Enheduanna. *How dare it?* And then thought, *well it dares, either because it knows nothing, or because that's the only word it knows.* Enheduanna decided to err on the side of *child,* and waited. The thing reached inside its folds of skin. It pulled out a packet of something. It removed a wrapping. It took a bite, and chewed. Strange, but plain enough. Then it handed the packet to the manna-eyed one who, one-handed, began to devour it, like the vermin that it was.

Enheduanna was about to order them onward, when a file of tray-carrying Porters approached. There was no choice but to make way, lest they drop their load. The creature raised its hand in a rude gesture, and made a noise. It did it again, and again, and again. It finally dawned on Enheduanna that it was indicating manna drying-bowls. Enheduanna said: "*khkhkh!*" the aspirated "k" rolling three times, followed by a click.

The creature replied: "*khkhkh!* Bowls," its mouth making an odd lip-pursing movement as it spoke.

Nearly-lipless Enheduanna replied: "Muuulls. *khkhkh!*"

The creature reached inside its skin again, and removed a small ewer. It touched the manna-eyed one. It pulled a stopper from the ewer, and held it to the manna-eyed one's mouth, tilting the ewer. But the ewer was empty. It held it inverted, then shook it, to show that. One drop of water splattered and alighted on the creature's hand. It raised the hand. It made a noise. It touched the manna-eyed one, and said: "*khkhkh!* [noise] *khkhkh!* [noise]," all the while making the same rude gesture at the water drop as it had used to indicate the *bowls*. It offered the ewer, then made the noise—no, *said the word*—again. Enheduanna thought, then said "Ater. *[drip]*." The creature replied instantly: "*khkhkh! [drip]*." It had to use one of its hands to say *[drip]*, flicking its face with one finger, but it said it nonetheless.

On impulse, Enheduanna called to one of the crushing floors: "Dip me a bowl of manna juice." The worker's posture looked skeptical, but it did so. Enheduanna waved it aside, and with a twitch of posture indicated the creatures. They drank strangely. The manna-eyed one tilted its head back and drained the liquid in three large gulps. Enheduanna called for a second bowl. The skin-draped one sipped more slowly, but drained it as well, with that same lip-pursing, back-tilting gesture, then handed back both bowls. If the worker was surprised or intrigued by these beings, there was no way to tell. Enheduanna was amazed that they seemed to require sustenance after so short a time. They had only marched two days, and that slowly.

Enheduanna grasped the manna-eyed one, clenched her gripping hand in the small of its back, then pushed backwards on its torso. It was amazingly flexible. She grasped its face, and moved it side-to-side. It was shocking how its head could swivel. It was no wonder it needed to drink already. Water dribbled from its eyes. She turned to the other. Unprompted, it leaned: backwards, then forwards, then swiveled at the hips (poorly), then at the neck (amazingly). Enheduanna reached over, and pinched its loose skin. It stayed motionless. Enheduanna pinched harder. Still nothing. Enheduanna reached to pinch with the gripping hand—and the creature blurted "Hold!"

Angered, Enheduanna stepped forward, but with one swift movement the creature raised its hands to its throat, twiddled with its fingers—and whipped the skin away, repeating "Hold!" Then, swiftly, before Enheduanna could react, the creature put one hand to its midline, and pulled. More of its skin peeled away, revealing—pink skin, the same color as its face and hands. Enheduanna reached and pinched *that* skin, and the creature flinched. The skin felt odd: smooth, dry, nearly hairless, warm.

Laurel was shivering. Asach at least had eaten and drunk on the march, but this was the first opportunity there'd been to share with Laurel the meager day's-worth of rations that Asach had packed away three mornings ago. Those gone, there was nothing left to offer but some warmth. Asach didn't dare part with the cloak. While the others stared, (presumably aghast, but how would you know?) Asach peeled out of vest and tunic, re-donned the vest and cloak, and walked to Laurel. A Warrior still held one arm in a death-grip. Asach turned to the white, and, enunciating very clearly, said, "Please ask it to let her go for a minute."

The white did not respond. Asach pointed to the Warrior's hand, then, grasping Laurel's other arm, mimed, and said, "Let. Go." It took three repetitions of this little acting out, but the white responded with a chickadee-trill—and the Warrior released its grip.

Gently, Asach said to Laurel: "You're going into shock. Put this on. Tastes like crap, but I think that water will help in a little while."

Laurel stood mute, still shaking. With infinite tenderness, Asach helped her into the tunic, took her by the hand, and whispered: "Laurel, I think it's going to be really important that we show some backbone."

At this, Laurel turned her head slowly, dumbly, away, releasing Asach's hand.

"Laurel?"

Silence.

"Laurel?"

Laurel croaked, barely audibly: "*He is not a Faceless God! May we turn our Gaze from those who refuse to See, praying fervently that they may not remain Blind.*"

Asach sighed. Some were harder to fix than others. "OK, kiddo. Have it your way." Asach would have given just about anything for a dose of Collie Orcutt right about then. "When we get back, you can tell it to your uncle." He'd have been a lot more useful. "Come on, then."

For all her shunning words, Laurel fell in step behind Asach. The Warriors looked to the white. Enheduanna barked. They fell into a cordon, fore, aft, and sides, but kept their hands to themselves.

Enheduanna remarked this: *it was no longer clear, which was the owner; which was the cattle.* Enheduanna also remarked: *it knew one word, but when it made that word, it Spoke.* Enheduanna remarked: *Not imitated, Spoke. Nothing else would ever have stopped a Warrior.*

As they neared, the city seemed to swell with a sunny glow. Laurel actually flashed a *look* at Asach, spitting: "You see! The angels have borne us to their city of light!"

It was not walled, precisely, but as the scale became apparent, it was clear that no entrances penetrated the lowest few meters. Instead, the outer surface was a polished green, darkened nearly to black, slick as glass. There were indeed other paths, all spiraling in to intersect at the one major entrance that offered admittance to the mound. Flanking that were two largish cave-like openings, with rows of laterite benches in their forecourts, and white shapes flickering in the rooms within.

There was a fair amount of traffic now, of differing shapes and sizes. There were heavy Porters, carrying enormous baskets filled with dried reed-cakes. There were whispers of light that streaked past them chittering just on the edge of hearing. There were smaller, brown versions of the white who led them. And flanking the forecourts were ranks of Warriors. Laurel gasped as a new shape trundled toward them, dense and peering like an enormous mole.

"There!" she cried, pointing, "There! You see, there's one! There's a True Angel!"

"Please, explain. I don't know what you mean."

"'*And His angels will cover your wastes with manna, making green fields of desert and Heaven of barren worlds.*' We have been waiting, for so many years. We knew, that if we were faithful, and prayed, He'd send His angels to rescue our fields. And there's one."

Asach peered at this new variety of creature. "Your fields?" The marshland extended in all directions as far as the eye could see.

"Yes, our fields. We're only five miles from Butterfield Station."

"But what do you mean? What fields? We're in the middle of a river delta."

Laurel was emphatic. "*No.* I know *exactly* where we are. We're south of the seep at Ocotillo Wells. We're east of Butterfield Station. This was all desert last year."

"Last *year?* Surely you mean last *gathering.*"

"No! Early last year! Well, OK, nearly two years ago, but still! Now do you believe?"

Asach thought: *Well, maybe some massive irrigation project could be done in a year, but…* "But surely this was here." Asach's hands spread to take in the city. The extent of the glass-and-stone construction was massive, and deep. It looked accreted over centuries.

But Laurel was shaking her head. "No, no, *no!* I'm a Seer. It's my *job* to know *every* route into and out of Swenson's Mountain." She stopped abruptly. Flushed. "I mean, His Eye. When the time approaches, I re-ride every route, checking whether His Eye awakes. Last month, I skirted past here, and saw an Angel, and saw that they had come."

Asach groaned. "Just in time for the Revelation."

"Yes!" nodded Laurel emphatically.

Asach began another question, but Enheduanna shouted "Hold!" pulling them up so abruptly that the Warriors behind nearly ran them down. The hissing started again.

Asach shifted focus to the traffic at the tables. Every Porter stopped at one or another of them. Whites came out to inspect every load. Their fingers clacked; they removed part of each; they reached into buckets beside the tables, scooped a gob of something, smacked it onto the container, stamped the gob with a carved stone sigil, and conveyed the reserved goods inside. The operation was efficient. Laurel stared, openly. She'd grown up on New Utah. She'd been to Bonneville. She could count. Simultaneously, she and Asach blurted:

"It's a tithe house!" "It's a customs house!"

Then Enheduanna chirped, and Warriors closed in, and began pulling at their clothes. Laurel screamed. Asach shouted "Hold! Hold!" but this time there was no effect. In a moment of sheer stupidity, facing the looming creature, Asach physically shoved between Laurel and a Warrior, and furiously disrobed. Laurel gasped. Enheduanna barked. The Warriors backed off as Asach let the last article of clothing drop. Then, before the others could react, Asach snatched up the vest, shouting "One!" while holding up one finger, and laid it on the bench. Then the trousers, "Two!" and two fingers. Then the belt, the underwear, the socks, the boots. Finally the cloak. Holding it as a screen, Asach hissed to Laurel: "Strip!" Laurel shook her head emphatically: *no*. Asach hissed again: "Do it! If you don't, they'll do it for you! I won't look! I swear! I'll hold up the cloak!" The Accountant examined the articles of clothing piled upon the table.

Trembling, Laurel peeled, her eyes riveted on her own feet. When she'd done, Asach wrapped the cloak around her, then, facing the accountant, back to Laurel, repeated the counting-clothes performance, standing buck-naked in the sun. The Accountant ceased twisting a boot to watch them. Frantically, Asach scanned the ground; spotted a small, white pebble; shouted "One!" and made a scratch-mark on the counter. "Two!" This time two scratch-marks, and underneath the numeral two. "Three!" And so on, until ten, when Asach circled all that had gone before, made one more mark, then wrote the digits: the one, the zero. The Accountant looked down at the table; up at Asach. Reached forward, seizing Asach's wrist with its gripping hand. Asach did not resist. Pulled Asach's hand forward, palm-to palm with its own. The sizes were not vastly different—save for the Accountant's second opposable thumb, located where Asach had no digits at all. With its second hand, it placed the pebble into Asach's arrested one; guided it to the counter beside the "10." Forced Asach to make two more marks, then let go. Without hesitation, Asach wrote "12," then offered the pebble to the accountant. The Accountant quickly scratched a glyph that looked like—two hands, clasped, edge on. Asach reached for the pebble. The accountant paused, then handed it over. Asach circled the twelve, circled the glyph, then drew a line to the ten and dropped the pebble. Holding up both hands, Asach said: "Base ten!" Reaching forward, cautiously, but firmly, Asach took the Accountant's hands: "Base twelve!" Then pointed to the numerals again: "Ten! Twelve!" and the glyph: "Twelve!"

The Accountant listened carefully. Then, cautiously, made the same hand-gesture, indicating first the numerals. "Ten!" it said. "Twelve!" Then, very slowly, it indicated the glyph, leaning forward toward Asach "*Ten!*"

"Yes!" said Asach, "Ten, *base twelve.*"

Assured, the Accountant moved rapidly, holding forth one of its hands. "Base six," then seizing Asach's two hands, "base ten." It grabbed the pebble, made six chalk marks, then wrote one-zero. "Base six," it said. Then made ten chalk marks; wrote one-zero. "Base ten," it said.

Asach made a huge sigh of relief. "Can we get dressed now?"

The Accountant said to Enheduanna, "You can inform the Protector that this one knows advanced mathematics. I have recorded it as *entire.* The other one—the shrieking one, with manna-colored eyes—I have recorded it as *anathema.* Let me know if that assessment changes. For the record."

Enheduanna swept one arm, indicating *of course.* "Give me a Protector's Runner."

"Supplied."

As the Runner streaked ahead, a path opened for the entourage, now ordered triple-file with Enheduanna at the head, followed by Asach, Laurel, and the senior hand leader, plus ranks of Warriors on either side. The Warriors adopted an odd, half-turned, outward-facing, click-step-click-step-click-step gait with gripping arms extended that Asach presumed was some sort of formal march. It had the effect of making each rank a moving, living barrier fence. Sandwiched as they were inside the formation, it was difficult to see much. Laterite pathways led to gaping openings; pockets of green filled most blank spaces between the lumpy mounds.

Then, at one turning, in a glimpse Asach saw a team of brown workers engaged in creating additional space. The process looked more like a complicated mining operation than home-building. One pair excavated earth. Another packed some kind of powdered coating onto the freshened wall. A third employed a series of mirrors and lenses to vitrify the tunnel mouth. A different team spread the newly-excavated clay as guttered paths, then used reflectors with a rolling, tunnel-like contraption to dry, pre-heat, and bake it to brick in place. Smaller versions of the mole-like one packed earth into baked depressions with narrow drain-grooves adjoining the gutters. The entire operation seemed slow and labor intensive. On the other hand, Asach reflected on the legions of stone cutters, brick-makers, transporters, house-builders, and landscapers that would be required to achieve the same purpose, and concluded that for the scale it was extremely efficiently organized. It also made Laurel's assertions more plausible.

They were shortly to find themselves incarcerated in the end result of such an operation. The room was domed, the ceiling high. Rosy baked-earth steps, hard as concrete, rough-polished like travertine, led them downward into a glassy space, its swirled rainbow-green-black walls slick and hard as tile or thick obsidian. There was no join at the floor: it appeared that it, too, had been vitrified, then overlain with more warm-colored laterite. Windows ringed the uppermost reaches, giving the feeling of a cathedral cupola. The room was chilly. Laurel huddled in the warmth of the sun's rays.

"Honey, I need the cloak for a minute. We may not have much time."

Laurel did not respond.

Asach gently peeled away the garment, warm from its days soaking in the sun, and quickly set up the transmitter. There was no way to know direction, let alone azimuth. There was no external power source. That meant short message, multiple burp, and hope something got through. The line-of-sight angle out of the windows was bad. There was no telling what the glass was made of, or how it would refract the beam. There was nothing to stand on. Asach composed the message. Minimum words, one precedence character, one encryption character, one validation character.

"Laurel, I need you to do something for me."

The girl just sat, immobile, sullen.

"Laurel, *'It is the duty of every island to give aid and support to the Seers, that they may be of aid to all pilgrims.'* Right now, I'm it. I'm your only island. I am trying to help you. I'm trying to help your Uncle Collie. I'm even trying to help Agamemnon."

At that, Laurel began sobbing. Great, racking sobs, like to tear her heart from her chest.

"It's just so hard. So hard. I've lost everyone. And now—oh, poor Agamemnon."

"I'm sure he's fine."

She shook her head. "No. He'll be left, hobbled, for my return. Only...only..."

She was broken in grief.

Asach walked over, physically pulling her to her feet, Laurel a rag doll hanging by her arms.

"Come on then! On your feet, girl! Help me send a message of revelation. And an instruction for Agamemnon." It was a blatant lie, but they were running out of time.

Laurel smeared her eyes on her sleeve and nodded.

"Hold this." Asach handed her the transmitter cowl. Laurel nodded.

"Come here. Climb on my shoulders." Asach squatted down, facing the wall.

"Good, now, on three, I'm going to stand. Then, you stand too. Then I want you to do this: Point the middle of that low out the window, then say *now*. Then point it middling out the window, and say *now* again. Then high. Can you do that?"

Laurel nodded.

"Good. Show me."

Laurel demonstrated. Around the room Asach sidled, three bursts per stopping point, approximately every fifteen degrees. The cloak was depleted. It would need hours to recharge. Asach had just finished packing everything away; re-wrapping the girl with aquamarine eyes, when the door opened. Two Warriors stepped inside. Then, down the steps, with a bearing unmistakable in any species, strode the biggest, whitest Motie that Asach had ever seen. Meaning, bigger than Ivan, the only Master in the newsreels. It entered alone.

Damn, thought Asach. *Where are the Mediators? The newsreels all show Mediators who learn fluent Anglic in no time.* But there was just the big white one.

Blaine Institute, New Caledonia

The Blaine Institute for Advanced Motie Studies had found itself in more-or-less constant uproar during the year since *Sinbad's* explosive return from the Mote System with a

Khanate fleet on its tail. After defeat, the Khanate had thrown their lot in with the Traders, and to ensure that they no longer posed a threat, the genetically modified C-L worm was pumping anti-maturation hormones into the digestive tract of every Khanate member. Whether Bury's will had cemented, or thrown a spanner into, the Motie trading alliance that now policed the blockade still remained to be seen.

But with their lines now doomed, would the Khanate remain true? Unless the Institute could engineer a way to *regulate* the worm: to make it possible for Moties to reproduce at will, instead of at necessity, there seemed little hope that the Mote System could ever be stabilized. With the worm, Moties could live out a natural lifespan—whatever that proved to be—but at the cost of becoming sterile. Without the worm, Moties had to breed or die. Their alternatives were at present stark indeed.

The only beneficiaries were Motie Mediators. Diplomats, linguists, social savants: those brown-and-white crosses between Masters and Engineers were sterile anyway, and as such doomed to radically truncated lives. With the worm, they might gain the advantage of actually living long enough to become elder statesmen. Yet even among Mediators, the assessment was universal: to a Master, the C-L solution was *anathema*.

So, the Blaines' immediate take on Barthes' New Utah business was: theoretically interesting, but not of immediate concern. However much the Founder's-Era frieze might *look* like Moties, it was centuries old, and the accompanying historical report was very clear. It described an *indigenous animal*, not some space-borne infiltrating wave from Mote Prime. Sadly, an apparently *extinct* animal, as well. Had there been an immediate danger to the Empire, given their voracious reproductive rates, Moties would *already* have overrun the planet. Just to clarify this enigmatic message from the past, there was no point in diverting any Naval vessel from the blockades, where there were *definitely* Motie vessels—some days, hundreds of them—attempting to break through to human space.

Of course, any input that might bear on Motie reproductive physiology was important. After the Accession talks, one way or another, they *would* get a copy of all the historical data on Swenson's Apes now "classified" in the True Church archives. Until then, while C-L work continued around the clock, a couple of bright graduate students played with the implications for various models of convergent evolution and *panspermia*.

They tried sending to Barthes, but received no reply, which was unsurprising. So they sent a courier via the next outbound ship, and settled in to wait.

Then Quinn's terse communication arrived, and all Heaven broke loose.

FLASH Renner Eyes Only.
Motie presence confirmed. Communications, translator, critical. Locator on. Contact Barthes. All Due Haste. Quinn.

Lord Blaine himself called the emergency session, pulling in his Motie-raised daughter, every available Mediator, and the linguistic team in charge of the Motie Alexandria Library. They worked late into the night. The questions were simple: Who or what should they send, and how?

"Focus on the who and what," instructed Blaine. "I'll worry about the how."

Renner's head and shoulders, floating holographically at the end of the conference table, were even more succinct.

"Focus on the what," he said. "You work out the details. Meanwhile, I want Ali Baba here, now."

Glenda Ruth opened her mouth to interject. Lord Blaine waved her down. "His ship, his ward."

Ali Baba was impassive. "As you say, Sir Kevin," and rose to prepare for departure. Inwardly, Ali Baba's heart was on fire. Outwardly, he showed only mannered calm. The meeting wore on.

House of Sargon, Mesolimeris

"Enheduanna says that you can Speak. Enheduanna reports that you may be an Accountant." Unfortunately, these words were not spoken in any language that Asach could understand. Sargon regarded the pair without emotion. It was regrettable that the manna-eyed one had been separated from its red, four-legged Porter. But Sargon had given orders that it be brought unharmed, and that was proving to be problematic. The thing fought like a Warrior, ran like a Runner, and had the senses of a Farmer. It had struck out with its forefeet, and a young, inexperienced Warrior had accidentally severed its restraints. Short of killing it, they could not catch it. It had disappeared into the wastes.

Asach was an anthropologist, not a xenobiologist, and certainly not an expert on Moties. But these were clearly social animals, and in all social colonies ever known, only three rules of organization applied: schools, swarms, and hierarchy. Indeed, the closer one looked at the former two, the more they broke down into the latter. These were clearly sentient beings, and apparently hierarchical, so in some fashion status was important. The great unknowns were: how do you get it, and how do you show it? Anything from *give it all away* to *keep it all for yourself*, from *hide it if you've got it* to *if you've got it, flaunt it* applied in human societies.

Go with what you know, thought Asach. "I am Amari Selkirk Alidade Clarke Hathaway Quinn, Second Jackson Commission Representative of the Empire of Man. This is Laurel Courter, Seer and Defender of the Church of Him in New Utah. While we appreciate your escort and hospitality, we must inform you that we require food and water. *Khkhkh! [drip]!*"

Then aside to Laurel, "Tell anyone that and I will kill you and your entire island. I mean it. I won't like it, but I'll do it."

Laurel looked supremely puzzled. "Tell them what? Your name?"

"My position."

Laurel looked confused. "I don't know what all that is. But everyone already knows you're an offworlder."

Asach saw another opportunity, and snapped "Hold!" in perfect Mesolimeran. Thankfully, Laurel fell into silence.

Sargon was impressed. There was no record of *any* human *ever* having learned a *single* word of Mesolimeran. Sargon gestured to someone unseen to comply with the request, then assumed a pose of formal introduction. Mentally, Sargon reviewed a Keeper's tale to find the right verse, and then, with formal gesture, in perfect, MP-accented Middle Anglic, said, "Get the flock outa my fields, fuzzball [rifle report]!"

Well, it's a start, thought Asach.

Laurel fainted.

Odd, thought the Master. *It's from the tale of my line's arrival in Mesolimeris. I thought that was a nice touch.*

The water arrived a few awkward moments later. Sargon considered the options. To know the enemy mind required communication. To know the enemy body required experimentation. The two were not mutually exclusive. The Doctors could wait, Sargon decided. The order was Spoken.

"Send for Lagash." A blur left the room, like a play of light on the edge of perception.

While they waited, Asach attempted to revive Laurel. There were few comfort options, save a splash of water about the face; propping her feet on the lower step—as it happened, at Sargon's feet— for a bit of elevation. With a flourish, Asach re-covered her with the cloak.

Sargon got the message, and barked at Enheduanna, who barked in turn to beings unseen. The room was a flurry of activity shortly thereafter. Several Porters arrived bearing large blocks of baked clay. Another arrived carrying a ceramic container filled with silty mud, accompanied by a mirror-and-lens team. Asach watched, fascinated, as they constructed in short order two contoured benches by laying out blocks, then annealing mud to the top surface. One of the Miners went from Asach, to Laurel, to Asach again, and with a combination of pantomime and manhandling tested the curvature of their spines, hips, and heads.

When complete, one of the Porters scooped Laurel from the ground and deposited her gently on one of the benches. She sank into it as if on a featherbed, her head, shoulders, hips, and knees perfectly cradled. The bench was still warm from the baking process. It radiated heat, and Laurel's shivering finally ended. She dropped immediately into deep, impenetrable sleep.

Asach ran a hand over the second bench, expecting a rough, dusty surface. Instead, it had the silky feel of soapstone, or polished wood: not slick like tile or glass, but warm like burnished pottery. Which was, Asach thought, essentially what it was. However, while Sargon stood, Asach did as well, in a stance of patient waiting, which the others seemed to find inoffensive. The furnishings team departed. The sun moved across the room, its rays warming the couch bases from every direction. Clearly the dome shape; the windows; the couches themselves had been situated to catch the warmth and light. Asach drank. The Moties chittered.

Then, Asach *heard* absolute silence, but *felt* an eldritch noise, like a disturbance in the very bones. Like jump shock, but without the disordered mind. Like grease sliding beneath the skin. Sargon stepped aside, and another framed the doorway. Its hair coat was beyond white— it shimmered platinum, even in the yellow sunlight. It was stooped, and its gripping hand rested heavily on the shoulder of the younger, smaller Enheduanna. The greasy feeling became prickly. Asach resisted the temptation to brush away a thousand centipedes. Laurel groaned and turned on the couch, but did not rise.

The feeling stopped abruptly. It said, "*Halo,*" in a booming voice.

Asach nearly dropped in surprise; recovered; answered. "Hello. I am Asach Quinn. This is Laurel Courter."

The creepy feeling resumed briefly, then faded. "*Halo,*" it said again, "*Mipela nem Tokkipa. Yu nem wanem?*"

Asach felt dizzy. Of all the things on all the worlds possible on that day, hearing an alien being speak Tok Pisin was not among them. Meeting an alien *named* Word-Keeper in Tok Pisin ranked in likelihood right up there with purple cows. But there was nothing for it. Asach took the plunge.

"*Mi nem* Amari Selkirk Alidade Clarke Hathaway Quinn. *Dispela nem* Laurel Courter."

The creepy feeling began again.

Had Asach benefited from Colchis Barthes' find in Saint George, an ancient creature's command of the language of servants and field hands would have been a good deal less mystifying. But operating while mystified was Quinn's element, and Asach forged ahead, thankful for this Rosetta Stone even if its origins were at best incomprehensible, and at worst profoundly terrifying.

Asach was as aware as anyone of the perils to humanity attendant on a Motie breech of either of the two blockades at Alderson points entering human space. The first and oldest, called the Crazy Eddie Point, was held by the Navy. A shift in that point the previous year had nearly allowed the fractured remains of a dozen warring Motie factions to burst through from the environs of Mote Prime. Holding it consumed most of the Navy's resources—and placed a tremendous burden on Imperial taxpayers. That much was general knowledge.

The second jump point, called The Sister, was policed by an alliance of Motie traders. That alliance was cemented by their collective interest in the profits to be made through technology transfer from the Mote System to the Empire. Were the Navy's incapacity to hold two simultaneous blockades insufficient incentive to maintain this shaky endeavor, Bury's Imperial Autonetics legacy gave at least some humans additional venal motives for trans-species cooperation. The Sister too was under constant assault from shifting factions of the many enemies of their Motie allies.

The intrigue surrounding The Sister was *not* general knowledge—at least not yet. The Empire had spent the better part of three decades convincing a public scattered among a hundred worlds that humankind's very survival depended upon keeping all Moties out of human space. The message that survival now depended on Moties policing themselves was proving difficult to spin. Regarding the Motie inheritance angle, the terms of Bury's will were private. They were known only to Bury's immediate family, those who had been present at the reading (including Renner and the Blaines), and an inner circle at Imperial Autonetics. The fact that Moties now held a forty-plus-percent stake in the Empire's largest and most powerful industrial giant was not a statistic the Board wished widely known. Asach had not exactly been in touch with the latest news, let alone at the center of Imperial policy-making, during that sabbatical on Makassar.

So, in Asach's mind, the *only* way that Moties could be present on New Utah was if one of the blockades had been broken. But, if that were so, where was the Motie technology? Where was the spaceport? Where were the Engineers and their Watchmaker helpers? Where were the sterile Mediators—the only caste allowed into human space? Was this—a worst-case-scenario—a new Motie farming colony? If so, the Empire's worst fears had already been realized. The phenomenal Motie reproductive rate would soon overwhelm New Utah. *How could this have happened without Imperial knowledge?*

Powers of detachment served well, as several days of intensive language acquisition wore on with questions burning in the back of Asach's mind. The old Master held the rank of Keeper-of-Words, charged with maintaining the legends associated with Sargon's line. Lagash sifted these for human phrases. Most of these were in Middle Anglic. Asach painstakingly built a vocabulary from Tok Pisin to Anglic. They worked through numbers, nouns, actions. They called in other Masters, including the customs Accountant. They called in Doctors. They called in Miners. The young Master kept records, and had a phenomenal memory. Eventually, they exhausted the confines of the room, and Asach was allowed outside. They called in Farmers. They learned enough to carry on crude conversations. Laurel sat in stunned silence on the sidelines. Asach tried to draw her out, but received in answer only stoic tears.

Asach requested food.

"I will ask the Lord," said Enheduanna.

Dizzy with hunger, Asach managed to send another round of bursts that night. Laurel moved like an automaton, muttering prayer.

"Wait!" called Asach, as a pinhead-sized light fluttered. "Hold it there!" This time, there was a reply:

> FLASH Quinn Eyes Only.
>
> Read attached Barthes report. Are 'Swenson's Apes' Moties? Is Motie presence: New? Expanding? Threat? Re: pre-Accession rules—prime directive applies, plausible deniability authorized. Possible translation keys attached. Advise efficacy. Barthes unblocked. Will provide him full Library data. Comms relay authorized as needed. Standing by for jump. All Due Haste. Renner.

Next came a copy of Barthes' message with the Swenson's Ape report, and a stream of sound files. Telemetry followed, with transmission windows and azimuths to the satellite.

Asach swore as the last of the cloak's stored energy drained, and pondered the options. The bottom line was: *Do what you can, and do what you have to, to protect the Empire. Screw pre-Accession rules if you must. Use Barthes if you can. You're on you own until we get there. Oh yeah,* thought Asach, *screw it up, and we'll swear we never knew you.* Well, that was just about right. At the moment, resources included a nineteen-year-old suffering a crisis of faith, a librarian half-way across the continent, some files that would remain unreadable until daylight, and not even a pot to pee in.

'Let's get some sleep," said Asach. "Big day tomorrow."

At least this time Laurel nodded.

Blaine Institute, New Caledonia

Another team was pulling an all-nighter. They were working and reworking numbers from the nearly five-hundred-year-old Naval Initial Assessment Report, because that's all they had to go on.

"But sir, *there's nothing there!*"

"Look again."

The Lieutenant was adamant. "It was just a standard Naval Level-1 prospecting survey. No orbital industry, no significant orbital ores, no radiation of any kind, no industry reported. Except at the known urban centers—Bonneville and Saint George. And the few known mining camps."

"Determined how?"

"Standard auto-classification array. Two full passes, one-hundred-percent coverage, data dumped for software recognition and mapping of vegetative cover, hydrology, man-made features, and specified geology."

"Well, run it against the new Motie data."

"Sir, I did. Nothing. There's just no signature indicating pre- or post-industrial development whatsoever, except for the known colonies. Hell, their *atmosphere* is even clean. They just plain skipped hydrocarbons. At least as fuel. If there are any. The survey identified no seeps, and they never developed any petrochemical industry. They went direct to solar at founding."

"Then do it the old fashioned way. Put human eyes on it, *and look at the ground.*"

"That's a lot of ground sir. It could take—"

"Start with these coordinates." The team leader passed them over. Neither knew where they'd come from. Renner knew. Lord Blaine knew. They were the last transmitted location from Asach's tracking collar. At close range, the cloak knew where the chip was. The satellite knew where the cloak was. As long as Quinn and the cloak stayed in close proximity, whenever the cloak talked to the satellite, Renner knew where Asach was.

"Pull it up."

The lieutenant waved hands about, and New Utah appeared on-screen in a three-dimensional swirl, already rotating and zooming down so fast that contours of weather systems; continents; oceans; poles; were gone before they'd even registered. The pale blue pinprick with a surrounding scatter of pink and red fields that was the fledgling Bonneville swept past in a wink. Then they swooped over the flat, white panne of The Barrens, followed by a spooky disjoint of seeming to fly *through* a mountain ridge, then bursting forth over a brilliant field, now emerald; now aquamarine in the shifting light.

"Pull back, then stop."

Even for a jaded pair of terrain analysts, the view of the brilliant river delta, slashed between ranges of scrubby mountains, was breath taking.

"Zoom in again."

But there was nothing there, save scattered earthen mounds dotting the lustrous fields.

"Can you pull in closer?"

The lieutenant shook her head. "That's it, sir. Ten meter's the limit on a Level 1 Survey."

Meaning that anything smaller than ten meters wide didn't even appear. The major nodded. "What's the vegetation?"

"Best guess is some kind of cyanobacteria. We'd need a full assay to be sure."

The major nodded again. *Everybody* knew what that was, and it was no surprise on a world with a native oxygen atmosphere. Without blue-green "algae"—really a photosynthetic bacteria—there wouldn't *be* an oxygen atmosphere. It was a primary adjunct to all terraform maintenance. The stuff grew everywhere: fresh water, salt water, inside rocks, hell, even in the coats of some animals. It formed globules, mats, filaments; partnered up with funguses to make lichens and rhizome mats; survived under ice caps, so long as light could get to it. Finding a form that grew in grass-like-stands in a river delta on a planet subject to climate extremes did not require a huge leap of evolutionary imagination.

"Do we have *anything* else for this area? *Any* comparator?"

"No sir. That was the only survey. It looks like Maxroy's Purchase only surveyed as far as their base colonies."

The major nodded again. Survey was expensive. A full planetary survey was probably well outside the budget of a religious order.

"What about the first Jackson expedition?"

"That was a just a delegation shuttle, sir. No survey mission."

The major nodded. "Right." She got up to leave, then thought again. "What ship?"

"Sir?"

"What was the shuttle vessel?"

The lieutenant consulted records briefly. "Oh." Looked again. "Private registry, sir. Imperial Autonetics. *Nauvoo Vision.*"

The major smiled at this. "Ah." Smiled again. "And by any chance, lieutenant, has *Nauvoo Vision* filed a survey record?"

"Like I say, sir, private vessel and—oh." The lieutenant tapped some more. "That's odd." More tapping. "It looks like—somebody—posted *restricted* files—sir that's not a Naval cipher."

"Uh huh. Filed when?"

"That's what's odd. They weren't filed with the original commission report. They came directly from—um—" The lieutenant had the very chilling sense that this was *not* something it would be good to know.

"Captain Renner?"

"Yes sir. Yesterday. I'm not on original distribution, so I didn't see them. They're IA proprietary." The lieutenant looked nervous.

"Relax, L-T. Bury leant the ship to the Jackson Delegation back in the day. You can't blame Imperial Autonetics for sneaking in a bit of survey on the side. Looks like Renner dug it up for us. Open sesame," said the major, punching an access code.

The fly-down played again. This one was more limited. It covered only the track from orbital entry to the parking spot at a geosynchronous station above Saint George. But that was all they needed. They ran the pass in reverse. During the intervening half-millennium between the reports, mountains had spilled their guts onto the plains below. Bonneville had grown from pinprick to splodge, rail lines and a highway now connecting it to Saint George. The brilliant flash of the DAZ-E field, the flat, fenced expanses of the Hopper strips and Lynx port, and the endless rows of associated warehouses were now clearly visible. The flat, white panne of The Barrens was now punctuated by scratches of roads and tracks; crossroads and pumping stations; emerald wheels of circle irrigation. An airstrip made a creamy, scrub-bounded cross against the white glare. This time they brushed the range top, then bursting forth over—a vast expanse of gridded, lifeless grey, featureless beneath the imager's lens. A rectangular black slash of water marked where the once-meandering delta's estuaries had been.

"See?" said the lieutenant. "Nothing there. Fits in with that Swenson's report about what happened around Saint George. At some point, they went in, cut drains through the marshes, laser-leveled the fields, and brought in heavy cultivators. Didn't last, though, and once it wore out, they abandoned it. Pity. They turned really productive wetland into salt desert, for the sake of a few decades of crops, at best."

The major nodded, and rose to leave. "Ok. Get some sleep, but keep looking for *anything* important. I'd ask better questions, but I can't think of any yet. See what you can come up with."

12
Paternity Suit

Enki answered Ninmah: "I will counterbalance whatever fate—good or bad—you happen to decide."

Ninmah took clay from the top of the sacred water in her hand and she fashioned from it first a man who could not bend his outstretched weak hands. Enki looked at the man who cannot bend his outstretched weak hands, and decreed his fate: he appointed him as a servant of the king.

Second, she fashioned one who turned back the light, a man with constantly opened eyes. Enki looked at the man who turned back the light, the man with constantly opened eyes, and decreed his fate: he appointed him as a servant of the king.

Third, she fashioned one with both feet broken, one with paralysed feet. Enki looked at the one with both feet broken, the one with paralysed feet and decreed his fate: he appointed him as a servant of the king.

Fourth, she fashioned one who could not hold back his urine. Enki looked at the one who could not hold back his urine and bathed him in enchanted water and drove out the namtar demon from his body.

Fifth, she fashioned a woman who could not give birth. Enki looked at the woman who could not give birth, and decreed her fate: he made her a weaver, fashioned her to belong to the queen's household.

Sixth, she fashioned one with neither penis nor vagina on its body. Enki looked at the one with neither penis nor vagina on its body and gave it the name eunuch and decreed as its fate to stand before the king.

—*Enki and Ninmah, The Electronic Text Corpus of Sumerian Literature*

PATERNITY SUIT

House of Sargon, Mesolimeris

Moties weren't given to emotional displays—at least, not to displays that humans could easily interpret—but Lagash's reaction to being greeted in a stream of archaic languages was unmistakable. The old Keeper visibly wobbled on Enheduanna's arm, and the bone-wrenching feeling that Asach was beginning to recognize as sub-audible communication between Masters ensued.

Before they could react, in the mish-mosh of languages they thus far shared, Asach said: "I talk Anglic. You hear many words. You stop you hear words you understand," then punched on the auto-translator, now beefed up with fifteen languages judged by the Blaine experts as the widest-possible cross section in time and space known from the Motie Library of Alexandria.

"Good Morning." Fifteen possible variations screeched and twittered from the cowl of Asach's cloak.

"My name is Asach. You know this already." Trilling and rumbling ensued as the cloak sent the translations.

"Do you understand any of this?" Zipping and—then Lagash shouted the word that even Laurel could understand.

"Hold! What is that?"

Asach glanced at a sleeve, noted the indicator, and set it as the default translator.

"I have made lists of words. Do you understand?"

The Masters heard in their own language something akin to: *I awrát weaxbredu tala ealdspræca. ðu ackneaow?* That is, it was about as close to Mesolimeran as Old English was to Modern Anglic. It meant nothing to Enheduanna. But to Lagash, it was very like the language of the oldest form of the oldest myth known.

"Listen," said Asach, "then repeat in your own language." Asach activated an auto-learn program. It was crude, but it rapidly built a syntax and lexicon by comparing the projected phrase to the one spoken back.

Lagash was fascinated. It appeared that overnight Asach had acquired the ability to speak by projecting words directly from the chest and throat, without involvement of the mouth or lips. The interactive program itself was also interesting. Motie-designed, it was succinct. It did not suffer from the agonizing slowness of working directly with the human. Within an hour, it was as smart in Mesolimeran as a bright child. And it already knew Anglic. Enheduanna joined in. Machine-assisted, their mutual patois came faster and faster now.

"We must have food now. We must have cleanliness. We must have these feces and urine removed. We will sicken and die. We already feel ill from hunger."

"The Protector grants meals. It is not in our power."

"Please inform the Protector that we request an audience."

"The Protector is aware of your request."

Asach was finally irate. *"Inform the Protector now!"* Interestingly, what boomed from the cloak was not merely a translation. There came a greasy undertow to the air: transmissions in the sub-audible. Enheduanna flinched. Lagash answered.

"Yes, milord. We inform the Protector now."

Bowls of dark green jelly arrived within the hour. It looked like slime. It tasted like manna. Next came a cleanup crew, and chamber pots. Next returned Lagash and Enheduanna.

Then the real work began. Five thousand word groups are enough to communicate like a five-year-old child. Ten thousand enough to make your way about as an adult in a foreign land. Twenty thousand enough to speak with the expertise gained by a university education. The simplest Mesolimeran myth contained thirty thousand word groups, with tenses and cases unknown in any human language. The Masters worked until they had exhausted the downloaded vocabulary. Then they all worked until they had exhausted their shared Tok Pisin and Anglic. At the end of the day, Asach's headache was blinding. Enheduanna seemed unfazed. The working group had bonded. They could communicate with relative ease. Simple questions followed.

"Where are we?"

"At the House of [*idiomatic translation of a proper name for a powerful and fertile leader with jurisdiction over former wastelands, descended from wanderers=Sargon*], [*idiomatic translation for a formal rendering of the proper name for the-land-between-the-mountains =Mesolimeris*]."

"Why are you holding us?"

"At the order of Lord Sargon."

"For how long?"

Lagash answered. "Tomorrow, Lord Protector Sargon will begin the interrogation. Then the Excellency will decide."

Then, thankfully, they departed. Asach beamed everything to Renner and Barthes, with a simple request: "Send More. Find us."

Asach awoke before dawn, surprised to discover the cape draped at the foot of the stone chaise, and Laurel bustling about the room. How it was possible to bustle in an unfurnished space containing nothing save two couches, two chamber pots, and a washbasin was unclear, but that's what it felt like. Laurel's outer garments were neatly folded; she was vigorously splashing and rubbing and running fingers through her hair. Asach observed this though half-closed eyes, then pointedly yawned and stood, facing the opposite direction, fumbling about in the cape.

"Here." Asach proffered a comb, and a sliver of soap, one arm stretched rearward.

"You have *soap?*"

Asach shrugged. "I travel light, but carry the essentials."

"Essentials?"

"You'd be surprised how many diseases are prevented by judicious hand-washing."

"You can turn around, you know."

"But I thought—"

"I just didn't want to reveal myself to *them*. People are all right."

"So you're not shy? Embarrassed?"

Laurel snorted. "After twenty years of *camp* life? Please."

Asach sat on the chaise while Laurel lathered. "You seem to be feeling better today."

Laurel nodded.

"Welcome back."

Laurel paused, mid-froth. "Back?"

"You've been sort of on auto-pilot."

Another scrub; a rinse, her answer bubbling through the water. "Auto-pilot?"

"You know, like—oh, never mind."

There was nothing to dry with. Casting about, Laurel settled for the back of her tunic. "I just had a lot on my mind."

"I'd say."

"But now, I've been fed manna by the hands of Angels. Just like the prophesy. So I feel fine."

Asach groaned inwardly.

"Manna?"

"Yes."

"That green slime?"

"Yes." Interestingly, her manner was not at all defensive.

"Is that what you call it?"

"That's what it *is.*"

"I see. Where does it come from?"

Laurel looked at Asach with that aura of incredulity reserved on any world for a rural denizen comprehending the utter stupidity of an urban gobshite. In most cases, this had the odd effect of making the rube look stupid in the city slicker's eyes. Asach was, however, better attuned to the reality.

"Humor me."

"Well, what do you think we've been walking through for—however long it's been."

"Grass of some kind?"

Laurel snorted. "*Grass?* Grass won't grow here. Uncle Collie went broke trying."

"So manna is—?

"Manna. It is what it is. The angels grow it. We cut it for hay when we can, but they don't like that."

Asach's head reeled. Then the introduction to the Swenson's Ape report swam into focus. Then the lower-case tone of *angels* registered.

"And where do—angels—come from?"

Laurel gave the I-can't-believe-a-grown-person-is-this-ignorant look again, then shrugged. "This is the first time they've come back to the Outback in my lifetime. I guess from the Way Outback, but I don't know."

"The Way Outback."

Laurel smiled. "Well, this all used to be the Outback, but after the rigs moved in, we had to call everything the other side of those mountains something."

"The rigs."

Laurel nodded. "The sand miners. Upriver. They are totally poaching, but there's not much we can do about it."

Asach was getting more than a little confused about this chain of revelations, and decided to return to first principles.

"OK, so, the angels come from—further east, beyond those mountains, and when they come, they grow manna. Is that about right?"

She nodded. "Or south. From downriver. They didn't manage to drain it all. There might have been some left along the coast."

"Some of what? Angels? Manna?"

Exasperated, Laurel sighed. "Both, of course. You don't get one without the other."

Asach pondered this for a moment. "And, how long, would you say, the angels have been here?"

"Here? Like I said. A year—two, tops."

"No, I mean on New Utah."

"On Heaven? Oh, forever, I guess. Before the Founders."

Asach had a spinning sensation in the pit of the stomach. "Before the Founders? How would you know that? How would anyone know that?"

"Well, I just know they were here when he got here. That's what kept him alive?"

Asach was confused by the religious possibilities of this statement. "He? Do you mean he, or do you mean Him?"

Laurel rolled her eyes. "Well, of course He has been here, for all of eternity. But I meant him."

This did not help. Asach plunged forward. "Him who? Which him?"

"Swenson. John David Swenson. Swenson's Valley, where we are now. Swenson's Mountain. Where you saw His Eye."

Swenson's Apes, thought Asach. "But *before the Founders? How?*"

Laurel was dressing now. "Well, duh. He was the *surveyor*. Came out with Murchison in 2450. I mean, how do you think

Founders got here—threw a rock and got lucky? Swenson was the First Colony's *guide*."

"But I thought he was some kind of local suttler. Provisioning settlers; surveying new claims, making records of local fauna along the frontier…" Asach trailed off, as Laurel rolled her eyes again.

"Uh huh. It's not like he came once and just *died*."

Asach was dumbfounded. Days of work, and most of the answers had been sitting right here all along. *Stupid*, to underestimate the literalness and pragmatism of these people. Find a planet where you can escape open persecution? It's Heaven. A rock looks like an eye and shoots radiant beams of light into the sky? It's God's Eye. Animals arrive and grow food in deserts where nothing can survive? They're angels growing manna. No further supernatural explanation required.

"Why didn't you say? Why haven't you told me any of this before?'

Laurel shrugged again. "You didn't ask me. And you made fun of me when I tried."

Asach sighed. It was easy to forget how intimidating even the smallest offhand remark made—or not made—by the middle aged could be to one so young.

"Well, thank-you. For telling me now. I apologize. Please believe me. I never intended to make fun of anyone. I'm sorry for it. I actually hold you in very high regard. You are extremely capable, and you have not had an easy life."

Laurel nodded once, and handed back the soap and comb in silence.

"So, how *do* you know all this?"

"Swenson? Everybody knows that. Well, everybody in Bonneville. I couldn't say for Saint George. And anyway, he was my Great-Something-Great Grandfather. On my mother's side. Technically, I still own all of this. All of it. Land, water, timber, fish, game, mineral, and near-space rights. Not that any of that gets recognized. Or that I'd do anything much with it if they did."

Asach nearly choked. On any *Imperial* world, that big a holding meant—well, a lot. Probably a title. The questions were piling on. "But you're a Himmist?"

Laurel looked genuinely puzzled. "Yes?"

"And so was your mother."

"Oh, yes, definitely."

"But Swenson—"

Laurel laughed. "What, you think no Himmist every married a Sixer? In *Bonneville?* You think that, you don't know much about people, what?"

Asach remembered the ecumenical microcosm that was Michael's household and smiled.

"Religion's in your heart and mind, not in your *genes*. Otherwise, why'd a Sixer like you be here as a pilgrim?"

Asach paused. "That's a big assumption. Is it that obvious?"

Laurel smiled. "Just a guess. It's nothing you've said. But you have a way about you. The way you react to what others say sometimes. The way you put questions. Anyway, I know now."

Asach nodded. "Fair enough. Why isn't your claim respected?"

Laurel slumped to the couch, downcast again. "When the True Church came from Maxroy's Purchase, early on they claimed jurisdiction over land rights administration. The first thing they did was disallow *all* prior claims, pending 'review of standing.' That didn't mean much for a very long time, because for all their bold claims, they were only a tiny outpost colony, and Sixers still held the majority. It got worse when the True Church took over on Maxroy's Purchase, because then they claimed control of the New Utah tithe to MP. Even so, there was nobody much out here. But when the TCM started enforcing tithe collection," Laurel shrugged, "that's when it got really bad. If I claim my rights, they'll claim back tithe. Then they'll own it all. That's how they bankrupted Uncle Collie. "

"But if you could enforce your claim?"

"I wouldn't. Well, I would—enforce the rights—but I wouldn't farm."

"Why?

"Because that's what Great-Whatever-Grandpa wanted. It's written in his old Book. He said they'd made a big mistake trying to farm this. He said that if we just left it alone, the angels would return." She looked up beseechingly at Asach. "And he was right. They did. Just like he said."

Asach nodded firmly. "Absolutely. Angels and manna."

Mind reeling, Asach headed to the washbasin, but was spared disrobing decisions by Sargon's arrival.

Once again, the Master filled the doorway. "I am informed that you are most certainly a Master."

Dumbfounded, Asach dropped the soap but did not reply.

"Explain to me," boomed Sargon's voice, "the meaning of 'Second Jackson Commission Representative of the Empire of Man.'"

Calmly, carefully, Asach crossed to the couch and donned the cloak; switched on the translator. "Excuse me, your Excellency. Could you please say that again?"

"Perhaps I was unclear? I was correctly speaking Anglic, yes?"

Asach bowed. "Certainly, your Excellency."

"In that case, *explain*. Also explain the meaning of 'Seer and Defender of the Church of Him in New Utah.'"

Against all reason, Asach felt compelled to comply. It was, after all, *their* planet. But Laurel leapt into the breech before Asach could work through what that meant in terms of non-interference.

"I am a Keeper of the Eye on Swenson's Mountain that heralds your return."

Sargon turned slowly from the waist. "Swenson?"

"Yes."

"Eye?"

"His Eye, on the mountain."

Sargon turned back to Asach, without comment.

Asach sought to clarify the untranslatable. "The light. The green light that shines every twenty-one years, from the top of the mountain. Where your Warriors, uh, *found* us."

Behind Sargon, hissing erupted out of sight down the corridor.

Sargon's voice was level, in a chanting pitch that combined a benediction with machine translation. "Ah. The light. On Beacon Hill. How amusing. It does not beckon *our* return. It beckons Swenson's."

"Swenson's?"

"Swenson befriended our lines. Swenson was an *ally* against the *vermin.*" At this, Sargon descended the steps with two strides, jerked Laurel close with the gripping hand, pulled her head forward, and stared directly into her startlingly aquamarine eyes. "And you, *vermin*, claim to be of *Swenson?*"

Asach froze, startled by Sargon's sudden fury; afraid to move; afraid not to, expecting Laurel to dissolve into depression. Surprisingly, she did not. "Yes," she said firmly, "I am. The Defenders kept the mountain and this valley free of settlement. He said 'keep this covenant, and you will be fed manna at the hands of angels.' So we did. And you've come back, and today you fed me manna. As Seer, it is my duty to proclaim your return, and beg sustenance for the faithful."

Sargon released her. She did not move. Now it was Laurel who stared into Sargon's inscrutable eyes. Sargon's third eyelid closed; opened. "You lie. Even now, your *vermin* destroy my *ar.*"

"*Ar?*" queried Asach, hoping to break the tension.

The cloak answered. *Ar. Noun, all-gender. Productivity, fertility, capacity, capability, duty, responsibility, land, land-value, allotment, profit, rate of production, production value, production unit, amount of produce, unit of land measurement approximately equivalent to*—

"Stop!"

Sargon swiveled to ponder this odd Master that stood conversing with itself. Asach spluttered for words, but once again Laurel was the faster.

"No!" she shouted, shaking her head emphatically. "Not us! You mean the sand miners, right? The poachers? The sand miners operating out of Watson Station?"

Sargon snapped back before she'd even finished, in the same disgusted tone used to say *vermin.* "Miners! No! No *Miner* would behave so! They waste labor! They use huge constructions to gouge out pits bigger than a hundred Houses! They fill the air with vile smoke and flood the valley with poisoned water! They are *vermin! They destroy the ar.* It costs me a bloody *fortune* to restore it! At least three additional Miners and a dedicated Farmer.*"

Rather than showing any upset at this reply, Laurel was nodding agreement. "That's them. They came in after the First Jackson delegation—" she looked daggers at Asach— "and drove us out. I had to reroute the Gathering to work around them. That's when I ran into your—Farmer?"

Well, thought Asach. *There's my job simplified. Let's just let all the locals go sort this out among themselves, shall we?* Asach interrupted before Sargon could reply. "Perhaps, Your Excellency, I should explain about the Jackson commission?"

"By all means," responded Sargon dryly.

"Before I began, milord, might I ask you a question?. You mentioned a beacon? To recall Swenson?"

"Yes," said Sargon. "Swenson's line."

"And where is it that—Swenson's line—are to return from?"

Sargon spread all three arms wide, in a stance that even the humans could read as incredulous. "Well, like you, of course. From the stars."

"Ah," said Asach, head pounding. Clearly, the first commission should have gotten out more. "Then perhaps I *should* explain about the Empire of Man."

"Yes," said Sargon, with growing impatience. "John David Swenson, of the Empire of Man. He pledged that, one day, his allies would follow."

Ah, thought Asach, *and, against all probability, here we are. Well, now I'm violating nothing by telling them we exist. Always a treat when colonials make promises on behalf of Empire.* "Jackson is the name of the Governor of Swenson's home world now. The Jackson Commission will arrive soon to offer New Utah membership in the Empire. If New Utah decides to join, the Commission will decide its status. My duty is to make preparations for the Commission's arrival."

Sargon grasped immediately many possible implications of that statement. "Offer? Offer to whom?"

"The planetary government."

"Explain *government.*"

"Legitimate authority."

"Legitimate how? Authority for what?"

And there's the rub, thought Asach, *because legally I can't tell them what the classification standards are, lest they change to meet them.* Asach found a neutral reply. "To make agreements. To decide. To keep the peace."

"The Meeting decides. The Masters police their Houses."

Asach did not respond.

"The Protector, the Masters of the six cities, with their Accountants and advisors. Keepers and Defenders of *ar.*"

Still, Asach made no reply. Sargon resumed the offensive.

"What *status*. What *preparations*?"

"Regarding status, that is not for me to say. I serve only as advisor. Regarding preparations, I arrange—things—for the Commissioners."

They were interrupted, as Laurel balled a fist, pounding her own thigh in fury as angry tears welled I her eyes. "It won't matter. It doesn't matter. They won't *come* out here. They won't *listen* to us. Not *any* of us. The True Church controls the TCM, and the TCM controls the tithe. It will be like last time. The Commission'll go to Saint George and do whatever the True Church says."

Sargon was exasperated. Why did this *anathema* even dare to speak? It—*she*—claimed to be of Swenson's line. If so, that line was clearly at an end. Sargon pointed to Asach. "*You* evade." Then to Laurel. "*You* lie. You are *anathema*. You are incomplete. You carry no lines." Then back to Asach. "*Things. Preparations.* Your words mean nothing. *Why* are you here? Tell me now: *why! You* are a Master. *You* are entire. Do *you* bring Swenson's lines?" Sargon's voice was not actually louder, but Asach's intestines began to writhe. It felt like being microwaved: from the inside out.

Groggily, Asach remembered details from Swenson's report on reproductive physiology. It dawned that, quite probably, Sargon meant something very specific, and important, by *lines,* and *entire.* That perhaps the Accountant had reported rather a lot of detail from their initial disrobing at the customs house. This might prove tricky. But just possible…

"Laurel?"

She looked up with haunted, angry, eyes.

"What do Himmists know about Angels?

For an instant, she was shaken from anger to exasperation by this *non sequitor*. "What I've told you. They raise manna. They—"

"No, I don't mean that. I mean, what are they *like?* How are they *made?*"

"Made?"

"Are they *made* in His image?"

She snorted. "Well, *obviously*, no."

"How not?"

She rolled her eyes. But she did not speak of superficial things like one ear and three arms. "Surely, even *you* know that. Humans are made in His image."

"Meaning?"

"Meaning '*male and female He made them.*' Angels aren't. They're—different. They're neither man nor woman."

"You mean neuter. Sexless."

"Oh, for His sake! Can you *really* be this thick? That's the point. Angels are perfect in His gaze. They're complete. They're—" and suddenly Laurel's eyes went wide. She looked at Asach with growing horror—"*entire.*" She backed away, then sat abruptly as her exit was cut off by the sleeping couch. "What *are* you?"

But Asach deflected the question, instead answering directly to Sargon.

"I think, Laurel, that it might be useful if you explained to *Archangel* Sargon something about your *lines.* Beginning with your *parents.* Your *mother* and your *father.* I think that might help The Excellency to understand why you claim to be *allies.* And I advise, Your Excellency, that among humans, *she* is very far indeed from being counted as *anathema.*"

But Sargon was finished, and with an exasperated wave, departed. "Enough. Explain this rubbish to Enheduanna." Then, in a rumble that rolled down the corridor, "Summon the Doctors. *I would know my enemy.*"

I am not, thought Asach, *going to enjoy this physical exam.*
Enheduanna waited, interested but passive.

"Laurel, unless you want to disrobe for what passes as the medical establishment here, I'd start talking. Now."

They talked for hours. Enheduanna, by now aware of the humans oddly insatiable need for daily sustenance, ordered more green goo and water. As Laurel worked her way through generations of begats, Enheduanna asked the same questions over and over. "And...*he* was? And...*she* was?" At first the hes and shes were hopelessly confused, but as forenames repeated and the pattern became clear, Enheduanna's pronouns became unerringly accurate.

"So, your—people—*always* have two parents?"

Laurel gave the are-you-too-stupid-to-breathe- look, but simply nodded. "Yes."

"And without two parents, all get are—*impossible?*"

She nodded again.

"And one parent is always—*male*, while the other is always—*female?*"

"Yes, of course," she nodded. "That's true for everybody. Humans are all made male and female."

Enheduanna swiveled to face Asach, who remained impassive. "I would like this to be recorded by the Doctors."

Laurel writhed with discomfort. "I don't want—"

"Of course," said Asach. "Me first." Staring intently into Enheduanna's eyes. "Then Laurel. You'll find *her* to be a *perfectly* normal *female.*"

Enheduanna gestured and made purring sounds. Laurel shrank back, but the Doctors—long fingered, hare-lipped, lips pulled back slightly to expose olfactory pores on the roofs of their mouths—first walked directly to the corner, to examine the contents of the chamber pots. They sniffed deeply; rotated them;

peered into their depths; exchanged them. Involuntarily, Laurel made an I-can't-believe-how-disgusting-they-are curl of her nose and one eye.

Satisfied with the pots, the Doctors next approached Asach, and sniffed carefully, head to toe. They paused and sniffed as Asach inhaled and exhaled. One steadied Asach's back lightly with the gripping hand, placed its twelve spidery fingers carefully over Asach's abdomen and torso, and made a continuous, barely audible humming noise. The other bent at the waist and circled Asach, its ear held close. The humming stopped abruptly; the Doctors chattered a moment in a high-pitched burring; the first one rearranged its fingers, and then began again. They repeated this exercise a dozen times, until the finger placement had covered one hundred forty-four points. None of it was particularly uncomfortable. Asach was too tense to be ticklish, but twitched involuntarily as the probing fingers crept down the abdomen, eventually landing to ring the lower edge of the pelvic girdle.

Then they traded places. This time, the examination appeared to be muscular, skeletal, and circulatory. While one hummed, the other felt for, and found, multiple pulse-points: throat, armpits, elbows, wrists, ankles, knees, inner thighs, groin. On the way, it probed major muscle attachments, manipulated all of Asach's joints, carefully examined the structures of the hand, and curled and uncurled Asach's spine with as much evident interest as the Miners had shown.

Other than removal of boots for a foot examination, to everyone's relief at no point did they require Asach to disrobe. Then they turned to Laurel. She blushed. The Doctors noted this immediately, with some excitement. Enheduanna translated, indicating Laurel's face. "Is this normal? This change in skin color?"

Asach smiled. "Yes. It is an involuntary response. It is triggered by many things: fear, anxiety, anger, excitement."

The Doctors sniffed especially carefully at Laurel's breath; immediately felt for pulse points; chattered between themselves, then continued the systematic examination as they had done for Asach. When they got to the lower abdomen, they stopped, puzzled. They traded places, and repeated the exercise. They purred at Enheduanna, who translated.

"The Doctors have questions."

"Yes?"

"You both have—"

Asach interrupted before Enheduanna could finish the sentence. "I am assuming that your Doctors can *see*—can form mental pictures, based on the sounds they make—inside our bodies?"

Enheduanna chattered something to a Doctor, who replied. "Yes, after a fashion."

"And *smell* very precisely? Smell the—chemical compounds—that make up our bodies, and that we excrete?"

"Yes."

"Then tell them that Laurel is a *complete* and *typical* human *female,* with *usual levels* of female sex-determining and reproductive hormones." *I hope that's true* Asach thought, gesturing in the direction of Laurel's chamber-pot. "Including a normal *womb,*" Asach placed both hands over the lower abdomen, roughly wherein the uterus would lie, "where *female* eggs are fertilized by *male* sperm, and the zygote grows until it passes out of the *female* body via the birth canal."

Enheduanna conveyed this information, and received more emphatic purring in reply.

"Yes, that is their question. It seems that—"

Asach interrupted again. "A *typical, complete* male does not have these organs. The male usually has only two testes that produce sperm, which are ejected from the organ that houses the urine tract. A typical male has very low levels of the same hormones, but very *high* levels of *male* hormones."

Enheduanna conveyed this to the Doctors, who answered only briefly this time.

"And other configurations are—"

"Are *normal*, but not *usual*. They are more common in some populations than others. Some are reproductively viable, some are not. Whether they are considered to be *acceptable* varies by culture. In many, they are seen as what you would call *anathema*."

Enheduanna considered this. "How very odd."

But Asach's dodges were insufficient. Laurel had grasped the undertones of this medicalized conversation. This time, her response was more angry than frightened. "What *are* you?" she snapped, marching toward Asach. "Are you a *man*, or a *woman?* I thought you were—"

Now, Enheduanna interrupted, with a tone that had finally mastered the quizzical. "This one is like us. This one is complete. You do not find this acceptable?"

Laurel fumed, with an anger Asach knew all too well. The deceived one. The betrayed one. Although there had been betrayal of nothing, save the undiscussed presumptions of another. Asach answered with practiced, weary patience. "It's probably best if you just stick with whatever you've presumed all along. That usually works out best. Stay in your own comfort zone. And when my actions—when I—don't quite match up to your presumptions—which I won't, always, because I can't— just remember, *it's not intentional*. It's not a *judgment*. It's just *different*."

Enheduanna comprehended this with amazement. Moties could not shake their heads, but somehow the gesture was conveyed by voice. "We could not have survived in this way. We are too few. Too widely disbursed. Too hunted. Especially the Masters."

Laurel plunked back down onto the couch. "Tell me." she said woodenly. "Tell me how *you* do it."

Across the gulf of species, language, age, and experience, Enheduanna could not and did not understand what ran through Laurel's head. Surely the actual mechanics of reproduction could not possibly be so upsetting. In Enheduanna's experience, only a threat to the *ar* could be this upsetting. Enheduanna understood what every Master did: Enheduanna understood the *ar*. *Ar* was at the center and heart and soul of anything. The *ar* of the land; the *ar* of the people; the *ar* of the lines. So Enheduanna sought to explain, at the highest possible level, the role of *ar* and reproductive mechanics in Sargon's House.

"We Masters are fashioned from All. All are in us. That is how we can Speak with the Voice to All. We can mate, Master to Master, but when We do, we cannot know, for certain, what will result. We risk the false Master: a Keeper, who remains ever-sterile. He may nurture our storehouses, administer our cattle, but cannot Speak and so cannot defend the *ar*. A Keeper will live long, but over time his *ar* will dwindle, and his name will be blown back to the dust whence it came. Masters always risk losing the Voice. We may bear one who speaks, but with a Voice for only the few. And we risk *anathema:* the four-armed ones. The incomplete ones. The ones like you humans: half-ones, one thing, or another, *male*, or *female*, but never whole. The ones with no *ar*.

"To *guarantee* continuity, a Master must make the Royal Marriage. Carry all in them. Bring forth *children*. But when they do this, it is their last. The Royal Marriage is a marriage with eternity. It can only be made once. A Master must always know *when* to make get, or try to make children. Too early, or too often, and they must divide their *ar*; splinter their *ar*, or sell their own as cattle—as Vermin must do. Too late, and the Marriage will fail.

"But only very, very rarely does even the Royal Marriage make a Great Master. They know that they have succeeded if there is only one. Only one *child*. If it is to be a Great Master, all the children they carry will be merged into one, and they will bear that one. But the bearing will exhaust them. The bearing of all, requires all. They will be as a Runner, at the end of a run. No Doctor can save them then, nor would try. But *that* child will be reared by all, and thus will Speak to All.

Asach pondered this. "So, this Royal Marriage, is made—where?"

"With All, before all."

"In public."

"Yes, it must be."

"And with—all what? All who?"

"All castes. The best from all castes. Farmers. Warriors. Miners. And every Master line."

"But how do they control this?"

"They control who receives the darts. Both partners inject darts before they exchange sperm. Both partners carry eggs. The darts determine which will carry the get to term. If one only receives them, that one will bear the get or children."

"How does a Master control who receives the darts?"

"They prepare the day before. They prepare by ejecting all of their own. Any get will be raised to staff the new household. Those sent to make the Marriage must prepare as well. Eat properly. Build and retain their darts."

"But this means the Great Master would receive darts in the—hundreds?"

"At least. Perhaps thousands."

"But that is impossible. Physically."

"Some do not survive."

"But those that do?"

"Carry every line. Perhaps. Some lines may fail. But even if the Great Master is alone, many lines will not. If the *ar* is poor."

"If the *ar* is poor, the Great Master will bear many children."

"No. The Master will bear many *get*. Many *castes*."

Asach thought back to Swenson's report. "So, when Great Masters are driven from their *ar?*"

"They make the Royal Marriage before they go, and leave the rest behind to defend their retreat. They flee, and bear their get where it is safe to begin a new colony. This is how my ancestors came to Mesolimeris. Sargon's ancestors."

"But if the *ar* is rich?"

"Then they may have a *true* child. A Great Master, born to a Great Master. A Great Master, who also carries All, was raised by All, and Speaks with the Voice of All."

"Like you."

"No, not like me. I am only Sargon's child. A Master, yes, who Speaks to the Household. But not a Great Master. Sargon is the first in a very long time. This is why Sargon has no family. This is why Sargon was named Protector. Sargon Speaks to All. All Cities, all Houses, all Lines. Sargon commands the Master's Grip. Sargon is Protector of the *ar* of Mesolimeris. The *ar* of All."

"And beyond Mesolimeris?'

"Beyond Mesolimeris lies fallow. Beyond that is the sea."

They broke off at a quiet sob from Laurel. She sat on the floor, hugging her knees, rocking slightly. She coughed once. "Sorry." She choked on her own quavering voice. Cleared her throat. "Sorry."

They waited.

"It's just that—it must have been horrible. Horrible. They came, they plowed your fields, and all your—people— were left to be shot, gassed, poisoned. And then your—Great Masters—had to cross The Barrens, somehow, all alone, to come here, and start all over."

Enheduanna made the sign for *great shame and sorrow.* "Yes. It is The Great Lament. Beyond The Barrens were our best and richest colonies. Many lines, all gone. "

"But don't you see," she cried, "that's our story too. The Great Weep. Driven from New Scotland. Driven from New Ireland. Driven from Maxroy's Purchase. Driven from Saint George. Driven out from Bonneville, into The Barrens. Driven from our homes, then our lands, and all by *them.*" Her eyes flashed. "By the *vermin.* And now they've come again. " She climbed to her knees, hands clasped, and addressed a plea, not to Asach, but to Enheduanna. "*I beg you.* We *have* helped you! *We* defended this land so that you could return. Me. *My* family. *Our* lines. Now *please*, help us! Tell Archangel Sargon to help us drive them out forever!"

Pulling herself to her feet, pulling herself together, wiping away her tears, Laurel aged about ten years before Asach's eyes, and took Asach's hands with genuine anguish. "I'm sorry. I am so, so sorry. I thought you were my—problem. My burden. When really, you were my guardian angel."

That remains to be seen, thought Asach. *The chips may fall without regard to you.* "I think you'll find," Asach said, patting and releasing Laurel's hands, "that you did most of the work yourself."

13

Tortious Intervention

Cunning leads to knavery. It is but a step from one to the other, and that very slippery. Only lying makes the difference; add that to cunning, and it is knavery.

—*Ovid*

Saint George, New Utah

The *blart* from the flash pager was so loud that as Colchis Barthes flailed awake he nearly landed on the floor.

It wasn't clear what he could *do*. He'd cajoled the True Church archivist for direct access to Swenson's data, without success. He'd answered Quinn's brief questions about the Swenson's ape report: *Where? How?* He'd played go-between as needed, downloading, pre-processing, and passing updates between Quinn and the Blaine Institute linguists. He guessed that Quinn must be locked up somewhere, with a narrow communications window to the satellite. He spent tense days, hands on notional business, mind elsewhere, ready to jump out of his skin at the *blart* that unpredictably but invariably arrived at odd hours of the night.

So, Barthes was startled, but he wasn't exactly surprised, until he saw the length of Quinn's usually terse communication.

FLASH EYES ONLY

FROM: QUINN

TO: RENNER

CC FOR ACTION: BARTHES

1. Prime assessment:

No immediate threat to Empire. No immediate threat to trade or commerce. No immediate violations of prime directives. Human-"Motie" contact is centuries-old and of local origin. No offworld information or technology transfer observed. No immediate military action required. No immediate economic sanction required.

2. Accession Considerations:

Implications are strategic and political, not military.

a. Prior Claims of Status: New Utah "Moties" unified. Claim pre-human residence, expulsion from native residence by True Church colonists, historical First Empire contact with Swenson as Imperial Surveyor under Murcheson, pledge of enduring mutual aid and assistance, no subsequent resistance to Imperial or colonial claims or actions, no participation in Secession Wars, and current request for renewal of previous ties. No evidence of contact with or awareness of Mote System aliens or other offworld entities. *Human* legal status would be: Active Request for Accession by Neutral Allied Prior Colony.

b. Planetary Government: Procurator (Senior Master) "Sargon," representing "Moties," may form alliance with Barrens Himmists re: alleged land and rights violations from sand mining. Attitude actively defensive. No active resistance to TCM government, but extremely hostile to further expansion into jointly claimed territories. If legal interventions not instituted, potentially destabilizing to planetary unity.

c. Space Travel: No capacity observed.

d. Prior External Claims: Unknown. Lillith Van Zandt reported on-planet. Possible link to sand mining. Coordinates, Ping image follow for interp.

3. Tactical Assessment:

Military strength, deployment unknown. None apparent. Few Warriors observed, serving as household bodyguard. Himmists have no apparent military organization but do organize for self-sufficient pilgrimage. Claim TCM holds monopoly of force in region.

Junior Master "Enheduanna" reports six cities, population unknown. Population my location estimated 3-5,000, all castes. No Mediators observed. "Enheduanna," older Keeper "Lagash" fill this role. No Engineers observed; may = Miners. No "Lesser Apes" (=Watchmakers? War Rats?) observed.

4. Economic Assessment:

"Moties" possess staple-financed state-administered economy with accounting, higher mathematics, surplus warehousing, and distribution organized by city-states with overarching common defense of western borders. Observed optical and ceramic technologies are highly sophisticated and use solar concentrators. Primary observed agricultural and food base appears to be a filamentous, human-palatable cyanobacteria ("blue-green algae") grown in reclaimed wetlands. Himmists prize this crop as livestock forage.

Himmist ranchers subsist in church-organized community cooperatives with secondary, opportunistic income from opal meerschaum sale in Bonneville. Primary agricultural activity is stock-keeping, although this is becoming stressed by climatic change. Aggressive TCM tithe-collection practices have fostered the stripping of mineral resources for quick cash. Primary mineral activity is silica-sand and related mining in support of Bonneville solar-optical industries. Moties prize Himmist buffering and protection of land areas around my location from further development.

Major resources: Unknown. Disputed sand mining may be in pursuit of fine grade silica sands for New Utah solar-optical industries. Himmist sacral sites characterized by raised seamount geology.

5. Status: In no immediate danger. Tracker active. DO NOT ATTEMPT RESCUE. Negotiating return to Bonneville.

6. Recommendations: Assess impact of sand mining dispute.

7. Instructions to Barthes:

Find current registered ownership; review prior claims by family names Swenson, Courter, Orcutt, registered Bonneville. Ollie Azhad, TCM Security, Saint George; Zia Azhad, c/o Michael Van Zandt, Bonneville may help.

USE EXTREME CAUTION. Azhad children recently murdered/kidnapped, Saint George. Michael van Zandt estranged from mother Lillith, but relationship complicated.

Barthes was now wide awake, very excited, very relieved, and reading the entire message a second time. He'd been worried about something—martial. A requirement for a fumbling commitment to an action at once bellicose and futile. As a Librarian, he would have been poorly cast, Boy's-Own-Story-Reserve-Lieutenancy to the fore, doing something very *keen* like heading up some brave little army in defense of the Crown.

But he understood what he was reading here. Any decision that established an Imperial precedent regarding non-human accession would be made at pay grades orders-of-magnitude above those on the Jackson Commission. It would be governed by forces in play on Sparta; in Mote space; at The Sister; on the Board of Imperial Autonetics; in the corridors of Naval power. New Utah's importance had never been particularly economic. It had just become *extremely* strategic. Strategy likes predictability. It despises careening spoilers. Unknown to themselves, the economic parasites that swarmed beneath the rocks of accession politics were about to be exposed to some very bright lights.

And, as a senior librarian with a lifetime spent poking in the shadows of what people wrote, doodled, and archived, conflict-phobic Colchis Barthes was no master of derring-do, but he was ideally suited to the role of Imperial spy. He listened, and people talked to him. He showed interest, and people showed him things. He picked up bits and bobs, until he'd curated brilliant collections.

As weak, grey light seeped behind the curtains, he began by doing what he did every morning. He donned his brocade bathrobe. He moved deliberately into his kitchenette. He carefully, neatly, made a pot of tea, and laid it out on a tray with full service. He quietly sat to drink it. Behind him, a distant *boom* shuddered the windows and rattled the tray. It had a familiar, comforting quality. The distant sirens played sweetly, like astral music.

Buried deep within her basement office, Linda Libiziewsky's fingers drummed on the desktop as she stared at the tacked-up mountain scene that passed for a window. Hugo Azhad dripped from every picture-bough. The picture-meadow bloomed with the purple flowers of Marul's eyes.

Deela's laugh splashed along the picture-brook, her brothers' footsteps sprinting up the picture-red-earth track.

Linda wasn't particularly close to the Azhads, but *everybody* knew Ollie. He was a bright spot in the TCM. While MP blow-ins fired up their fanatical goon squads, Ollie hired and trained all-local boys for supplemental security contracts. He kept them supervised and out of trouble. He was intolerant of thugs and bullies. He cultivated good relations with the civil police; with Zone and Church authorities. His recruitment net was ecumenical. "It's a warehouse," he'd shrug, "not a sanctuary." His lads were quiet, effective, nearly invisible, and in high demand. New Utahans were pragmatic.

No local, drummed Linda's fingers, *would have done this. Not at all; and not like this.* What was the point of kidnap? Ransom? There was no percentage in it. TCM Security profits went to the Church, not Ollie. The Church didn't ransom kidnap victims. It ruthlessly hunted down the perpetrators, declared them and their families excommunicants, confiscated their property, exiled them to The Barrens, and placed them under shunning orders. There was nowhere to take the money and run *to*. Extortion? Over what? Warehouse security? VIP escort? Nobody local would pick *that* fight lightly. Ollie was too astute a politician and businessman. He was a decent man, but he controlled the equivalent of an infantry division with eyes and ears in every community on the planet. There wasn't a contract out there worth measures as extreme as murdering his eldest son and stealing his youngest kids, because there wasn't a contract out there worth the potential retribution.

No, this murder smacked of offworlders: offworld prejudice, and offworld threat. It was meant to look like a local cock-up. That was the prejudice part. It was what an offworlder might imagine a local blood feud would look like; some offworlder framing of negotiation hostages. But New Utahans didn't *do* blood feuds. They did litigations and shamings and shunnings and banishments. They might tie each other up in court for decades determining just compensation, but they didn't tie each other up in trees for public guttings. They didn't steal one another's kids.

So, it was a message. A disgusting, public threat. *To whom? To whom? To whom?* drummed Linda's fingers. To Ollie? It just didn't make sense. To Moorstown? It had certainly soaked the community in fear. Street play all but shut down. Parents hovered over their kids. Whispers and rumors flew everywhere. But to what purpose was that? What message was sent? Why shouldn't kids go to and from work, or play outside?

The drumming stopped. Linda went icy all over. She felt physically sick. *Because nobody can protect them,* she thought. *That's the message. Nobody can protect you. Not even Ollie Azhad. Not even the TCM.* Now she went hot all over. Her faced flushed bright red. The message was bright and clear, to anyone who knew how to read it: *deal with us, or you'll have no future here.*

Suddenly, all the random violence made sense. At some level or another, Linda knew most things of any consequence in the Zone, because she paid all the bills. She didn't need to pull up Trippe's travel reimbursements. She knew them by heart. One FLIVR fuel receipt, for a weekly out-of-Zone community relations meeting with the current lessees of the old Founder's Retreat. She reached forward; pulled down the picture, and thought deeply as she examined the cliff face, capped by the façade of the mountain aerie now occupied by Lillith van Zandt.

Blaine Institute, New Caledonia

The IA communications satellite was tiny. It didn't hold a lot. It didn't do a lot. It served a specific purpose, which was to burp transmissions at light speed and hideous expense to like-minded state-of-the-art transponders-cum-shuttle pods parked within eyeshot of the daisy-chain of Alderson points tenuously connecting New Utah to the rest of Empire space. That's why Asach had dropped it into geosynchronous orbit above the Bonneville plains all those years ago.

It did have a minuscule image acquisition system, which didn't cover many bands. It had no onboard atmospheric correction, nor could it record data needed to accomplish same. It was lousy at punching through clouds. It was pretty worthless at night. But on a clear day, if nothing else was going on, if anybody asked it to, it could record whatever happened to lie beneath it. It couldn't see a lot. It wasn't strictly speaking directable, but you could fiddle with the aperture slit, so that it looked out at an oblique angle. If you had those settings, you could correct the image so that it looked something like vertical. If you knew *exactly* where you wanted to look, you could use *all* of your available storage to bump up resolution and get as much detail stuffed in as possible. Using it was like waving a camera above everyone's heads at a concert, and hoping whatever you got would turn out well.

Given those constraints, it was pretty amazing that they got anything at all. Anything much smaller than a house was little more than a dot. Waist-high scrub along dry washes was reduced to darkened streaks. Multi-story dunes appeared as hazy smears obscuring the white scars of bulldozed access roads.

It didn't matter. They stared at the scaffolded contraption with shock and awe. It looked like a skyscraper's innards mated with an octopus. The tiny yellow cab must have been bigger than a house, or it would not have been visible at all. But what was most stunning was the sand it mined. It was not the stuff of palm-swept holidays or Scheherazade oases. Linear mustard yellow dunes banded with greenish black spilled like vomit across a vast expanse at the base of scruffy mountains. The octopus had chewed away square-walled sections seven stories high, and re-spewed the multi-colored grains into a bracelet of neatly-sorted conical piles. In turn, SunRail spurs chewed away at these, ferrying gemstone-colored open boxcars in a necklace that cascaded to a ring of smelters, fired by a solar concentrator big enough to cast a shadow across the entire yard.

But the alignment was not cooperative. They stretched. They rotated. They enhanced and cropped and magnified. But they could not get any clear image of insignia; branding; printing: anything at all that indicated the identity of the operators of the mine. So they called in Chief Snow, a Warrant Officer who was himself older than the sands of time. He looked at the mining booms. He looked at the operations layout. He looked at the SunRail boxcars. "Local," he grunted. He looked at the smelters. "Nice adaptation," he rasped. Then he shifted the view slightly, and looked at outbuildings; latrines; bunkhouses; warehouses, equipment yards.

"Come 'ere," he wheezed. His breath was foul. "That," he said, his tobacco-stained index finger poking at one nondescript building among many, "is the primary flinger house. And *that*," he said, circling the array; walking his hangnailed, callous-encrusted digit along the lines and paths and buildings, "is a Van Zandt Mining Number Four-A layout." He turned away, grey stubble glowing in the backlight; dandruff flecks carpeting his shoulders. "Colony concession model. Unmitigated, total extraction, open cut-and-strip. Not silica sand. Wrong geology, wrong color. You got a lot goin' on here. That ridge is an old sea mount—undersea volcano—that went dormant, got ringed with reefs, then raised up, then baked in sun, then weathered down. Those sands are eroding out of an exposed shoulder of the mountain core. Best wild guess, rare earths, based on that geology and color."

"Rare earths?"

Snow grunted. "Yeah. Only thing is, rare earths ain't. Depending on where you are. Something out there's worth some startup, though. Look at the height of that tower feeding the smelters." He drew the triangulation of the solar concentrator's height and shadow, then punched in trigonometry based on standard heights for the warehouses. A number appeared. They all gave a low whistle. "Plus or minus, either way, if they went in legal, they did this *fast*. You either need big payback quick, or a guaranteed long haul to make that investment worthwhile. And no overhead."

They looked at each other. Snow was old and good. He was also old and—old school, to put it politely. *No overhead* was a euphemism. It pretty much meant *slave labor.*

They asked him some questions, but Chief Snow was done. "Told you what you need. Your job to figure it out." He stumped off down the hall. They began waking up geologists. One of them slipped out, and woke up Renner himself.

Bonneville, New Utah

Zia stared at the ceiling with red-rimmed eyes. She was too cold, or she was too hot. She couldn't decide. She threw off the blankets, and shivered in the breeze that soughed gently through the carven shutters. The muezzin lulled her to sleep. The muezzin woke her up. The soothing white noise of the fountain trickling in the courtyard beyond her window was drowned out by the plunk of a faucet dripping two floors above on the opposite side of the compound. Marul was a comfort. Marul was an impossible burden. Her children were dead. Her children were alive. She had grieved passed caring. If she could not find them, she would die.

She grilled Ollie daily for another detail; another sign. She walked Marul through her steps again and again, until she herself walked the path through the early morning frost. She remembered her own role on that morning. She arose. Ollie arose. Hugo arose. The little ones rose. Again and again they sat to table in the last breakfast of her mind.

Hugo left to make morning pickups from the warehouse. In a jocular display of big-brotherly good temper, Deela and the boys went along for the ride. Ollie left to open the market stall that served as office, grocery, and teahouse. Zia left to fight her way through the traffic and trash; dead dogs and severed signposts that pointed to the dreary procurement ledgers at Orcutt Land and Mining.

As dawn broke, exhausted by her nightly march from home to office; warehouse to tea stall; daily routine to the horror on Philosopher's Way, Zia finally drifted off. Doves cooed in the eaves. Sparrow cheeps and kitchen clanking echoed in the courtyard. The Stirling thrummed with a whisper of vibration that the Lads had been unable to fully banish. Good Lads. Ollie had hired them off the loading docks.

Zia sat up, her head full of echoes and clanking and thrumming and loading docks and all the other sounds and smells of a warehouse. Their warehouse. Number 27-A. Mostly used for security equipment storage. Handy to the market supply bays in Lane 26, and also to the guarded, leased commercial storage on Lane 28, with rear bays that loaded directly onto the SunRail spur. Location was everything, said Ollie. People need to be able to chat with you, anywhere, all the time. Put your office in the market. Store your equipment where you'll need it most. Save money. Save time.

It suddenly occurred to Zia that she'd lost track of that. Really, she didn't know who she'd worked for, at the end when OLaM had changed hands yet another time. Just the general meeting; the announcement of a consortium buyout; but no transfer of property and equipment since they remained registered to the company. Just a minor aside, from her administrative standpoint—the movement of durable goods from TCM Lane 29, on the opposite side of the tracks, into the leased commercial lane. Most of Orcutt's stores were held on-site, but TCM had warehoused one lot in transit pending movement out to the mines. Months had passed since they'd sold off the claim, and they wanted to clear their warehouse. She'd been on the run, and signed the work order on the fly one morning, in the middle of a mountain of other paperwork. The warehouseman already had the cipher keys.

"Just sign here, please, ma'am," he'd said, in a bit of a fluster. "An' me an' dese pelas get going." She could see his coveralls. She could see his cap. She could see his calloused hands and his sacks-of-melons muscles and his wraparound shades. She scrubbed at her memory, but she couldn't see his name, and she couldn't see his face. Authorization for six loaders, two FLIVRs, two cargo handling teams. To transfer contents TCM Warehouse 29-C to Leased Warehouse 28-A. Lessee: Van Zandt Mining. She'd drawn a stroke through Van Zandt, wrote OLaM, initialed, and signed. It now occurred to her that maybe the clerical error was right the first time.

Zia rose, and dressed, and woke Michael.

Founder's Retreat, Oquirr foothills, New Utah

It was a gala affair, and Jeri LaGrange was supremely pleased that she'd been invited. It was a working invitation of course. Five hundred years ago, Founder's Day had begun as a solemn procession from the Tabernacle in Saint George to the Founder's Retreat in the Oquirr foothills, where the Saints would sing a sunset prayer of thanks for the bounty spread before them in the valley below. Now, the Temple procession kicked off a parade, the singing kicked off a city-wide festival, and the Founder's Day Ball was *the* annual event.

Crowd and traffic control always required weeks of preparation. Given current tensions, security coordination had become an absolute nightmare, particularly since the Retreat itself no longer fell directly under Zone administrative control. Finding it increasingly difficult to subsidize the expense of maintaining Retreat properties year-round, the True Church had found an ideal tenant in the person of Lillith Van Zandt, Margravine Batavia, who pledged her household *delighted* to give over Retreat facilities as needed to continue tradition. To Captain LaGrange's immense frustration, the Margravine's security team showed no evidence whatsoever of sharing in that delight.

Four security organs managed the chaos. Saint George civil police were fully occupied with city traffic management and crowd control. LaGrange's own TCM Zone security company was called out in force to control Zone access, secure the Temple, and patrol installation boundaries. The Maxroy's Purchase True Church Militant Saints Battalion served a ceremonial role as the leaders and official escort of the processional parade, whence it marched on in orchestrated fanfare to man formal posts on the Retreat's approaches. It was the highlight of their Mission on New Utah. TCM Contract Security provided backup to everyone, filling gaps, patching holes, and providing rotational relief so that most could nip in for a bit of the festivities. The Margravine's generosity had extended to bearing the expense of maintaining household security via the offices of her private bodyguards. They were an odd bunch: professional, tough, inflexible, and *exceedingly* visible. The overbearing presence of their bulging Plate was only slightly mitigated by the Delft blue of the household livery donned for the occasion.

LaGrange's favorite place was not the airy opulence of the ballroom, nor the lofty sweep of the grand staircase and reception hall. Rather, it was the cramped bustle of the cloak room, rendered fabulous by the bright splashes of satins and sabers; gild and glitter that adorned the outerwear and inner linings of capes and greatcoats; *kepis* and saucer hats worn once a year, on this day only, by every institution on New Utah. Colonels and Primates; Guild Masters and Police Chiefs; Surgeons and Attorneys General; junior officers, senior community leaders, and the Saint George Mayor himself rubbed arms and twisted shoulders as frantic ladies scanned tags and issued chits in a hopeless effort to stem the tide of fabric slithering across the counter. It would be a long night, most of it spent checking in and out with security posts and security counterparts, but the cloakroom was a magical snapshot of what it was all about.

    Colchis had seen the phenomenon before, but never failed to be impressed. Lillith Van Zandt fairly glowed with charm. Whomever she greeted—her hands in a warm clasp, her couture hairstyle betrayed by one floating wisp, her smile jovial as she made a conspiratorial half-bob of favored recognition, her Delft blue sash sparkling in both the icy cluster clipped below her shoulder and the depths of her periwinkle eyes—felt drawn in to a private circle of exquisite friendship, when in reality, each was only one of hundreds plowing past in the receiving line.

    The Margravine graced the role of Guest of Honor, each citizen handed forward by the Mayor and her husband with an accompanied name and position uttered by the ceremonial aide-de-camp appointed from the Saints Battalion. Trippe looked the part and played it well, back straight, regalia pressed, voice clear without shouting. She greeted each with no trace of condescension; as if genuinely surprised by joy at the once-in-a-lifetime opportunity to meet water reclamation department heads, gunnery sergeants, and cheese mongers.

    Lillith's smile broke like dawn as Barthes approached. "Colchis! How wonderful! I'd no *idea* that anyone else was here!" *Anyone else* being a euphemism for *anyone else like us. Anyone else from Court.* Which Barthes knew was bollocks on two counts. Firstly, Saint George was by now fairly crawling with unofficial advance teams of every description, most of them holed up in the same less-than-satisfactory hotel, but what could you do? Secondly, there was very little that Lillith Van Zandt did *not* know, if she cared to, and the composition of the advance team for the accession delegation would certainly be something that she *would* want to know.

"Dame Lillith! Imagine my joy!" He swept a hand to encompass the holographic plinths that lined the stairway and dotted the room beyond, forming convenient conversation points. "Your usual flair! It's what brings you here, I suppose?"

The projections had an eerie physicality. Some of the nearer plinths sparkled with crystals; others looped images of working machinery dating back to DaVinci. Notably absent was any reference to asteroid mining.

"Oh, yes!" she gushed. "And all done with *local* technology! Isn't it divine? The Mayor is *quite* enthusiastic about an exchange! She's promised some *exquisite* examples of opal meerschaum folk art! " Meaning a cultural exchange; specifically, a curatorial exchange with the Imperial Museum of Minerals and Mining, of which the Margravine of Batavia was a noted patroness.

"Really Colchis, we *must* chat when I'm done with the line. We need to get our people together to go through your archives!" Meaning the New Utah archives. Meaning to establish precedent for what was, and what was not, allowable portrayal of technology.

Which, thought Colchis, *should have been done well before I ever entered this receiving line. My, my Lillith. What* are *you up to this time?*

It was autumn crisp on the evening mountain. Clegg shivered. To Tanith skin, the brisk air was Siberian, and to Tanith eyes, the valley view was grey. Rather, Clegg's *body* shivered. Clegg himself was not acutely aware of physical sensations. Like breathing, they existed somewhere in a vague background noise of physiology. Notions like *discomfort* had no easy purchase in his mind. As the light faded, and the torch lights that lined the processional Way winked on far below, Clegg's attention was occupied by his eyes and ears, not his gooseflesh. While those organs did their jobs, his mind wandered, pondering the utterly asinine bullshite that meant he was outside wearing shadowflage, not inside wearing Delft.

The bullshite had a name, and its name was Major Johannes Trippe. Clegg had no time for Trippe, because Clegg had no time for pomposity, heroes, or heroics. Heroes were for the most part naïve, bombastic rogues who failed to coordinate their actions and called attention to themselves. This made them difficult and dangerous to protect, if you worked *for* them, and dangerous to be around, if you worked *with* them. You accomplished the mission by focusing on it and training people to task, not by encouraging heroics. Heroics just got people killed. Take guard mount that evening. There'd stood Trippe, the pompous ass, blarting on about proud traditions and The Saints Battalion and The Mission on New Utah Making Men out of Maxroy's Purchase Boys. *Get on with it,* thought Clegg. *Quit filling their heads with tripe, or they'll wind up wearing it just like that boy down below.*

Which was why he was out here in the cold, listening. His contract guaranteed the personal security of Dame Van Zandt, her household, and her guests. Trippe-the-hero could bluster away all he liked about Clegg's so-called mission post beginning at the mansion's doors, but in practical terms, that's where Clegg's brief *ended.* If Clegg let an external threat pass through those, he hadn't done his job. If Dame Van Zandt was threatened by *her own* staff; by *her own* guests, that was her problem. *Clegg's* problem was that Trippe's brats were uselessly manning fixed posts while visions of sugarplums danced in their heads. If some Mormon-tea-addled guest went after the Margravine Batavia with a cocktail toothpick, the household goons in Delft would handle it. Clegg was concerned with forces rather more sinister.

Clegg's philosophy was simple. People who shot at you were your enemy. Things that tried to eat you were your enemy. Those that did neither were, for the moment, not your enemy, until they got pissed off or hungry. That pretty much summed up life on Tanith. The only way out of that vicious state of affairs was to *buy* your way out—which, for Harlan Clegg, was never going to happen unless he got paid out on this contract. He vaguely imagined an alternative reality where people just got on with their lives, whatever that meant. It was hard to picture, since he'd never seen it, but it lurked back there in some racial memory of a home and a farm and domesticated animals. Nothing drastic. Nothing idyllic. Long days of work and short nights of sleep just fine. Just a bit less kill-or-be-killed.

So he'd appreciate it, thank you very much, if half-assed *heroes* would quit complicating his business, act moderately professional, and leave his people the flock alone. Like that Ollie Azhad character. His lads were good. Shitey business about his kids, but there you were. Trippe had this flocked-up notion that Azhad needed a reminder of who was running the show. Clegg wasn't so sure. Maybe that cowboy shite worked out here—who knew where the flock they were?—but on Tanith pissing off a guy with eyes in every neighborhood was not an attractive path to career success. Or that TC Zone Captain. No *drama*. Just kept those shite-for-brains kids from flocking up in some wise spectacular, which is about as good as it got with amateurs.

Branches snapped. Clegg concentrated. On Tanith, things ate you if you couldn't figure out how big and where they were. *On the subject of Azhad,* thought Clegg, *it's that flocking Sauron dinosaur. All brawn, no brains, like something crawled out of a flocking swamp.* Clegg listened. Three people, one big—that would be the Sauron—two average, moving away, downhill towards the FLVR pool. *Off to spike the fireworks.* Clegg shrugged. *That* was Trippe's call, for better or for worse. Not his problem if Trippe's nasty little buddies played at heroes—at least not until these lunatics pissed off enough people that they figured out who to come after to get even.

All the same, it was a shitey business about those kids.

North Badlands, Borrego (Swenson's) Valley, New Utah

Sargon struck. If the swarms of humans meeting on the mountain were nothing to do with these vermin in the sand hills, there was no reason not to. They had no interest to defend. They might even be allied. Sargon's orders to Enheduanna were simple. "Return them where you found them. Have them muster if she speaks the truth. Kill them if she lies." With that, Courter and Quinn's incarceration abruptly ended, and Porters, Runners, and Warriors swept them back up the trail they'd originally descended, moving at the double-time.

Then Sargon struck, in the late afternoon, when half the camp was blinded by the solar field of light. Sinkholes appeared in the barracks floors. Chittering creatures poured forth like roaches from night-time drains. Half-dressed men sleeping off the night shift dove from windows and doors, sweeping fire behind them, running their weapons dry, abandoning the buildings to horrific-looking six-legged rat-like things with nasty teeth and voracious appetites. The monstrous sand miner reeled and waved as cutting beams severed its primary arm. It toppled to one side, the operator dangling from the cabin, stranded seven stories high. Guards boiled up from everywhere, shouting and running and firing until dust devils burst from the sand at their feet, when they grunted and died, their brief, last memory a high-pitched whine. The heavy weapons platoon fell back on the smelters. Most of them were burned alive. The cooks formed a valiant but doomed defensive line, shielded with skillets and brandishing butcher knives.

It was over before it started. Within the hour, Farmers were demarcating toxic zones, and Miners were swarming over the concentrator tower, calculating lines-of-sight. Cleanup teams were searching every facility, with Accountants to assess and tally anything of value for salvage. Assay teams were already working their way through piles of crystal samples from the smelters. By nightfall, the poisoned ground would be vitrified into an inert, multi-hued sea of glass. By morning, the disassembly squads with their legions of miniscule, four-armed helpers would depart, leaving wind and sand and glass and gutted buildings.

Perhaps it was providence that Hand Four were descended from the Household Grip *Lagash's Own*. Perhaps it was only to be expected: these wastes lay in a desolate corner of Lagash's old *ar*. The Grip was Sargon's now, but they'd had their history from the ancient Keeper: who better to know their lines? And with it, they'd heard from Lagash himself about the strange conversations between the human Master, the manna-eyed one, and Enheduanna. "Because," doddered the old Keeper with over-dramatic flair, "Lord Sargon would *know the enemy*." Unmoved by Lagash's voice, inwardly they yawned.

Or perhaps it was only luck that Hand Four was assigned to sweep the kitchen cellars. They were efficient and ruthless and disciplined and several cook's helpers died by the time they came to a final locked door and heard muffled whispers inside. But when the Hand burst through, revealing several huddled vermin, the Leader barked "Hold!" before they could strike. These were different from the others. Smaller. Their color was odd. They offered no resistance. They appeared unarmed. For a second that seemed eternal, the Hand Leader watched a tableau vivant of five Warriors staring down two awe-struck boys, who cowered behind grim-faced, eleven-year-old, green-eyed Deela Azhad. *Lord Sargon would know the enemy*. It barked orders. One Warrior bolted to fetch a Runner. One stayed on guard. One moved out to inform the Mining Communicator to prepare for a message relay to Beacon Hill Station. The rest moved on.

Founder's Retreat, Oquirr foothills, New Utah

"Ladies and Gentlemen!" announced the Mayor, "It is my *great* pleasure to introduce the True Church Temple Junior Choir!" The room dissolved into cheery applause as well-scrubbed children in lapis robes filed in to bracket the long, blank, curving reception hall wall that dissolved to reveal the purpling landscape and twinkling lights that lined the road to the pinking blush that was Saint George. "Please join them, as they lead us in our annual Founder's Hymn of Thanks!"

The first note surged just as the final ray of sun struck the Angel Moroni at the tip of the distant temple spire, casting a golden glow onto the sunset wash that painted the stones below. Though Mormon-led, the hymn was shared, and it welled up from the childhood hearts of every New Utahan in the room, in varying approximations of the key set by the choir. It was not long, but for its few verses, the scattering of guests from Maxroy's Purchase and parts beyond felt themselves very much outsiders to the alien tune that filled the room.

The city fell into shadow as the final chords died away, and the room burst into another round of spontaneous, cheery applause. All surged forward to play the inevitable round of can-I-see-my-house-from-here?, while the Mayor's husband pointed out key landmarks to the invited offworld guests. LaGrange drew back, as her silent pager went off. She plugged in the 'tooth, noting with mild shock that it was not the Duty Officer, but Linda Libiziewsky who had called.

"Jeri! Get back here! Get everyone down here! It's the MPs! They've seized control of—" but her words were interrupted by a distant flash, then boom, then another, then another. The crowd gasped as the distant Temple flared a brilliant white. Other flashes popped across the city; imagination filled in activated sirens.

Suddenly, every officer in the room moved to a Saint Vitus's dance of slapping pockets. The Police Chief hunched, one hand cupped to ear, barking "Status! Status!" the other extended toward the Mayor in the universal *wait* sign. The Mayor herself was icily calm. The Bishop stood gap-jawed in horror.

LaGrange barged through to the Mayor. "I need the police to secure His Grace!" The Mayor looked to the Chief, who did not interrupt his conversation, but nodded.

LaGrange spoke to the Bishop. "Your Grace, I've just activated a Zone Emergency order. Zone security has been breached. The city police will escort you to a safe location away from the disturbance. I will take control of the Zone Escort that brought you here." The Bishop nodded and moved off to consult the Choirmaster. The children dissolved away in the company of their parents.

Major Trippe made an elegant show of calling out: "Guard! To me!" as the ceremonial posts formed up inside and out, ready to spring to the city's defense, but the effect was lost on its intended audience. The room rapidly emptied, as to a person the Saint George natives shouted words or punched codes to activate emergency contact with Ollie Azhad.

Shite, thought LaGrange. *Shite, shite, shite. How do I avoid the MPs and get off this mountain?* She called Linda again. The line was dead. So was the line to the D-O. She looked around. Trippe was preoccupied with something. The house guards were stripping off their Delft. She moved deliberately, identifying a few TCM locals. "Go in with the Battalion!" she hissed. "Then secure the command post. Local orders only! Pass the word to those you *trust!* The MP battalion's compromised!"

And then LaGrange found herself face-to-face with Dame Lillith van Zandt, accompanied by Slam-Dunk Hooper himself. "S-TWO?"

"Sir!"

"What the flock's going on down there?"

"Sir, I can't raise the D-O. I'm heading down to find out."

"No, you're not. You're relieved, Captain. The Mormon Battalion is heading out to restore order. Major Trippe now has operational control. Report to him."

Like hell I will, thought LaGrange. "Sir," she said.

As LaGrange departed, Lillith van Zandt maintained her mask of empathetic horror. "Please excuse me, Colonel. You clearly have much to do." He made a half bow. She turned to leave the room, and spied her target. "Colchis! Oh my, it's *too* horrible! You *will* be all right? *Where* will you go?" She did not, he noticed, actually expect a reply. "Please excuse me. I really must inform Governor Jackson. He *assured* me that New Utah was perfectly *stable*. I *really* don't see, under the circumstances, how we can move forward."

Barthes was non-committal. "Yes, things do seem to have become difficult."

"Very sad, these outbreaks of civil disturbance. I *must* tell the Governor how *fortunate* it is that we have his Saints Battalion here to restore order."

She was grace and light personified as she glided from the room flanked by her security detail, but he heard a sharp change in tone as her voice echoed down the corridor. "*What?!* *When?* Unacceptable! Find out! *Not* my problem! Do it!"

Now that, he thought, *is the Lillith I know.* It was time to get hold of these Azhad people, and Renner and Quinn, pronto.

Van Zandt then passed beyond Barthes' hearing and out of sight of all but Clegg's hand-picked escort. They left the building, stepped into her personal shuttle, and sped toward the Lynx port.

14
A Sharp
Correction

Gudea, the ruler in charge of building the house, the ruler of Lagash, presented the Temple with the chariot "It makes the mountains bow down", which carries awesome radiance and on which great fearsomeness rides and with its donkey stallion to serve before it; with the seven-headed mace, the fierce battle weapon, the weapon unbearable both for the North and for the South, with a battle cudgel, with the mitum mace, with the lion-headed weapon made from nir stone, which never turns back before the highlands, with dagger blades, with nine standards, with the "strength of heroism", with his bow which twangs like a meš forest, with his angry arrows which whizz like lightning flashes in battle, and with his quiver, which is like a lion, a piriĝ lion, or a fierce snake sticking out its tongue—strengths of battle imbued with the power of kingship.

—The building of Ningirsu's temple (Gudea, cylinders A and B): c.2.1.7

East slope, Swenson's Mountain foothills, New Utah

A subtle play of sunlight and shadow on lichen-stained rocks rippled down the slope toward them. A Runner slowed and stopped to address Enheduanna, who called a Warrior forward. The Warrior wore a belt whence it pulled a hand-sized object, then turned so that it faced midway between the early evening sun and a distant ridge capped by a promontory that leaned outward from the mountain.

The object flashed, and the pair became aware of an answering twinkle. A fast, three-way conversation with overtones of a mixed-breed kennel ensued among the Mesolimerans: rumblings, twittering, barking.

Enheduanna addressed Asach and Laurel. "The Lord's Grip has found three creatures. They are small. So high." Enheduanna's lower right hand hovered near Laurel's waist. "One is *female*. Two are *male*. My Lord Sargon wishes to know: what are these?"

Laurel looked appalled. "You've captured *kids?*"

Enheduanna was confused. "You believe these to be the offspring of grazing animals? They appear human, except that, in proportion to their bodies, their heads appear to be larger than yours. Also their coloring is different. These are another caste? They were found—" Enheduanna paused to consult briefly with the Runner—"in a food preparation facility. Perhaps they are edible?"

Now Laurel was confused. "No. I mean *kids*. Human *children!* I cannot believe this! Is this how you *help*? You'd steal *children?*"

Enheduanna ignored the outburst. "These were found, not stolen. My Lord would know whether they are helper castes. Subordinate species, like—" Enheduanna muttered a word. Unhelpfully, the cape translated [*Pit ponies. Probable cognate: Watchmakers.*] The first term meant nothing to Enheduanna; the second meant nothing to either of them. Enheduanna grappled for words. "They are like Miners, but smaller, with four arms. If left to themselves they become vermin."

Laurel shook her head. "No! We have nothing like that!"

Enheduanna's tone became sharp, firm. "But we know that you do! Your people are *often* accompanied by four-legged creatures that carry you and your burdens!" The Warriors bristled.

Laurel looked incredulous for a moment, then burst out laughing. "*Ponies?* You mean *horses? Mules?* Those are *animals*, not humans."

Still pondering the implications of a cognate for *Watchmakers*, Asach decided that it was time to step in. "Yes, Master Enheduanna, this is true. But the creatures they use as Porters are not related to humans. Seer Courter believes that what you have found are human *children*. Bearers of *lines.* "

Enheduanna paused and thought for a moment, then barked again. The Warriors relaxed. "In that case, I understand your concern. Please, understand the Protector's concern. If these were like Miner's Helpers, and shared your physiology, it would have been important to keep them segregated. To prevent an outbreak of vermin."

Laurel had a sudden image of three terrified kids, separated and manhandled by Doctors. "They'll be scared. In shock. How long have you had them? Where did you find them? We need to *talk* to them!"

Enheduanna ignored the questions. "Yes, this is why the Runner came from the signal station. Please speak. "

Laurel looked around, confused. "I don't understand. You will take us to them?"

"You will speak to me. This Warrior will send your words to the beacon station. The station will relay the message to the children. There is a similar arrangement at their end. None there speak Anglic, but Runners will assist them to signal exactly what was said. The Grip is also in communication with Lord Sargon."

Great, thought Asach, *a three-way conference call using hand-held mirrors among an overgrown teenager with a chip on her shoulder, a bunch of aliens, and three terrified kids. I predict an early end to this alliance.*

But the mirrors were more sophisticated, and Laurel more practical, than Asach had imagined.

"OK, ask them their names."

"Please, you must say *exactly* what you want us to send. Most of this will be phonetic. None but me—and, we hope, the children—will actually understand anything but my translation. It would be better if we had a Mining Communicator. They are best and most precise at this. But this Warrior will do what it can."

To Asach's surprise, Laurel nodded, as if what they were about to undertake was an everyday occurrence. "OK, got it. First, say this: *Don't be scared. I am just a big Tweety Kitty. I am talking to you for some friends.*"

Asach's first thought was: *so they do know what Tweety Kitties are.* Asach's second thought, looking at a Warrior, was: *If one of those things piped up claiming to be a Tweety Kitty, I'd have nightmares.* Asach's third thought was: *If that Warrior playing mouthpiece on the other end ever finds out what a Tweety Kitty is, we're all dead.* Asach had no time for a fourth thought, because an answer came in, in an odd warbled jumble that distorted the vowels and scrambled the consonants. Nevertheless, if you unfocussed your eyes and let the bits you couldn't quite make out slide past, the tone sounded *exactly* like three different children all speaking at once.

"That is *so* cool! How did you *do* that"

[Whispered.] "Shut *up* Damien! Didn't Dad teach you anything?" *[Shouted.]* "Prove it!"

"Dee-Dee, I'm *hungry!*"

Less experienced a linguist, Laurel needed more concentration. But she'd had a lot of practice disentangling pilgrim's accents, and that talent served her well. "OK," she said. "They don't sound *too* bad. Say this: *Hi! My name is Laurel.* Then ask the biggest one first: *What's your name?*"

Further progress was hampered by what seemed to be a combination of incomprehension—questions like "What's your island?" and "What's your number?" and "Were you at the Gathering?" being met with silence mingled with interjections like "Huh?" and "What island?" and "We were inna *building,*" that made no sense— and the girl's intransigence, questions like "Where are you from?" and "How old are you?" being met with interjections like "Ow! Dee-D*ee!*" and "Shut *up!*" and "Don't be *stupid.* They could be *anybody!*"

Finally, it was the youngest of all who broke the impasse, when he whined in the background: "Deelie? I don't understand! Didn't Daddy send the Tweety Kitties to *rescue* us from the bad men? I need to *pee!* I want *Hugo!*"

To Laurel, this made no sense. She'd assumed all along that the kids had somehow strayed—or been snatched from— the Gathering camp. She broke off her posture of concentrated listening and spoke directly to Enheduanna. "I don't understand. Who found them? Where did they find them? When? Where are they? What building are they in?"

Enheduanna made motions of surprise. "The Protector acted as you requested. The sand mines are cleared of vermin. These *children* were found an hour ago, in a basement. They are outside that building now. The Protector concluded that they might be a variety of vermin because no *females* were in evidence. Are they past the age of requiring *parents?*"

Deelie, Hugo, bad men, rescue, Warriors, mining camp and the past tense suddenly added up to gooseflesh. While Asach pondered the interstellar implications of news that Motie Warriors had just wiped a remote, undefended outpost off the map of a human world, Laurel remained focused on the practical problem of communicating with frightened kids.

"Did they kill anyone?"

"The *children?*"

"No, of course not. The Warriors. Whoever Sargon sent."

"Yes, as I said. They exterminated all vermin. Farmers are clearing it now."

Laurel blanched, as she pictured the slaughter of an entire mining camp, its crew consigned to a compost heap. But she stayed on task.

"Did the children see dead bodies?"

Enheduanna conferred briefly. "Yes. Outside the food preparation area."

Laurel thought a moment, but reached a quick decision. "OK. Do this. Remove the bodies. Tell them: *Laurel says its time for lunch.* Take them inside, to the kitchen. Use a clean route. Don't let them see bodies or blood. Tell them: *you can eat anything you want.* No matter what they say, answer *yes.* If they want to prepare food, let them. Just don't let them have knives. Be *sure* there are no human bodies or blood in the food prep area before they go in! Tell the boys: *find the bathroom.* Follow them, but let them go in alone. They will know what to do. Listen and report what they say. Bring them back out when they have eaten."

"And then," interjected Asach, "get them to us as fast as you can." *Because the fate of your planet may well depend on it.* There were a lot of ifs here. *If* the mine was operated by unlicensed offworlders, and *if* they were poaching mining rights on somebody else's land, and *if* Ollie Azhad could prove kidnap, and *if* they could all get back safely, then *maybe* Sargon's raiders could be painted as extrajudicial heroes working in favor of human interests. But if word got out that *Moties* had attacked or harmed human kids—well, that was pretty much it. Anything reported five hundred years ago by an oddball scientist about local wildlife would be chaff in the wind.

Asach pictured an interstellar escalation from there that would serve *no* interest. Asach thought of The Lads, waxing mushy over Deela's green eyes. The chances that nobody at that camp had reported the attack were remote. They *had* to assume the worst. It was *essential* to control the spin. Renner had to know what was up. So did Barthes, for his own safety. And of course, so did the Azhads. *Non-interference* be damned.

Asach begged off for a bathroom break around the bend, and flashed the message.

Founder's Retreat, Oquirr Foothills, New Utah

LaGrange slipped from the building, dodged into shadows, and could not believe her luck. Of all the possible vehicles in all the city, Majlid's pulled up, his scruffy farm-boy cousin riding shotgun. Two of Ollie Azhad's best boys. Straight-shooter TCM, but local, and no friends of Maxroy's Purchase. The tall, silver-haired Imperial emerged to wave them down just as she stepped forward to seize the door handle.

He was kindly, unflustered. "I do beg your pardon— Captain? Is it? I'm not very good with insignia. May we help you?"

She was well aware of the strictures: those were quite clear. No, strictly speaking, he *couldn't*. That is, he was not allowed to interfere with her official capacities. And who knew *who* the MPs were in bed with? She hesitated with indecision.

Majlid broke the impasse. "Hey Jeri! Need a lift? Is it OK with you, Mr. Barthes?" He grinned. "Zone Security, so you're safe with her!" Then to her, earnestly, "Do you believe this shite?"

At which moment Trippe emerged, thankfully buried in conversation with Hooper. LaGrange ran out of options. Without waiting for a reply, she dove. Trippe looked up to see

Majlid's bulk, apparently opening the rear passenger door for the Librarian. The goofy cousin waved and grinned from the front seat. Barthes' aquiline nose caught the lamplight as he climbed in. They pulled away, and Trippe bent back to his conversation.

Barthes spoke first. "Would you perhaps be more comfortable on the seat? There's plenty of room." Although, he noted, not as much as there had been. Full Plate now lined the floor and every door.

The scruffy cousin answered. "I think she's best right where she is for awhile." Suddenly, his grin did not look disarming. He looked very armed.

LaGrange's cramped voice mumbled up from the floorboards. "Guys, what's going on?"

The Lads looked at each other, then looked at Barthes in the rear-seat monitor. Barthes stayed mum as they careened through the downhill hairpins.

"Guys, just tell me. If there's a *problem*, we can sort it out later. I'm gunna puke." She sat up, but stayed on the floor.

Majlid nodded. The little one spoke, but his eyes stayed fixed on Barthes. "When the Temple blew up, the MPs went crazy. They turfed us out of all the Zone posts, took control of the command center, killed the gate guards and anybody else who objected, and then a bunch of them wearing civilian clothes went on a rampage in Moorstown. They smashed up half of Araştırmak Kadesi before our guys in the Storefronts Guild managed to stop them. We caught a couple of 'em alive, but"—he shook his head—"so far nothing. Wait. Get down."

Ahead on the valley floor, vehicles clogged the roadway, held up at a checkpoint. They could see the bright sashes of the Maxroy's Purchase Mormon Battalion reflected in distant headlights.

"Shite," said Majlid. Without slowing, he killed all running lights. They hurtled through darkness. Barthes was acutely aware of the hum of their passage reflected off guardrails, the precipitous drop beyond, the lashing of trees whipped by the wind of their passage, and then sudden silence, all sound swallowed by blackness. He heard Majlid counting, calmly, slowly, under his breath, and then his stomach lurched as they jerked right, straight off the roadway.

Barthes expected a slow fall, followed by sudden death. Instead, he felt a ca-clunk and slither, then heard the crunch of gravel, then started as his window was whipped by overhanging brush. They hurtled on, banging and bouncing. LaGrange grunted as she bumped about against various bits of floor pan. Finally, the ground leveled, and as Barthes' eyes adjusted to the dark, he realized that they were heading west, circling north of the city on farm tracks that cut across the fields.

"Your call, Jeri, but I can't do too much of this. I'm low on fuel."

LaGrange untangled herself and rolled onto her back, speaking to the roof as she gazed upside down at Barthes.

"They can't guard everything. There aren't enough of them."

Majlid said nothing, but turned left at the first crossroad. Barthes shuddered involuntarily as he saw the Temple spires looming over the city, illuminated by the fires below. As they drew nearer, distant gunfire and wailing sirens seeped like dreams through the deathly quiet. He started when LaGrange spoke again. "Sir, I may need your help to get in."

"Excuse me?" Barthes tried to make sense of her upside-down lips and chin. It was bizarrely fascinating. They seemed to bear no relation to the spoken words.

"Your Imperial credentials. These guys are your formal escort, right? Assigned by TCM?"

Barthes nodded.

"Well, your credentials and escort pass will—probably—get you to wherever you need to go. If the MPs capture *me*, they'll probably kill me. If they find me with you, they may kill us both. If you have a problem with that, I need to get out here and take my chances."

Barthes thought this over, slowly. Then, with great deliberation, he straightened his heavy overcoat, lumped on the seat beside him. "It cannot be comfortable there," he said. "You must be cold." He draped it neatly over LaGrange, covering her head to toe, assessed the effect, tugged it into several casual folds, pulled his neck scarf through a sleeve, and half-draped them up onto the seat. He then slumped back, clasped his hands in his lap, and closed his eyes.

The effect was remarkable, and his timing was impeccable. As they coasted into the glaring lights of a desolate checkpoint hastily erected across the road, the peering sentry saw only an elderly, dozing gentleman who had not noticed that his coat had slithered to the floor. The boy spoke briefly to Majlid, then rapped on the glass. Barthes started awake, looking groggily into his stern, expectant face as Majlid lowered the window.

"Credentials, sir?"

"Ah, yes." Barthes bent down, his body blocking the sentry's view of the floor, deftly twitched fabric, then righted himself, the brilliant flash of the Imperial Seal drawing the boy's attention as Barthes flipped open the case and handed them over. The private proudly scanned the identity page, read the result, looked Barthes full in the eyes, then rendered a sharp salute as he handed them back.

"Travel safely, sir. It's crazy in there!"

Barthes smiled, warmly. "I'm sure we shall, thanks to your efforts. Please, carry on!"

The lads bobbled and grinned. The sentry looked at them fiercely and barked "Move along!" as he saluted again and waved them through.

Barthes exhaled. He fumbled in his pockets, searching for the 'fone that talked to his rooftop dish. He cursed under his breath as he realized that he'd turned it off for the reception and left it that way. He fumbled and muttered at it, unable to figure out how to stop the auto-download so that he could start to compose a message to Renner—and then stopped trying, when he realized that a FLASH from Asach had come in. Waiting for it to scroll, without looking up, he said "I need to find Ollie Azhad. Can you get me to him?"

LaGrange sat up. "Why do *you* need Ollie Azhad?"

Barthes stared fixedly at the tiny screen, flicking text past with his finger. "I have my own reasons. Among them, at the moment, I need to inform him that my colleague appears to have located his children."

The Lads shouted in unison. "*Deela?*"

"Yes," nodded Barthes, "and two small boys. They appear to be unharmed."

After the adventures thus far, Barthes expected some dramatic response: a lurch of acceleration; careening around corners. Instead, Majlid meandered through the city with intense concentration and caution, pulling up in a shuttered alley lined with low warehouses that backed up to the stall fronts facing outward into the public street. It was heavily patrolled by grim-faced farm boys, who nodded at the lads in silent greeting.

Inside steamed with body heat. Men with weapons sprawled across their laps slouched in chairs lined up along the walls, silently, unquestioningly, waiting. Ollie was slumped over a battered desk, head in his hands, listening carefully to Linda Libiziewsky, but barely responding. A cluster of town luminaries, still wrapped in evening finery, gestured and pleaded with Ollie in low tones. At Barthes' entry, the low tones died to a murmur, then died away completely as the plaintiffs stood and stared. LaGrange stood aside to let him speak.

"Mr. Azhad?"

Ollie looked up.

"I have some news which may not be relevant to the present difficulties, though I suspect that it may well be. If I might speak to you privately?"

Azhad's eyes narrowed.

"I am a colleague of Asach Quinn."

Azhad nodded curtly, and several chair occupants detached themselves from the wall. They politely but firmly escorted the luminaries to an adjacent room. LaGrange and Libiziewsky huddled to one side.

Barthes leaned forward, spoke to Ollie in low tones, then handed him the 'fone, queued to Asach's message. Ollie's eyes went wide, then narrowed. One way or another, he currently had twelve thousand men and women under arms, patrolling every VIP residence, office block, parking lot, and hotel in the city. Until that moment, they'd been acting in fractured discord, each doing the best they could to guard their assigned bits of pavement and street.

Now, stripped of the threat to his remaining children, the broken man rose up from his chair suffused with righteous indignation, a general in command of an army. The transformation was terrible to see. Things moved very quickly. They pooled their knowledge.

There had been at least three explosions in and around the Temple. Two were superficial and external, and burned with low intensity, but very brightly. They were clearly meant to be seen. The third was caused by a vehicle exploding in the loading bays on the public side of the facility near the archives. It was burning fiercely. When it went off, so did numerous smaller fires, scattered throughout the city. Saint George Casualty Suppression was stretched beyond breaking.

The Zone Security Duty Officer that evening was from Maxroy's Purchase. He'd rotated on just before the explosions. He declared Zone Emergency immediately, sealed the post, and announced a general curfew. Civil personnel were ordered to leave. Linda stayed. Then, an MP platoon made the rounds, replacing TCM Zone and Contract Security guards with their own. They simply shot anyone who objected. As word spread, some joined the MPs; some fled the post; the rest were locked up "pending investigation." Finally, all non-MPs were ejected from the command post, to join their incarcerated brethren. They worked out the timeline: all of this had happened *before* Captain LaGrange was formally relieved. Which meant that Colonel Slam Dunk must have known about it. Then the comms tower went up. Linda hid until she could slip out a back gate into Moorstown.

The motive for the rampage in Moorstown was pretty clear to everybody as well. It was happening all over the city. It was supposed to look like spontaneous looting and rioting— but spontaneous looting and rioting didn't fit in very well with the local mentality, which was far more inclined toward Maintaining Peaceful and Orderly Communities.

Saint George citizens were veterans of this particular tactic. On a low level, it had been going on for months. On this scale, it had been done before, around the time of the first Jackson Delegation visit in 3035. Back then, irate residents had taken to the streets, made citizen arrests, forced the perpetrators with funny offworld accents to clean up the mess, marched them sixty miles in the general direction of Bonneville, and released them without shoes, food or water.

But, unknown to the good citizens of Saint George, shortly thereafter the "looters and rioters" had piled into cargo trucks headed toward an undisclosed location, and the city awoke the next morning to find Friedlander urban assault vehicles patrolling the streets, sent in by the True Church Militant to "restore order." Citizen resistance was fierce for awhile, but collapsed when it realized that Maxroy's Purchase fanatics were willing to destroy the city in order to save it. They went home quietly, and enrolled their sons as drivers for TC Contract Security.

This time, when "spontaneous" looting and rioting broke out, they were ready. They had become masters at playing the cat-and-mouse game of keeping their heads low while serving as eyes and ears for the civil police. This time, no looter or rioter made it more than a block or two down any street. They were all arrested, or killed while resisting same.

On their own initiative and as best they could, TCM Contract Security reported in which regular TCM units remained loyal to the city. It was a patchwork out there. It looked like those who had received LaGrange's whispered "local orders only" directive had slipped off to join their own and were holding fast. Others were taking their orders from MPs. Ollie's people had been cautiously backing up Saint George Casualty.

There was no holding back any more.

Barthes now remembered his first flight in and all the subsequent nights of dread with crystal clarity: the burned-out junk, the threadbare corners of the city. He understood now: for the second time in as many decades, New Utah—or, at least, Saint George—veered on the brink of civil war. He looked around him; felt the depth of commitment, and community, and, overarching that, the feeling of anger fueled by the toxic allegation of illegitimacy. How could Maxroy's Purchase make such outrageous claims? How could the True Church there declare New Utahans outsiders on their own planet? That much hubris was difficult to conceive. He sat awake, waiting for anything from Asach, while Ollie tried again and again to get through to Zia in Bonneville, and more experienced hands curled up in corners and nodded off around him.

North Badlands, Borrego (Swenson's) Valley, New Utah

The Operations Officer snarled as another light winked out. "What the flock is going on?"

The command post was filled with chatter. A left-chevron of position indicators swept forward, paused, flashed green to indicate battery fire—and then, one by one, went blank. He heard agitated communications chatter.

"Pull back! Pull back! Retrograde, Route Alpha!" This was ridiculous. It wasn't in the mission plan. What were they doing out there: playing Outies and Imperials?

"Lieutenant, Report! Why aren't you executing the training plan?"

The Fire Control Officer stayed focused on the board as he shouted his response, watching lights change colors and wink out. "Sir! Star Dawg's down. Phud Pucker's down. Killjoy, Backscratcher, Harm's Way—down, down down. Two total kills, two weapons kills, one mobility kill."

"Well, tell 'em to quit flocking around. We will blow our contract if we don't finish Phase Three Weaponization Tests on schedule."

"No! Sir! I mean they're *really* down!" As the board went dark, the lieutenant frantically sifted comms chatter.

"*What do you mean 'really down'?!*" This was ridiculous, and nonsensical. They were doing practice gunnery tests on a live-fire range. The 'enemy' were fixed targets. There wasn't even anybody out their role-playing an opponent.

"The w-kills and m-kill were reflected fire. The other two—Sir, somebody dropped a rock on 'em."

"A *what?*"

'Rocks, sir. Great, big, flocking rocks."

"*How?*"

"Flingers, I guess. We can't acquire."

"Well, *duh*, but how?"

The Fire Control Officer shook his head. "We're just getting scattered intel now. It looks like—" the lieutenant stopped to listen for a second. "Sir, they're opening sinkholes somehow."

"*Sinkholes?*"

"More like sink trenches. The vanguard moved out max overland, and then—poof—the ground just dropped in front of 'em. They fell into defilade, and before they could engineer out, a bunch of rocks just—dropped out of the sky. Along the whole trench. Like they'd pre-registered. We're running ground-penetrating radar now. It's like Swiss cheese under there."

"Show me."

The lieutenant pulled up the last-known positions for the killed amour, and pointed. "Here, here, reflected fire. BFR's here. Sorry. Big Flung Rocks. Open trenches here. Swiss cheese rendering now."

The image angled to its plane, showing a subsurface maze of threads transecting their line of travel.

"What were they firing at?"

"Nothing, really sir. Just dusting the path. They'd done their fixed targets, and were lasing lines to assess the scatter."

"And what shot back?"

"Nothing, sir, apart from their own EeRWigs."

The Major didn't like this at all. Enhanced Eradiation Weapons did not just bounce off shiny rocks to return their own fire.

"S-TWO!"

The intelligence officer also had both hands flying, 'teeth in both ears. "SIR!"

"What the HELL is going on! We are supposed to be shooting sunbeams into a sand pit a hundred clicks from the nearest *farmer!*"

"Nothing, Sir! I find nothing! No ground surveillance radar signatures, no infra-red trace, no counter-fire trace—nothing."

"Show me!"

The lieutenant put the remote sensing array results on screen. Auto-classification showed nothing. No armor, no artillery, no weapons masses, no blurry red dots indicating infantry radiating heat.

"Look forward."

The lieutenant changed scan range and repainted. The Commander pointed at an aquamarine splash, punctuated by grey-brown dots.

"What's that?"

"River delta, sir. Marshes."

"What about the dots?"

The lieutenant shrugged. "Doesn't tag anthropogenic, sir. Geology of some sort."

"Gimme a side scan." The lieutenant drew a box to shift the sensors again. The commander stopped him. "No, opposite those trenches."

The S-2 reoriented and punched. "On screen, sir."

There was nothing. The commander squinted. "What's that?" He pointed at aquamarine streaks arrayed along what might have been washes and gullies.

"More plant life, sir. The local stuff shows up this weird color. The invasives around Saint George show up pretty normal, but out here—"

The commander cut him off. "*Plant* life, you say?"

"Sir."

"Then, why is it *moving?!*"

The lieutenant peered. It wasn't fast. It was—walking pace. Not even. *Low-crawl* pace. But moving on line, inexorably forward. And the tank battalion, diverted by the collapsing trench system, was already turning directly toward it.

"Holy crap!"

They both started shouting orders.

The tank commander threw the hatch, muttering about what-the-flock was wrong with his track, and what-the-flock was wrong with his comms and—*What the flock?*

He couldn't see much.

And then he couldn't see at all.

He fell back inside, screaming and clutching his eyes.

His gunner couldn't see anything to acquire. Then his viewfinder fried white, dazzling him.

It was just as well. They would not have liked at all to see what came next.

It took the Warriors a minute to clear the tank. It took the War Rats another fifteen to strip it. They weren't as efficient as Miner's Helpers.

They flashed CLEAR. The Side leader sent in a Mining and Accounts team. There was a lot that the Miners did not understand, but they understood the laser weapons components in principle. They were like cutting beacons. *There* was the collector, and *there* was the charger, and *there* was the pump, and *there* was the fuser-cutter generator. It was odd that they had modified the assembly to serve as a weapon. This would not enhance *ar.*

They extracted the crystal. Judging from its affect when reflected back onto its source, this was quite valuable. This was what the vermin produced in the dirty smelters that reduced *ar.* Their own vitrifying fusers worked just as well, but not in so small a space. They required a team of three, but this seemed to require only one operator. The miner assessed a temporary bowl value. The Accountant issued orders to the Warriors. The Miner began calculating net *ar* required for production, but had to stop until they could consult a Farmer. A Runner streaked past, carrying a crystal sample to Enheduanna. Porters departed. Work finished, Warriors exterminated War Rats, except for a few personal pets. It was kinder. They could not survive out here. There was no *ar*.

With no one there, the Gathering camp was high, windy, and desolate. Gone was the eerie chanting; gone the fires and smells of cooking. Gone were picket lines and tents. The space was cleared as if never inhabited: rocks re-distributed at random; tracks brushed clean; manure burned and ashes scattered. Asach marveled at how the mind worked: how emotions waxed nostalgic over something that was so recently so strange. Stars punctured the evening air, twinkling in the distant lake.

Enheduanna made to leave, leaving Asach alarmed at the emptiness. Laurel was unconcerned. "Another island will come," she said. "Tomorrow—maybe the day after that. It depends on the rains." Asach huddled within the cloak, the night breeze chill after their days of sun-soaked confinement, imagining a coming misery of muddy damp.

They heard the edge-of-hearing chitter they now associated with Runners. One materialized as from the air itself, with a small package and a message for Enheduanna, who called for light. It appeared, from a distant, unseen point. The Runner everted an iridescent ruff of hair around its head that settled into a mirror-silver cowl focused on the packet. Enheduanna extracted three crystalline disks, and rolled one in each hand. The first was clear as a window pane. The second was the warm, fading lavender of sunsets. The third glinted with the bright, clear aquamarine of Laurel's eyes. Enheduanna explained.

"These are from the sand mines, and from—conveyances, hardened with ceramic covers, carrying weapons. The weapons flash green, like the Beacon." Enheduanna proffered the hand-sized lavender gem, sides and back dulled silver by the ceramic reflective jacket in which it was cradled. "Then they cut with light." With the gripping hand, Enheduanna extended the transparent crystal, almost invisible in the near-dark. "This is what they mine. This is what they make."

"Weapons?" asked Laurel. She grasped the thing. It dwarfed her hand. "Like tool and die cutters?"

Asach marveled at one so young, and from a farmstead so remote, that the rolling fire of mercenary gunners had never swept her life. "Good God. How many did they find?"

"A Grasp at least, maybe an Accountant's Hand, of each."

Asach struggled to remember the collective nouns of Mesolimeran commodity accounting, and gave up. "Show me, please."

Enheduanna flashed fingers: six times six times three times six times three times six—somewhere between two and four thousand. Asach made a low whistle. It didn't take an officer's commission to figure out that there were enough military-grade laser cores stockpiled there to equip an army.

With the slowness of the utterly unexpected, Enheduanna's words soaked in. Were explained. Were received with an involuntary shudder and closed eyes. Asach could taste the actinic blood and cold bile of fear that had welled in those poor sods who'd had nothing more than a day's work on their mind before they'd died at the, for want of a better word, *hands* of aliens. The likelihood that Sargon's attack had been communicated to—someone—was now overwhelming. They were out of time.

"Enheduanna, how long until the children arrive?"

Voices chattered. Lights twinkled. Time passed. Clouds scudded past, blocking shreds of stars. "Soon," was the only reply. They waited.

Enheduanna peered intently at Laurel. "You have pledged your *Swenson's people* as allies. Their assistance is now required."

Laurel shrugged. "Here? Tonight?"

Asach's skin crawled with foreboding. "Laurel, we *have to* get back. I *must* communicate with Bonneville. You *must* talk to Collie."

She shook her head. "And where would I do *that*? On foot? At night?" She shrugged. "The nearest 'optic jack is at the old OLaM strip on the other side of the mountain. That's a full day, even with mules, in daylight. Unless there's some other way *you* know of." She stared meaningfully at the point where the cloak's clasp lurked in the shadow below Asach's chin.

Then conversation stopped, as opaline ghosts flickered across the underside of scudding clouds. For a few moments, both Laurel and Enheduanna followed the iridescent play, then instinctively averted their eyes. Asach was nearly blinded by the sudden emerald dazzle that shot up through the hazy sky. The overcast was thickening. The Eye's reflection cast the valley in an eerie greenish glow, made the more ghastly as its pale shine caught and released the upward-falling snow of thousands of fluttering wings that spiraled heavenward, searching for true starlight.

Enheduanna picked up the thread of conversation, gesturing at a line of dark shapes disappearing into the night. "The rains have begun. The Protector's Army is on the move. It will reach The Barrens tomorrow, marching from the south. Others will follow you, over the passes to the western slopes. To prepare, a Grip of Miners and Farmers is moving forward now."

Laurel shook her head again. "Why now?"

"Because they will come," said Enheduanna, one hand still clutching a laser core, gesturing westward. "Won't they? Won't the Masters of these come now?" With the gripping hand, Enheduanna waved east and south. "And when they do, they will be destroyed by Sargon's Army. So, we will need all our allies. To make clear who is *friend* and who is *foe*. To prevent them being reinforced. To prevent fear within *your* cities. To help hold passes through the mountains."

Asach shuddered. *Or to be cannon fodder for Friedlander armor.* "I can send a message to colleagues in Saint George. Maybe they can get through to Bonneville, and from there to Collie. It may take all night."

Enheduanna showed interest, but did not question this statement, instead speaking again to Laurel. "Perhaps it would be faster if you ride? Runners could accompany you to relay messages. As we did with the *children.*"

"Ride? Ride what?" Laurel's head swiveled side to side.

"Your Porter. We attempted to bring it to you, but it does not like us. It shies away. It strikes out and bites. So we left manna every night for that beast and three others. They seem all right." Enheduanna gestured toward the distant lake. Several dark shapes stood like boulders against the dark shore, distinguished only by the absence of reflections in the water where their bodies blocked the light.

Then Laurel heard a distant *whhooo,* like a giant blowing warming breath into cold, cupped palms. The wind shifted slightly, accentuating the ripples that blew away from them across the water, and by contrast, the silhouettes at the shore.

"*Agamemnon?!*"

A sharp whinny pierced the night, followed by raucous braying from three long-ears.

Laurel was already running, her words trailing out behind. "You bring the kids. Radio whoever, take the mules, and bring the kids to the OLaM strip."

"But I don't know the way!"

"Leave at daylight. Follow the marked trail. Take every turning west or north. Give the mules their heads. It's the closest water. They'll find it." Laurel's voice was growing fainter in the distance.

"But wait! What will you do? What will you tell Collie?"

Laurel stopped, and spun in her tracks. "That the revelation is nigh! That behind me follows a Host of Angels!"

The ghastly light winked out. They saw nothing. They heard low rumbling nickers, followed by snorting and snuffling and stamping. Then hoof beats, as a black shape departed the valley in the blackness. Then Laurel's silvery voice, sliding away down the hillside: "I'll be there by dawn!"

Enheduanna made a murmur, and two ghosts slipped away to follow, fluttering wings marking their passage into the night.

Asach bent to one knee, already unzipping hood from cloak.

15

Final

Accounting

If you are going to sin, sin against God, not the bureaucracy. God will forgive you but the bureaucracy won't.

—Admiral Hyman G. Rickover, New York Times, 1983

For the sin they do, by two and two, they must pay for one by one.

—Rudyard Kipling, Tomlinson

Bonneville, New Utah

There was pandemonium at the Bonneville Lynx port when Lillith Van Zandt arrived. She marveled. News of the sand mine massacre had spread like wildfire. It was a secret operation, conducted by secret contractors, in a secret location, on the other side of some barren mountains across a barren wasteland on a world no civilized person had ever heard of, yet ITA hangers-on were already hopping into port like fleas from a drowning rat, while the rest of Bonneville slept on.

Almost the rest. The warehouse district abutting the SunFreight spur was ablaze with light, and the source of the "leak" became obvious. Sergeants were barking and waving their arms about in a midnight dance of getting armored vehicles onto flatcars. Access to OLaM's leased bays was tightly restricted, but the Klieg-lit movement from the concealment hangers was visible throughout the yards. They were odd-looking lumps assembled from local components and materials, including Plate recycled from older, derelict equipment.

She found the Friedlander commander, and spoke only one word. "Well?"

He shrugged. "Your contract specifies cost control. There was no apparent threat. There's nothing out there. Wasn't. We sent out a platoon for Phase I weaponization testing with light security, but held the heavier stuff here pending full-scale fire-and-maneuver. We're shipping out to re-secure the location in two hours. Obviously, we're not too happy with this outcome either."

"*Re*-secure." Her tone bespoke icebergs. "Against *whom*, exactly?"

"Not sure. Bandits. They were already there, whoever they were, which I guess means Himmists. Not really like them, but—" he shrugged again. "There's no-one else out there. We'd have known if anybody had moved from here. Not to worry. They've got nothing that can stand up to *this*." He waved a hand at the long line of flatcars.

"And restoring operations?"

He shrugged yet again. The quirk was beginning to irritate her. "Whatever they are, not our contract. I guess you'd need to talk to Trippe about that. It's his operation, as I understand it."

She smiled thinly. "Yes, it is." Mentally, she was weighing the cost of the survivor benefits clause against her growing annoyance and wondering whether, in this case, it was worth it. "And ensuring that they are *secured* is yours. I can't say that I particularly approve of your *cost-control measures*. They have become *very* expensive."

He shrugged for what she decided was the last time. "Usual cost of doing business, on an outworld. One way or another. With all due respect, ma'am, our contract calls for us to secure *our own* operations, which is the weapons testing. It doesn't include point security for yours. So from here on, you're effectively getting an added bonus. At least until testing is over."

"Indeed. I'm sure that you appreciate the risks better than I would." She turned away from the commander, called Clegg forward, and spoke to him, almost inaudibly. He nodded once, curtly, and faded into background again. "I will have a full damage assessment report—when?"

"Two days, at the earliest. They're finishing switch reprogramming now. We'll rail to the end of the line at the old OLaM hopper field, offload, and move out overland from there. We'll hook south around that mountain and either flush them out or tag them in the hills. We'll move the assessment team in as soon as the location is secure. Trippe has the plan."

But he was talking to himself. Lillith Van Zandt was already leaving, followed by Clegg and his men.

OLaM Station, The Barrens, New Utah

Agamemnon stood spread-eagled, head hanging, chest heaving, sweat steaming from every pore, air blasting through his nostrils with the force of bellows. A stock tank stood within five paces, and his belly ached with longing. But, throwing herself from his back before he'd even staggered to a lurching halt, Laurel had shouted "Stand!" So he stood, heaving and gasping, a Good Boy, doing as he was told. They'd left at dusk; now it was dawn. He'd covered a hundred rough miles and left the Runners collapsed at the trail side.

Red-gold morning crawled toward them across the plains as the rising sun crested the mountain behind them.

They rested in deep shadow, the deafening whum-whum-whum of the windmill field above them. The fusion glow of the SunRail collectors were lighting up the path back to Bonneville.

The airfield appeared deserted. The dusty junction of two roads to nowhere anchored the desolate shells of mud-brick and stone houses that had once served various functions for workers at the abandoned mines. An empty flinger gantry presided: a wingless heron on an empty beach. Only dust-devils played on the flat cross of the taxiways, two level strips in the level flats that stretched from the foothills into infinity. But Agamemnon threw up his head and stared into the far distance, so Laurel guessed that a train was coming.

Agamemnon's breathing eased. She felt inside his jaw: his pulse was still fast, but slowing. She walked with him the few paces, and let him sip some water a bit at a time. The easy way would be to ride down to the operations shed and call from there. It had everything, including an 'optic line. But she didn't want to get trapped on the airfield, and she didn't know what was coming, or how soon. There was no regular service here, and it was the wrong time for a pilgrim charter. If Agamemnon could already hear it, that did not leave much time.

She climbed back on. He swiveled his ears, not sure where they were going, because neither was Laurel. Then she decided, and feeling the twitch of nerve fibers that presaged actual body language, he abandoned the trail and plunged straight down the hillside, slithering and sliding and sending little avalanches of stone bouncing along ahead of their progress. Agamemnon jumped the last chunk of slope and broke into full stride, carving his own wind through the morning chill as he sprinted for the operations hut across the taxiway.

There was a window. There was a rock. There was Laurel inside. There was Agamemnon outside the door, hip cocked in rest, just waiting. Every Seer knew what to do, and Laurel did it: She activated the emergency lines. She got through to Collie. Her first words, however, were not about the kids. Her first words were simple: "*Uncle Collie! They're coming!*"

He listened to it all. He didn't say much. "Just get those kids to me, " he answered. "We'll take it from there. We'll get 'em home safe. We'll secure OLaM Station. We'll secure the mountain. We'll have every gathering in The Barrens backing us. We'll see it's done right this time."

And then Agamemnon was off like a crossbow quarrel, back the way he'd come, retracing his steps back up through the foothills to find the Runners and intercept Asach somewhere along the trail.

Bonneville, New Utah

There wasn't a city clerk alive in Bonneville who thought it the least bit odd that Zia Azhad would request access to titles and claims recorded at the public records office. Nor was it odd that she'd be at the door, awaiting morning opening. They'd known her from birth. She'd worked in the business since maturity. She'd spent the last decade in OLaM procurements. They did find it odd that she asked for Founder's–era land tax rolls, but public records were public records.

The basement was close and stuffy. Zia cursed under her breath. It was Barthes that was wanted here, not her—she had no idea how to access these archaic files. She fiddled with the clunky machine, trying to follow the pictogram instructions. She tried and failed to change the sort order and sort criteria.

She struggled to figure out how to open a search. The interface was incomprehensible. Nobody there could help her.

Finally, she resorted to thumbing down, page-by-page, eyelids drooping, eyes gravel-raw as she scanned for *Orcutt, Courter, Swenson; Ocotillo Wells; Butterfield Station; Swenson's Mountain; Swenson's Valley;* and a bunch of survey coordinates, moving backward through time on the reverse-order ledgers. Scrolled, and scrolled, and scrolled, and scrolled, in ever-increasing frustration, until near tears, she backhanded the screen, hitting—something—that made the file jump to its end.

And there it was, on the oldest cadastral survey recorded in Bonneville. She froze, not quite believing what she was seeing. She moved the image up and down a bit. In that funny old syntax, laid out plain as day, was an original Imperial deed, complete with surveyor's map and description. It showed a geologic fault line on the eastern border of The Barrens, running at the base of the foothills. Everything to the east of that was not only ceded, but entailed in perpetuity to "John David Swenson's heirs female." The True Church *couldn't* lay claim to it, because it was land that *couldn't* be bought, sold, mortgaged, pledged, or given away. It could only move down Swenson's line. If abandoned, it would revert to the Crown. Anyone who tried to poach it from Swenson's heirs— heiresses— was, from a *legal* standpoint, poaching from—the Emperor himself. He'd even personally sealed it, "in gratitude."

Zia sat for a moment, tingling with that odd sort of numbness that follows a shot of adrenaline. Then she moved over to a conventional terminal to work on the easy part. It wasn't even complicated, once you bothered to look. There it was: OLaM's new owner-of-record: some blabbity-named consortium, majority shareholder: Van Zandt Mining.

Zia pulled up the plat books for The Barrens. She'd never really had any reason to look at the old Orcutt landholdings: she'd only been concerned with getting things into and out of active mines. Once she did, the pattern was clear: over four generations the Orcutts had assembled a patchwork of parcels that added up to most of the land just *west* of that geological fault line, plus two big panhandles extending to Orcutt Station and along the OLaM SunRail line. Collie had held onto the family station itself, but everything else had been OLaM, not personal, property—first swallowed up by the TCM, and thence to Van Zandt.

Zia switched next to the True Church genealogy index—and suddenly all of it made sense. The next-to last in Swenson's female line was Serena McClellan Orcutt. Collie Orcutt's youngest sister. Laurel Courter's mother. The Orcutt men had been consolidating access to Swenson's Mountain for four generations—ever since they'd arrived from New Ireland as outcast Himmists in 2964. By maternal line, Orcutt's mother had been a Swenson.

Collie Orcutt had had a vision, but he'd gambled wrong in his vain attempt to secure a promised land. Now Lillith Van Zandt had murdered and kidnapped and cheated and bribed and poached her way through to the other side with a very different vision of her own.

Zia's lips were white. It all went back to the warehouses. Warehouses in Saint George, where her own children were seized to paralyze Ollie; warehouses here, where Michael was scammed, presumably so that he'd shut down and slink away somewhere to hide. Warehouses full to the brim with the nasty detritus of Lillith Van Zandt's scheming mind. Zia pictured it all again. This time, instead of Michael's twenty-two kilos of opaline glitter, she saw the packing boxes, full of sand, like geological calling cards. She pictured her boys, and green-eyed Deela, and thanked Him for holding them in his Eye. And finally, leaving to tell all to Ollie, Zia began to cry.

OUTIES

Orcutt Station, The Barrens, New Utah

To the untutored eye, they were a posse of broken old men. They slouched in trucks wearing battered hats. They sat their horses like sacks of potatoes. Their faces were burned to leather; their movements a study in conservation of effort. They ringed Collie Orcutt's house, waiting for news of those kids.

The signal lights twinkled first—a head's up none of them missed. They'd used the method themselves, more than once, organizing; practicing; marshalling all those years. Then the lights were obscured by haze, as a dust cloud boiled ever-nearer. Then its edges shimmered with half-seen movement. Then a shrill chatter reached their ears.

Trucks didn't react, but horses did: blowing and snorting and sending mules shying, riders sliding along with them like an outer hull of their own skin.

And then there she was: Agamemnon's head hanging, bobbing as he walked, catching his feet on every tick in the ground, neck curly-haired with dried sweat, flanks and belly tucked in, but ears still pricked.

And then there they were behind her: wide-eyed and towering above the dust: a girl and two boys, bobbing along, hands in a death grip on their Porters' ears, one great, hairy arm securing each pair of legs, the other swinging in the marching time of the pace.

And behind that, Asach, on a braying mule, its compatriots in tow.

And behind that, a Legion of Angels.

"Well?" said Collie.

The old men nodded. "Yep," said one, "we see 'em." Then they called every gathering, instructed every Seer, and within the hour were passing Laurel reports of every movement on or along the SunFreight line; to or from or through OLaM Station; into or out of the OLaM hopper field.

And Agamemnon got a long-deserved drink, and a rubdown, and hay, and even treats.

Near Butterfield Station, The Barrens, New Utah

The armor plowed southward like ships through whitecaps, each vehicle's progress demarcated by a bow-wave froth of sheer skin wings edged and veined with aquamarine, the fat little bodies sparkling in the sun like splashing water. Hundreds; thousands; millions of the creatures emerged to molt, and fly, and mate, and die during the brief promise of desert bloom that followed the first winter rains. The tracks plowed through and over squat cycad trunks already fat with water, a-fuzz with the first emergent green of bud stalks, and bejeweled with umbrellas of the creatures extending and testing new wings. Startled to flight by the whining engines, they answered with their own sharp buzzing, boiling into the sky like silvery clouds of fish schooling off an ocean reef. The roar was both piercing and deafening.

So, from a distance, the company lines approached like a thunderstorm rolling forward off the sea. From a height, they looked like lines of arrows drawn on a sand table, the better to indicate their objectives. Surprise was a sheer impossibility.

The Warrior lines danced northward, the half-Runner Cavalry sprinting ahead; leaping with sheer exuberance to snatch and crunch the meaty little bodies from the air. They became living, jogging trees themselves, as the emerging nymphs struggled to climb any height; as the newly fledged saw them as handy roosts for hasty test-landings. They traveled light, surrounded and suffused with all that they could ever want for perfect food and drink. From a distance, they could not be seen at all: mere ripples in the flowing field of crawling aquamarine.

The Miners wasted little time or effort. Assuming that *they* intended to recapture the sand mines, *they* would have to turn through the neck that led to Butterfield Station. South and west of that was already mired in marsh, the basin filled by early winter rains. Eastward was the mountain. The neck was an old, compacted river levee, now slightly elevated above the silty plain long since scoured away by the incessant wind. It was the only option for moving quickly.

So, the conclusion was foregone. If *they* stayed on the levee, they would fry in their own reflected fire, or the fire of concentrators operated by the Mining teams. If *they* slithered down banks greased with the bodies of winter flies, they would be mired in the seasonal back swamps. If *they* attempted to breach the banks to the north and east, a honeycomb of sand-traps awaited them. From a hundred points, the trebuchets awaited, ready to commence flinging. Signal watchers lined the hills, day-dreaming of the feast to come, already tasting sweet winter fly meat. Farmers lined the levee, listening for *their* approach.

The battle was vicious.

The battle was brief.

Those who survived remembered the buzzing din of Beelzebub; the grinning faces of demons; the sinking of an armored battalion beneath a rising sea of aquamarine.

Like castaways, faces red with burns, eyes shielded with torn strips of rags, raw lips cracked and bleeding, they staggered back the way they'd come. Reduced to sucking bugs for juice, many fell to the slimy ground kicking, sweating, trembling, their pupils shrunk to pinpoints. The smarter scraped mud into shirttails, and sucked on that instead. The water squeezed out green, then brown, then not at all. Their wounds began blistering and peeling.

Eventually, a clutch of Himmist kids on horseback was the best thing they'd ever seen. As they approached, the kids chatted briefly among themselves, then wheeled and bolted, horse's tails flagging in the air like retreating banners. Some stood dumbfounded. Some sank down, sobbing. Some cursed. A sergeant said: "We'll camp here." Here was nowhere. No-one objected. Some were not going to make it. The least wounded commenced to digging. A few hours later, a shriveled old man in a pickup truck genuinely *was* the best thing they'd ever seen.

Bonneville, New Utah

It was a quiet coup. The first to notice were the devout, at four a.m., who did not awake to the strains of a muezzin. The next were the sacristans, who at four-thirty found themselves quietly, but firmly, escorted to join their brethren in Allah for morning coffee. At five, after it had been explained that they would be escorted by a number of burly young men employed by TCM Security, the remnants of the TCM tithe committee found it reasonable and expedient to accept an invitation to an ecumenical breakfast. By five-thirty, when the SunFreight pulled into the rail yard, the assorted primates, bishops, patriarchs, elders, imams, aldermen, and dignitaries discovered their plans for morning prayers and services drastically rearranged.

For their part, SunRail yardmasters and transit police learned very quickly that the inbound cargo and passenger list from OLaM Station also had been altered rather dramatically from what they'd originally sent in the outward bound direction. By six, hands of Warriors and squadrons of Himmist cavalry had fanned out through the city, in time to greet the shift changes at the DAZ-E field, Hopper strip, transmission stations, and city police.

By six-thirty, the assorted dignitaries had all been briefed. The message was simple: an alliance of TCM Security and The Church of Him wished to ensure that there would not be any disturbances such as those suffered in Saint George. Bonneville's cooperation was expected. Absent cooperation, the Himmists could and would prevent movement of anything at all into or out of the city by any means save the Lynx. Indefinitely.

There were, of course, questions regarding how this might be done. Some of the questions were not especially politely phrased. Butterfield Station survivors were brought in to explain. Several in the audience expressed even less polite disbelief. A hissing Warrior led by a gleaming white Master was brought in by way of show-and-tell. The various factions recognized them in their own ways: Angel; Demon; Ape; Motie. When Enheduanna then addressed them in their own language, they nearly fell from their chairs. When Enheduanna gestured gently to the wings, to be joined enthusiastically by three goggle-eyed children, the youngest of whom proudly told the tale of how Tweety Kitties had saved him and his siblings from *bad men*, then reached out and took a hand of a sinewed Warrior, the buzzing of disbelief ensued again. When Enheduanna then explained the alliance of forces under the command of Sargon the Protector, two fainted, and all began to sweat. It was, the bishop would later explain, a rather *sudden* introduction to the neighbors.

The need for haste was impressed. A common press statement was achieved. By eight-thirty, it was released. By nine, the various guests were released as well, and rushed to explain the rules of order to their flocks, islands, and employees. Saint George was notified by ten o'clock that morning: the city stood under His protection.

"It's no good, mother. You are finished here." Wind whipped sand across the Lynx port hard enough to sting exposed skin. Lillith pulled her tunic's hood close around her face.

"Meaning?"

"Meaning that they've already recorded appeal. It's public record everywhere now—not just in Bonneville. Saint George, Maxroy's Purchase, and filed for protected status at accession. They all know. You forcibly poached an existing mining claim."

She snorted. "Appeal? By whom? Protected? By whom? They'll be admitted in Colony status, and we'll have the concession. We hold all the cards from here. This setback is merely temporary. They've no basis. We bought out the Orcutt and TCM claims in legal, recorded transactions. The rest is commons."

Michael stared at his feet, the wind whipping his whites around his ankles. His face flashed resolute; quavering; blank; near tears. She reached out a languid hand, brushed hair from his face, patted his cheek—was startled when he snatched her wrist in a vice grip. He snarled without raising his head. "Appeal? By the legal heiress—who still lives. You screwed that up royally, Mother—or your keen little go-to did. As you well know, Orcutt's claim only extended to the foothills. The Swenson line holds the rest. And get this, mother dear." He looked up now, face contorted with disgust. "That patent wasn't local. It was Imperial. So the claim *will* be heard by the Judiciary. We'll be laughingstocks at Court, thanks to your nasty little mess. Or worse."

At this, Michael yanked her around and pointed into the dark. "And protected? By *that!*" A hand of hissing Warriors stepped forward from the shadows, heavily armed. "Nothing was ever enough for you. You've brought us to this!"

Clegg made a move. Michael snapped, "I'd advise against it." He was trembling—with anger? Fear? Disgust? It was difficult to assess. Lillith knew him like this. There were some things of this universe that were just too ugly for Michael to contemplate. They'd found the one thing that gave him backbone: sheer contempt.

"You may think you have his ear, but the Emperor will never, *ever* forgive this. We'll never see Sparta again." He pulled her around to face him, his nose curled and eyes narrowed. "And more to the point, from what you care: neither will Imperial Autonetics, the ITA, or the Bury organizations. You've *ruined* us. I'll be stuck here *forever.*"

Lillith returned his look with an unruffled, unwavering stare, as she reached up and pried away his hand. "I wouldn't worry about that, my dear. They'll take it well enough. It's only business."

But Michael was done. "Get out," he spat.

"Gladly." She barked at Clegg. "Do whatever you must to get me off this planet under safe escort."

Clegg took a moment to think through this. He folded his arms, mentally calculating. He unfolded them, and counted off numbers on his fingertips. "That's now Extreme High Risk. Extreme Hazardous Duty Bonus, with Lifetime Survivor Benefits."

"Yes, yes." She was already turning toward the Lynx. Clegg did not.

"You approve activation of the survivor benefits clause on behalf of Van Zandt Mining?"

"Yes, I said! Just get me off this planet! Get on with it!"

Clegg looked at Asach. *"Witnessed?"* Asach nodded.

But still, Clegg remained immobile. "Then call it in."

Lillith gaped, about to object, but was confronted with the blank pane of Clegg's shaded eyes. Whipped by stinging sand; confronted by those *things* hissing at the edge of the airfield, she was suddenly overcome with chill, sharing her son's disgust at the sheer horribleness. "Oh, all right," she snapped, and activated a 'tooth, turning up the volume to cope with the howling wind. They could hear Van Zandt Operations in the background. She spoke briefly. The duty officer checked down his list of standard questions. "Yes," came her icy answer to the final one, followed by her personal authorization. It was done. And then they crossed the tarmac and left, the Lynx's engines flaming blue as it spiraled away to Saint George.

Saint George, New Utah

Trippe ran with devils on his tail. He was desperate, now. It was over. The battle was lost, the murder found out, and as far as everyone else was concerned, it was all his fault. He was out of facts on the ground. If they caught him, he'd hang.

He ran through the shuttered streets of Moorstown, where no-one even dared look out, shedding his uniform as he went. He was down to his pants and boots. He cut through an alley and nearly jumped out of his skin at wild braying. A man looked up, startled himself. He'd been about to untether a mule, now spooking at the end of its picket rope.

Trippe didn't even pause. He shot the man, then shot the mule, scudding to a stop even as the poor creature fell. Trippe ripped off the man's vest, then tunic, then baggy pants and boots. He jerked off his own footwear and uniform remnants; pulled on the dead man's clothes. Slung his own utility belt as a bandoleer, slashed the picket rope at the stake, unbuckled the hobble from the dead mule's foot, and coiled the rope as he ran.

He headed for a section of fence behind the FLIVR pool hanger. The FLIVRs were all out. There was nothing to guard. He took a gamble, and won. He hurled the hobble at the top of the fence. It caught with a banging clang, first try. He scaled the fence, unhooked the hobble, jumped down, ran on.

He snaked through abandoned buildings. There were no more battle sounds. He headed uphill, away from the surrendering ranks. His lungs were bellows. He kept the rope, but ditched the utility belt as he ran on.

He hit the back fence. No-one was there. He did the rope trick with the fence a second time. He looked up, up, up past the Oquirr foothills, into the mountains beyond. He could see the Van Zandt compound. Sun glinted off the glass wall like a beacon as he ran. He settled in to marathon pace. He was dumb as a post. He had the judgment of a jellyfish. But God, could he run.

His plan was simple. Nobody would guard the sheer cliff face. So he'd climb it. He'd climb it, like Alexander's Macedonians taking the Rock of Sogdiana. They'd never see him coming.

Trippe was nearly right, but for the wrong reasons. He might have saved himself a good deal of effort with more brains, and less brawn. Van Zandt's personal security detail were contractors. They were contracted as personal bodyguards, in a civil zone. They were not an army of mercenaries. Per contract, they had delivered Lillith Van Zandt to a secure location—her own compound. They had fulfilled the terms of their contract. Then, they had withdrawn. Except for one.

Fit, but the worse for the battle, the run, and the climb, Trippe hove puffing into the corridor leading to the conference room. The rest of the building was empty. There was nowhere else she could have gone. She'd be there anyway, watching his progress on the big screen. Or, from her viewpoint, the blinking, stationary pip that was his utility belt, lying within the Security Zone.

Harlan Clegg blocked his way. "I figured you'd come."

Trippe did not wait to find out how, or why. He aimed high and fast, above the Plate, but Clegg was faster, and already diving for the ground. Trippe just kept running, and aimed dead center the second time. He heard the *bam* as Clegg hit the wall then thudded to the ground, face down. Trippe skidded; grabbed the conference doorframe, spun to a stop, facing Lillith Van Zandt down the long, long length of the room.

Van Zandt was tap-tap-tapping on the conference table. As Trippe filled the doorframe, it went completely dark.

She looked up, the unruffled, polite gaze of a social hostess. "Dressed for carnival?" she smiled, "how delightful!"

He stood blinking for a moment, not comprehending the joke. "I'm not going down for this alone."

"How droll. Who's going with you, then?"

But there was to be no interesting repartee, not with Trippe. His long passages of militaria were memorized by rote. He possessed no wit of his own.

"You are. It's over. Azhad got to the MPs and shut them down. The Bishop's confined the TCM to barracks. Your invincible Friedlander Amour is burning in The Barrens. Your own security detail's run. And *they* hold the landing zones. There's no way off the planet. There's no way out of the Zone. Hell, there's no way out of the *building.*"

She contemplated him without answering. She thought she'd chosen him well. Duty, honor, die gloriously for Empire, and all of that. This was simply tiresome.

Trippe said, "I am *not* going to hang for treason. You tricked me."

"Treason? Tricked you?"

"Just *shut up.* Just shut up, and get up. I'm not going down for this alone. You're going to come with me, and we're going to surrender, and you and your family lawyers are going to *save me* from the Tribunal."

"I am?"

"I *trusted* you. I came to this godforsaken dirt ball because you said to. I served you well. "

"Not well enough, it would appear."

At that, Trippe snarled, and lunged forward. Van Zandt folded her hands on the tabletop, unperturbed. "Care to dance?" she said, as Trippe tumbled to the floor.

It had felt like—just a tug, really. A little tug, like—like tripping over a wiry icicle. He tried to stand, but stumbled again. Something was wrong with his foot. Suddenly, the pain was incredible. He looked down; couldn't make out what he was seeing. Half of his right foot was missing. Not missing exactly. There it was, in half a boot, lying behind him on the floor.

"Oh, dear. When dancing, you really *should* watch where you put your feet." The pretty mask twisted into a snarl. "Because I really *don't* like it when people step on my toes!"

Trippe was shaking now. Involuntarily. His heart was racing. Adrenaline was fighting with shock. Shock seemed to be winning. Forcing deep breaths, he scanned the room, searching for the nearest piece of wood; fabric; anything combustible. A carpet runner circled the baseboards. It was beautiful. Design played along it like brook water; like flower fields; like thunderstorms in mountains. The patterns changed as you turned your head. The very threads were holographic. Things were moving very slowly. This way autumn; that way spring; they changed with the play of light.

"No!" screamed Van Zandt, then forced controlled composure. "Oh, how could you. That carpet's irreplaceable, you *boerenkinkel.*"

Trippe looked at his hands. The laser pistol played back and forth, back and forth, along the line of the runner. Curls of acrid smoke swirled above the floor now. It smelled like burning dogs. In what was probably the sole moment of poetic clarity of his entire, boarding-school life, he intoned: "Like Alexander's gift to Zoroaster, I dress your table with fire, milady."

Actually, it was not original. He'd read it somewhere. But his brain had registered: table; fire, and unbidden the quote had come. Trippe scanned the room, and saw what he was looking for. The smoke revealed only the one laser-thin line of light: only the one nasty little tripwire. He held the gun steady now, drilling a hole through the baseboard. The laser winked out.

Now Van Zandt was standing. Lurching, grasping the table for support, Trippe stood too. He leveled the gun, began to say, "You *will* come with me now," but blinked, groggy, because something new was wrong. Lillith held a grenade in an outstretched hand, her thumb in a thumb-sized depression. The play of light in a halo showed the grenade to be charged and armed.

"On the gripping hand, you seem to have a little problem now, no? Shoot me, I drop this, we both go." She smiled. "I prefer a different scenario. I leave, and maybe I toss you a little *party favor* on my way out—or if you *continue good service* maybe I don't. Do you play cards?" She stepped forward.

Trippe swung on his good foot in a desperate move. With one hand he grappled for the picket tether and slung it around the massive table leg, the hobble at its end whipping the rope around in a spiral, then lunged to snatch Lillith's free arm with the other. Lillith was strong, but he was heavier. His dead weight pulled them both to the floor. He was fading now. He tensed to force blood into his brain and tossed the gun, freeing both hands, rolling to pin Lillith's free arm under his body. He struggled to buckle the hobble to Lillith's wrist as tight as it would go, threaded the tether end through the ring, snapped the lock, and rolled, heaving on the rope with all his strength. Lillith's free hand jerked up, cinched to the table leg. Trippe crawled to the far side, and tied the rope off to another leg, far from Lillith's reach.

He was panting now, adrenaline gone, limbs gone limp, body shutting down from shock. "Turn it off," he croaked. "They'll be here soon anyway. Your security detail's gone. It's over."

Lillith Van Zandt pursed her lips, then sighed. "You people really are so tiresome." Then she dropped the grenade, and matter-of-factly straightened and patted her clothing. "I've no intention of submitting to Imperial interrogation," she said. She closed her eyes. Lights pulsed a countdown. It seemed to be very slow.

Trippe croaked, then screamed, then sobbed, as he tried, and failed, to lunge for the grenade. "No! Help! Stop! No!" But there was no-one to hear. No one but Clegg, face down in the corridor.

Yet, in Clegg strode, face impassive behind his shades, his eyes confined to a little secret universe unconnected to the mayhem unfolding around him. The pale sun had brightened the sky to a clear, winter blue that suffused the window wall. It cast his shirtfront with a bluish glow. He paused a moment. His brow furrowed slightly. He inhaled sharply. He stepped forward, staring blankly at the now-blank screen of the window wall, out into the blue space beyond, down into the solid grey mist that carpeted the valley floor.

There was a kind, hard edge to certainty. You could decide, right or wrong, but just decide, and then you stopped being virtual, and started being hard and certain and real. He did not hesitate. He fell forward. One fall, covering the grenade with two inches of solid Plate. Then everything went very, very quiet. Then he sailed right through the screen and into another life.

The blast wave snapped back Lillith's head; jerked her body backwards, hard against her tethered arm. She looked up at the underside of the conference table. Was appalled to see chewing gum stuck beneath the edge. Then a chunk of Plate tore past her eyes, striking Trippe squarely in the forehead.

FINAL ACCOUNTING

16
Chairman of
the Board

Sometimes it is said that man cannot be trusted with the government of himself. Can he, then be trusted with the government of others? Or have we found angels in the form of kings to govern him? Let history answer this question.

—*Thomas Jefferson, First Inaugural Address*

Sinbad, holding for jump to Maxroy's Purchase

Quinn's report was long. Quinn's report was thorough. At beginning and end, Quinn's report cut to the chase. Barthes had read it, and privately concurred with its findings. Renner finished reading it, and sharply sucked in air. Oh, how very ironic. If Bury had known, those few years ago, that unknown to all and sundry "Motie" castes *were* there, New Utah would now be a ball of glass, and *no one* would have a stake here.

Instead, a decision hung in the balance that would change human space forever. If the Van Zandt claim held up in Imperial court, there would be no doubt as to New Utah's status at accession: Colony world, entailed to Maxroy's Purchase, with Van Zandt Mining holding a ninety-nine-year concession for production of weapons-grade doped YAG. Human population reduced to serfdom, and—what to call them? They weren't Moties. They had not come from the Mote system; had never seen Mote Prime. They had gone *to* the Mote, in some age past, and it would be a very long while before anyone knew just when. Swenson's Apes, maybe, for the moment, though they surely were not that either. Maybe what they called themselves: *Mesolimerans*, the people between the mountains. Whatever to call them, Van Zandt's actions would march in time with past precedent: the Miners, possibly, would be enslaved, and all others tagged for extermination.

And what would that do to human-Mote relations? Set the tone for things to come: slavery, or annihilation? Renner shifted uncomfortably in his chair. He had twice survived passage through the Mote system. This was hubris. *That* tone would doom them forever. If the Motie-patrolled second blockade were to fail, human space would not survive. It could not defeat an alliance of Motie enemies. Even xenophobic Bury had seen that light in the end: human survival depended on an alliance of Motie friends. Quashing the Van Zandt claim was the only option.

And what would that mean? For starters, that would define Lillith Van Zandt as a traitor, and Van Zandt's illicit operations on New Utah as treason. Treason which had *not* prospered: treason, loud and clear. The Emperor was as ruthless as needs must. Lillith herself would be for the chop, with Michael appointed the new Margrave by way of consolation. Lillith too had been young once: charming, graceful, powered by ambition. Would Michael prove to be any better over time?

For New Utah it meant accession in—what status? Unless a miracle was conceived, Colony, yet again. Ridiculous though that seemed for a world that was at heart as technologically advanced as any in the sector, and no clear threat to anybody—at least, not in the military sense. But New Utah had no planetary government and, if you excluded the offworld craft, no space presence: no travel, no orbital technology.

For all his years at Bury's side, Renner was a pilot. He plotted a course, then reacted to events. It gave him a headache, thinking through this mess.

He called Blaine. It was never the same as in person, no matter *how* high-end the holo-D. It wasn't just the blotches and delays. It was the absence of subliminal input: body language in peripheral vision; changes in odor and breathing. But they had been friends, on and off, for so many years, that Kevin could fill in the gaps. Rod was pissed off and edgy, even though he wasn't saying.

It began amicably enough. "Rod, why'd you pick Quinn?"

Blaine shrugged. "Originally? The first Jackson Delegation? Simple, really. That Mormon thing. It was all muddy Church politics, and Quinn was handy."

"No, this time."

"Precedence, really. And this time I had Bury's testament about past and future reliability."

Renner was confused. "If Quinn was unreliable, why send—"

Blaine burst out laughing. "*Quinn? Unreliable?* You *are* joking?"

"Well, who then?"

Blaine sobered. "Oh, for Christ's sake Kevin, *do* try to keep up. You were even *in* on it. Jackson, of course. And Lillith. Though I can't say Lillith surprised me. really."

Renner sat back, blinking. "But Jackson *fought* the Outies. That's what earned him his Knighthood. And the Governorship."

Blaine snorted. "I know you think I'm just being an elitist prick, but Jackson played the oldest hand in the book. Bury would have found it himself, if you all hadn't gotten sidetracked with the Motie scare and the real threat at the Sister. For all I know, he did. You remember what he said: *There was too much money flowing through that system.* Jackson allied himself with Lillith Van Zandt—or, should I say, Lillith spotted Jackson's ambition early on—then he *invented* an Outie threat—bankrolled by Lillith—and defeated it. Handy, really. As you say, it earned him a title and Governorship. I no longer recall in which order. Of course the Emperor knew some of it even then, but he admired Jackson's ambition, tenacity, and capacity for accommodation. And there was the original Motie angle, of course."

"His prior service."

"Yes, in my first command."

Renner chewed on this. "Then along came Bury."

"Yes, Kevin, along came Bury, but more to the point, along came you, and your *incredibly* inconvenient dedication to creating and investigating the Motie Scare on Maxroy's Purchase. You nearly got my children killed, you know."

"That's unfair. You know that—"

"Oh, of course Kevin. It all worked out in the end. Children intact, Empire saved, alliance patched to blockade the second jump point, and now you arsing about on pins and needles waiting for Senate confirmation of your Mote System governorship. But think a moment. What did *any* of that actually have to do with New Utah? And *who supplied the ship* for Jackson's first accession delegation? That was Bury. *You* got lucky, because you were along for the trip, which put you in the right sector to go and have your second joyride through Motie space. But regarding New Utah, it was *Bury* who was right in the end: *There was too much money flowing through that system.* Bury, who'd had a stake in purchasing unregistered ships from New Chicago. Who better—"

"—to spot a world where somebody had a stake in manufacturing unregistered weapons systems."

Blaine answered by way of silence.

"So, this will cost Jackson his governorship."

"Oh, I should think so. He can hardly claim to be the innocent. He may have thought using Lillith as proxy would keep it all at arm's length, but no arm is long enough to distance him from this."

Renner saw doors opening and closing. For himself; for Imperial Autonetics. He also saw a quagmire of politics. Who would become his enemies at the fall of Lillith Van Zandt? Aside from Jackson, of course. "Rod, I'm not sure what to do here. I don't want to lose that Governorship. I've *got* to get back to the Mote."

And now Blaine was white-lipped. "You are asking *me* for advice? Kevin, *advice* is your responsibility. What will secure Acrux? What will secure my House? What will secure my *family?* A poke in the Emperor's eye for backing the wrong horse? A running feud with the House of Van Zandt? Welcome to *real* politics. Some of it *is* talk, not action. You are sitting on the fence chewing your nails, scared to death of what you might not get. What do you *have* that you care to defend? Your own ass? Your ship? Your stake in Imperial Autonetics? Our friendship?"

Bonneville, New Utah

The True Church Elder muttered hostile prayers as Ollie Azhad escorted him from the room. He'd been dragged from his bed and flown to this godforsaken wasteland, and at his own expense to boot. The corridors of Bonneville Citadel were ugly and crude. Its windows faced east, the view across the endless Barrens a reminder of the waste from which Heaven had been hewn.

He thought the use of the old Founder's Bowl a bit of cheap theatrics. Beyond the stage, there was nothing but the dusty plain stretching to infinity. Across the tiered semicircle,

Bonneville whites predominated, but the ecclesiastical garb was many-hued. They'd brought a small delegation from Saint George, including the Mayor with that female Captain as escort, but he suffered no delusions. *Planetary government my eye*, he thought. *Constitutional convention be screwed*. This was about *him*: about how far *he'd* bend; about Church and State and what *he'd* do.

He'd not been in Bonneville these past days. He'd arrived by night. His hubris might be excused.

Sinbad, above Maxroy's Purchase

A human might have paced, or drummed fingers, or raided the food locker. Ali Baba hummed, in a range inaudible to humans. It was a thrumming pitch, like a drawn-out groan, that both expressed discontent and soothed.

For the thousandth time, he played the recording of Bury's voice on the testament cube. It helped him forget how afraid he was; how alone; how misused. He desperately needed something to *do*.

So he did what he always did when bored: he hacked. There wasn't an onboard system he couldn't break into. *Everyone* had long since learned that the only encryption immune to his many prying fingers and miraculously accurate imitations of voice were a triple combination of biometrics and randomly-generated codes.

So, obviously, Kevin meant him to find this. He might as well have drawn circles and arrows. Ali Baba called up the files, and listened transfixed to a medley of non-human voices. They were *nothing* he'd heard from the Mote. They were *everything* he'd heard from the Mote. He found the translation packets. He worked through those. They *mimed* the words, but they missed all the notes. They were right, sort of, but *all wrong*. He listened to the originals, and then the translations, over and over, and trembled. *"I would know my enemy." "Legitimate government." "Allies." "From the stars."*

Bonneville, New Utah

The hoppers floated on transparent albatross wings, their descent rippling toward them from the horizon in a rolling mirage. As they approached, the Elder felt a vague trembling in his seat, and craned his neck, trying to make sense of the non-relationship between the ground vibration and the approaching gliders.

A wiry man, at least the Elder's age, moved across the stage in a careful series of folding and unfolding joints. It was the stride of a man who, for a very long life, had never walked anywhere if he could ride. Beside him strode a lanky girl, who looked up at them all with piercing aquamarine eyes. Beside her was an odd-looking chap in a ridiculous getup: The City Gates Uniform, representing the privy council of Bonneville. He looked like something from the top of a Christmas tree.

The vibration increased slightly, and resolved into separate pulses. It was like sitting inside a giant cup, with a giant finger tapping on its side. The Elder's eyes narrowed. It had been a score years, or more, since he'd last set eyes on Collie.

The acoustics were incredible. The old man spoke out clearly, and no amplification was required. "Ladies and Gentlemen, my name is Collier Staten Orcutt, and this is my niece, Laurel Courter. On behalf of all pilgrims and The Barrens gatherings, I'd like to introduce you to some friends of ours." The Gatekeeper merely nodded.

Orcutt stood impassive as the source of the vibration became loud and clear. Ranks marched in from behind the Bowl. TCM Security tramped in to line the aisles. Wave on wave of Seers filled the orchestra pits and choirs, ranging in age from infants-in-arms to older-than-God. And then, with a steady tramp-slap, tramp-slap, in concentric arcs to complete the circle on the far side of the stage, marched half a Side from Sargon's Army. It seemed to go on for weeks. The Bowl sat, awed into eerie silence.

The hoppers settled to ground, sun glinting from their wings as they coasted to a halt beyond the troops, lined up side by side. A path opened through the ranks like a parting sea. The Elder felt his bones tingle; his intestines begin to writhe. Then, as the sound rose to human-audible registers, and washed over them in a terrifying tide, the Seers joined in, overlaying the alien strains with the eerie polyphony of The Gathering Hymn.

Even the Elder was wide-eyed. There was nowhere else to look. There was nothing else to see. Down through the ranks of demons strode seven stately figures, twin arms folded, gripping arms extended, fur a blinding white. One topped the others by a head and shoulders. Except that none of them *had* shoulders. Only when they had reached the stage did the alien cheer and Himmist Hymn subside.

Laurel stepped forward, eyes bright. "It is my privilege to introduce The Excellency Sargon the Hand, Procurator of Swenson's Valley, Protector of Mesolimeris, Defender of *Ar,* and the Masters of the Six Cities, with whom all of The Barrens are allied."

There was silence, save for the wind, whipping through the various flags of ecumenical fabric. The Elder was started from shocked reverie by sharp, echoing clapping that arose from a pair of hands directly by his side. He turned and stared, heart sinking, as he watched Ollie Azhad rise and step away. Fuse lit, the applause whipped down the rows; across the aisles, following the TCM lines, and the thought finally came: *Good Lord. I've lost them. TCM Contract Security has defected to their side.* He looked out across the amphitheatre. He had no MPs. He had no TCM Zonies. He had no Temple. He was just one among patriarchs. He looked again. And matriarchs. He looked again. And—*them.*

The Bonneville Counselor spoke for the final time. "The First Constitutional Convention of New Utah is convened. Will official delegates please join us inside."

Sargon hadn't the patience for this. It fell to Enheduanna. Who hadn't the patience, either, but an order was an order. Humans were infuriating. They argued about *what ought to be,* instead of negotiating *what was.* Now the Elder was shouting something.

"*Facts on the ground?* I'll give you facts on the ground. TCM tithe collection *is* this planet's government. There's no other institution that governs *both* Saint George and Bonneville."

"*Governs?* More like *poaches.* Strips us all of tithe to pour into Maxroy's Purchase and that misbegotten Temple!"

"And well-placed, too! Without the Maxroy's Purchase True Church—"

"Without the MPs we'd be dealing with two thousand fewer common thugs!"

This last outburst came from the Mayor herself, much to the shock of the Elder. He was genuinely hurt. "Madam, do not forget the sacrifices the True Church has made to make this planet habitable. Selenium supplements. Medical supplies—"

"Which we wouldn't need if you hadn't leached the topsoil." Now the Himmists were back in the fray.

The babble was cut short by Enheduanna. "We will repair this. We will restore *ar.*"

The Elder bridled; refused to face the *ape.* "I fail to see why this—creature—has a place at this table. We are making decisions regarding accession to the Empire of *Man.*"

The Bonneville Counselor spoke up. "Well, I can't say we're *thrilled* about it either, but, you know—" she looked at

Enheduanna— "there's rather an *army* of 'facts on the ground.' And that army's *not yours*."

For hours, the arguments rolled 'round in circles. Asach, observer, sat in the corner, doodling the same words, over and over. Then added curlicues, baubles, leaves; the words peered out of gewgaw forests. Coffee. Pie. People. Different. Fixing. They broke; returned; broke; returned; made no progress backward; made no progress forward.

The Elder wanted his True Church. Bonneville wanted—Bonneville. Eclectic, anarchistic, metropolitans-in-the-desert that they were. The Barrens wanted manna. The Mesolimerans wanted to be left the hell alone. Who was left to tip the scale? Asach was out of options.

At the next break, Colchis Barthes, with quiet aplomb, approached Jeri LaGrange, still assigned to protect the chief Saint George dignitary of the no-longer-one True Church. They chatted softly and briefly. At the break after that, he stepped over to Ollie Azhad; asked quietly: "might I have a word?" Next came the Saint George mayor. The University president. Like Lillith at a grand soiree, Colchis Barthes greased the herd.

The next morning, as conference broke for Sabbath prayers, the Mayors climbed aboard one of the gossamer birds.

It was, all-in-all, an earthy delegation. Farmer John peered out from beneath his grandiose ear. The Lads, shorn of weaponry and excess hair, certainly cleaned up good. The President of the Saint George Grange was new upon the scene. Collie Orcutt was bracketed by Laurel and his younger self, a sinewy Professor of Agronomics from Zion University. They'd worked all night. Their staffs had worked all night. In the case of the university, a bunch of students had worked all night. The delegates filed in, bleary-eyed themselves, and were met with nothing less than a model world.

It was three dimensional. It spun and swirled. By inserting hands inside, it could virtually stretch; by squashing it outside, it could be shrunk; by bracketing points, a section could expand to fill the whole wall. In depth; in detail; in beautiful illustration, they explained and showed what it took to actually feed all *eight* cities on their world.

The Mesolimeran cities were dazzling. They sparkled topaz, ringed with aquamarine fields. Beauty aside, the statistics were sobering. Mesolimeran farming was at least *six times* as productive as even the best of Saint George farmland. Its primary philosophy was *intensive,* where Saint George's had always been *extensive*. Direct to the heart, if allowed to extend their methods to The Barrens—which the gatherings would wholeheartedly encourage—they could produce sufficient selenium supplementation to serve the entire human population of New Utah within a year.

Which meant the True Church could use its *legitimate* revenue to rebuild.

As could Bonneville.

The Elder was intrigued, but suspicious, still. "And what do they want in return?"

Enheduanna answered, personally, with one word. "Citizenship."

The Elder looked blank.

"We want the same rights as humans."

His eyes narrowed.

"And we want Sargon appointed Defender of *Ar* for all of New Utah." Anticipating the next objection, Enheduanna interjected: "We care *nothing* for your Church."

The Mayor of Saint George spoke up. "Ladies and Gentlemen, on behalf of the Mayors of the Eight Cities," she paused a moment for that number to sink in, "I'd like to circulate a draft Constitution."

17
Intellectual Property

What a piece of work is a man, how noble in reason, how infinite in faculties, in form and moving how express and admirable, in action how like an angel, in apprehension how like a god! the beauty of the world, the paragon of animals—and yet, to me, what is this quintessence of dust? Man delights not me— nor woman neither, though by your smiling you seem to say so.

—*William Shakespeare, Hamlet, Act II, scene 2*

Saint George, New Utah

"I don't understand. Why can't we just use the Lynx?" The voice was gruff; querulous.

There were six groups clumped around Lillith Van Zandt's conference table, with one from each more-or-less shoved to the fore. What had been her conference table, now moved to another room. It was early. Frost still lay on the valley, spread far below.

At the head was Sargon himself, with old Lagash, Farmer John, a Doctor, the senior Keeper of the Storehouses, and a knot of Miners arrayed behind him. Two warriors stood as Sergeants-at-Arms.

To Sargon's right was a cluster of religious heads representing the assorted patriarchs, elders, bishops, presbyters, pastors, imams, and rabbis of the various Christian, Muslim, and Jewish denominations. Only Laurel Courter and the New Utah True Church Elder were pushed up to the table. Next to them was seated the Chair of the Board of Physiology of the New Utah College of Nurses, Physicians, and Allied Healing Arts.

To Sargon's left sat Asach, and beyond Asach was a knot of civil servants, including the Mayors of Saint George and Bonneville, departmental chiefs of the utility and transportation authorities, and Michael Van Zandt, along with Zia and a senior TCM warehouse accountant. They were more-or-less clumped behind Aloysius Geery, chair of Zion University's College of Technical Science, Engineering, and Urban Planning, along with the senior research librarian and the college's lone astrophysicist, a mostly self-taught junior Fellow. Oblivious to any potential issues of protocol or propriety, the engineering operations chiefs of OLaM, SunRail, SunFish, DAZ-E, FLIVRBahn, and the Saint George spaceport were sprawled in various elbow-leaning, leg-bouncing attitudes in the conference chairs, messing with the on-table graphics and passing e-notes back-and-forth to their field staffs, even as they argued.

At the foot of the table were the Imperial Observers, in the persons of HG, Colchis Barthes, and the ITA representative. Barthes smiled inwardly. HG was clearly annoyed. He'd only just returned, and still suffered from the delusion that Asach was his personal aide-de-camp. That Asach was not fulfilling that role was annoying enough, but Asach's privileged seat at the table next to Sargon's gripping hand was likely to turn HG apoplectic before the meeting was over. It was the Librarian's self-appointed private responsibility to remind HG that he was there in an official capacity, and keep him sitting on his hands.

The spaceport ops officer repeated the question. "The Lynx? Why can't we just use that?"

"Because *it's not ours*. It's FairServ's. We didn't design it. We didn't develop it. We didn't build it. It's not based on indigenous New Utah technology."

"Well, an ITA landing craft. Or *Nauvoo Vision*. That's what *they* came in on, right?" With a hike of the thumb in HG's direction.

"Same logic."

"OK, a True Church shuttle, if we have to!"

"And there's the rub, *again*. *It's theirs*. Maxroy's Purchase's. That makes us an MP colony, *not* an independent Classified world. Haven't you been listening? You *must* grasp this! The Empire of Man *will not recognize* space flight unless we develop it ourselves. We can't just buy it."

"This is ridiculous. We may not be industrial giants, but we *are* a fully developed world! We've *masses* of indigenous technology. *Masses* of indigenous aircraft."

"Like?"

"FLIVRs, strictly speaking. SunFish hoppers."

"I won't comment on FLIVRs. And the SunFish is a powered glider."

"A *solar*-powered glider, capable of round-the world hops."

"And used, I might add, for *planetary* tax-collection."

"By *you lot* of the TCM, *while* you were still under MP control, which is not *really* the precedent we want to reinforce, eh?

"But not, sadly, for orbital flight. It's an air-breather. No air, no flight. Or should I say, in air, no spaceflight."

"Oh, for heaven's sake. Mining flingers, then. Pushed to the max, they deliver payload on an extra-atmospheric ballistic trajectory. You can't claim we bought those!"

"Well, I wouldn't bray about 'em too loudly. Any child with a ruler, six magnets, and a handful of ball bearings can make a coil gun."

"Not one that uses solar power to shove a ton of payload over mountain ranges! Go try it yourself, you *people mover*."

"Again, sub-orbital. And anyway, incapable of carrying a *living* passenger, *rock pusher*."

"But we had *no reason* to invest in independent spacecraft development, let alone launch capacity! We could have done. For God's sake, after the First Empire collapsed, Aldrich Saxe sketched designs for a manned, orbital Flinger in *2699*. The story is not apocryphal. He was half-drunk one night, and did it on a bet, on the back of a cocktail napkin, within twenty minutes! I've *seen* it! But there was no point in developing it, because *there's nothing to mine up there!* We've one rocky scrap of an asteroid moon, and *that's it*. We're a small place. We have small, dispersed settlements. We built to appropriate scale. Space vehicles sufficient to our needs were already here! *They did not need re-inventing!* We concentrated on developing efficient solar technology that we *could* use. You might as well say that *Sparta* isn't an independent developer!"

"But they could be. They have the infrastructure. They have the University. They have the Library. The knowledge is already there."

"The knowledge was *already here!*"

"But we can't prove that."

"We can't prove that, *because Lillith Van Zandt*"— murderous glare toward Michael— *"burned down the Scriptorium!"*

"In which case, the knowledge was lost. The space technology available to New Utah is built, maintained, and launched from offworld, specifically from Maxroy's Purchase."

"That's insane. You think that bunch of god-bothering, seed-spitting Snow Ghost hunters pulled a spaceport out of their agricultural communes and genealogy charts? They *bought* the whole damned thing, kit and caboodle. And a beat-up pile of space junk it is to boot, from what I've heard."

"That's different." HG had that adolescent trump-card look about him again.

"*Why?!*"

Barthes cut him off before he could blurt out something childish, like 'because I said so.' "Because on Maxroy's Purchase the Navy was presented with a done deal. The MP economy—trade system, technology exchange, the whole lot— was already integrated with New Caledonia. The genie was already out of the bottle."

"Well, so was ours, until the embargo. The economy, I mean."

"Should have joined up when you had the chance." There was no end to HG's smugness.

"What chance was that? As a Maxroy's Purchase *colony?* You've seen enough by now to know that would have meant *civil war.* We did our best to avoid that, and bloody well did, *in spite of* Lillith Van Zandt's best efforts."

"And so, we are back to no planetary government.*"

"*Well then how the hell did we get labeled as a bunch of dangerous, piratical, space-faring Outies if we're so backward and primitive that we can't even be Classified?*"

"That's rather the point, isn't it? The bottom line is: when the Navy pops through that door, if they don't see developed, orbital technology, they become rather determined to keep things that way. Lest you *become* a threat to the Empire."

Sargon grew increasingly bored with this. He Spoke.

Asach thought long and hard, then interpreted. Not translated—there was no simple string of literal words that could convey the concepts involved—but interpreted, as best possible.

"There is planetary government now. Anyone who disagrees may leave." Asach paused briefly. No-one stirred. Asach posed the question on Sargon's behalf. "If there is no spaceflight, what becomes of the *ar?* The land? What becomes of the productivity of the land?"

"You lose control of it."

"This we will never allow."

HG exercised usual tact. "You'll 'allow' it, or the Navy will fry the planet."

Sargon was horrified. "They would do this? These Imperials? They would *destroy ar?"*

Asach answered, softly, for the benefit of the room, "They would destroy everything that lives." That stopped the chatter, even among the engineers.

Sargon swept three hands backward impatiently. "I do not mean the living. I mean the *ar.* The potential. The potential of the land to produce life."

Now Barthes answered. "If they thought the threat great enough, they would turn the soil to glass."

Sargon's response was involuntary. Although it involved no movement, every being in the room felt a tremor; a temblor; a wrenching, eerie *wrongness* in the bones, not unlike the feeling during a jump. It was the feeling that accompanies a near-strike of lightning, or rolling thunder, or the eerie noises that echo through deep caves. All shivered, or squinted their eyes, dimly aware that their bodies and brains had heard something that their ears had not.

Then Sargon Spoke. Again, Asach interpreted.

"Then you will cease arguing. You will make a solution. You will begin the work with all due haste."

The humans looked about, confused by this. Now, the Miners began earnest conversation among themselves. Enheduanna barked orders. Farmer John had already motioned to a Runner before Asach explained.

"The Protector has just placed the entire means of this planet at your disposal. He has authorized you to procure whatever, or whomever, you need to accomplish this task. Unto death, if necessary—which I should explain is something that The Protector does not entertain lightly."

"Just like that? Wave our hands and, *voila*, a solution?"

"Consider it a vote of confidence. For him, the decision is simple. The *ar* of this planet is threatened, and Sargon is the defender of the *ar*. Anything you can imagine— wealth, power, life, sanctity, even just plain getting laid—is summed up in that word. Without *ar*, nothing else matters. Nothing else exists."

"Well, rationally speaking, there could of course be some level of compensation, not to mention personal preservation, that would—" The ITA representative stopped abruptly as the eldritch feeling passed through everyone again.

"Excellency, I believe The Protector feels that this is not a good time for philosophical discussion."

"Right," said Geery. "Down to business. What are the rules. What's the minimum we can get away with?"

"Ah, there's the rub. We aren't allowed to read the rules. We have to get there on our own."

"Oh, please."

"Regarding the minimum necessary, there is a precedent that we could invoke."

Heads and bodies swiveled. The astrophysicist had finally weighed in.

"Prince Samual's World. About thirty years ago. Just after Maxroy's Purchase joined the Empire. Around the time of first contact with the Mote. Maybe just before that. Twenty years before the first Jackson delegation arrived, anyway."

"Care to explain, for the benefit of those of us who weren't exactly tuned in at the time?"

The astrophysicist sighed. "I'm afraid I don't really know the details. Before my time. I was just a kid. I just remember people talking about it—how this industrial world achieved space flight before they had even developed aircraft. "

"Well then, a good thing you included at least *one* octogenarian on this panel." The Himmists were shocked at this interjection, and showed it. They'd expected no cooperation from the True Church Elder whatsoever, let alone support.

"Call it an old man's pride," the Elder continued, "but I see no point in denying common knowledge, even if it isn't common to anyone in this room but me. And anyway, it's a matter of public record, and I'm getting pretty tired of all this Imperial bureaucratic grandstanding, as if we were a bunch of *apes*. " With this he glared at the row behind Sargon. The row ignored him.

"Prince Samual's World. Iron and steel industrial. Navy stumbled across its threshold, and the Sammies got wind somehow"—at this, a glance toward Asach—"that if they didn't have spaceflight, a bunch of aristos would be granted colonial concessions, and they'd not be admitted as a Classified world. So they upended a big salad bowl, mounted a chain cannon in it, and plopped a tin can on top. Stuffed in a girl and a bunch of artillery shells and gyroscopes. Not in that order. Fired artillery shells non-stop into the bowl. The blasts drove everything up. Damned near killed her, but she made it to orbit."

"What about re-entry!"

"No need. Put out a distress call when she got up there, and the Navy obligingly picked her up."

"And *that* got them a Classification?"

"The main thing was, nobody could—or, anyway, nobody *said* they could—prove that the design had come from offworld."

"Did it?"

"Well, there were rumors. One was, they found it in a Temple archive on Makassar." Another rheumy glance toward Asach, who again did not respond.

"Makassar? Why Makassar?"

With an uncharacteristic but perhaps understandable lack of reserve, Colchis Barthes interrupted. "Why anywhere? I'm always amazed that people are shocked to find things *in archives*. That's what they're *for*."

"Well, yes, amen to that, but I was really referring to the fact that she wound up exiled there."

"On Makassar?"

"Yep."

"How do you know *that?*" Barthes marveled silently at HG's capacity to greet *any* new bit of information as a personal affront.

The Elder continued with tired patience. "I really must ask what they teach you people in school these days. I'm an Elder of the True Church. It's my *job* to know where people come from. And go to. And what their genealogies are." He delivered this last glaring directly into Asach's eyes, did not drop the stare when he'd finished, and continued. "Not sure my memory is still up to a word-for-word quote, but I think the ruling was something like:

> 'in the absence of challenge by any interested party, we conclude that the craft qualifies as a spacecraft of marginal performance characteristics, and may be accepted as evidence of limited space-faring capability

existing on Prince Samual's World at the time of application for membership.'

That about right?"

Barthes spared Asach making any reply. "Verbatim, actually. And lest anyone feel tempted to slander *me* with a charge of treason for confirming that quote,"—this to HG— "I will tell you that I first read those words in the New Utah True Church Temple Archives last month."

"Why?!"

"No idea. They were queued up on a reader when I arrived."

"Who!"

"Again, no idea. It was a public reader. I can only presume some *local* space buff." And, tit for tat, Barthes was looking directly at the Elder now.

"Why did you not *just say*—"

'Forgive me, but I think it has been made quite clear that I am not at liberty to *say* anything. I'd just hoped that, the point having been made, we might move on, because *as an observer*, it is also clear to me that anyone attempting to charge that the newsreader in question did not already exist here would simply be wasting *more* of His Majesty's time."

"Newsreader?"

"Yes. Bog-standard news release, for general circulation. Clearly, it circulated."

"ENOUGH!"

Apart from Asach, the humans in the room started as one and snapped their attention to Sargon's amazingly, perfectly, human voice.

"You will cease endless talk. You will list ways to launch. You will list ways to orbit. You will list ways to carry passenger. You will list ways to communicate. You will defend *ar* of this world. YOU, and YOU," pointing to Barthes and HG with two right hands, "will record this Meeting. You," pointing to Asach with the gripping hand, "will help explain words. You," pointing to Laurel, "will speak for Him. You," pointing to Geery, "will speak for human Engineers. You," pointing to Michael Van Zandt, "will keep order. Begin. Explain."

They sat for a moment, still stunned. Asach broke the silence. "Michael, I will interpret as needed, but, I think you will find that The Protector has rather a broader grasp of Anglic than you realize."

"It's no good," Geery said. "It won't make any damned difference. It's not just the mass of the passengers that's at issue here. It's the mass of life support, and landing shields, and stabilizers. Hell, there'll be eight gees of *spin* on that thing, never mind the launch. You could put a *kid* in there, but they wouldn't survive the trip."

"But how much mass are we talking about here? What do we really need for re-entry? And eight gees—so what? I mean, during the first flight *ever* Yuri Gagarin stayed up an hour and three-quarters, hit over eight gees on re-entry, then still managed to eject and land by parachute. Alan Shepard stayed up there over fifteen minutes, withstood six gees on takeoff, and then a whopping 11.6 gees on reentry. And that was over *a millennium* ago! Surely we can manage that much?"

Geery shook his head emphatically. "Look it up. Check your space history. Their rocket launch programs rested on the backs of huge existing military infrastructure and a few hundred million people. And then, even after nearly *half a century* of pretty regular orbital flight, *two* of *five* space vehicles broke up—one on take-off, one on re-entry. We get one shot at this, and we have—how many weeks?"

The—what to call it?—New Utah Planetary Executive's

rapid-fire internal discussion sounded like a cross between an aviary and an open-pit mine. The conference table vibrated with every basso communication; the window vibrated with the highs. Sargon spoke.

"You will explain again ways to launch and show Miners."

Michael operated the conference table. The window darkened, so that what was projected on the table top in front of each seat was also projected on-screen for all to see. Asach spoke slowly. In summary. Among them, Sargon, Farmer John, and the Doctor interpreted. The engineers pulled and showed schematics.

"One. Rockets. We have a fireworks industry. We use small chemical rockets to launch weather instruments. The physics are known, but we have nothing capable of delivering a payload as large as an adult human, plus the fuel required, to orbit. We could use Lynx-type pocket rocket technology, but we run the risk of a ruling that it is of "offworld" origin, not our own.

"Two. A Prince Samual's World-type chain cannon. Ironically, *too* primitive. Again, the physics are known, but we do not have the right style of heavy industry. We have no way to build either the cannon or the shells in time."

"Three. Magnetic linear accelerator. The New Utah solar-powered mining flinger was unarguably developed from pre-Empire, local technology. It can handle the payload. Under ideal conditions, we *might* be able to push that payload to orbital velocity without blowing the top off the rails. But, in the time allowed, we can't do it without killing the passenger."

"Four. Space Planes. Back to the Lynx problem. This time, not with the motor, but with the airframe itself. We don't have one. The SunFish is a long-wing solar glider. We could push it up to high-altitude atmospheric limits, but there's no way to put it into orbit. It might work as a launch platform for something else, but what? We are back to the small-rocket problem. We don't have anything big enough to carry a passenger plus life support into orbit."

"Five. Laser launcher. We got excited about this for a minute, because no one can dispute our leadership in solar and light technologies. We arrived here with 'em, and never lost 'em. Even when spare parts became a problem. In theory, we could pool all of our laser capacity—rip everything we've got out of all that Friedlander armor; remount and refocus all of our mining cannons, you name it—pool all of our solar capacity to power it, and then drop a spinning, shiny thing like a child's top, with a gas expansion chamber below it, into the photon stream to launch it. Two problems. Three. First, it's not like shining a bunch of flashlights. We can't get all of that aligned into one coherent beam. Second, payload. It takes a lot of light to do that. Third. Power. We'd definitely suck the grid dry and induce a planetary blackout. Not a great way to greet the Imperials: Hi! We have spaceflight, but no lights or refrigeration! Did I say three? Four. Fourth is spin. That's what we were just talking about. Let's assume that we could overcome the rest, and make a capsule big enough to hold a person. We'd have to put tremendous spin on it to stabilize its launch trajectory. Too much. We'd probably kill the passengers. Centrifuge the blood right out of their heads."

The room was quiet, hushed in the dark as the screen dimmed. They had, at best, weeks before the tramline opened and the Imperial Navy arrived. Never mind the engineering constraints; all humans there—clergy included—could see that none of the options were *socially* doable in time. They required too much coordination; too much cooperation; too much explanation.

A Miner boomed, quietly. Farmer John answered. They both swiveled toward Lagash. Lagash consulted his accountants, and then chirped in reply, apparently to the Miner.

Hesitantly, the Miner stepped forward to the table. It boomed again, to Sargon. Sargon actually leaned toward Asach, but spoke directly.

"The Miners ask: why not make a sailboat?"

The TC Elder snorted; his nearest ecumenical colleagues heard him mutter, "You see? Apes!" under his breath.

One of the more Asperger-ish engineers sneered, "Because sailboats don't *fly.*"

But Sargon was immune to the implied insults. Another short consultation with Asach followed.

"The Miner means: a Phoenix."

"Well, at least they're talking *birds* now."

"The Miner will show you."

And to the amazement of all humans except Laurel and Asach, the Miner's hands began moving very quickly on the surface of the table. Its left hand drew a crooked cross with a very long axis, then a line traveling along the cross, into a spiral. Simultaneously, its lower right hand drew a concave slope, with a dished depression at its top, while the upper right hand drew parallel lines emanating from the dish. It slashed an arc intersecting the parallel lines, with the spiraling line also intersecting just below it, fizzling into a scatter of dots. Above the arc, it drew a bullet-shaped object, with an arrow encircling its base, and what looked like a handkerchief floating above the nose end. Then, it drew a series of glyphs to the right of the image, with a line from one to the base of the parallel lines. Finally, next to the bullet, it drew what looked like two small bowls, with a slash through each. With no prompting from Michael, it pressed the thumb of its gripping hand to the table edge, and stepped back. The image appeared on the window screen.

The reaction was mixed. Before it disintegrated into cacophony, Sargon drew a circle around the spiral.

"This is Phoenix."

Then a circle around the bullet-with hanky.

"This is sailboat."

At which point, HG actually jumped from his chair, then gasped and sat again as Barthes kicked him under the table.

"What is that?"

"Wait. That looks like an airstrip."

"Not *an* airstrip. *The* airstrip. The SunFish hopper strip at the Orcutt concession outside Bonneville."

"The one on Orcutt's ranch?"

"Not Orcutt Station. OLaM Station. The SunRail mining terminal. Mined out now, though."

"So what's the squiggle?"

But the answer was overlaid by a simultaneous interjection.

" What's that bullet thing?"

"What do you mean, sailboat?"

"Why the dots?"

"I don't see where this gets us."

"What the—"

"What *is* this?"

They all stopped when Laurel spoke. She circled one glyph, hesitantly, then another. "I know those. I mean, I think I do. I must. I have seen them, over and over. Now I think I know. That's His Eye." The line pointed to the dish atop the slope. "And beside it, That's His Eye, Opened."

Several of the clergy groaned. Laurel froze, staring at her feet.

Michael interjected. "Please, to order. I believe that *Defender* Courter has information we might *all* benefit from."

Laurel closed her eyes. It was like being back in Sargon's House. She was very afraid, and very alone. She listened to her own breathing for a minute. Harsh, loud, like

Agamemnon's, when he had shivered before Farmer John on that first day, a lifetime ago. She looked at Farmer John. That permanent smile. Like a rock, embedded in soil. His Eye was no longer hers alone.

"Please, forgive me. I can only use the words I know. But I am the only Gathered human here"—she resolutely did *not look at Asach*—"I mean, the only *human* who has seen the Earthly Eye. This mark *here."* she circled again, pointed again, "you find it in the foothills. It marks all the safe routes into Swenson's Mountain. So I guess it's just a road sign, really. 'This way to Swenson's Mountain.' But this one," she circled the glyph beside it, "this one rings the Eye itself. It marks— well, you don't go past this, ever. Lest you be consumed by His Gaze."

There was some pained murmuring. This time, Laurel cut it off herself. *"Hear me out!* I never went to school. I studied at home. I don't know what you know. But you don't know what I know, because you've never been there. What I know now. I have thought about it since that final day, when *they* fought on the plains. Fought the Friedlander amour. I saw them there, those bright green lights, and I thought it then: like little eyes, blinking open and shut. The laser cannons. Blinking open and shut. Like His Eye."

She looked around. Sargon's delegation simply waited, patiently, for the very slow humans to comprehend. Asach stared carefully at folded hands. HG squirmed, uncomprehending and bored. The ecumenical council, attuned to the subtext of personal spiritual insight, had fallen silent. Laurel raised her eyes, and met the stares of the— *unbelieving*—engineers. "It's a laser. His Eye. It's a giant, giant laser. A giant laser that blinks on and off, once a day, for sixteen weeks, every twenty-one years."

The shoe finally dropped for Michael as well. "In the volcano? The opal meerschaum? It erodes out of the volcano?"

Laurel nodded. "And we Gather there. In His sight. Every twenty-one years. Only—" she looked to Sargon—"only, *they* were there first. And Swenson knew. That's why he claimed the mountain. That's why his daughters led us there. To protect it, so no one else would come."

And then the astrophysicist rose, hands to his mouth, creating a ripple of craning heads as he blocked the big-screen view. He waved a hand at the screen. "Do you see that? Do you *see* that?!"

He turned and pointed at the Miner. "That man's a genius. A *genius*. We can do this. We can *do* this. We can *do* the engineering." He swiveled between the human and non-human doctors. "Can we do this? Can we do the life support? Can we do enough life support to get them up there?""

"A genius?"

"Do what?"

"What genius?"

"What does he mean, gen—"

"Life support?"

The astrophysicist was flapping his hands about to quiet the room. "Ladies and Gentlemen, what you are looking at here is Aldrich Saxe's napkin. This Miner—your Excellency, does this Miner have a name?—This Miner has sketched for us a way to put a capsule in orbit using existing technology, plus *the Eye* as a laser cannon."

Forgetting the conference table, he ran up to the screen.

"Look at this. This is the old OLaM airstrip. It's the closest to Swenson's Mountain. You strip a SunFish of everything—*everything*—non-essential, and load it with a space-worthy capsule. You use thermal uplift to gain airspeed, and use airspeed to gain altitude, as high as you can get. Then you use all remaining onboard power for the final whip up to the top of the atmosphere—and time it to drop and glide *straight down into the Eye* on its last leg. The airframe gets burned up, but that puts the laser capsule into the photon stream at the top of the troposphere. *That's the Phoenix.* Same system as we talked about earlier—the laser ablates the bottom surface of the bullet to create thrust, and it heats the air chamber, forcing superheated air out of a hole to create stabilizing spin. But it doesn't have far to go now, so it doesn't need so much spin, and it does not need it for so long. You get a—I don't know how many seconds, I'll work it out in a minute—countdown, until you are out of atmosphere. Then you pop out a light sail. *That's the sailboat.* We aren't *going* anywhere in particular, just parking in orbit, so we don't really *need* to steer it. We just get the extra push, then jettison the sail and tip into orbit. At this point, we might not even need attitude adjustment. Depends on how far out we want to go, how long we want to stay up, how much total mass, how precise an orbit."

He broke off and, shoving past now-furiously-scribbling engineers, threaded his way to the head of the table, behind Sargon, clasping the now very befuddled Miner, right hand thrust forward.

"Sir, I want to shake your hand—" momentary confusion—"er, hands. What *is* your name, sir?"

The Miner made a burbling warble.

Asach smiled. "Might I suggest Alhacen?"

As the engineers huddled in working groups to put meat on the bones of this concept, Asach and the accountants helped with the arduous process of translating the mathematical notations to understandable equations, and the numerical notations to base ten from base twelve. Even the civil administrators followed along eagerly, but this left the ecumenical council with little to do. Until the High Church primate cleared his throat.

"I have a—concern."

Michael looked up. "Yes?"

"Am I to understand that the SunFish—breaks up?"

One of the engineers looked up. "Burns up, more like. It'll be diving down the throat of—"

"Yes, yes. I see. But my concern is: What happens to the pilot? Does he—or she—parachute out?"

The engineer laughed. "Oh, there'll be no parachuting. That'd burn up too."

"So, I repeat, what happens to the pilot?"

Suddenly, the light came on. "Oh. Uh, well, he—"

"Or she."

"Yeah. Uh. Either way. He. Or she. It'll be, uh…"

"A one-way trip?"

"Well, yeah. A fast one. Pretty much as soon as they dive in. They'll flash, break up, and burn. See, the capsule will protect whoever's going on up, but…"

"But we will be sending the pilot on a suicide mission."

"Pretty much."

The primate spoke up. "Is there anyone in this room aside from myself who finds this morally reprehensible?"

He was looking directly at Sargon.

"It is for the *ar.*"

"We hold to rather higher standards regarding the sanctity of human life."

"The *ar* is all. We would never like to destroy a *line*, but the *ar* is all."

"I cannot condone it. To send someone on a mission of *certain* death? To gain a political end regarding *political status?*"

There was a murmur of assent from among the council.

Sargon understood this. The undercurrent was clear. Sargon did not yet understand humans very well, but there'd been chance enough in battle to understand this much: This man would not even know the pilot. The pilot would go willingly. So this was not really about the principle. This was about control. Sargon boomed. One Warrior stepped forward. The movement was fast, sure, over.

"This Warrior will go. This Warrior has get and children. This Warrior's lines are secure. You will teach this Warrior to fly the Phoenix. This Warrior will defend the *ar.*"

The primate fell silent. The SunFish engineer was already texting his office, and mentally calculating the Warrior's mass. The primate spoke again.

"And in the capsule? Who will go in the capsule.?"

The engineers waved the doctor and Doctor over. They joined the huddle, discussing time, g-forces, mass, and oxygen.

18
Opportunity Investment

An academic reactor or reactor plant almost always has the following basic characteristics: (1) It is simple. (2) It is small. (3) It is cheap. (4) It is light. (5) It can be built very quickly. (6) It is very flexible in purpose. (7) Very little development will be required. It will use off-the-shelf components. (8) The reactor is in the study phase. It is not being built now.

On the other hand a practical reactor can be distinguished by the following characteristics: (1) It is being built now. (2) It is behind schedule. (3) It requires an immense amount of development on apparently trivial items. (4) It is very expensive. (5) It takes a long time to build because of its engineering development problems. (6) It is large. (7) It is heavy. (8) It is complicated.

The tools of the academic designer are a piece of paper and a pencil with an eraser. If a mistake is made, it can always be erased and changed. If the practical-reactor designer errs, he wears the mistake around his neck.

—Admiral Hyman G. Rickover, Paper Reactors, Real Reactors, 1953

Bonneville, New Utah

DAZ-E line number six ran continuously. Retooled from machining solar reflector "flowers," it now stamped and sealed silvery inverted mushroom caps beneath silvery inverted cones, sandwiching in tiny chips for brains, transmitters that looped twenty seconds of speech, and deployable hair-wire antennae.

The bigger stuff was on line number three. There, SunRail engineers struggled to mount a magnetic bearing into a larger version of the mushroom, and use it to suspend an insulated tin can, around which the mushroom-cone sandwich could then spin, in vacuum, without friction, freely, like an inside-out centrifuge. They called in more experts from the wind turbine fields to help them stabilize vibration.

Their first three attempts lost internal alignment and blew apart spectacularly. They retooled, retried, and got it working up to three thousand rpm. Then six. Then eight. Then ten.

They had to work around the bearings they had. There was no time to customize them. They measured and re-measured essential payload. They calculated and recalculated air compression. They stripped out all safety margins. They called the physiologists again. How much could their phoenix chicks take?

They revisited SunFish cargo bay plans. They put together a mock-up, correct in size and weight. They started miniature launch tests. They moved real equipment into place.

Swenson's Mountain (Beacon Hill), New Utah

It looked like a deranged, open-air bottling plant. In fact, some of it *was* from a bottling plant, disassembled in Bonneville and shipped to OLaM Station by express SunFreight. It was a testament to brute labor. Flingers dropped canisters filled with parts onto landing pads down near the lake. Hundreds of Porters hiked them up over the rim for assembly. The Eye itself crawled with Miners, polishing imperfections away in a process they could barely explain, but that was reviewed and approved by DAZ-E mirror manufacturers. The islands set up bunk tents and mess lines. Enheduanna's Side kept the manna flowing.

The bottles were replaced by the cone-capped mushrooms, held vertical by tiny brackets that allowed them to initiate rotation. During launch windows, Miners cleared the Eye, and the tiny satellites whipped off the edge of a ski-jump gantry as lines of spinning tops. They flashed as they hit the Eye's photon stream, invisible in the broad light of day, sputtered to life as each base superheated, and twinkled up, up, up out of view like a squadron of heaven-bound fairies. Each of their little chips of brains ticked off its list of imperatives: *Count off the seconds. Use yourself as a flywheel. Pop open your solar collector-sail. Spin away into the cold, black vacuum. Poke out your little antenna. Beep.*

They didn't all make it. Some burned through. Stabilization was tricky. Some wheeled out of control, falling back as chunky, silver hail. Some lost attitude, tumbling along in decaying orbits only to wink back to earth, burning up as miniscule shooting stars somewhere over a New Utah sea. Some shot too far, escaping orbit altogether to sail into endless, black infinity. The engineers did not sleep. They tinkered with the coatings. They tinkered with the gyroscoping flywheels. They tinkered with the delivery line. They tinkered with the gantry. They tinkered with the initial rotation, and with the timing of release. They got better, daily.

No-one knew how long they'd last, beyond "long enough." There was nothing sophisticated about the payload. Each one was pre-programmed to do one thing: send a simple beacon, with a simple message, on a narrow band of frequencies. Each batch used a different set of these. No-one knew exactly where or when the Alderson Point would open, nor the delegation's approach trajectory, nor on what channel they'd be listening. But no matter when or where or what that was, they were sure to get the message:

> On behalf of the Government of New Utah, welcome to New Utah space. Please proceed to geosynchronous orbit at the following coordinates. Please contact New Utah Spaceport on the following frequency to coordinate escort and reception.

It was stop-and-go, but by the end of the week, there were hundreds in orbit, girdling the globe in a spreading band of cacophony. They called them winter flies.

The day finally came. Geery sent the magic words: "We're ready."

Over OLaM Airfield, renamed New Utah Spaceport

The Warrior hissed in shear exaltation. There was *nothing* to flying, really. There was *everything* to flying. Ridge and wave and thermal lift sent the gossamer craft whipping ever-faster, ever-higher, spiraling up toward the top of the troposphere. Up, up, up, and then the tip, the rush, the weightlessness of plummeting earthward toward the target, in perfect verticality.

It did the practice simulation of tail separation in zero-g, then pulled up, hissing and trilling and tasting pure manna. It liked the name: Phoenix. Its solo exam was complete.

The SunFish pilot trainer called in. "We're ready."

New Utah Spaceport Hangar Six

Some things you could train for, others you could only test for. They picked carefully. They tested two dozen, and eliminated all but six. They started training, and eventually whittled down to three.

It became a set drill. "Ventilate!" They stepped up pumping their bellows of chests. "Pack!" They exhaled to extreme; inhaled to extreme; gulped down air to extreme.

"Hold!" They switched off, into a trance of waiting. "Run!" They moved out. Meters rolled by. They held it still. Blood vessels constricted. Blood moved to brains; extremities grew weak, screaming with a pain they no longer felt.

They improved quickly. Five minutes. Nearly ten minutes. Breathing pure oxygen, almost fifteen. Then the same without it.

They climbed into the centrifuge, and started all over again. Three gee. Five gee. Ten gee. Fifteen.

"Now do it with the set tasks."

Leaden and tired and out of air, bodies squashed flat by a ton of gravity, eyes covered with blackened hoods, they repeated the drill. *Confirm chronometry. Confirm altimetry. Engage flywheel to slow external rotation and store energy. Lock exhaust port for attitude control. Slide out of propulsion stream, roll, and brake. Vent any remaining compressed air to cabin. Wait. Blow hatch. Exit. Greet.*

Finally came the pure misery.

Never mind doing it blindfolded, backwards, under pressure. They practiced until they could do it with arms of lead, deaf and dark, without breathing, stuffed three-deep inside an old packing barrel.

The chief of physiology called in.

"I think they're as ready as can be."

Sinbad, above New Utah

They fell out of jump, systems shut down, computers running recovery test sequences. Ali Baba was a flailing misery; a little starfish hauled from a hostile sea. The ITA rep threw up. Except for the young fit crewmen, for all his age, Kevin recovered most quickly, but it mattered little, until *Sinbad* itself was out of its misery.

There were odd little sparkles in the Langston Field.

Oh criminey, thought Kevin. What he actually thought was unprintable on most planets, but there was good reason for his ecumenical blasphemy: the jump point had shifted from their calculated trajectory, and they had actually emerged *inside* New Utah's meteor belt. Not that it had many, but they were heating up, ever so slightly, from collisions with space trash.

Then he remembered that there shouldn't be any.

Then he rallied enough to have the sailing master take a look.

Then Sinbad rallied enough to make that possible.

"Sir?" said the sailing master.

"Umph."

"We're receiving a lot of very-low-power RF energy."

"That's a contradiction in terms."

"I mean, like, a hundred itty-bitty transmissions, on, like, a hundred frequencies."

He tuned one in. He grinned at Renner, and punched it on. "This," he said, "you ain't gunna believe."

Two hours later, HG arrived, Barthes in tow, ranting about the indignities involved in using the FairServ shuttle, and *Sinbad* moved to the designated coordinates.

19
Formal
Accession

An anthill increases by accumulation. Medicine is consumed by distribution. That which is feared lessens by association. This is the thing to understand.

—Ovid

Of course, it should have all gone wrong. What was meant to take days should have required weeks, not the other way around. The Eye should have closed early. The Alderson point should have opened early. The mountain should have fogged in, scattering the beam.

But none of these things came to be. Instead, something happened when human engineering got mixed up with…*Swenson's Apes.* Things just…kept moving. Once they worked right, they *stayed* that way. If Miners and Miner's Helpers moved onto the line, *every single time* it happened *exactly the same way.* If something didn't work—it didn't work. It moved on to the next test, without frustration or waste.

They were exceptional at innovation, but in an incredibly methodical way. Things marched along. Even the weather cooperated. Bright and clear, except for one sharp lens of cloud indicating a mountain wave. And over the Eye: nothing at all. Not a single cloud, the air dead calm, not a particle of haze. And then came The Day.

What were the chances? That on such a day, the message would come, All Due Haste?

"The tramline is open. They're here."

Enheduanna was in direct communication. Had to be, for orders relay. The Phoenix would soar to the edge of flight possibility, but its dive must be timed with the Eye's pulsing phase. They'd call it directly from the ground. The Seers would know how to wait.

The crew sealed in with a thimble of air; the rapid climb; the stunning view; the pulse; the tip to orient the gleaming silver egg. The weightless drop into garnet depths, like the big red target out there on the airway. The flash, the flames as earthly feathers burned away.

It shouldn't have worked on the hundredth try. Nevertheless, against all the odds, the diamond egg streaked away.

Sinbad, above New Utah

The capsule was small. Too small. Barely big enough for one grown man, pretzeled into a fetal position. The crew milled about it, confused. One tentatively reached forward, rapped on its blunter end, and jumped back at an answering *thump* from within. He jumped just in time, because the thump was followed by a reverberating ba-ba-ba-BAM as explosive bolts blew the hatch a few feet across the bay.

More thumping ensued. Renner barked: "Help them!"

Two Boatswain's mates sprang to action, just as a limp, brown arm flopped from the opening. They half-wrestled, half-dragged a dead weight from the port. The Miner's body emerged; slid along the capsule skin; thumped to the floor with the mates scrambling down after it.

The crew froze in collective shock. They counted limbs. They counted again. Saw the brown fur. Saw the rictus of a smile, plastered across the alien face, even in death. Did the math. Were stupefied on their first contact with what they saw as a dead Motie Engineer.

But of course, for one of them, this was not a first contact. Ignoring the body, Renner himself went to the capsule; grasped the edge; peered through the hatch. Two shivering shapes, twisted to conform to the narrow confines and entwined nearly as one, their chests heaving, gasped for air. Without thought; without hesitation, on reflex, he reached in and placed a hand gently on the nearest head.

"It's OK," he said, without knowing whether they could even understand him. "You made it. You're here."

The creatures did not move, save to tremble harder. Their breathing was ragged. Renner tugged, gently, at one arm, but nothing happened. He stood up, and thought a bit. Thought back on everything he knew of Moties, far and near. Thought of Moties on Mote Prime; on Mote Beta; on Mote Gamma. Thought of Base Six and the Treasure Comet and the Trojans. Thought of Ivan and Jock; of the Khanate and Crimeans and even Vermin City. Thought of everywhere he'd been, thanks to Bury and *Sinbad*. And then had a moment of clarity.

He looked across to the Delegation, and spoke softly. "Ali Baba. Your Excellency. Would you please join me?"

The little Mediator, with the bearing of a prince, grasped its gripping hand with both arms, and did so.

"Your Excellency, please do something for me." Ali Baba went stiff with diffidence. Renner paused. "I mean, not for me. I want you to do something for—" Renner leaned, and whispered, so that only Ali Baba could hear—"*your Grampa Horace.*"

Ali Baba made that odd little bow that Moties did instead of a tilt of the head, because they had three jointed bones instead of spines. Renner cupped his hand, and whispered again.

Everyone on deck started as two words boomed across the cargo bay in the authoritative voice of a Horace Bury restored to life and vigorous youth; the compelling Voice of a Great Master who could not be denied: "RUNNERS! REPORT!" Then, they cringed at what they could not hear, but felt, as he repeated the same in the Master's speech of a Mesolimeran.

As one, the huddled shapes sucked in a lungful of air, rallied in the low ship's gravity, pulled themselves upright, and climbed out, supported only by Renner's free hand.

They unfolded to full height, and gripping hands united, grasping hands outstretched, spoke clearly, in unison, in Anglic, in the Protector's Voice, colors rippling down their arms in the Royal Greeting:

"I am Leica, 10 John, Royal Emissary of Sargon the Hand, Procurator of the Mesolimeris Northern Protectorate, and by Acclaim of the first Constitutional Gathering appointed Protector of Ar and Seer of New Utah. You are hereby notified that you have entered New Utah space, and by extension, the New Utah Protectorate. Any who may hear this message are respectfully requested to hold in current orbit and await the Protector's Representative, the Excellency Amari Selkirk Alidade Clark Hathaway Quinn.

"Any duly appointed representatives of the True Church of Maxroy's Purchase who may hear this message are hereby notified that the Excellency is a direct descendent of Quinn of the Six, by right of decent and accomplishment appointed Elder of the Reformed Church of Jesus Christ of Latter Day Saints on New Utah, and by acclaim appointed Defender of the Mormon Faith on New Utah. By order of the Defender, the True Church security zone has been demilitarized, the Maxroy's Purchase paramilitary wing of the True Church Militant in New Utah has been disbanded and

disarmed, the urban centers of Saint George and Bonneville are now patrolled and administered by the Protector's Accountancy, and her Excellency Laurel Courter is co-appointed as Defender and Seer of the Church of Him on New Utah, with spiritual oversight of the non-human populations of the Six Cities.

"Any duly appointed representative of The Empire of Man is hereby notified that, having independently achieved planetary government and sentient space presence, New Utah makes formal application for admission to the Empire of Man as a Classified planet. As proof of commitment to the binding Laws of Empire, the Protector requests permission to remand one Lillith Van Zandt to Imperial custody, as a traitor to New Utah and the Empire of Man, for judgment under His Majesty's Courts.

"I am Leica, 10 John, Royal Emissary of Sargon, Procurator of Mesolimeris, and by Acclaim of the first Constitutional Gathering Protector and Seer of New Utah. I have undertaken a dangerous journey to further the interests of New Utah and the Empire of Man. I have spoken the full and complete truth, and at the behest of my Lord now request sustenance and medical attention."

As the hanger broke into complete pandemonium, two limp, bedraggled, slate-grey bodies collapsed onto the deck.

"Help them!" shouted Ali Baba, who stood, rigid, Kevin forgotten, Bury forgotten, staring at a point beyond the messengers' sagging heads, his own bones aching, ears ringing, hope soaring, riveted by the fading echoes of his Master's Voice.

Not a soul took any notice whatsoever of Jackson's blurted expletive.

Even Horvath's Goon was left speechless.

And then, as medics rushed to the Runners' aid, Sir Kevin Renner threw back his head, pulled out his pipe, and laughed himself blue in the face.

Epilogue

Bonneville, New Utah, 3051

On Saturday afternoon, the eighteenth of August, Amari Selkirk Alidade Clarke Hathaway Quinn sat down with a silk-smooth pen and a stack of creamy parchment, and stared at five faded, underlined words: <u>Pie</u>, <u>Coffee</u>, <u>People</u>, <u>Different</u>, <u>Fixing</u>.

The view of the city was stunning. Up there, above the urban canyons, it was windy, and the night was turning cool. The soft air and crickets recalled so many other evenings, filled with crickets, or peepers, or cicadas, or all three. It was amazingly soothing to hear late evening traffic in the distance. Fireworks sparkled over some celebration or other further off in the hills. A wedding was going on down below, with attendant laughter, chatter, music, song, arrivals, departures, and fireworks of its own. Finally, as the light faded, a muezzin made the midnight call to prayer.

Wind played through the tamarisk trees. Asach sat on the roof, wolfing down pie and sucking down aromatic draughts of coffee. Watched people making their way through the ancient alleys. Watched the changing light cast the city rooftops in shifting shades of green. Watched curiously as a hefty, three-armed shape made its way down the lane, raised a fist, and pounded on the door below.

Appendix

Map of Inhabited Areas of New Utah

As drawn by John David Swenson, c.2450.
Annotated to indicate major Lines of Communication

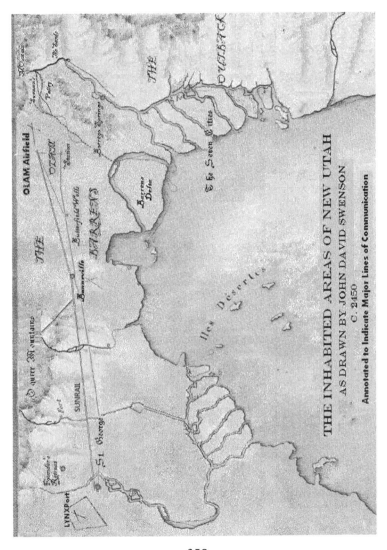

True Church of Mormon Organization

From: *The Evolution of Mormon Religious Faith Practices in the Trans-Coal Sack Sector*, A.S.A.C.H. Quinn

On Maxroy's Purchase and New Utah, the relationships among arms of the so-called True Church of Mormon and its military wing, the True Church Militant, can be confusing. The definitions below will be especially helpful to those who have had little or no direct experience of Mormonism as practiced in the Trans-Coal Sack sector.

MORMONISM. Religious communities that trace their origins to the teachings of Joseph Smith in the United States of America in the 1830s, and include the Book of Mormon as a part of their religious canon. Adherents refer to themselves as "restorationist" Christians and do not adhere to Roman, Eastern, or Protestant orthodoxies. All believe that God was not always originally a corporeal human being, but become a deity by following Mormon teachings on another world, and that human men may also become deities. Whether women can do so as well is ambiguous and controversial in some groups. Most also believe that because human souls are the literal offspring of God, human increase is necessary to provide corporeal bodies to populate the many planets.

CHURCH OF HIM. Founded 2882, on New Scotland, by Howard Grote Littlemead. Not strictly speaking a Mormon religion, but early adherents were drawn from many faiths, including LDS Sixers, LDS members from the Pacific Diaspora, and Fijian Christians.

The Church of Him teaches that the Coal Sack nebula visible from the New Caledonia system is literally the face of

God, and that the red giant star "Murcheson's Eye" visible therein is literally the eye of God, staring out from beneath a hood. Near the time of founding, a smaller star, known as the "Mote in Murcheson's Eye" appeared to flare—an event interpreted by Littlemead as God awakening. This flare—now known to be a laser cannon launching a probe powered by solar sail from the Mote system—winked out in 2902, an event now referred to by Himmists on New Utah as "the Great Weep."

Following persecution in the New Caledonia system, in 2908 the Church of Him dispatched a mission to Maxroy's Purchase, where many adherents were recruited among those persecuted, expelled, and excommunicated by the True Church of Mormon during several purges there. In 2964, a "sister" Himmist mission was dispatched to New Utah, where Himmists made little attempt to settle in the True-Church-dominated capital city of Saint George. Instead, they migrated eastward to and beyond Bonneville, eventually coming to dominate the desert and steppe lands known as The Barrens. Located beyond view of the Coal Sack, New Utah Himmists have developed interesting local variants of literalist liturgical practice, and proved remarkably pragmatic in their ongoing relations with other religious adherents.

CHURCH OF JESUS CHRIST OF LATTER DAY SAINTS ("LDS CHURCH"). From the movement's founding in 1830 until the late twenty-third century, the largest denomination of the Latter Day Saint movement, headquartered on Earth in Salt Lake City, Utah, with established wards and temples Empire-Wide. Founded on a pioneering tradition in the hostile terrain of the Old American west, the LDS organization was extremely effective in organizing and managing early First Empire colonial efforts. However, with the destruction of the "home" Temple in Salt Lake, LDS membership waned and eventually was eclipsed by that of the Reformed, or "Sixer," movement.

REFORMED CHURCH OF JESUS CHRIST OF LATTER DAY SAINTS ("LDS SIXERS"). Founded in Los Angeles, California, United States of America, Earth, 2066, by the descendants and followers of six LDS Church scholars excommunicated for apostasy when their works contradicted traditional LDS Church history.

The Reformed LDS Church strongly upholds scholarship and scientific inquiry, arguing that resolution of best-known fact with mythical and metaphorical belief is a necessary component of deepening adulthood faith. It also teaches absolute equality of all sexes, and openness regarding gender identity. The "Sixer" movement initially gained traction among the many excommunicants effectively exiled to urban areas, but its pragmatic approach to changing lifestyle circumstances led to its popular reception among multicultural urban communities, offworld transportees, and members of the spacefaring trades. In this millennium, ties between the LDS and Reformed LDS churches are strong and mutually cooperative.

TRUE CHURCH OF MORMON ("TRUE CHURCH" OR "TC"). Founded 2456, Maxroy's Purchase, by a self-organized, fundamentalist, ruralist, masculinist splinter faction of dissident Mormons who established the initial colony. In 2553, their numbers were swamped by over 100,000 transportees settled on Maxroy's Purchase, among them many LDS and Reformed LDS members unsympathetic to TC claims.

Citing "withdrawal from urban decadence," in 2567 the Temple of the True Church was removed to a remote outpost in Glacier Valley, and dispatched a colony to New Utah with which it maintained close ties for several hundred years. Following a massive pogrom in 2864 that claimed to "purify" urban LDS and LDS Sixer churches—generally by burning them down and executing or exiling their members—the TC declared its Temple the governing church of Maxroy's Purchase.

When the Alderson tramlines from the Maxroy's Purchase system to New Utah collapsed shortly thereafter, the TC continued expensive shipments of selenium supplements, fertilizer, and medical supplies and equipment, receiving partial payment-in-kind in opal meerschaum. This trade was possible once every 21 years, when an orbiting neutron star temporarily reopened tramlines—although, following MP's accession to the Empire of Man in 3007, it was technically illegal, since New Utah remained an outworld.

The True Church of Maxroy's Purchase considered itself to be the governing body of its New Utah counterpart throughout this period—but the combination of remoteness, sporadic contact, and normal social evolution on New Utah put considerable strain on this relationship. This became clear in 3035, when the New Utah True Church averted open civil war by refusing an accession offer that would have codified that subordinate relationship.

TRUE CHURCH MILITANT ("TCM"). The military arm of the True Church of Mormon. Formally organized in 2567 as a Temple Guard in Glacier Valley, the TCM became enforcers of TC canon, and conducted the purges of 2864. One TCM wing is formally organized as the so-called **TC Mormon "Saints" Battalion**, which "supports" the TC "mission" on New Utah by rotating young men there for three-year tours in the **True Church Temple Security Zone**. TCM service is considered equivalent to a proselytizing mission.

The **New Utah TCM**, under pressure to exact sufficient payments to meet its obligations to the TC Maxroy's Purchase, evolved away from church law enforcement. Instead, its primary mission became canonical tax ("tithe") collection.

Rather than suffering judgment under TC law, non-conformants and non-adherents are subject to heavy (even extortionate) tithe levies, and the TCM New Utah is tasked with universal collection.

The TCM New Utah is also responsible for protection of and order within the **True Church Temple Security Zone**—a sprawling administrative complex that includes the Temple itself, its archives, tithe and trade goods warehouses, various ministries, and key transportation hubs. Law and order outside the Zone is the responsibility of civil police. The **Maxroy's Purchase TCM Mormon Saints Battalion** is housed within the Zone and nominally attached to the Commander, Zone Security.

Unique to New Utah is a TCM auxiliary arm, called **TCM Contract Security** (short name: **TCM Security**), which allows the True Church New Utah to minimize expenses for standing paramilitaries—and generate a revenue stream from visiting dignitaries. Originally cultivated from past members of various home-and-farm defense militias, TCM Security is organized as a private-sector company offering skilled drivers, pilots, escorts, bodyguards, security guards, and allied personnel who are pre-cleared by the TCM, but can be called up and hired on service contracts as-needed. Members are recruited on a city zone and rural regional basis, so are intimately familiar with their home territories. Members may also hold reserve appointments in one of the TCM branches. Many are members of landholder families from estates outside Saint George.

Catechism of The Great Weep

From: *An Ethics of Tears: Variants of Practice among New Utah Adherents of the Church of Him*, A.S.A.C.H. Quinn

The Great Weep variant of the catechism of the Church of Him is practiced by all Himmists of New Utah, known locally as "gatherers."

His Gatherings

2450   His sisters sail to New Caledonia to create islands of peace, and He smiles with joy.

2600   Consumed by Mammon, the brothers of New Scotland and New Ireland turn their faces from Him, and attack all those who would Gather.

2800   The brothers and sisters cease Gathering.

2860   He Awakes! The Great Opening, also called the Revelation of His Face, in which he reveals his true substance as a quadripartite God.

2880   The First Gathering! He sees our Prophet Littlemead and founds His Church on New Scotland.

2900   Alas! The Second Gathering! The Gathering of the Great Weep! He gathers his cloak about His Face, and closes His eye, as it is filled with angry tears. Our Prophet is sent in haste to plead for His mercy. We flee to the island of our sisters in New Ireland, and begin The Great Wandering. We wander for three Gatherings.

2910   Our sisters dispatch His Mission to Maxroy's Purchase, to found a new island. The sisters make many islands of the sisters cast out by the True Church Militant.

2960   The Great Wandering Ends! He dispatches His Mission to Heaven! Our Foundation Gathering, also called the Fifth Gathering.

2980   Our First Gathering, in which His Earthly Eye is Revealed! Also called the Sixth Gathering.

3000 Our Second Gathering, also called the Seventh Gathering.

3020 Our Third Gathering, also called the Eighth Gathering.

3040 Our Fourth Gathering, prophesied the gathering of the Revelation. Also called the Ninth Gathering.

His Numbers

Five fingers to a hand, four hands to a gathering. His perfection is Revealed in Fours.

One century plus one half had we peace.

Two centuries had we war.

Three gatherings had we rebellion, until we Gathered.

Alas! Began the Great Weep, and we Gathered.

Three Gatherings we wandered, until we found Heaven on Earth.

We met the Gaze of His Earthly Eye, our First Gathering in Heaven.

Three Gatherings have we waited! May His Face be Revealed!

A Seer spans two Gatherings. My Gathering is number [*my Number here.*]

His Tenets

It is the duty of every pilgrim to sail to her island for her Gathering, to prepare pilgrims for the next Gathering, and to honor the wisdom of the pilgrims of Gatherings past, who have gazed into His earthly Eye and believed.

It is the duty of every Seer to maintain the Watch for the Waking of His Eye, and to guide all pilgrims in safety and secrecy to the Gathering.

It is the duty of every island to give aid and support to the Seers, that they may be of aid to all pilgrims.

In His Gaze, we are all pilgrims, we are all Seers, and all islands are One.

His Creed

The quadrine perfection of God the Father, the Son, and the
Holy Spirit, is Revealed to all in His true Face.
[Amen]

He is not a Faceless God! With His Heavenly Eye, He Sees all
who See Him.
[Amen]

He is not a Faceless God! With His Earthly Eye, He Sees all
who See Him.
[Amen]

On the Day of Revelation, will His true Face be Revealed.
[Amen]

On the Day of Revelation, will He Gather all Churches to Him.
[Amen]

He is not a Faceless God! May we face one another and pass
His Gaze among Gatherers.
[Amen]

He is not a Faceless God! May we face the worlds and pass His
Gaze to All.
[Amen]

He is not a Faceless God! May we turn our Gaze from those
who refuse to See, praying fervently that they may not
remain Blind.
[Amen]

In the name of Him who has shown His Face, may we all truly
See.
[Amen]

The Gathering Hymn

The pilgrim's song. Sung in procession to Gatherings of the Great Weep.

'Twas brother's peace with brother for
One hundred fifty years
Then brother smote his brother for
Two centuries of fear.

Three score of sad rebellion
Three score of hate and ire
Three score of living hell, then
Awoke His watchful Eye!

For twenty years we faltered
For twenty years we hid
And then He sent his Prophet:
Our speaker, Littlemead!

Oh Lo! We were not faithful!

Oh Lo! They did not heed!
He pulled his cloak about Him
Oh Lo! How he did Weep!

Three Gatherings we wandered
To seek his gracious eye
Dispatched to gather faithful
Across the starless skies.

A Gathering we struggled
A Gathering we cried.
Each Gathering he shows us:
Salvation Day is nigh!

Oh weak were we to flee that Face
And weak were we to fear
For through our sin he closed His eye
And shed His awful tears.

So now we wait in endless toil
For gifts and grace He sends
And when His angels cross our doors
We'll know we've made amends.

Arise! And leave no stone unturned!
Arise! And plow each field!
Arise! Believe! That all who yearn
Will see His Face revealed!

We fled in fear His awful Gaze
But with His Earthly Eye
He sees, He knows, He sends His Grace
Across all starry skies.

So shoulder all your burdens!
For when your time is done
Revealed at last! His angels
Will make all Churches one!

Mesolimeran Tables of Measure

From: *New Utah "Motie" Accounting Systems*, A.S.A.C.H. Quinn

"Three-Hand," or "Cattle" Accounting

Living beings that can be entailed, leased, loaned, bought, or sold, and that are entitled to ration allotments from their "holder," are accounted with the so-called "three-hand," or "cattle" system. Classed as "digits," these entities include livestock, slaves, adopted children, widows, orphans, lower-ranks military members, various laborers, and powered vehicles, equipment, and appliances.*

"Three-Hand," or "Cattle" Accounting

Base		Unitary	Military
Mote	*Ten*	*Name*	*Equivalent*
1	1	Digit	
2	2	Thumb	
4	4	Palm	
10	6	Hand	Squad, Maniple
100	6x6=36	Side	Platoon
1,000	3x36=108	(Real) Grip	Company, Century
10,000	6x108=648	(False) Grip	Battalion, Tribune
100,000	6x648=3,888	Master's Hand	Brigade
1,000,000	36x648=23,328	Master's Side	2 Divisions
10,000,000	108x648=69,984	Master's Grip	Army

Note that both "1,000" and "10,000" are called a "Grip." The difference is generally inferred from context.

---

*A considerable body of religio-legal precedence grew from litigation surrounding classification of individuals in this schema. In this body of work, three underlying principles came to guide juridical decision-making. These were that the individual concerned (a) is not entitled to, or is incapable of, independent food production, (b) is not entitled to, or capable of, independent food procurement by other means, and (c) is entitled to be fed by someone else, as a matter of both legal and sacred obligation. By extension of these principles, powered vehicles and machinery also came to be accounted in this way. In the figurative sense, like fingers that grip and

manipulate, but wither if cut off from blood supply, "digits" add power to the hand that wields them—but at a price.

In "three-hand" accounting, units 1-"10" represent the six digits of the first hand. Each unit of "10," or a Hand, is then tallied on hand two, up to the total possible "100" (6x6=36), or a Side. Finally, each Side is transferred to the three fingers of the gripping hand, for a possible grand total of "1,000," a Grip. Thus, in the Motie trihexagesimal system, "1,000" does not represent (6+6)2, as we might expect from our own finger-based base-10 analogy, but 6x6x3—in keeping with a Master's finger tally.

Land Accounting

Land is measured and accounted by the "*ar*," or "Farmer's Grasp" system. *Ar* accounting is based, not on physical surface area, but on productivity estimates. The basic unit, an "*ar*," or "Farmer's Grasp," represents approximately 1 cubic meter of fertile, arable soil.

In some terrain, one *ar* might be thinly spread over many square meters of surface area. In others, one square meter of surface might actually extend several *ar* deep. Land payments and allotments are made in *ar* by a Landholder (usually, a Master), to an *ar*-holder (usually, a Farmer). In return, rents and taxes are paid in produce by the *ar*-holder to the Landholder, Creditors, and the *ar*-holder's Cattle.

Thus, it is generally in everyone's interest to conserve and increase *ar* value. For the Landholder, a rise in *ar* promised an increase in available allotments, and the revenue derived therefrom. For the *ar*-holder, it meant the possibility of beating the system by getting more produce out of an allotment than it was originally worth.

However, since arability varies with moisture, friability, and other factors, a given plot of land's value in *ar* was a matter of continual, intense agronomic negotiation, accounting, and legal dispute between *ar*-Holder and Landholder. The most vicious disputes arose at two crucial times: (1) following natural disaster, when the *ar*-Holder tried (often desperately) to shift the burden of responsibility for failed crops or dead Cattle onto someone else; and (2) on an *ar*-Holder's death, when final reckoning for all accounts due the Landholder and other Creditors took place.

Land, or "Farmer's Grasp" Accounting

Number of Ar		
Base Mote	Base Ten	Unitary Name
1	1	Ar (Farmer's Grasp)
10	6	Span
100	36	Post
1,000	3x36=108	Concession
10,000	6x108=648	Field
50,000	3x648=1,944	Farmer's Grasp
100,000	6x648=3,888	Master's Hand
1,000,000	36x648=23,328	Keeper's County
10,000,000	108x648=69,984	Procurator

Commodity Accounting

Harvested commodities and materials that are consumed in manufacturing, such as foodstuffs, ores and minerals, are subject to multiple (generally volumetric) systems of measure and reckoning. These are based upon what have come to be standardized in-kind payments and delivery quotas for the commodities in question.

Humans find transaction negotiation across these systems extremely confusing (if not outright litigious). Within the Empire of Man, such contracts are concluded using standardized pricing structures derived from ancient currency-based monetary institutions. Outside the Empire, exchange rates are set by local commodities markets—many of which are *de facto* pegged to the Imperial Crown.

Moties, however, have no difficulty making simultaneous calculations in several reckoning systems, while applying current, local conversion rates and standards on-the-fly. At any given time, these conversion rates and standards appear to be universally and intuitively understood by all parties, including the leveraging effects of variables like transportation costs and availability across time.

The actual negotiation process for Motie commodity barter is poorly understood. Current research suggests that Motie commodity transactions presume perfect cost-factor knowledge, and that the opening phase of any commodity barter negotiation includes an extremely rapid exchange and verification of all underlying fiduciary assumptions. Thereafter, the subject of negotiation and litigation is never one of relative commodity value. Rather, the substance of discussions seems to treat issues of rank, duty/privilege, and ability of litigants to extract commodities by force, should negotiations collapse.

Commodity, also called "Keeper's Grasp" or "Bowl" Accounting

Number of Bowls		
Base Mote	**Base Ten**	**Unitary Name**
1	1	Bowl
10	6	Table
100	36	Post
1,000	3x36=108	Concession
10,000	6x108=648	Field
50,000	3x648=1,944	Accountant's Grasp
100,000	6x648=3,888	Accountant's Hand
1,000,000	**36x648=23,328**	**House**

Asymmetry, Chimerism, and Hermaphroditism in New Utah Swenson's Apes: An Adaptive "Gene Banking" Mechanism?

New Utah Founder's Day Plenary Address prepared for presentation at the twenty-seventh Irregular Meeting of the New Caledonia Chapter, Interplanetary Association of Xenobiology, 2867

Introduction

I begin this paper with what will at first sound like a digression into some arcane points of New Utah history. Please bear with me: they will, in the end, prove relevant. And, for those of you unfamiliar with our little, far-away, home-grown university, this dip into our admittedly short history may even prove interesting.

Probably the best-known thing about us is the tendency among residents of Maxroy's Purchase True Church "outback" communities to imagine (and refer to) New Utah as "heaven" or "paradise." Indeed, this is an oft-cited example of a "Golden Age" mythology, wherein subsequent generations suppress memory of actual hardships and create legends attesting a simpler, more abundant golden age in the past. Kroeber described this phenomenon in Old American Navajo myths that attested "endless flocks" of sheep with "pastures beyond the horizon" prior to European contact—an obvious example of false reminiscence, since sheep did not exist in Navajo lands prior to European arrival.

We have had little to go on in assessing the facts of New Utah's "golden age" presumption. Two documents existed: the New Utah True Church Founder's Report to the Elders of Maxroy's Purchase, filed 300 years ago by the First True Church

Colony in New Utah of 2567, and the Imperial Navy's Initial Assessment Report (IAR), filed at the turn of the following century.

The Colony Founder's Report refers to New Utah as a land of endless, green bounty, teeming with huntable game. That Colony, founded at what is now the New Utah capital of Saint George, was laid down in the silty plains of the Oquirr river delta. As we shall see, it may well be that, at the time of landing, the plains *were* covered with bright green vegetation similar in appearance to Spartina grasses, as well as animals that depended on those "grasses" for sustenance. Further, at the time of founding, the True Church on Maxroy's Purchase itself had just withdrawn to Glacier Valley. The expenses of that withdrawal were massive; as a consequence, the Saint George Colony was not well-funded, and the primary goal of the colony was to establish a self-sustaining agronomic base. In short: at its beginning, the TC colony at Saint George was fully occupied with survival, and conducted virtually no exploration outside the Saint George plains. Therefore, the Founder's Report may in fact *be* accurate, if it is understood as applying to those plains, and not to New Utah as a whole.

On the other extreme, the Navy IAR reported a planet that, while habitable, was largely devoid of interesting ores, characterized by brown, steppic expanses, and devoid of significant indigenous life. Once again, the context of these fly-bys must be noted: they were never intended as systematic surveys. Conducted by sector patrol ships just prior to outbreak of the Secession Wars, their primary aim was to ascertain what, if any, profitable industries might be quickly established in New Utah's orbit. The Naval survey was aimed at identifying potential profitable resources for industrial-scale usage in space, *not* for local development needs. Since New Utah has only one moon—a small, lumpy, rock devoid of metals—and no significant asteroids, it was clear that any industrial resources would need to be planet-based, significantly increasing transport costs for either ores or finished products. Nothing likely to be profitable was identified in the IAR, and the report did not recommend undertaking the expense of more intensive follow-up.

Thus, from the perspective of New Utah colonizers, New Utah *was* heaven: readily available surface water, arable land, abundant grazing for pastoral production, and sufficient game to see the colony through the first few winters. Further, as compared to the extreme winter temperatures of Glacier Valley, the Saint George climate was exceedingly mild. However, from the perspective of the Imperial Fleet, there was nothing of interest that was not more readily available from (already remote) Maxroy's Purchase or the recently terraformed planets of New Caledonia. Indeed, at the time, there was a good deal of political pressure to provide justification for the high investment made to terraform New Ireland and New Scotland.

By local standards, the New Utah colony *was* a quick and enduring success. According to MP True Church records, within one decade the Saint George colony not only became self-sustaining, but stockpiled the rotating four-year surplus advocated by LDS doctrine. At the conclusion of that decade, explorers and provisioned settlers had established farmsteads on the fertile plains surrounding what is now Bonneville, and TC tithe-houses quickly followed. Stock-grazing expanded rapidly, and the 20-year report shows in-kind payments of course and fine mohair fabrics made to the Colony Foundation. Urban centers at Saint George and Bonneville grew and, for a time, even thrived, fueled by locally developed energy resources, particularly solar. Although New Utah remained fairly remote, additional settlers trickled in via Maxroy's Purchase, gradually increasing the urban population. Many of these were non-dogmatic Mormon "Sixers," excommunicated and shunned by the True Church expansion on Maxroy's Purchase, who passed through Saint George and on to the Bonneville frontier.

The question then becomes: what happened during the intervening three centuries? Until now, we knew only that the agricultural boom did not last. As early as sixty years after foundation, Saint George tithe records show that net production began to decline. The colony remained "successful," but remained in stasis. Little or no further exploration was undertaken, and no new colonies were established on New Utah. This trend continued until, at this writing, Saint George crop and livestock production had become completely dependant on rare earth mineral supplements, in particular, selenium. Data are not available for Bonneville, which from shortly after foundation operated its affairs semi-autonomously. If Bonneville filed annual reports with the main Temple at Saint George, they have been subsequently lost.

No doubt the onset of the Secession Wars played a role in this. New Utah and Maxroy's Purchase were distant even from New Caledonia, and both remained largely neutral. It is likely that no external capital—from either Imperial or Secessionist forces—for further exploration and colonization was available. The True Church did (and does) continue to finance a Mission to Saint George, providing selenium-enhanced fertilizers and nutritional supplements, but New Utah agricultural operations now operate on a break-even sustenance, not a profitable surplus, basis.

More complete answers may lie in private, family records in Bonneville. From the outset, Saint George was a True Church Farm Colony (and protectorate). Farming was conducted along strict doctrinal lines, with emphasis on high-yield production. The colony did not include a geochemist, xenobiologist, xenobotanist, or any other member dedicated to basic science. Although a TC institution for higher education was soon established, its focus was strictly vocational-technical.

None of these observations is intended as criticism, rather as a description: this was a working colony, and could not afford much in the way of overhead.

Bonneville, however, was, from the outset, a good deal more eclectic. "Sixers," while Mormon, are descended from six LDS dissidents of the twentieth century who advocated freedom of rational intellectual inquiry. For them, investigation of basic questions is not merely a matter of interest: it is of a matter of religion. Given the severe limitations on access to information they endured—no Imperial libraries, no Universities, not even access to the True Church Archives in Saint George—most of these personal intellectual quests were at best amateurish.

Nevertheless, amateurs often prove to be very keen observers, and some are even keen recorders. Which brings us, finally, to the crux of this paper. Although we have virtually *no* official surveys of the flora, fauna, or natural history of New Utah, one such keen observer and recorder did exist there. In the course of his occupational travels, during the first 50 years of New Utah's colonial existence, John David Swenson, professional provisioner and amateur naturalist, traversed the length and breadth of all inhabited areas. He observed, imaged, and recorded the behavior of dozens of species, but became particularly enamored of a class of animals, now extinct, herein referred to as Swenson's Apes, in honor of his discoveries.

Swenson's records might well have been lost to posterity, had they not on his death in Bonneville been ceded to the newly founded Saint George Technical Institute, where, he said in his will, "he hoped they might do some good." That Technical Institute grew to become the Saint George College of Arts and Sciences, and finally Zion University. During those growth years Swenson's notes were not in fact doing anyone much good. Due to lack of interest, they were never scheduled for data migration, and so eventually became unreadable. However, during the run-up to New Utah's 300th Founder's Day celebration, for her senior project an industrious Zion undergraduate took it upon herself to dredge up and transfer as many founder's era records as possible to current media. In the course of this endeavor, she discovered Swenson's remarkable material, and brought it to my attention.

Swenson's recordings are nothing less than phenomenal. At the time, these animals were classed as agricultural pests, and subject to local extermination. Swenson saw them otherwise, and became determined to record all he could before they completely disappeared. In addition to his meticulous observations, he acquired many killed specimens, conducted meticulous autopsies, and rendered three-dimensional holographic recordings. He made equally meticulous investigations of their reproductive habits, nutritional requirements, and of the plants on which they primarily depended. In the course of his work, Swenson became convinced that the creatures—or at least some of them—were sentient and deserving of protection. The Church disagreed: his work was ridiculed and suppressed, and thus his work, save the keen perception of one sharp student—was very nearly lost for all time.

In this paper, I will not only present the first summary of Swenson's observations to see the light of day in nearly 250 years, but demonstrate that they constituted a cautionary tale. Had they been appreciated at the time, New Utah's agricultural collapse might well have been prevented, and New Utah would not now be dependent upon selenium supplementation from Maxroy's Purchase. As it is, they attest an exciting and possibly unique biological adaptation to extreme conditions and highly variable climate. I present it here at this conference in the hope that xenobiologists from every world will review this data, as it is directly relevant to questions of how life begins on and propagates across many worlds.

The Planet of the Apes

Swenson observed and recorded dozens of now-extinct animals on New Utah, but in this paper I will focus on several related species divided into two groups herein classified as Swenson's Greater Apes and Swenson's Lesser Apes. Swenson himself did not refer to them as "apes" at all; he was quite clear that despite their physical appearance, they were not even mammalian, let alone Earth primates. However, their general hirsute appearance, bipedal locomotion, direct manipulation of their environment with arms and hands, and absence of tails made them appear ape-like to early settlers. The chief physiological distinction between the two groups is that the Lesser Ape species are six-limbed and bilaterally symmetrical, with two legs and four arms, while the Greater Apes (in general, as we shall see below) are not, possessing only three arms.

Swenson viewed these creatures directly, as well as conducting detailed interviews with farmers and construction workers. Early observers presumed that there was only one species of Swenson's Ape, but that it was highly variable in size and color. The presumption was natural. The animals lived in colonies widely dispersed among the vast "grass" marshes of the Oquirr delta, about which more later. Each colony included animals ranging in size from that of a newborn human infant, to some (at the largest) approaching two meters in height. The tallest individuals were generally white in color, and the smallest brown or black, although this was not always the case. Colors included white, brown, black, and occasionally striped individuals, locally called "zebras."

Interestingly, Swenson soon determined that these size and color variations actually corresponded to *separate* species, not size and color variations *within* a species. Further, *all* colonies appeared to be multi-species, and *all* apes appeared to live in colonies. Within each colony, one species, brown in color, dug and maintained elaborate tunnel systems, with galleried nesting dens. Another species engaged in rude cultivation, planting and propagating the "grasses" in exposed mud flats. A third species "stood guard" at the colony perimeter, making gestures quickly understood as threatening by early settlers—this species proved most troublesome to settlers, at is possessed sharp, chitonous, cutting spines which it used to fatal effect until colonists began shooting them on sight. Another species, more massive than the others, burrowed water diversion channels that created new mud flats for planting. Swenson believed that the two species of Lesser Apes, named Swenson's Marmosets and Swenson's Shrews, were commensals—animals that lived only in association with the colonies, but had no specific role within it. Both scavenged food and material wastes and created smaller sub-colonies ringing the main dens. They may have been tolerated for their "alerting" function, as they became quite agitated on the approach of any person or animal. The largest species, usually white, but sometimes black, in color, served no visible function, although it prowled widely within the colony itself and throughout the surrounding "fields."

Swenson found the apparent stability of this "social symbiot" colony structure to be remarkable, because the colonies were few and far between, none of them large, with most colonies including no more than a few individuals of any one species. How, he wondered, did their populations remain viable?

Zebras, Mules, and Truth Stranger than Fiction

Swenson noted that, on various occasions, each species had been observed carrying what were clearly offspring, but no offspring had ever been observed among the "zebras," which were also least numerous. Swenson initially presumed that "zebras" were sterile hybrids, often called "mules," the result of a chance mating between two Ape species. However, the fact of interspecies generation of offspring aside, it became clear to him that appellation "mule" was a misnomer— a fact with profound implications for understanding the reproductive agenda of all Swenson's Apes in general.

Swenson found that "zebras" were not, strictly speaking, hybrids. Hybrids form from the fusion of *gametes* (egg and sperm) from two species to form a single *zygote* (fertilized egg) that will develop if and as possible. For example, an actual hybrid mule is the offspring of a male donkey, which has 31 pairs of chromosomes, and a female horse, which has 32 pairs. The resulting offspring has 63 chromosomes. This odd number of chromosomes results in an incomplete reproductive system, which is always sterile in males, and usually sterile in females.

Swenson's Ape crosses are not "mules" in this sense. Rather, they are chimeras. Chimeras result from the physical mixing of cells from two *independent* zygotes (fertilized egg cells). "Chimera" is a broad term, applied to many different types of cell mixing. Although cross-species mixing is possible among species that are closely related and share similar developmental physiology, most chimeras result from the mixing of cells within a species. Chimeras can often breed, but the fertility and type of offspring depends on which cell line gave rise to the ovaries or testes. Intersexuality and true hermaphroditism may result if one set of cells is genetically female and another genetically male, and as we will see, this is nearly *always* the case in Swenson's Apes.

Nevertheless, we can use the cross-species equid analogy to clarify how *chimeras* differ from *hybrids*. As stated, crossing a male donkey with a female horse produces a hybrid mule. That is, one sperm of a donkey fertilizes one egg of a horse, resulting in a mule that shares the DNA and characteristics of both parents. It gets long ears from Dad, a short, glossy coat from Mom, and a DNA test of either its ears or its coat would show DNA from both parents.

A chimerical animal would result if one fertilized egg of a donkey (with both male and female donkey parents) were mixed with another fertilized egg of a horse (which had both male and female horse parents). Such an animal would develop so that some of its organs were "pure" horse (with 32 pairs of chromosomes and 100% horse DNA), while others were "pure" donkey (with 31 pairs of chromosomes and 100% donkey DNA). In addition, depending upon how the growing cell lines migrated, the animal's coat might have patches of shaggy, grey donkey hair alternating with patches of slick, brown horse hair. A DNA test on such an animal *would only show the DNA for the specific cell type and location tested.* The DNA for the shaggy, grey parts of the coat would be pure donkey; the DNA for the slick brown parts of the coat would be pure horse. To have the "full" genetic picture for this creature, you would have to draw DNA samples from multiple locations. Notably, in Swenson's Ape crosses, classic chimerical Blaschko's lines (fur striping) occurs, with the colors showing the boundaries of the cell lines.

Finally, whether a chimerical donkey-horse was interfertile with either donkeys or horses would depend on which cell line comprised its reproductive system. *Even if the rest of its outward appearance were that of a donkey,* if it had 100% horse cells in its reproductive system, when bred to a horse, it would produce a 100% fertile horse, with a full 32 pairs of horse chromosomes, and *no* donkey characteristics whatsoever.

Understanding this distinction is crucial for understanding Swenson's Ape reproductive physiology and secondary sexual characteristics, *because Swenson subsequently found that all Swenson's Ape species are profoundly chimerical.* Chimerism not only occurs within and across all Swenson's Ape species; it is both a usual and an essential part of their reproductive lifecycle.

Most Swenson's Ape matings result in multiple zygotes (fertilized cells), that is, fraternal twinning. Thereafter, any or all of four types of chimerism may (and usually do) occur. These are: stem cell transfer, tetragametic, germ line, and parasitic chimerism. This means that Swenson's Ape offspring may inherit multiple cell lines from each parent, and these cell lines may or may not be fused n vivo. In the upper classes, *parasitic* chimerism results in asymmetry, as discussed below.

Stem cell transfer occurs via cross-placental blood-vessel connections between twins, and is especially common for stem blood cells. In this case, the individual's bloodstream, immune system, and bone marrow will have different DNA from other parts of its body.

Tetragametic chimerism occurs through the fertilization of exactly two ova (two gametes) by exactly two sperm (two more gametes), followed by the fusion of the zygotes (the two fertilized eggs) at a very early stage of development. This results in an individual with intermingled cell lines. That is, the chimera is formed from the merger of two fraternal twins. The resulting individual can be male, female, or both. In Swenson's Apes, for reasons as yet not well understood, both is most common.

Similarly, *germ line chimerism* occurs when multiple ovi are *each* fertilized by one or more sperm. The fertilized eggs then divide, and the resulting blastocysts (cell clumps) may or may not fuse to form one or more chimeric embryos. These embryos exist for a fairly extended period prior to implantation, and then may attempt to implant at the same hemophore (blood vessel node.). In this case, the embryos merge. If this happens, one embryo atrophies, except for the reproductive cell lines, which complement those of the other embryo. The twin then develops normally, except that it bears the reproductive cell lines of its sibling. If the merged embryos were of opposite sex, this results in a truly hermaphroditic individual. Again, in Swenson's Apes, for reasons as yet not well understood, this is the most common outcome.

Parasitic chimerism occurs slightly later in embryonic development, when a "male" embryo attaches to a "female," eventually fusing into a single, hermaphroditic individual with a shared circulatory system. "Male" and "female" are indicated parenthetically, because at this stage of development, the embryo consists of little more than an undifferentiated alimentary canal, with no developed digestive capacity or limb differentiation, and either or both embryos may *already* be stem cell, tetragenetic, or germ line chimeras.

The War Between the Sexes

In a further elaboration of this trend, *all* asymmetric Swenson's Apes (that is, classes excluding Swenson's Marmosets and Swenson's Shrews) are chimerically hermaphroditic, and are formed in vivo from the "parasitic" attachment of a "male" germ line embryo to a vestigial genital pore formed at the side of the head of a "female" germ line embryo. On contact, an enzyme digests the lips of the (attaching) mouth and the (attached to) pore. At this point, as blood vessels form, the circulatory systems of the pair fuse.

"Male" development then continues as follows: First, the attaching embryo forms and injects male gonadal stem cells, which migrate to colonize the (female) birth canal. Given appropriate hormonal triggers, these gonadal colonies form multiple testes, one or more of which may or may not produce viable sperm, and may or may not descend, depending upon various factors that affect hormonal regulators, including rank, age, courtship rituals, and nutritional status. Most commonly, multiple testes produce sperm, but none or one testis descends. Second, in response to hormonal and enzymatic triggers, the axial limb buds migrate dorsally, and continue growth as the "gripping" hand and arm—creating the "asymmetrical" physiognomy of the "upper" Swenson's Apes.

Under specific circumstances, reproduction within a caste may proceed sexually, asexually, and/or chimerically. *All* Swenson's Ape matings are spermatozoically competitive. During mating, the hermaphroditic pairs exchange sperm packets. Because of the chimerically redundant testes, these sperm packets may (and usually do) contain sperm from multiple germ lines. Sperm may be stored in special ducts for long periods, perhaps even years. This means that once a Swenson's Ape has mated, under some conditions it is capable of continuing to bear offspring until its stored sperm is exhausted or dies. Because of the prevalence of hermaphroditic chimerism, all fertile Swenson's Apes are also capable of self-fertilizing without ever mating at all, although this seems to be rare and has not been observed in the upper castes.

An additional factor accounts for previous reports of so-called "sex changing" in Swenson's Apes. In the case of sexual reproduction, two Swenson's Apes initially engage in elaborate courtship ritual and display, which stimulate associated hormonal production. At the end of this first phase, a bank of highly muscular sacs are excited and contract. These eject up to 144 chitonous "love darts," similar to those produced by common land snails. Thereafter, sperm packets are exchanged.

Received packets are "split" by an enzymatic process that both triggers ovulation and dilates storage ducts, releasing stored sperm. All sperm—the recipient's own, plus all lines within the received sperm packet— then "compete" to either re-enter storage, or ascend the birth canal and fertilize all available eggs. Sperm that do not reach the "safe haven" of a storage duct or an egg are scavenged by digestive enzymes. Conception normally results in multiple zygotes, for both parties.

However, the mucous coating on the "love darts" contains a powerful hormonal cocktail that blocks further production of androgenic (male) hormones and excites production of oogenic (female) hormones. This leads to retraction of the testis and growth of a placental bed, enabling embryonic implantation. At this point, given sufficient hormonal injection, a "darted" Swenson's Ape becomes "female" for the purposes of gestation and birth. It is therefore theoretically possible for *both* Swenson's Apes to become pregnant as a result of mating, but this has not been observed. The prevailing theory is that Swenson's Apes sequester a significant proportion of available oogenic (female) hormone precursors in love dart mucous, thus rendering their bodies so depleted that they are unlikely to "receive as much as they give." Thus, it may be a matter of chance that one or the other Swenson's Ape will have further developed "love darts," and thus have give up the chance at "being female."

Where Have All the Flowers Gone

At this point, we might well note: these creatures have a *bizarre* reproductive physiology. We might indeed ask: *why!?*

In the absence of *any* physical specimens, I can only speculate, but speculate I will. To begin, we must turn back to that basic foodstuff of the Swenson's Apes: the "grasses" distributed thickly on the mudflats of the lower Oquirr delta. As is well noted, vegetation on New Utah is now sparse, but on first arrival our Founders reported vast, lush, green fields, glinting "almost aquamarine" in the long, sunny days. The "pastures" nourished man and beast alike: among its other ingredients, an old Founder's soup recipe calls for "one measure marsh grass, dried and powdered."

In fact, those pastures were not grass at all; they were the tall stalks of a semi-terrestrial plant, more closely akin to so-called blue-green algae (cyanobacteria), that survives its march up out of sea water by forming dense, root-like, rhizomous subsoil mats that wicked water and dissolved nutrients upwards from the (saline) water table. In a unique adaptation, excess salt is excreted in small beads that form at the tip of each stalk. Almost no stands now exist, because under True Church direction, all of the Saint George plain and most of the Oquirr delta were quickly put to the plow, followed by pivot irrigation and drainage systems to combat soil salinization. Once the rhizome mats are destroyed by plowing, stands do not regenerate.

It was the plowing of these algae fields that led to the first contact (and conflict) with Swenson's Ape colonies. Early on, construction and agricultural activities in close proximity to colonies themselves did not seem to result in anything but excitation among the Lesser apes. However, the first team to run gang plows through adjacent "grass" stands met with a quick and bloody end. Swenson was fairly certain that this algal grass was a primary colony food source, and that the attacks on humans had been made in defense of "colony-owned" fields. Thereafter, colony clearances were conducted as part of plowing operations. Colonists were quick to identify and pick off the "watchdog" species; thereafter, the other Greater Apes generally fled. The commensals were more problematic: colony clearance was generally followed by a local population explosion. Considerable effort went into their subsequent extermination, generally by gassing and poisoning.

This provided Swenson with hundreds of specimens of Lesser Apes for dissection and analysis, and he came to a startling conclusion. In brief: primitive blue-green algaes require and utilize selenium and iodine as powerful, highly-soluble antioxidants, readily available in sea water, to excrete excess oxygen during photosynthesis. However, this becomes problematic on land: because it is highly soluble, selenium quickly leaches from soils, especially under conditions of high rainfall—or artificial irrigation.

In general, terrestrial plants cope with the absence of these antioxidants by manufacturing their own, such as ascorbic acid, polyphenols, flavonoids, and tocopherols. However, some terrestrial plants, like aquatic seaweeds, actually accumulate and store selenium and iodine, and the New Utah algal grasses are among these. In these "grasses," selenium uptake is regulated in the rhizome mats. Hence, when the mats are destroyed, so is the uptake mechanism—and thereafter selenium is quickly leached from the soils.

Also in general, terrestrial animals can and do utilize many antioxident forms, as well as sequestering trace amounts of selenium and iodine in the thyroid gland, or its equivalent. However, in the case of Swenson's Apes, or, at least, in the case of the Lesser Swenson's Apes, selenium deficiency resulting from collapse of access to the algae fields was especially dramatic in its effects on reproductive hormonal regulation. Absent selenium, "love dart" manufacture all but stopped. Initially, this resulted in increased oogenic ("female") hormonal levels and "feminization" of the population (since no female hormones were being withdrawn from the body for dart manufacture). At the same time, reproductive drive increased, as did copulation rates. Given the total number of live births, Swenson postulated that hermaphrogenic reproduction also took place, but he was unable to prove this. In any case, the immediate effect was a local population explosion. However, the second consequence of selenium deficiency became manifest in isolated individuals: spontaneous, habitual abortion and miscarriage. Outwardly, apparently "female" Swenson's Apes gradually sickened and died, as internal egg and sperm stocks were repeatedly fertilized, aborted, and reabsorbed.

Conclusion

So again, *why* this *bizarre* reproductive physiology? Our research resources here on New Utah are, to say the least, limited, and I am more historian than xenobiologist, but I will draw some tentative conclusions from what I know of old Earth specimens.

Chimerism and hermaphroditism are most common in (especially) aquatic species characterized by low population densities and high potential birth rates. These include angler fishes, marine and terrestrial mollusks, and other animals that live in isolated populations that rarely encounter one another, including some of the lower primates. In these animals, chimerism and hermaphroditism ensure that multiple germ lines are carried within each individual, maximizing the potential for genetic diversity with each "chance" encounter—or, in the absence of an encounter, via hermaphroditic reproduction within the "individual" itself. A Swenson's Ape colony is, in effect, a "gene bank," representing germ line biodiversity far beyond that of the number of its members.

The prevalence of these modes of reproduction in Swenson's Apes, plus their apparent dependence on selenium for efficient reproductive regulation, suggests two things. First, that we might well search for maritime origins for this bizarre set of creatures. Their physiology is certainly more akin to that of widely-dispersed benthic mollusks than that of terrestrial mammals. Second, that these animals are reproductively adapted to extreme and variable conditions.

The paucity of indigenous flora and fauna on New Utah has been the subject of much conjecture, but little science. We *suspect* that we may now be experiencing a climatic optimum, but we have no way of testing that assumption. Basic geology has not even proceeded to the point of developing local radiometric curves. We have insufficient samples to establish normative carbon isotope uptake and decay, so we cannot validate radio-carbon curves for carbon dating. Similarly, we have not yet established local thermo-luminescence norms. Even if we could, we have virtually no paleontological record to draw from—let alone any archaeological record or deep-time historical sources. Thus, we can only construct a circular argument: we *presume* that climate in the past has been subject to extremes, in part because Swenson's Apes' reproductive physiology is so well suited to surviving them.

More importantly, we might well take a lesson from what we do know: the observed practices of Ape colonies. We should investigate methods for re-establishing selenium-concentrating algal fields for livestock forage and local nutritional supplementation. Doing so would eliminate New Utah's dependency on imported fertilizers and vitamins.

And lastly, we might well ponder: Swenson insisted that these were not mere animals, but sentient creatures like ourselves. When faced with destruction, some Swenson's Apes fled. Where did they *go*? So much of New Utah remains unexplored by science that perhaps, one day, we will be able to ask them ourselves.

Acknowledgements

I owe debts of knowledge and gratitude to many people who informed the science behind this story. Special thanks are due Aleta Jackson of XCOR Aerospace, for providing personal tours of the world of privately-financed space tourism, rocket planes, Mohave Spaceport, and the XCOR Lynx production line. McArthur fellow Prof. Guillermo Algaze of the University of California, San Diego introduced me to the early complexities of Mesopotamian accounting, trade, industry, and labor systems. Professor Lisa Levin of the Scripps Institute of Oceanography illuminated the improbable world and reproductive habits of benthic mollusks. Finally, the owners, operators, staff, and impeccable security teams of Neareast Resources kept me alive and safe amidst the chaos that was postwar Iraq. My debt to them is unlikely to ever be repaid.

About the Author

Dr. J.R. Pournelle is an archaeologist and anthropologist best known for reconstructing landscapes surrounding ancient cities. A Research Fellow at the University of South Carolina's School of The Environment, and past Mesopotamian Fellow of the American School of Oriental Research, her work in Turkey, Iraq, and the Caucasus has been featured in *Science, The New York Times* and on *The Discovery Channel*. In a former life, she received numerous decorations for service as a United States Army intelligence officer and arms control negotiator, and as a civilian conducted reconstruction work in Iraq.